# THE GRENDEL AFFAIR

*A SPI Files Novel*

LISA SHEARIN



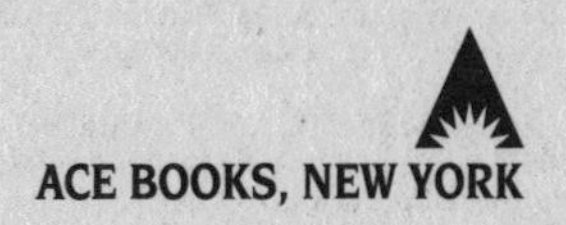

ACE BOOKS, NEW YORK

**THE BERKLEY PUBLISHING GROUP**
**Published by the Penguin Group**
**Penguin Group (USA) LLC**
**375 Hudson Street, New York, New York 10014**

USA • Canada • UK • Ireland • Australia • New Zealand • India • South Africa • China

penguin.com

A Penguin Random House Company

THE GRENDEL AFFAIR

An Ace Book / published by arrangement with the author



For information, address: The Berkley Publishing Group,
a division of Penguin Group (USA) LLC,
375 Hudson Street, New York, New York 10014.

ISBN: 978-0-425-26691-5

PUBLISHING HISTORY
Ace mass-market edition / January 2014

PRINTED IN THE UNITED STATES OF AMERICA

10 9 8 7 6 5 4 3 2 1

Cover art by Julie Dillon.
Cover design by Judith Lagerman.
Interior text design by Kelly Lipovich.

PRAISE FOR

# THE GRENDEL AFFAIR

"Lisa Shearin always delivers a great story. Fresh and exciting, humorous and action-packed, *The Grendel Affair* is urban fantasy at its best."

—Ilona Andrews, #1 *New York Times* bestselling author of *Magic Rises*

"Throw Stephanie Plum, *The X-Files*, and tequila in a blender and experience it all explode in your face with murder, mystery, the supernatural, tea-drinking dragons, and a hot partner who always has your back (and he might have a little more if given half a chance). Nonstop action, hilarious klutziness, romance, and lethal Lotharios everywhere. What could be better?"

—Rob Thurman, *New York Times* bestselling author of *Slashback*

"In Lisa Shearin's SPI Files series, seer Makenna Fraser brings Southern sass, smarts, and charm to the mean streets of Manhattan as she battles monsters and other magical beings. An action-packed mix of monsters, magic, and mayhem that will keep you turning the pages."

—Jennifer Estep, *New York Times* bestselling author of *The Spider*

"One of the best parts of being an author is getting to read books like *The Grendel Affair* before they're published. One of the most frustrating parts is sitting here asking, 'When does the next one come out?' before book one is even in print. This was great fun, with engaging characters and plenty of fast-paced action. But seriously, when does the next one come out?"

—Jim C. Hines, author of *Codex Born*

*continued . . .*

PRAISE FOR THE RAINE BENARES NOVELS

## ALL SPELL BREAKS LOOSE

"Exceptional . . . Shearin has proven herself to be an expert storyteller with the enviable ability to provide both humor and jaw-dropping action." —*RT Book Reviews*

"*All Spell Breaks Loose* not only lived up to my expectations but was even BETTER!" —*Dangerous Romance*

## CON & CONJURE

"Tons of action and adventure, but it also has a bit of romance and humor . . . The complexities of the world that Ms. Shearin has developed are fabulous." —*Night Owl Reviews*

"Action-packed and fast-paced, this was a fabulous read." —*Fresh Fiction*

"A great addition to a wonderful series." —*Dear Author*

## BEWITCHED & BETRAYED

"Once again, Ms. Shearin has given her readers a book that you don't want to put down. With Raine, the adventures never end." —*Night Owl Reviews*

"*Bewitched & Betrayed* might just be the best in the series so far! . . . An amazingly exciting fourth installment that really tugs at the heartstrings." —*Ink and Paper*

## THE TROUBLE WITH DEMONS

"Lisa Shearin's fun, action-packed writing style gives this world life and vibrancy." —*Fresh Fiction*

"Lisa Shearin represents that much-needed voice in fantasy that combines practiced craft and a wicked sense of humor." —*Bitten by Books*

## ARMED & MAGICAL

"Fresh, original, and fall-out-of-your-chair funny, Lisa Shearin's *Armed & Magical* combines deft characterization, snarky dialogue, and nonstop action—plus a yummy hint of romance—to create one of the best reads of the year . . . Shearin [is] a definite star on the rise."

—Linnea Sinclair, author of *Rebels and Lovers*

"An exciting, catch-me-if-you-can, lightning-fast-paced tale of magic and evil filled with goblins, elves, mages, and a hint of love interest." —*Monsters and Critics*

"Dazzling wit and clever humor. It's gritty, funny, and sexy—a wonderful addition to the urban fantasy genre . . . From now on Lisa Shearin is on my auto-buy list!"

—Ilona Andrews, #1 *New York Times* bestselling author of *Magic Rises*

"An enchanting read from the very first page . . . [Shearin is] definitely an author to watch!"

—Anya Bast, *New York Times* bestselling author of *Embrace of the Damned*

## MAGIC LOST, TROUBLE FOUND

"Take a witty, kick-ass heroine and put her in a vividly realized fantasy world where the stakes are high, and you've got a fun, page-turning read . . . I can't wait to read more of Raine Benares's adventures."

—Shanna Swendson, author of *No Quest for the Wicked*

"[Shearin] gives us a different kind of urban fantasy . . . Littered with entertaining characters and a protagonist whose self-serving lifestyle is compromised only by her loyalty to her friends, *Magic Lost* is an absolutely enjoyable read."

—C. E. Murphy, author of *Mountain Echoes*

*Also by Lisa Shearin*

*The Raine Benares Novels*

MAGIC LOST, TROUBLE FOUND
ARMED & MAGICAL
THE TROUBLE WITH DEMONS
BEWITCHED & BETRAYED
CON & CONJURE
ALL SPELL BREAKS LOOSE

*For Derek, the perfect husband for a writer.*

*For my in-laws, Ron and Roma Shearin. Though to me, you're Dad and Mom. Your love, encouragement, and support mean the world to me.*

# ACKNOWLEDGMENTS

To Kristin Nelson, my agent. What would I ever do without you? You rock!

To Anne Sowards, my editor. You're simply amazing to work with! And on top of everything else you do for my books, thank you for helping this Southern girl get the New York details right.

To Colleen Lindsay, Melissa Hastings, and Brad Brownson, my marketing, online promotions, social media, advertising, and publicity team at Ace Books. You guys are awesome!

To Julie Dillon, my cover artist. Thank you for bringing Mac and Ian to vibrant life.

To Mary Pell, my copy editor. Thank you for your sharp eyes and meticulous attention to detail. Your hard work made this a better book.

To Joe and Joey Romano, my fabulous father-and-son fans, for the inspiration for this book's title (and the next two as well). Thanks, guys!

# 1

MOST people grabbed a coffee on the way to work. I was clinking my way to the liquor store checkout with three bottles of Jack Daniel's. One bottle would probably get the job done, but I snagged an extra pair for insurance. There was no way in hell I was doing this twice.

The clerk's eyes went from the bottles to me and back again before scanning them into the register.

"For the morning staff meeting," I said. "Gets the week off right."

The man gave me an I-just-work-here grunt. "Need a bag?"

"Got it covered."

I started loading bottles into the messenger bag slung across my chest, winding an old towel I'd brought with me around and between them, careful to keep the bottles away from the borrowed thermal night vision goggles that were almost as critical as the booze for tonight's job. I wasn't far from where I was going, but I was trying to avoid any icy sidewalk accidents on the way there.

It was two days until New Year's Eve. The temperatures

hadn't risen above freezing the entire week, and since we had gotten an extra half foot of the white stuff last night, it felt at least ten degrees colder than it actually was. Though when you added in a wind that was cold enough to give an icicle frostbite, a couple of degrees one way or another didn't make a hill of beans worth of difference.

The liquor store was a block from the subway station, and it was only two more blocks from there to Ollie's, so I walked and slipped and clinked. A man sitting propped against the outside of the liquor store heard that telltale sound and looked at me like he was a Lab and I'd just bounced a tennis ball. He started to get up, staggering as he did so. I pushed back my coat, giving him a good look at my gun. I wasn't big, but my gun was.

It was also a fake.

I'd learned real quick that there was a big difference between owning, carrying, and shooting guns in the big city and doing the same back home. There were lots of rules that the NYPD got real bent out of shape about if you messed with. As a result, my new employer had yet to deem me qualified for a company-issued gun, so I'd bought myself one of those water pistols that looked exactly like a 9mm. If the sight of it wasn't enough of a deterrent, I'd loaded it with tequila. Aim for the eyes then run like hell. It wasn't much, but it was something.

The man looked at me for a second or two, his eyes shadowed under a tattered hat, and apparently decided that while a small blonde sporting a ponytail wasn't scary, the gun told him the risk probably wouldn't be worth it. He actually smiled at me through a couple of days' worth of dark stubble as he sat back down. Good. Strange, but good. I really didn't want to start my evening by squirting a homeless man.

I'm Makenna Fraser. I'm from a place called Weird Sisters, a small town in the far western point of North Carolina that doesn't show up on Google Earth, was named in reference to the three witches in *Macbeth*, and where the first word of the town name perfectly describes most of its citizens. I'll be the first to admit that includes me. I'm not what most people would call normal, never have been, never will be, and I'm fine with that.

Weird Sisters had been settled by the kind of people that normal people didn't want to have living next door. Most times, they couldn't put their reasons into words; it was more of a feeling than anything else. Other folks could put words to what they felt while in town just fine. Heebie-jeebies, the creeps, or just plain spooked. Outsiders passing through town instinctively knew whether they belonged there, or if they ought to just keep going.

Weird Sisters was said to be located on a ley line that supposedly magnified psychic and paranormal energies. I didn't know if there was anything to that or not, but something attracted people—and non-people—to stop and stay there. Quite a few of our townsfolk didn't exactly qualify as human. They looked human enough, and sounded like regular folks, but make no mistake—they were something else entirely.

Creatures from myth and legend are real.

Members of my family could see them for what they really were. We were what my Grandma Fraser called seers. We could see through any veil, ward, shield, or spell any supernatural could come up with as a disguise. Some used magic; most didn't. Veils were a survival mechanism, much like how a chameleon changed its colors to blend in with its surroundings to protect itself from predators. Or how predators looked perfectly harmless until something—or someone—they wanted to eat wandered by.

Down through the years, my family has taken it on themselves to protect the prey from the predators. Since the town's founding in 1786, there's been a Fraser as marshal, then sheriff, and now police chief. I chose my own way to expose the truth. Supernaturals didn't have the market cornered on predatory behavior. As a little girl, I dreamed of becoming an investigative reporter for our local paper.

But with the coming of the New Age movement, our main street became lined with shops, cafés, and tearooms populated with psychics, mediums, crystal healers, tarot and palm readers, clairvoyants, and way too much more. Between that, the influx of tourists from Asheville, and the advent of the Internet, it didn't take long for our newspaper and its website to become just another way to market the town. And when I came back home with my shiny new degree in journalism, I realized that in a town with more than its fair share of psychics (some of whom were the real thing), unsolved crimes were few and far between.

I decided it was time for me to leave for good.

I came to New York with the dream of running with the big dogs at the *New York Times*, or even sticking close to my hometown roots and writing for the Weird News section at the *Huffington Post*. But all I could get was a job at a seedy tabloid called the *Informer*, where only stories like "Donald Trump Is a Werewolf Love Child" had any hope of making it to the front page. If a story was the truth, great; if not, lies worked just fine. The majority of our gullible readership thought everything we printed was the gospel truth anyway. That particular headline had been an obvious lie—at least it'd been obvious to me. No self-respecting werewolf would have hair like that. But my stories had been the truth and had the dubious distinction of having been on the front page more than once, which had been good for keeping food in the fridge, but bad for my professional pride.

I could write about the weird and the spooky because I could see it. Implying that a mob boss on trial was less than human didn't make anyone bat an eye. Making the mistake of telling my now ex-editor that said mobster had horns and a tail, and that his lawyer was a literal bloodsucker had made me the darling of his black, profit-loving heart.

As luck would have it, that same story had also put me squarely in my new employer's sights. By that point, any job that'd let me regain my self-respect was a job that I'd gladly take—even if it took me back into the family business. When SPI recognized me for what I was and made me an offer, I'd literally skipped to my editor's office to resign.

Now I work for Supernatural Protection & Investigations, also known as SPI. They battle the supernatural bad guys of myth and legend, and those who would unleash them.

My family was thrilled to hear about my new job.

And I realized I couldn't run away from who and what I was.

Most supernaturals come here wanting the same things as the rest of us: a good job, nice house, 2.5 kids, and a dog. The others? Well, their powers are stronger here, their greed is bigger, and any treaties or bindings that might have made them behave back home don't mean squat here. They don't just want their slice of the American Dream; they want the whole pie, and they don't care what they have to do, who they have to kill, or how many city blocks they have to level to get what they want.

SPI's mission is twofold: keep the world safe for supernaturals and humans alike, and cover up the truth. Because when it comes to supernaturals, to paraphrase Jack Nicholson: people can't handle the truth. SPI has offices worldwide, and their agents are recruited from various alphabet agencies, top police forces, and military special ops, and are supported by the sharpest scientific and academic minds.

Then there's me.

My job as the seer for the New York office is to point out the supernatural bad guys, then step aside so the aforementioned commando-ninja-badass monster fighters can take them into custody—or if necessary, take them out. Doing my part to help keep the world safe is gratifying work, with regular pay, and my job description includes three of the most beautiful words in the English language: full medical coverage. If Bigfoot was on the rampage hurting innocent campers, I'd hunt him with a butterfly net if it meant having a dental plan.

But the bottom line was that I liked my job. Since starting at SPI, New York wasn't just the place where I lived; now it was home, a home that seemed to have supernaturals around every corner, kinds I'd never seen before, sitting at tables in every sidewalk café, and sharing every subway car with me. You'd be surprised at how many supernaturals lived in New York—then again, maybe you wouldn't. Perhaps that was why they liked it here; they were just another face in the crowd.

When I'd first arrived in the city, I discovered that New

York supernaturals were even better than the ones back home at disguising what they were and fitting in with their human neighbors. But I could see them, and they could see me seeing them. I'd give them a little smile and a nod whenever that happened, to let them know that I was cool with what they were. After an initial moment of surprise, more often than not, they'd smile back.

Yes, I'd traded the scent of mountain laurel for diesel fumes, and a ley line running under the mountains for a subway line running under the city, but New York had an energy all its own. I could see why it was called the city that never sleeps—it didn't want to miss one thing. And neither did I.

I loved New York.

A blast of wind that must have come straight from the North Pole brought my wandering mind back to where it belonged—keeping me from busting my ass on an icy street in SoHo. We got plenty of snow back home; it was pretty coming down and pretty when it landed. When I'd stand in the woods on the side of the mountain, it was as if the whole world came to a stop to watch in complete and awe-struck silence.

There wasn't nothing quiet about New York.

A man was walking toward me on the sidewalk. Only then did I notice that we were the only people I could see. That was beyond odd for SoHo, regardless of the time. Maybe everyone else had more sense than we did, and was at home and staying warm on a subfreezing night. The snow on the sidewalk was packed down and slick. I didn't want to risk falling, so I started to step aside and let the guy pass.

He beat me to it. Chivalry wasn't dead.

But the man was.

Though technically and clinically, he was undead.

Vampires were off-limits to me in my job. It didn't take a seer's skill to recognize a vamp, and my seer's skill wouldn't do squat to protect me from one. Most monsters would eat almost anything. Vampires fed on one thing and one thing only—human blood. I was human, and I had blood. The guy who had my job before me had gone and gotten himself exsanguinated in an on-the-job mishap involving a school of giant

North American sewer leeches. I wasn't going to meet a similar end on an icy sidewalk in SoHo.

My panicking brain told me what not to do: don't look him in the eye, don't act like prey. I knew what I wanted to do—run. But my brain was so busy telling me what not to do that it couldn't send the move-your-ass memo to my feet.

So I just stood there like a chipmunk cornered by a rattlesnake. I was shaking so hard, the liquor bottles were clinking together in my bag. If I ran, I'd probably just slip and fall like some B horror-movie actress. On the upside, if that happened, I'd probably die of embarrassment before he got his fangs into me.

The vampire resumed his slow approach. Anyone watching would think he was being careful walking on the ice. I knew he was playing with me, his dark eyes glittering like I was a hot toddy made just for him.

My hand fumbled under my coat for my gun, and I was kicking myself for not buying a second squirt gun for holy water. The vamp smiled, showing me fangs that were way too bright to be natural. Someone had gotten one or five whitening treatments too many. He was also wearing a fancy suit with no coat, though it wasn't like vampires had to worry about freezing to death. The strap of a laptop case was slung over one shoulder.

Aw jeez. Death by yuppie vampire.

That ain't gonna happen. I got my hand on my gun. A squirt in the eye with tequila might at least buy me enough time to get back in the liquor store. It might not stop him from draining me dry, but at least there'd be witnesses while it happened.

The vamp graciously inclined his head. "Miss Fraser."

I froze and my fingers went numb on the butt of my gun. I knew a handful of vampires by name, only one lived in New York, and this guy wasn't him. What were the chances that a fancy-suited, laptop-toting vamp who knew my name just happened to be walking where I was walking on a night when no one with a lick of sense was outside?

Next to nil.

Faster than I could react, the vamp closed the distance

between us and grabbed my hand, his bloodless fingers sliding past my gloves and up under my coat, his grip a paralyzing cold around my bare wrist. I opened my mouth, trying to scream, when the yuppie vamp's gaze darted over my shoulder and behind me. Now it was his turn to shake in his shoes, though I was sure his had to be much nicer than mine. I didn't want to risk taking my eyes off the vampire, but if there was something worse behind me, I needed to know about it.

The only other person on the street two minutes ago had been the homeless man. If the vampire couldn't get me, the homeless man would be easy pickings—that is, if the whatever-was-behind-me hadn't already gotten him. I didn't want either to happen.

I turned around.

I'd been surprised by a lot of things since starting at SPI, but this was near the top of the list.

The homeless man was the only person—living or otherwise—that I could see, and he might have been homeless, but right now, he looked far from helpless. He stood with no staggering this time; his movements smooth and predatory. Regardless of the battered coat and hat, if he had been a supernatural, I would have been able to see at least an aura of his true form. Yet, his face—or at least the bottom half that I could see—now revealed much more. Faint impressions of multiple faces, each different from the one before, were layered one upon another, stretching back into the distance, like looking into a wall of fun-house mirrors. My instincts told me that they had all been real enough at one point in time or another.

The vampire must have known or sensed something more about the creature that I couldn't. His expression went from thinking he'd found dinner, to wondering if he *was* dinner, as he actually jumped back and landed on his ass in the gutter then crab-crawled backward, desperate to get away. So desperate that he didn't hear or care that his pants caught on something in the street, ripping them when he scrambled to his feet. The vamp's fancy shoes found traction, and he ran across the street, slipping and sliding, half the ass torn out of his pants, showing the world one red-satin-boxers–covered cheek. I dimly wondered if there was a Santa on the front, or maybe Rudolph.

"Give my regards to your partner," said a silky voice from behind me.

I sucked in my breath and spun back toward the homeless man—or whatever he was.

Gone. As in no trace that he'd ever been there.

A real person couldn't have vanished that quickly. My seer vision wasn't something I could turn on and off. The man had been just that—a man. Maybe. Perhaps a man who had lived a lot of lives. That wasn't cause to freak out, but the little hairs on the back of my neck were telling me otherwise.

*Give my regards to your partner.*

My partner, Ian Byrne, had been a SPI agent for the past three years. For the five years before that, he'd been with the NYPD, and the prior seven had been in the military doing things that no one else at SPI knew about; and believe me, I'd snooped around. That information wasn't around to be had.

I stood there, unmoving, my quick breaths visible as tiny puffs of steam in the subfreezing air. I was alone on the street. That is until the next monster who knew my name or my partner showed up. I clutched my messenger bag to my chest, and got the hell out of there. Fast.

My destination tonight was Barrington Galleries, a glorified pawnshop on the edge of SoHo. The owner, Oliver Barrington-Smythe, called it a collection of antiquities, artifacts, and curiosities.

I called it a store full of spooky shit that only even spookier people would want. Most of Ollie's merchandise looked like it'd been dug up, either from the ground, a crypt, a basement, or a psycho's imagination. Among the stuff for sale that packed Ollie's place floor to ceiling were Victorian exorcism and vampire hunter kits, squishy things preserved in jars, dried things not in jars, funeral portraits, voodoo paraphernalia, and a sarcophagus that stood next to the counter with an actual, honest-to-God mummy inside. Well, there was until one of Ollie's saner customers literally caught wind of the occupant and alerted the city health department. So now the mummy was a well-wrapped mannequin.

Ollie's present problem was a stowaway in his latest shipment from Germany. He had a Bavarian nachtgnome running loose in his shop. Ollie liked money, and the green stuff would stop coming in real quick if word got around that something with fangs and an appetite for exposed body parts was loose in his shop.

That was where I came in. This wasn't an official assignment; nachtgnomes didn't register on SPI's radar, unless there were a couple hundred of the little critters overrunning Grand Central Terminal at rush hour. This was a favor for a friend—and my best information source for supernatural activity in the city. As a former reporter, I knew the importance of a good snitch. I'd only been working for SPI a few months, but I'd been introduced to Ollie during my first week. A big part of being a seer was knowing where to look for the bad guys. Any flake in town with supernatural connections or leanings was drawn to Ollie's place like a kid to a candy store.

Oliver Barrington-Smythe was short, beady-eyed, balding, and resented being all of the above, so it came as no surprise that Ollie rubbed most people the wrong way. I definitely wasn't most people, and liked the borderline rude little guy. I liked his accent, and he liked mine. We'd hit it off—once I'd made him understand in no uncertain terms that I wasn't a hillbilly—and he kept me in the know. To keep that gossip wheel greased and the goodwill coming, I was going to use a fifth of Jack to lure a Bavarian nachtgnome out of hiding and into a cage.

I'd never actually seen one before, but I'd studied the company manual. Nachtgnomes were short, shy, and wasted after one drink. Kind of reminded me of my last date. I'd had an easier time finding monsters in New York than a nice guy to spend time with. Ollie had promised to leave an iron cage to scoot the little guy into until morning. My job was just to catch it; Ollie had made other arrangements for getting it out of his shop. And no, I hadn't asked what those arrangements were, because I really didn't want to know. Though I suspected the population of the New Jersey marshes was about to increase by one. I'd learned in training that it was one of the more popular spots with the local criminals for getting rid of a dead body—or a disagreeable supernatural critter. On second thought, Ollie might not know that according to the manual, nachtgnomes could reproduce all by their lonesome. Maybe I should leave him a note.

At anywhere from a foot to eighteen inches tall, a full-grown nachtgnome would be big enough to drink right from the bottle. And as their name indicated, nachtgnomes were nocturnal, hence the NVGs. I'd learned how to use them in one of my training classes, so I saw no reason why I shouldn't take advantage of Ollie's gnome problem to get some practical application of my newly gained classroom knowledge.

I'd brought an old pair of plastic Scooby-Doo cups I'd dug out of the back of my kitchen cabinets. Needless to say, I wasn't going to be using them again after tonight. I bought two instead of one because I wanted the gnome to drink enough to make it catchable the first time. I'd fill up both cups and leave the rest of the bottle. First call should be last call.

I was about half a block from Ollie's place, and had been looking over my shoulder almost constantly, when a tall, shadowy figure stepped out of the shop's recessed doorway.

Aw crap.

At least I knew who the shadow belonged to, but I also knew that I'd been busted. Though right now, after what had already happened to me tonight, I was kind of relieved. Almost.

There was no mistaking Ian Byrne's silhouette of relaxed readiness. If I'd been someone up to no-good, I'd have given serious thought to crossing the street right then, or better yet, turning and running like hell. Actually, who was I kidding? Those thoughts had just crossed my mind. Considering his professional background, Ian Byrne's "Don't even think about it; I can kick your ass from here" stance came naturally. The impression was strengthened by the fact that Ian was at least a head taller than me.

The powers that be at SPI had assigned him as my partner,

though I think he saw himself as more of a combination of babysitter and bodyguard. One, I was a newbie; and two, I was a seer. Seers were rare enough that the New York office only had one in their employ at any given time. As a result, SPI felt the need to protect (and hopefully help preserve) their newest personnel investment. As much as I liked having my SPI-provided medical insurance, I tried not to think that I might actually need it.

Ian Byrne had never said it, but I knew he resented being assigned to me. And I would have liked him well enough, except I had no desire to be around people who didn't want to be around me. He was constantly watching me, like he was just waiting for me to screw up.

Ian stepped out to where he knew I could clearly see and identify his tall, dark, and dangerous self. As I got closer, I could see that his arms were crossed in front of his chest. Yep, someone was most definitely not amused by my show of professional initiative this evening. I thought it might be a good idea to keep my two earlier encounters to myself, at least until I'd finished what I'd come here to do.

I hadn't told Ian about my favor to Ollie, because I knew he had plans tonight, plans that didn't involve playing bartender to a nachtgnome. The only people who knew I was here were Ollie and Sam, SPI's armorer, the man responsible for the borrowed thermal NVGs. I'd tried to check out a gun as well, but that didn't fly with Sam. Apparently, he liked job security and health insurance, too.

Ian was also my shooting instructor for the still-to-be-issued company gun. Normally SPI didn't issue guns to their seers, but since my predecessor's exsanguination and subsequent departure to the great beyond, they'd adjusted the company policy. I'd been born and raised in a town where cough syrup meant moonshine and honey, and guns and hunting had been a big part of my upbringing. I mean, how many girls got a hand-me-down muscle car and a shotgun for their sixteenth birthday? I still wanted to kick myself for not hanging on to the 1970 Pontiac LeMans, but I still had the shotgun. I could shoot just fine. However, I was used to shooting beer cans off the back of an old washing machine, or at things that ran away from me that I intended to eat—not things that ran toward me with the intent of eating *me.*

I'd found that to be a significant difference.

I stopped. The bottles clinked.

His mouth was hard and unsmiling. "Agent Fraser."

"Agent Byrne."

"That's quite the traveling party you've got there," he said.

Back home, in my younger days, I'd been busted by our local sheriff for underage drinking, and it had only made it worse that she was my aunt. This felt exactly the same. Though I reminded myself that Ian Byrne was only a couple of years older than I was, and he could only make me feel like a delinquent teenager if I let him.

I wasn't going to let him. I wasn't doing anything wrong.

"Told you I was fun," I said.

Ian had what looked like a small camera bag slung over one shoulder. I looked closer. Nope, not a camera. NVGs. In a case identical to the one in my messenger bag. Apparently I hadn't been the only one signing out gear.

"Looks like Sam ratted on me," I said.

"I asked. He told. I'm not about to let you try to catch a nachtgnome by yourself."

"Excuse me? *Try* to catch?"

"They're mean."

I snorted. "They get drunk from a couple shots of booze."

"Then they're mean drunks."

It was too cold to stand out in the street and argue with him. "I didn't tell you because Ollie needed this done tonight, and you had a date." I grinned. "Or is this business before pleasure? Come here and bag a gnome; go there and bag a . . ."

"Lawyer."

Oh.

"I happen to like smart women," he continued.

There were only six words in that sentence; but to me, every last one of them felt like he was saying that he didn't consider me to be smart and he didn't like me. I squashed that line of thought. It seemed that every time I got around Ian Byrne, paranoia became my new best friend.

After a couple seconds of awkward silence, Ian jerked his head toward the door. "So what kind of liquor did you get for Shorty in there?"

"Three-fifths of Jack."

He raised an eyebrow.

"Accidents happen," I said. "I got some insurance."

I stepped past Ian and started working on Ollie's locks. He'd given me the keys and the code to deactivate the alarm system. Ollie had three dead bolts, each with a different key on what looked like a glass door with a wooden frame. Anyone trying to break in would be in for a surprise. The wood was steel and the glass was bulletproof.

I had to give the door a bit of hip action to get it open. A bell rang. I looked up. Ollie had one attached to the top of the door. Crap. So much for stealth.

"It's your party," Ian said. "After you."

A round red light at the top of the alarm system keypad started flashing. I had ten seconds before flashing turned to banshee shrieking. I fumbled the piece of paper out of my pocket that I'd scribbled the numbers on, entered the deactivation code, and the red light went out.

Ollie had never had a break-in. No surprise there. Anyone looking to score something to steal had always given Ollie's shop a wide berth. One, the place was spooky enough in the daytime; and two, when they went to fence what they'd stolen, the only person who'd buy stuff that bizarre was Ollie, which kind of defeated the purpose and the effort.

I closed the door behind us, successfully got the NVGs on and focused, and did a slow scan of the shop.

Nada.

Which meant absolutely nothing. From what I'd been taught in my classes, nachtgnomes tended to stay hidden—unless you made it interesting for them, either with whiskey or exposed skin. All my pieces and parts were covered and going to stay that way. I'd brought booze to this party, not snacks.

The gnome had to know we were here. Aside from the bell, it was virtually impossible to take more than three steps in Ollie's place without bumping into something. My goggles were to ensure that I didn't bump into anything that bit.

If I turned on the lights, we'd be able to see, but the nachtgnome would burrow his way into something dark and stay there. So the dark was to make him comfortable, and the Jack was to make him sociable. I scanned the area around the counter and froze. The mummy was registering red and orange—at least the head was. And the contents were . . . moving.

Sweet Mother of—

"Mice," came Ian's whisper at my left ear.

I damned near jumped out of my skin.

I shot him a glare that would have been a lot more effective if he could have seen my eyes, then something scurried over by a case of voodoo dolls, bare feet pitter-pattering like wet rubber on the wood floor. I had an immediate and overwhelming urge to jump on a chair, flap my hands, run in place, and squeal. I had to grit my teeth to keep from doing any and all of the above.

My thirsty customer had arrived.

It's just a nachtgnome, Mac. Just one. A small one. And it's probably more scared of you than you are creeped out by it. Get it drunk, get it caged, and go home.

There was a more or less clear area near the middle of the shop. Ollie had left the cage there, as promised. I quickly set up my nachtgnome bar—one cup at the cage door, another inside, and the bottle near the back. I sloshed some of the whiskey on the floor. I'd never poured Jack Daniel's into Scooby-Doo cups while wearing night vision goggles. My shaky hands had nothing to do with it. Nachtgnomes loved whiskey; they just couldn't hold it. The little guy should pass out after half a bottle, which was about what two Scooby cups held.

We didn't have to wait for long.

I knew that Bavarian nachtgnomes didn't look like that cute white-haired gnome with the British accent in the travel commercials, but this thing was closer to something out of *Gremlins*—and not the cuddly one. The drawing in my employee manual was accurate; however this specimen was larger than I expected. From the picture in the book, I knew that its skin was green, its wide ears rubbery, and its eyes yellow. From standing less than ten feet away, I knew that it had way too many fangs. Black claws curved on spindly hands and feet. No little blue jacket and pointed red hat for this thing; it was buck naked. The gnome had to use both hands to pick up the Scooby-Doo cups, but it tossed back both like it was doing shots of water. Then it snatched the bottle right out of the cage and did the same to it. It lowered the bottle and just stood there outside the cage door. Staring. At us. Its yellow eyes glittering with barely contained pissed-offness.

Uh-oh.

"I'd kind of hoped to take care of this quietly," I muttered. The chances of that happening were vanishing faster than the Jack had.

"Looks like you can kiss that big tip good-bye," Ian told me.

That comment deserved a response, but I kept my eyes on the critter, resisting the urge to look for the nearest chair, countertop, or exit.

The nachtgnome's upper lip peeled back to reveal jagged teeth that were thankfully less than clear in the NVGs. However, I got an all too good look at the lip rippling with a low snarl. The snarl increased to a growl.

"Mean drunk," was all that Ian said. The "I told you so" was clearly implied.

"Okay, fine. You were the cop. How'd you arrest an uncooperative drunk?"

"Human drunks don't have fangs, and they definitely can't jump six feet straight up."

I blinked under my goggles. "Six *what*?"

"They're jumpers. You didn't know that?"

"I read three feet, which was bad enough."

"When they get to be that size, it's six." Ian blew his breath out in exasperation. "Hand me another bottle."

Not taking my eyes from the gnome, I reached into my bag and pulled out a second bottle. Nowadays, I didn't drink anything stronger than ginger ale—unless it was moonshine with honey for medicinal purposes. If I drank, I got dizzy, and if I got dizzy, I got sick. No one wanted to see that. But I was considering going medicinal on that third bottle—if we got out of here without any bites taken out of us.

Ian unscrewed the cap, set the bottle on the floor, and pushed it as far toward the gnome as he could without risking digit loss. "There you go, big guy. Time to go nighty-night."

Ian moved back and the gnome stalked forward. He wrapped both hands around the neck of the bottle, swung it up to his thin-lipped mouth, and chugged it. We should have jumped him then, but we were both mesmerized by the sight of a thing not much taller than the bottle it clutched in its hands—and it draining it dry.

Two bottles of Jack gone in as many minutes.

The nachtgnome slowly lowered the bottle and belched so loud I swear it rang crystal somewhere in the shop.

"Damn," Ian said.

I blinked. "Ditto."

In response, the gnome threw the empty bottle at our heads. We barely dove behind a display case of shrunken heads in time.

"Someone wants to stay up," Ian noted.

"Someone should get shot," I spat. I stopped and quickly pressed my lips together. I couldn't see Ian's hard green eyes, but I could sure feel them.

"Sam said you asked for a gun." It wasn't a statement; it was an accusation.

"And he didn't give me one."

"Did anyone else?"

"No . . . not exactly . . ."

"Mac."

I drew my gun from my shoulder holster, but before I could open my mouth to explain, Ian had grabbed my wrist in some kind of mutant Vulcan death grip, my fingers went numb, and then Ian had my gun—all in about two blinks of an eye.

"Jeez, relax, will ya?" I tried to shake the feeling back into my hand. "It's fake, a water gun—well, a water gun loaded with tequila."

"What?"

I grinned. "Aim for the eyes then run like hell."

"Do you know how many people get themselves shot by waving one of these things around?"

"I don't *wave* it arou—"

He tucked my gun in the back of his jeans. "No guns."

I looked around the corner. No gnome.

My free hand fumbled next to the doorjamb at where the light switch should have been. It wasn't.

A growl was all the warning I got. I ducked as a jar of something shattered against the steel door frame where my head had just been. Something rancid soaked the alarm panel, and the jar's contents landed with a wet plop right next to me. I didn't look. No time, and certainly no desire.

I scanned the counters. Nothing. Just because I couldn't see him didn't mean I couldn't feel him seeing me. Completely creepy. I clenched my hands into fists to keep them from doing that girly flapping thing.

"See him?" I asked.

"Not yet." Ian was scanning above the shelves, a knife in his hand.

I had nothing.

I remembered that Ollie had a couple of sword canes in an elephant-leg umbrella stand next to the counter. I scurried over and snagged one. It was old, and the blade was rusty, but all I needed was what it still had—a pointy end. If that thing ran at me, tetanus would be the least of its problems.

Ian was focused on the ceiling. "Bingo."

I looked up.

The nachtgnome was crouched on one of the big ceiling fan blades, balancing on the thing like a freaking surfboard, and grinning wide enough to show us all of his fangs.

I couldn't believe it. "The little bastard thinks this is funny." Even more unbelievable was that he was able to balance on anything after two bottles of whiskey, including his own two feet. I didn't want to think about how he'd gotten up there, just like I didn't have to think about what I did next.

This time I found the switch I was looking for.

Ian actually chuckled as the ceiling fan speed went from Lazy Susan to propeller in three seconds.

"Who said nachtgnome hunting can't be fun?" I watched with satisfaction as the gnome clutched that fan blade with his arms and legs and hung on for dear life. "If I can't get him drunk, I'll take him dizzy."

"And probably sick."

I hadn't considered that, but if that's what it took, I could take a shower or three. Unlike Ian, I didn't have any plans tonight.

The ceiling creaked and bowed over our heads enough to make the fan wobble off balance. The nachtgnome squealed and hugged the fan blade harder.

Ian and I looked from the ceiling to each other. In that blink of time, Ian's hand now held his gun instead of a knife.

"What's up there?" he asked.

"Just Ollie's office."

"And Ollie's not here."

"He said he wasn't going to be."

Ollie used to have a stock clerk who had been nearly three hundred pounds of solid muscle. I'd been down here in the shop before when this guy had been upstairs. He hadn't made the ceiling bow, meaning who- or whatever was upstairs weighed over three hundred pounds.

A scream shattered the silence.

I didn't think it was Ollie, but then I'd never heard him scream. The scream rose into a shriek of primal terror, a sound that a human throat shouldn't be able to make.

A guttural roar overpowered the screams.

Ian ran to the stairs behind the counter. "Stay here," he ordered.

No way. I liked Ollie. Sure, he sold creepy things, but I liked the little guy, and I wasn't about to stand by while something big enough to shake the rafters and make that roar tore him apart.

The shriek ended in a raspy gurgle, and then the only sound was the moaning of an airsick nachtgnome.

I ran back to the switch and turned the fan off, then took the stairs two at a time behind Ian. The gnome was on his own. The city sewers could always use something else to keep down the not-mythical alligator population.

Working for SPI, I'd heard my share of screams. Some of them had come from me. When you ran around a corner and found yourself face-to-gaping-maul with something out of your worst nightmare, you *would* scream. Guaranteed. While you could hope it wasn't a girly shriek, you didn't get to decide how you screamed; the nightmare in front of you did.

Ian and I had reached the top of the stairs when a deep voice from behind the closed door gave a wet cough. Once. Twice. After the third cough I realized it was a raspy chuckle. The thing was laughing.

I death gripped my borrowed rusty sword.

There was the crash of breaking glass and what sounded like a muffled explosion that shook the landing beneath our feet.

It was getting away.

Part of me was completely fine with that, but apparently that part got outvoted, because there I was, right behind Ian when he kicked in the locked door.

The lights were on. And plenty of light shining on the contents of that office was something I could have done without.

I took one step into the room and didn't go any farther.

Scattered all over the office were pieces and parts of what may or may not have been Ollie just a few moments before. Blood sprayed the brick walls and ceiling. In the center of the floor, leaning against the desk was a headless and limbless torso, belly slashed open, the insides now on the outside, arms and legs torn from their sockets. One arm had been tossed in a corner with the legs. The second arm and the head were nowhere to be seen.

Bile rose in the back of my throat and it took everything I could muster to force it down. The mixed stench of blood, death, and disembowelment did things to my nose that my stomach was in no condition to handle. My sensory smorgasbord was topped off by what I could only describe as dead fish at low tide. The voice of reason in my head was reduced to incoherent jabbering, and the rest of my mind wasn't far behind.

Ian ran over to the shattered window, and looked out, down, and then up.

I stayed put. "See him?" I swallowed with an audible gulp. "Or it?"

"It's two stories down and the fire escape wasn't lowered, and there's at least ten feet of smooth brick to the roofline."

Meaning that whatever did this could either survive a two-story jump or fly or both. None of the above was reassuring.

Ian had his phone in his hand and hit a speed-dial button. I knew he was calling the office. SPI had investigators and a full lab, as well as a cleanup team that could make Ollie's office look like nothing had ever happened. I wished them luck getting rid of the stink.

"Is there enough here to have been Ollie?" Ian asked, waiting for someone on the other end to pick up.

The last thing I wanted to do was take a closer look, but fortunately it didn't take much looking to know that the mess on the floor wasn't, and had never been, Ollie. Ollie was almost as short as I was; there was too much here to have been him. Though with the head and one arm missing, I had no clue who it might have been.

"Not Ollie," I said, trying without success to breathe only through my mouth.

Ian gave me a sharp nod of acknowledgment, then focused his attention on the person on the other end of the line.

The only remaining arm, the left one judging from the position of the thumb, was on the desk, palm up, dead fingers curled loosely around something dark. My curiosity got the best of me and I went in for a closer look, careful not to step on or in anything that might remotely be considered a body part. Wound around two of the fingers was a tangled piece of hair, almost like a dreadlock. While interesting in its own gross way, what was really intriguing was what was on the man's palm. I got a Kleenex out of my bag and used it to remove the hair, giving me a better look. In the center of the palm was a tattoo of a bug. It had an Egyptian look to it.

A scarab? Who the hell would have a scarab tattoo on their palm?

"Don't touch anything," Ian said from right behind me.

I jumped and bit back a yelp, instinctively shoving the Kleenex in my pocket.

Ian went back to talking on the phone, so showing him my discovery would have to wait. I picked my way over to the office's one window. It'd been reduced to a gaping hole in the brick wall. Some of the bricks had even been knocked out.

"So much for what that muffled explosion was," I murmured.

Whatever had ripped a man to shreds and destroyed a window and half the wall had done it all in less than ten seconds.

Blood covered the pieces of glass on the floor; there were probably more in the alley.

Then I saw it.

A partial handprint wrapped around a section of brick, made by a massive hand that had to have been at least five times the size of Ian's.

"Police! Freeze!"

Two cops quickly moved into the room, guns drawn, a third guarded the doorway.

I hadn't heard a thing, and apparently neither had Ian.

"This isn't what it looks like," I insisted as the cop twisted my wrist around behind my back and cuffed me. Before he did, I got a glimpse of his ears. He'd look human to everyone else, but I could see his upswept ears clear as day. A lot of elves found their way into the NYPD. For some reason, they had a thing for law and order.

"It never is," the cop said, cuffing my other wrist.

Though I had to admit it did look bad: two people in an office with something that wasn't a person anymore, one with two guns and a knife, the other with a rusty sword, and both with NVGs pushed up on their foreheads. If I'd been the cops, I'd have thought we were up to no-good.

"Look at me," I told the cop. "I only come up to your neck. Do you honestly think I could have done this?" I jerked my head toward Ian. "And him? I mean, he's all lean and buff, but to do this? Get real."

"Thanks, Mac," Ian said.

"Just being helpful."

"Do you think you can stop being helpful until we get a lawyer?"

My right foot picked that moment to slip on the blood-covered broken glass. I lost my balance and fell against the brick wall, crushing the contents of my messenger bag—and breaking the last bottle of Jack Daniel's.

As the cop pulled me to my feet, the whiskey ran down my leg and into my boot.

A chittering came from downstairs that could have only been nachtgnome laughter. As the cops took us down the stairs, I saw the gnome dart out the now open door and into the night. *Now* the damned thing decided to leave.

I hoped the sewer gators won.

# 2

THE advantage to seeing a police interrogation room on TV rather than in real life was that you didn't have to deal with the smell. My nose was telling me in no uncertain terms that this particular room had recently held a suspect who had serious personal hygiene issues—and had sat in the chair where I was now sitting. Though with the right leg of my jeans sopping wet with whiskey, I was in no position to cast stones.

The buzz of the double-strip fluorescent light directly over the lone table and two chairs was giving me a headache. It had to be some kind of pre-interrogation softening-up technique. Eventually suspects would probably admit to anything just to get out of here.

Right now, I'd settle for a change of clothes, or at least jeans.

I knew my rights. I didn't have to answer a single question without a lawyer present. Yet there were only two chairs in the room: one for the suspect, and one for the detective. It was like they wanted you to think, "No chair for a lawyer, so no lawyer for you."

Ian and I had been separated from the get-go. We'd been brought to the First Precinct in separate cars, and not allowed to talk to each other from the moment we'd been cuffed. Ian had been on the phone with SPI when we'd been arrested. Hopefully, they'd send a lawyer. Ian had been with SPI long enough to warrant legal assistance. I'd been there only a few months. I probably warranted being fired and booted to the nearest curb, seer or no seer.

While no one at SPI had ever specifically told me not to hunt Bavarian nachtgnomes on the side, I knew they'd frown on anything that resulted in one of their agents sitting in a NYPD interrogation room. Getting arrested while doing a little freelance work for a friend risked exposure, and exposure of the supernatural was one of the very things SPI had been established to prevent. What I had done tonight—and by association, Ian—wasn't the problem. Getting caught was. In SPI's opinion, the resulting risk of exposure was the same as if we'd being caught running naked at high noon through Times Square in front of a church tour group from Alabama.

Ian and I had been seen, caught, and brought in for questioning by the mortal authorities in connection to a gory murder that had been perpetrated by something that in no way, shape, or form could have been human.

We hadn't been charged with murder, but when the police get an anonymous call about a murder, and the officers dispatched to the scene find two armed people in the same room with a shredded third person, questioning was a given. The cops had to have arrived almost while the murder was happening. In my mind, that meant someone knew there was going to be a murder and wanted to make sure that the police all but walked in on it.

In my TV-viewing experience, detectives either stood for the small talk then sat in the chair across from the suspect for the questions they really needed answers to, or stood and walked around behind the suspect the entire time trying to throw them off balance. This guy looked like a sitter, not a pacer. Good. I was in no mood to spend however long I'd be here swiveling my head around like Linda Blair to keep track of the guy.

Detective Burton had introduced himself as soon as he'd come into the room and shut the door behind him. Polite, yet businesslike, he looked more like an accountant than a detective. He was on the short side with practical black-framed glasses, yet his dark eyes were sharp behind those lenses. People probably tended to underestimate him. I was determined not to be one of those people. I couldn't see a third-string junior detective being assigned to question a suspect (or whatever they thought I was) in a murder where the victim probably had to be shoveled into a body bag. At the moment, he was making a show of reviewing what he apparently wanted me to believe was incriminating paperwork in a manila folder.

While I didn't have to talk without a lawyer, I wanted to know who had called the police to report a murder that hadn't happened yet. The trick was to find out if the police knew anything I didn't while saying as little as possible, thus avoiding having my potentially soon-to-be-unemployed butt being kicked to the aforementioned curb.

Ian and I had been up those stairs within seconds of the slaughter. Two minutes later, the police had arrived. The math didn't even begin to add up. I would've said that I smelled a setup, except no one knew I was going to be in Ollie's shop except Ollie, Ian, and Sam. Maybe Ollie had gotten talkative to someone else, perhaps to the guy with the bug tattoo. Why bug tat guy had been in Ollie's office, how he had gotten in, and why a monster had spread him all over the place like strawberry jelly then taken a couple of body parts for souvenirs, were more questions that needed answering.

Detective Burton closed the folder, lightly tossed it onto the table, and leaned back against the wall with the two-way glass, casually crossing his arms over his chest.

"Ms. Fraser, do you honestly expect me to believe that you and Mr. Byrne were in Barrington Galleries attempting to capture a rat?"

A cut-to-the-chase kind of guy. Good. I might get out of here before the buzzing light made me homicidal.

When dealing with small supernatural critters, the go-to answer for New York's SPI field agents was "big rats." Agency rule number one was to stick to the truth as much as possible.

"That's what Ollie told me it was," I said, sitting back and resisting the temptation to cross my own arms. Keep the body language non-defensive and not guilty. "That's what we were looking for. Due to someone being murdered upstairs, we didn't get to catch it. Though hopefully it ran out the front door when your boys left it standing wide open."

Detective Burton's sharp eyes narrowed.

Way to go, Mac. You probably just added an extra half hour to your fluorescent buzz torture. What happened to saying as little as possible?

"We have been trying to contact Mr. Barrington-Smythe to corroborate your statement, and to inform him of the crime that occurred on his property. However, we have yet to locate him. You wouldn't happen to know where he is, would you?"

"No."

I'd have put up with an entire night of a buzzing light if it meant getting Ollie alone for a very meaningful chat. I didn't believe he'd known that his office was going to be redecorated with human body parts while I was gnome hunting downstairs. However, I knew that Ollie dealt with some unscrupulous people. Oliver Barrington-Smythe's double-barreled surname was real enough, at least as real as Humphrey Collington or the five other aliases I knew about. And I'd bet my right to an attorney that Ollie could put a name to the hand with the bug tattoo.

"The officers on the scene reported that you and Mr. Byrne were found wearing state-of-the-art night vision goggles," Detective Burton said. "And you had three bottles of Jack Daniel's with you. One bottle was found empty, the other empty and then shattered as if it had been thrown, and the third was broken in the bag which was found on your person. Explain the high-tech gear and the whiskey."

Ian and I had both been given breathalyzers when we were brought in and hadn't blown a thing, so the obvious explanation of a whiskey-induced, NVG-enhanced party for two wouldn't work. I didn't have to answer, but these were questions I actually had answers for. I wasn't guilty of anything, and a little cooperation might go a long way—or at least get me out of here faster.

"Part of a bottle was for the rat," I said. "My grandma told me that rats like the smell of whiskey; must be the grain. The other two were for my New Year's Eve party Saturday night. And rats don't like light, hence the goggles."

"And the bottles were broken how?"

"I tripped. It was my first time using night vision goggles."

Burton raised an eyebrow. "The broken bottles were found in different sections of the shop. So you're saying you tripped twice?"

"I threw the second bottle at the wall because the rat was climbing up it. I don't like rats."

"There was more glass found by the door from a broken jar containing a"—Burton flipped open the manila folder and read with distaste—"monkey brain, according to the jar's label."

My frozen, open-mouthed grimace wasn't an act. I remembered the wet, squishy plop hitting the floor by my feet after the nachtgnome had chucked that jar at me. "I could have stepped on a *monkey brain*?"

Ollie only carried stuff he knew he could sell. I didn't know what disturbed me more: a monster on the loose that could tear off arms and legs, or some wacked-out collector scurrying around the city shopping for just the right monkey brain to go on his mantle.

"Odd thing though," the detective continued, sitting down across from me at the table. "Whatever liquid was in the jar shorted out the alarm keypad. So the jar couldn't have been broken before you arrived as you said in your statement, since you claim that you deactivated the security system using the code that Mr. Barrington-Smythe gave you."

I sighed and slouched in my chair. "Listen. I don't know anything about security systems. Ollie gave me the code and I used it. That's all. I have no idea what the alarm and the monkey brain did or didn't do before I got there."

Detective Burton leaned forward, elbows on the table, hands folded. "Ms. Fraser, I don't believe a word you've said. But as a former reporter at one of our city's least reputable tabloids, no doubt you're more than capable of fabricating what you need to fill in the gaps." He inclined his head toward the manila folder. "I see that you're presently employed by Saga Partners Investments. That's quite a move from a tabloid reporter. Exactly what do you do there?"

Saga was just one of the business fronts for SPI. Located off Waverly Place near Washington Square Park in Greenwich Village, Saga was an actual, working private securities firm, whose clients included SPI agents and employees. Saga had a few clairvoyants on staff, so our 401k accounts were in really good shape.

Having worked at a sleazy tabloid didn't make me sleazy. I was tired, I smelled like a still, and I wanted to go home. I sat up straighter and looked Burton in the eye. "I'm an investigator. I do background checks on the smaller companies we recommend, or don't recommend, to our clients."

Burton nodded absently. "And how do you explain this?"

He tossed a ziplock bag tagged for evidence. Inside was a small, blood-spattered photo.

Of me.

I just stared at it. I blinked and looked again. It was still me and still bloody.

In the photo, I was wearing the green sweater my grandma had knitted me for Christmas. I had a cookie in each hand, and was eating one of them. I wasn't doing that great a job of it, judging from the powdered sugar I was wearing in addition to the sweater. I'd worn it to work for the first time yesterday. Judy from HR had baked and brought cookies.

Someone at SPI had taken that photo. At SPI headquarters.

"It was found in the coat pocket of our John Doe," Burton said.

I'd heard the expression about your blood running cold, and at that moment, I knew exactly what it felt like. A photo of me was taken yesterday at the super secret—and supposedly secure—SPI headquarters and was found tonight on a dead man whom I'd never seen before. Who took the picture and why? At least at my old tabloid job, I knew who wanted to stab me in the back—everybody. I hadn't been at SPI long enough to have pissed anyone off that bad, at least I'd like to think so. At SPI, the stabbing could be literal and it could be anyone.

"I want a name, Ms. Fraser."

"So would I," I heard myself say.

"It's a stretch to classify as a coincidence you being at a murder scene where the victim was carrying a photo of you, don't you think?"

I didn't respond because I was officially beyond words. At that moment, I knew I really needed a lawyer. The sight of the photo combined with the smell of my own clothes and the chair I'd been sitting in made me feel more than a little queasy.

There was a knock at the door—as the door was being opened.

"Miss Fraser will not be answering any more questions, Detective Burton."

I knew that cool, lightly accented voice, and I didn't need to turn around for confirmation.

Alain Moreau, SPI lawyer.

Speak of the devil.

Most people would be glad to see a high-powered lawyer arrive to save the day. The day might be saved, but I wasn't, at least not for long.

Alain Moreau wasn't just any agency lawyer; he was SPI's chief legal counsel, right-hand man to Vivienne Sagadraco, the boss lady herself. Here he was at oh-dark-thirty elegantly attired in a black suit that probably cost more than I'd make this year; that is, if I still had a job come sunrise. It set off his always meticulously cut white blond hair, pale skin, and light blue eyes to perfection. I'd always thought he looked like Anderson Cooper, minus the giggling and sense of humor. Most people couldn't carry off that look in the middle of the night, but Alain Moreau wasn't most people. The night was the middle of his business day.

Alain Moreau was a vampire.

I was sure that plenty of people at SPI had been tempted to make the bloodsucking lawyer joke. An ill-timed vampire lawyer reference to my former editor was what had made me the target of his creepy attentions. So I, like everyone else at SPI, kept any joke urges to myself.

I'd been brought in to the First Precinct for questioning in relation to a gruesome murder.

Now I was really in trouble.

I'd rather have told Detective Burton the absolute and unvarnished truth and risked getting locked up for a full psych evaluation than have Alain Moreau here. Moreau meant that Vivienne Sagadraco had a personal interest in what had happened tonight—and in her two agents who had been there when it'd happened.

"Miss Fraser, if you will come with me." Moreau's tone betrayed no emotion whatsoever.

No part of this turn of events could be called good.

Burton stood. "I'm not finished questioning . . ."

"Yes, Detective Burton, you are. Miss Fraser has told you all that she knows. I have spoken with your captain and filled out the necessary paperwork. Miss Fraser and Mr. Byrne will be leaving with me."

Ian Byrne wasn't happy.

News flash. None of us in the agency SUV were happy. Not only was I not happy, I was downright terrified.

Alain Moreau sat up front with the driver. He was facing ahead, his eyes on the frozen tundra that was Lower Manhattan, his thoughts probably on the fastest way to terminate my employment and where to scrounge up a new seer on short notice. He hadn't said a word since we'd left the police station. I didn't know what he was thinking. Maybe he felt that it was just more efficient to ask his questions once we were in the boss's office. Maybe Moreau didn't like repeating himself. Probably he was just too pissed to talk.

Unlike the rest of us, the uniformed driver might not have had a bad night, but I couldn't see his face from where I was sitting, and he hadn't so much as glanced in the rearview mirror. Not that I could have seen his eyes anyway. He was wearing sunglasses. According to the blue-lit digital clock on the SUV's dash, it was nearly two o'clock in the morning. Who—or what—wore sunglasses at two o'clock in the morning? Not that I really wanted to know or find out.

Ian sat next to me, his profile in shadow, illuminated only when we passed a streetlight. "What did you tell them?"

I slouched back into my own little patch of dark. "We were hunting a rat, whiskey was bait, NVGs because rats like the dark, I didn't know the dead guy . . ."

"And?"

I really didn't want to have the rest of this conversation, but this wasn't one of those problems you could ignore and it'd go away. Ignoring it was liable to get me killed—or worse, fired. If I hadn't offered to help Ollie with his nachtgnome problem, none of this would have happened. Well, the murder still would have happened, but we wouldn't have been there to hear it and then get caught in the aftermath.

"The dead guy might have known me," I said.

Silence from Ian, though I knew that was temporary. And even deeper silence from the vampire lawyer in the passenger's seat.

I told Ian about the bloody photo and made sure Moreau heard every word. This was one story I didn't want to tell again.

"Are you sure the photo was taken at SPI?" Ian asked.

"It was the only place where I was eating cookies." I didn't like what it said about me that most of the time when someone aimed a camera at me, I was eating.

"Who had the camera or phone?"

"No one that I could see."

"Then who was standing close enough to get that shot?"

"A lot of people. Like I said, there were cookies."

"What time was it when you ate two cookies?"

"Uh . . . actually that should probably be *which* time was it. I ate two cookies at the same time more than once. They were really good—but they were small," I hurried to add.

"How many times?" Ian repeated.

"Three . . . or four. Yesterday was a slow day."

Moreau let a small sigh escape.

Way to make a good impression on the boss lady's right-hand man, Mac. Tonight you freelanced, got arrested and interrogated, and now Moreau probably thinks you spend more time eating than working.

"I'll have security pull the break room and adjacent hallway footage for the entire day," Moreau told us. His disturbingly pale blue eyes met mine in the rearview mirror. I guess that thing about vampires and mirrors wasn't true; I could see his disapproving expression just fine.

Unfortunately, the identity of the amateur paparazzi at SPI wasn't the end of my stalker worries.

I closed my eyes for a moment. Come on, Mac. Spill it. "And I'm pretty sure someone else is following me, too. Then again, make that two someones." I watched Ian's face. "And one of them knew you."

I told them about the homeless man and the yuppie vampire.

Ian was incredulous. "Why didn't you tell me when we—"

"Because you would have pulled the plug on my nachtgnome hunt at Ollie's." I didn't mean to snap, but I didn't try to stop myself, either. It was probably due more to emotion overload than anything else. I'd been shaking in my boots since I'd stepped into Ollie's office, and my night had yet to get any better. "I promised to help him, and I was raised to do what I promise. It wasn't like either one of these guys followed me to Ollie's."

Ian gave me a suspicious frown. "That you know of."

"Yes. That I know of. I checked behind, beside, in front, and above me the entire way there. And to be extra-super paranoid, I walked around sewer grates so nothing could grab my ankles."

Ian was watching me steadily. "Exactly what did the man say?"

"Give my regards to your partner."

"That's it?"

"That's it."

"What was his tone? Any inflections? Did he have an accent?"

"He had a silky voice. Kind of slimy, actually. Smug." I thought for a moment. "No accent that I could tell."

"Everyone has an accent."

"If he had one, I don't know what it was."

"And you could only see the bottom half of his face?"

"Right. The—"

"How about his hands?"

"Gloves. I think."

"You think?"

What little composure I had left went bye-bye. I felt like I was being interrogated all over again, this time by my own partner. "The first time he was sitting on the sidewalk in the dark. I couldn't see his hands. The second time, I had a freakin' vampire at my back." I froze. Oh shit. "No offense, Mr. Moreau," I quickly added.

"None taken, Agent Fraser. During the course of my lengthy life, I have been called many things, but 'freakin'' has never been one of them. I'll consider it a novelty."

Ian raked a hand through his dark hair and exhaled slowly. The tension level went down by a couple of notches. "I'm sorry I snapped."

If he could make the effort, so could I. "Me, too." I swallowed on a dry throat. "It's been a shitty night."

"Agreed."

"About the guy's face," I said. "He had . . ." I hesitated. I had no idea how to describe what I'd seen. "He had more than one, if that makes any sense. They were like images, layered one on top of the other."

That got everyone's attention. Even the driver's sunglass-covered eyes gave me a quick glance in the rearview mirror.

"I've never seen anything like it," I said.

"You're sure it wasn't an aura from a veil?" Moreau asked.

"Positive."

"Were all the faces human?"

I thought back to the fun-house mirror images that I'd seen. "The top few layers were. The others weren't as clear."

"How many were there?" Ian asked quietly.

"Too many to count. I'm sorry I can't give any more detail than—"

"That's okay." My partner's expression seemed to soften. Maybe it was just a trick of the shadows between the streetlights. "You can only see what you see."

I hesitated. "Do you know him?"

"No." Ian gazed out the window, his eyes narrowing in concentration. His thoughts were his own, and he seemed determined to keep them that way.

I slumped back in my seat, dropped my head into my hands, and closed my eyes for a blissful three seconds.

I raised my head. "So does anyone know who the vampire might be?"

"I don't know of any such individual personally," Moreau replied. "However, I am on good terms with the mistress of the Manhattan coven. I will make inquiries until I locate him."

"What about a man with multiple faces capable of scaring a vampire clear across the street?"

Alain Moreau almost smiled. "I especially look forward to meeting him."

# 3

WHILE New York was the city that never sleeps, sometimes it at least closed one eye. It was the middle of the night and absurdly below freezing. The only people out driving were those who had to be, or people who were crazy enough to want to.

The driver pulled into a private parking garage on West Third Street a block from Washington Square Park in Greenwich Village, and began spiraling down to the lowest level. The garage was dimly lit, yet the driver kept his sunglasses on and seemed to have no trouble seeing where he was going. I chose to ignore anything that implied, concentrating instead on my fear of being squashed. Let's just say I was prone to claustrophobia. Once we got to the bottom level, there couldn't have been more than a few inches of clearance between the top of the SUV and the concrete slab above it.

The driver pulled into a parking space near the back of the garage between a pair of concrete columns, turned off the engine, flipped open a small panel on the SUV's dash, and pressed a button. Almost immediately, the car began to sink, the only sound the low rumble of some serious hydraulics hidden in the columns and in the wall in front of us. I had been taken to SPI this way once before. I didn't like it then, and I didn't like it any better now. But when you had four people in a company SUV, there were only so many ways you could get to headquarters.

The elevator stopped with a disconcerting jerk, and a pair of steel doors ground open in front of us, opening into one of the city's many abandoned subway tunnels. In this particular tunnel, the tracks had been removed, and the ground smoothed and paved. The driver pulled out of the elevator and turned down the former subway tunnel as if it were just another street. After about a hundred yards, we came to what looked like a dead end. At SPI, things and people were rarely what they appeared to be. Moreau pushed another button on the dash, and what looked like a wall of rock and construction debris lifted, revealing another parking garage with seven black SUVs identical to the one we were in, two troop transport trucks, and a limo. All of the SUVs had sunroofs that weren't for admiring the view. They were for those occasions when our teams needed quick access to the big guns—and to get them back out of sight with equal speed. The NYPD frowned on rocket-powered grenade launchers or belt-fed machine guns being used in the five boroughs. I was glad to say that my presence hadn't been needed on any of those missions.

I much preferred the entrance I used on a daily basis. I'd go into Saga Partners Investments through the front door, walk through the office into the back room, open the door to the cleaning supply closet and step inside. All I had to do was put my hand up to the hand scanner, and that closet became a pine-scented elevator down to SPI headquarters. A pleasant scent, minimal claustrophobia, and the elevator opened near the break room with its life-giving coffee and occasional cookies. What's not to love?

Me, Ian, and Moreau got out of the SUV, but the driver stayed. Maybe he had more wayward agents to pick up at another police station. Moreau held his hand in front of what looked like a sheer concrete wall. There was an approving beep and a door-sized portion of the wall smoothly swung open. A short access tunnel and another hand-scan-activated door later, we were in what we called the bull pen.

SPI's New York headquarters complex was located directly beneath Washington Square Park, and it was nearly as large as the park itself. Just the bull pen area was ringed with five stories of steel catwalks connecting offices, labs, and conference rooms. The main floor was filled with desks, computers, people, and not-people. We ran three shifts a day, and operated 24/7/365. Not surprisingly, the largest shift was on duty right now—the graveyard shift. Even supernatural baddies that weren't nocturnal tended to do their thing at night. Humans were essentially the same, but without the fangs, claws, and paranormally bad attitudes.

I'd been introduced to Vivienne Sagadraco, the founder and CEO of SPI, at my final interview before being hired. Maybe she met with every new employee, or perhaps being the only seer in the New York office had earned me the special treatment. I'd heard that longtime agents referred to her as the dragon lady. I was slow on the uptake, so until I was face-to-uh-face with Vivienne Sagadraco, I didn't realize that was meant literally.

My boss was a dragon.

She could morph in and out of human form; but as a seer, I got a clear view of what she really was.

I'd figured the meeting had been set up as a final test. At the tabloid, I'd interviewed some scary people, though at least most of them had been human. What had kept me from running out of the room screaming during my final SPI interview had been the utterly surreal setting and situation—that, and I really wanted the job. That single fact was not only motivational, but had effectively put the brakes on any potential hysterics. I think I might have even smiled at my new boss.

So money and a chance to regain my professional self-respect had motivated me to sit and have a proper high tea with a proper—if scaly—British dragon.

To a normal person, Vivienne Sagadraco appeared to be an attractive and vital woman in her late sixties. My seer vision revealed a dragon with peacock blue and green iridescent scales, seated in a throne-like chair across from me, having just served me tea from an ornate silver tea service, now improbably holding a dainty teacup and saucer in her long, taloned fingers. A pair of sleek wings were folded like long shadows against her back. Definitely surreal. All that was missing was a nervous rabbit in a waistcoat running through the oak-paneled office with a giant watch freaking out about the time. Vivienne Sagadraco in her human form wasn't much taller than I was. However, a faintly glowing aura surrounded her, telling me that in reality the creature before me was much larger than she appeared.

I'd decided right then that I could go through the rest of my career at SPI perfectly happy not knowing exactly how large of a dragon Vivienne Sagadraco actually was. It was bad enough that during our interview my future boss's glittering eyes had looked at me much the same way as I had the finger sandwiches.

After what I'd done tonight, the boss might decide that her initial impulse was correct, and that I'd make a better snack than agent.

Being escorted to the boss's office by her right-hand legal eagle/vampire meant that what Ian and I had stepped in tonight wasn't just another crime scene with a monster perp.

We took an elevator up to the fifth floor and the executive suite. As Moreau escorted us into her office, Vivienne Sagadraco was standing with her back to us in front of a two-way glass wall—which bore an unsettling resemblance to an interrogation room's—gazing down into the bull pen. It was about two hours until sunrise, yet her tailored gray suit looked as crisp as it would have at the start of the business day, and her short, silver hair was perfectly styled. Vivienne Sagadraco wasn't nocturnal and she didn't live at headquarters, though rumor had it she kept a small apartment here for emergencies. Home was a penthouse overlooking Central Park West. Dragons liked to be able to survey their domain. So if this wasn't an emergency, that meant she'd made a special trip here just for us on a night with a subzero windchill.

I shot a quick glance at Ian. He didn't look like he felt

special or flattered, either. Then again, Ian always had any and all of his feelings securely locked up. The man of steel and stone.

Vivienne Sagadraco spoke without turning. "Good morning, Agents Byrne and Fraser." Her British accent was cool and smooth, rather reminding me of Judi Dench's M about to give James Bond some really bad news. "Please be seated."

We hung our coats on the brass coatrack by the door, then did as told. I perched on the edge of the chair with the only part of my jeans that hadn't been soaked in whiskey. They were relatively dry now, but the smell was still there. Moreau remained standing by the door.

"I will not waste any of our time," she told us, "since so little remains of it. Last night the mutilated body of a goblin noble was discovered in Chinatown. Kanil Ghevari was one of our own, and was a strong advocate with his people for keeping the supernatural realm hidden from the general population. Certain elements of his murder bear disturbing similarities to the incident at Barrington Galleries earlier tonight."

Detective Burton had homed in on me and Ollie, but only in connection with tonight's murder. Chinatown was close enough to the First Precinct, so why hadn't Burton grilled me about where I was last night?

"We have his remains here," Sagadraco said, as if she could read my mind. "The human authorities do not know of Kanil's murder, nor can they know."

"After his death," Ian told me, "any spells Kanil had been using to pass for human would've faded; within an hour, they would've been completely gone."

That would have been a big surprise for someone down at the city morgue.

"Kanil was the sole voice of reason with the radicals among their aristocracy," Sagadraco said. "They are rapidly growing weary of concealing themselves from humans. He will be sorely missed." Her steely blue eyes took in both of us in turn. "Tell me precisely what happened this evening. Leave nothing out."

We did. I started with Ollie asking me to catch the nachtgnome, included the run-in with the vampire and the multi-faced man who scared him away, and topped it off with the picture of me having been found on the dead man—a photo taken at SPI. Ian filled in his involvement as it came up.

Sagadraco scowled, then glanced past us at Moreau.

"I will locate the vampire and the man outside the liquor store," he said.

She nodded once.

"And I will know the identity of the photographer before dawn," Moreau promised.

"Notify me as soon as you do."

"Of course, ma'am. Permission to begin now."

"Granted."

The door opened and closed, leaving us alone with Vivienne Sagadraco.

Now her full attention was on me. "Did you capture it?"

"Ma'am?"

"The nachtgnome, Agent Fraser. Did you capture it?"

"No, ma'am."

I heard a distinctly draconic sniff of amusement. "Unfortunate."

"Yes, ma'am, it was."

"And this was after it had consumed two bottles of whiskey." She almost sounded impressed. "It must have been a large specimen."

"And a mean drunk," Ian added.

She almost smiled. "Agent Fraser, when we are finished here, please avail yourself of our shower facilities and a change of clothes."

There was nothing I'd like more. "Thank you, ma'am."

Her smile vanished. "Our source in the city medical examiner's office reported that there was a winged scarab tattoo on the dead man's palm."

"There was also a large, bloody handprint on the window frame," I said.

"How large?"

"At least five times the size of Ian's . . . uh, I mean Agent Byrne's."

Sagadraco nodded in acknowledgment as if that information wasn't news to her.

"Two units arrived within minutes," Ian said. "Someone knew there was going to be a murder, and called it in to make sure the police would arrive immediately after. I didn't detect any surveillance around the shop, but that doesn't mean that it wasn't there."

"I'd told Ollie that I'd be there around ten o'clock," I said. "Between the vampire and the icy sidewalks, I got there closer to ten twenty."

"Given the photo of her found in the victim's pocket, there is a chance that all this could have been a setup for Agent Fraser." Ian continued, "Though I don't know what the motive could have been. More likely would be that the caller wanted the police to find the body quickly; maybe even get a glimpse of the thing that did it. Though if they'd gotten themselves glimpsed, that thing would have probably added two more heads and arms to its collection."

Both possibilities strongly suggested that the caller wanted the human authorities to discover an inhuman murder scene—and me. Combine that with the murder last night of a known and vocal advocate of keeping supernaturals secret from humans . . .

"Could this just have been an attempt to draw unwanted attention to SPI?" I ventured.

"Among other things," Sagadraco said.

"Did our lab people find anything with Kanil's body that'd give us a clue as to what we're dealing with?" Ian asked.

"There were claw marks on his right shoulder consistent with a creature large and strong enough to tear an arm from its socket. The arm removal was done pre-mortem, yet there was very little blood found at the scene. The arm was not found with Kanil's body." She crossed the room to her desk and picked up a clear evidence bag like the one my bloody photo had been in. "However, this was." She gave it to Ian.

I leaned forward to get a better look. It was big enough that I didn't really need to, but morbid fascination got the better of me. The object was black, curved, narrowed to a fine point, and was at least five inches long.

"It looks like a claw," I said.

"That is precisely what it is, Agent Fraser. It was found caught on a rib adjacent to Kanil's heart."

My mouth went dry. "The thing that belonged to was on the other side of Ollie's office door?"

"We have every reason to believe so. And our examination of Kanil's remains confirms that all of his wounds—with the exception of the decapitation—were inflicted before he died." Sagadraco's eyes narrowed and a low rumbling briefly vibrated the air around me. I froze as I realized that Vivienne Sagadraco had just growled. Ian only saw and heard the human version; I got the full dragon experience in surround sound.

"There were five puncture wounds on Kanil's chest," she continued as if nothing had happened. "Our own medical examiner reported that they were indicative of a large clawed hand restraining him—also pre-mortem. She believes that Kanil's attacker tore off his arm, then held him down until he bled out."

There was dead silence.

Sagadraco scowled. "Measurements taken from the claw placement on Kanil's chest and the downward angle of the gash at the . . . amputation site on his right shoulder suggest a heavily muscled creature at least three meters tall."

Ian sat perfectly still. "A nine footer?"

"Probably closer to ten."

"The man in Ollie's office was torn limb from limb in less than a minute," I said. "And his head was taken as well as his right arm."

"The attack tonight displayed animal savagery. Kanil's murder was more the work of a sadist. I received a letter this evening from an individual who is claiming credit for bringing the creatures to New York."

"Creatures?" I blurted. "Plural?"

"Two, to be precise." Sagadraco took a piece of paper from her desk and handed it to me. "The letter was delivered to me at home earlier this evening. I took the usual precautions before opening it, and deemed it not to be dangerous." She scowled. "I was mistaken. Immediately after I read it, both the letter and the envelope it was in burst into flames. I wrote down the vital portions before it vanished from my memory."

Ian leaned over to read with me.

*I will cure humans once and for all of the absurd notion that they are, or ever have been, at the top of this world's food chain. To truly believe, they must see it for themselves. Their own literature abounds with predators that hunt them in the night. I have introduced two of them to this island teeming with prey.*

*I am certain that you will extend every courtesy to my guests as they sample the delights that this fair city has to offer—especially during the revelry that bids farewell to the old year, and will welcome what promises to be the beginning of an enlightened new age.*

That was about as clear as mud.

Sagadraco perched on the edge of her desk. "The letter was unsigned, but the envelope had a wax seal—stamped with a scarab."

I looked up from the letter. "Like the dead man in Ollie's office."

"Exactly."

That made no sense. "But wouldn't that mean that the dead guy worked for whoever wrote the letter? Who claims to be in control of the monsters?"

"It temporarily confuses matters," Sagadraco admitted, "but I suspect there was a reason. Dr. Evans has theorized that the derisive reference to humans and the mention of '*their* own literature' indicates that our adversary either isn't human, or believes him- or herself to be vastly superior, holding all others in contempt. Or both."

"Dr. Evans?" I asked.

"Our staff criminal psychologist," Sagadraco replied. "He believes that this individual will communicate again with us very soon; the megalomania evident in the letter will not allow them to remain silent for long." Her eyes glittered. "We will not wait for the next communication; and we will do everything in our power to prevent these monsters from killing again. I have our researchers compiling a list of creatures featured in literature capable of tearing off a man's head and limbs. And our contacts in the city medical examiner's office will let us know if anything was found with tonight's victim that may assist us."

I suddenly remembered that I hadn't had a clear look at the scarab tattoo. I'd had to move something out of the way first—something I'd stuck in my coat pocket.

I jumped up and almost ran across the office to the coatrack. "I think I can help. That is, if the police didn't take it when they searched me." I fumbled around in my right pocket until I found the wadded up Kleenex with the hair. Now that I knew what it probably belonged to, I extracted it with two fingers, not really wanting to touch it at all. If the police had come across it, they'd left it right where they found it. I didn't blame them in the least.

"I don't think you want to handle this," I told the boss, "or have it on your desk. Do you have a piece of paper I could put it on?"

Vivienne Sagadraco pulled a sheet of paper out of the printer behind her desk. I quickly put the hair and Kleenex on top, glad to get rid of it.

Ian came over as the boss took a pencil and peeled back the tissue, exposing the hair.

"It looks like a big dreadlock," Ian said, "made of wire."

"It's softer than it looks," I told him, "though not by much."

"Where did you find this?" Sagadraco asked me.

"Clutched in the hand of the man killed in Ollie's office. The hair was wrapped around two of his fingers. I was thinking he might have pulled it out of the monster during the struggle." I paused uneasily. "Or what there was of it. I had to move it to get a good look at the tattoo."

Ian scowled. "After I'd told you not to touch anything."

I flashed him a smile. "Nope, I did it before. And with the cops barging in seconds later, it's a good thing I did."

"This time."

Sagadraco leaned in closer to study the hair, close enough that the snout of her dragon aura hovered directly above it. When it came to sensitive schnozes, dragons ranked right up there with werewolves. She sniffed almost delicately, taking in its scent, then her human face twisted in disgust.

"I'll send the sample down to the lab for analysis," she said, "but I think we can safely deduce that it came from the creature that attacked our John Doe. Its scent is . . . most potent and distinctive."

Ian put the letter back on Sagadraco's desk. "Kanil was killed last night. John Doe tonight. From the contents of that letter, he—or she—has something extra special planned for New Year's Eve."

"Do you remember the siren infestation during Fleet Week two years ago, Agent Byrne?"

Ian went back to his chair and sat. "Yes, ma'am. That was a tough one to cover up. Though it helped that a lot of those sailors were drunk."

"Yes. It did. Unfortunately, three days from now, the television cameras and the world's communication technology will be intensely focused on this city."

New Year's Eve in Times Square.

Oh hell.

In less than forty-eight hours, New York would play host to the world's largest and loudest party. A million people there and billions more watching. I'd moved to New York in November of last year. I'd made a couple of friends by New Year's, and they said that everyone should do the Times Square New Year's Eve thing at least once. So I'd gone, and had subsequently filed the experience under "never do that again." I liked people, but I didn't like being in the middle of *that* many people. I couldn't imagine a pair of ten-foot monsters rampaging through that crowd. What the monsters didn't kill, the resulting panic and stampede could.

It would be the perfect coming-out party for a pair of monsters—and the undisputed end of hiding the supernatural from the world's population.

"Ma'am, I know this probably goes against agency policy," I ventured, "but shouldn't we notify someone? Like the army, navy, air force, and marines?"

"And tell them what? That a pair of literary monsters have been loosed on the city and will slaughter dozens, possibly hundreds packed together the way they will be in Times Square, during the night when the world's eyes are upon us? Which authority do you think will believe such a scenario, Agent Fraser?"

My silence was her answer.

"Precisely. Even if they believed that there was a threat, they aren't qualified to locate these creatures—or to deal with the one who released them. We *are* qualified and we *will* deal with those responsible. Whoever is behind this is probably providing another type of concealment for them. A veil of some kind would be most likely. A person who is powerful enough to control such creatures has more than enough talent in the magical arts to conceal them from the view of our agents."

Monsters concealed from view. It sounded like I was about to be drafted. It made me question just how important a 401k was to me. I didn't have a choice though.

"But first, I require your and Agent Byrne's assistance in an even more pressing matter. We must discover the mastermind's identity and location with the utmost speed. At the moment our only link to this person is the man who was killed in Oliver Barrington-Smythe's office—a person who had a photo of you that had been taken in a supposedly secure location. That detail does *not* make me happy. This man had your photo and was in that office for a reason. I want to know what that reason was, and I want to know if Mr. Barrington-Smythe has any connection to the murder of one of my people." Her eyes narrowed. "He is your source, Agent Fraser. Find him. If we know that there is a connection between the two of you, so does our adversary. You must find Barrington-Smythe first and discover what he knows. And if you cannot obtain that information from him"—she smiled in a baring of teeth—"bring him to me. Dismissed."

# 4

A hot shower and an even hotter cup of coffee didn't change how I felt about having to find two monsters capable of tearing a man to pieces. I was only marginally less enthused about having to hunt Ollie to the ends of the earth—or at least the five boroughs.

I got dressed, wolfed down a stale doughnut in the break room, snagged another doughnut and cup of coffee to take with me, and met Ian in the bull pen.

It was a little before six in the morning according to the clock labeled "New York" on the bull pen wall. We had clocks for every other major city and time zone around the world. If you were tracking a monster that got up when the sun went down, I could see why it'd be a good idea to know exactly what time it was. Here in headquarters, it was time for the shift change; yet there was no shifting or changing going on. No one was going anywhere. I had a feeling the next few days were going to be all hands on deck.

Ian and Yasha Kazakov were intent on a bank of computer screens in the corner of the room.

Yasha was one of SPI's drivers and trackers. In a city where at any given time there were more supernatural baddies than available parking spaces, having a reliable drop-off and pick-up guy was a necessity. Even better was one who had no problem with turning a rampaging monster into a hood ornament. And should a simple collar turn into a cluster, Yasha was always more than happy to take the fight beyond the driver's seat—especially during the full moon.

Yasha Kazakov was a werewolf.

Even if a person was using a spell to mask their true identity, my seer vision gave me a sneak peek of what they had going on supernaturalwise. In Yasha's case, it was like a large, furry, red-haired aura. I had seen a few werewolves before coming to New York, so it wasn't that much of a shock. The majority of werewolves had more control than people gave them credit for. At ninety-six years old, Yasha had had plenty of time to practice. There were two werewolf packs: one in Manhattan and another in the outer boroughs. Yasha wasn't a member of either one. He considered SPI his pack.

Older werewolves could change when they wanted to, but all werewolves, regardless of age, changed on the night of the full moon. Werewolves at SPI automatically got three days a month off: the day before, the day of, and the day after a full moon. Though some missions went better and got resolved faster when you had an irate werewolf on your team. Most supernatural baddies surrendered on the spot to keep from having a full-moon–crazed werewolf, who could do zero to sixty in six strides, turned loose on them.

But on those occasions when the moon was full, a werewolf agent was needed, and chances were high that the public might accidentally get a glimpse, SPI's Research and Development department had come up with a disguise for "that time of the month." Mood swings, cravings, anger, and irritability—trust me, you ain't seen cranky until you've seen a werewolf trying to force down their natural inclinations during a full moon.

I didn't understand how it worked, but it involved a little

science, a lot of magic, and worked on the same principle as a goblin being able to walk down Broadway while looking just as human as anyone else.

The disguise R&D settled on? A German shepherd. Readily accepted the world over as police and military dogs. Pair a K-9 with a SPI commando in a flak vest or body armor, and your average New Yorker wouldn't bat an eye.

Yasha glanced up, saw me, smiled, and waved me over. The big Russian was wearing his usual uniform of fatigues, combat boots, and a T-shirt. Today's T-shirt phrase of the day was: "In case of emergency, lift shirt, pull .44."

I liked Yasha.

All eyes were focused on a bank of six screens. Two of the images appeared to be from street cameras like the ones the city used to keep an eye on traffic at major intersections.

Kenji Hayashi was SPI's resident tech geek. He was also an elf. I didn't know if he was half elf/half Japanese human or all Japanese elf. Heck, I didn't even know Japan had elves, and I didn't know Kenji well enough yet to ask. Some supernaturals could be even more sensitive and PC about those things than humans. Multi-cultural was one thing. But multi-species? Not sticking my foot in my mouth would be next to impossible, so I had kept it shut on that topic.

What I knew for sure was that if information was buried deeper than a politician's past or encrypted six ways from Sunday, Kenji was the go-to guy to dig it out and make it sing.

During his in-office hours, he was surrounded by computer screens directing teams of monster-hunting agents. He did exactly the same thing in his off-duty time, only then it was called gaming. Not being a gaming, anime, or comic aficionado, I didn't recognize most of the figures and toys on every exposed surface in Kenji's workspace, but there were two that I did—a foot-tall Godzilla complete with glowing red eyes, gripping a headless Jar Jar Binks action figure. The head was in Godzilla's mouth. It was my favorite.

There was one toy that both Kenji and I had at our desks, as did everyone else on SPI's company paintball team—a semiautomatic paintball rifle. It was a company-approved and encouraged activity because paintballs could be easily switched out for balls filled with holy water, which I'd heard had come in handy on more than one mission.

"Hacking into the city's cameras again, Kenji?" I asked.

His lips quirked in a quick grin, his eyes never moving from the computer screen where he was scrolling through a black-and-white video recording. "Only when they're showing TV worth watching."

I moved in closer. "What's on tonight?"

"What we heard, but didn't see," Ian said.

"Huh?"

"We have a camera mounted on the roof of the building across the alley from Ollie's office," Kenji said.

I blinked. "You watch Ollie's office?"

"Occasionally watching but always recording," Kenji said. "Ollie knows several interesting people, and we like to know when they visit."

"The dead guy was one of them?"

"Never seen him before. But don't blink; you're about to see more of him than you ever wanted to."

I'd seen it once and I didn't want to see it again.

"About ten twenty's when it got interesting." Kenji's eyes stayed on the counter. "There it is."

The camera was aimed at a darkened window. Someone opened the door, flipped on the lights, and closed the door behind them. My heart beat like a hammer in my chest. I hadn't seen the man's face before, but I'd seen most of the rest of him. It was definitely Ollie's office. Who else would have a pair of shrunken heads tied by their hair and hanging on the back of the door? The soon-to-be corpse sat at Ollie's desk and booted up his computer.

Yasha was looking at the doughnut in my hand. "You going to eat that?"

I handed it to him. "Not anymore."

"Ian, the question you asked? Here's the answer." Kenji indicated the two screens on either side of the one showing

Ollie's office. "That's the front door of Ollie's place, and that's the back. I went through the tapes for the past twelve hours. Our man didn't come in either one."

"The only way to Ollie's office from inside the shop is the stairs we'd used," I said. "From the outside, there's just the fire escape."

"Does Ollie have a basement?" Ian asked.

"I don't know."

"The bar at end of block was speakeasy in twenties," Yasha said. "Trapdoor in basement leads to tunnels that go to East River. Great for smuggling illegal . . ."

"Hooch," Kenji said helpfully, never taking his eyes off the screen.

Yasha grinned. "Hooch. Smuggling hooch. Likely Ollie has same."

Ian nodded, rolled a chair over, and sat. "Can you get more detail on his face before . . ."

"He doesn't have a head anymore? Probably." The elf's fingers sped over the keys, and the man's face was magnified, the pixels increasing in size along with it. Then he did something too fast to follow with the mouse and a few clicks later, the resolution sharpened, and we had a clear image of the man's face.

Ian leaned in closer. "Got enough to run through facial recognition?"

"Oh yeah." Kenji dragged the image to the screen above and the software started doing its thing. It flew through what had to be thousands of photos—and surprisingly more than a few sketches.

"Why are some of them only sketches?" I asked.

"Not all of the beings in our files can be photographed."

That wasn't a warm and fuzzy thought.

A few minutes later the computer stopped on a photograph.

"Lady and gentlemen," Kenji murmured, "we have a match."

It looked like a passport photo. Blond, square-jawed, nice

smile. Wherever his head was, I'd bet it wasn't smiling now. Text rapidly filled in the other side of the screen.

Dr. Adam Falke, Ph.D.
Born: November 16, 1963, in Roskilde, Denmark
Education: University of Copenhagen—Bachelor of Arts, Nordic Mythology & History, 1984; Master of Arts, Archaeology, 1986; Ph.D., Archaeology & Antiquities, 1988
Conservator, Arnamagnaean Institute, University of Copenhagen, 1989–1991
Associate Professor of History, University of Copenhagen, Department of Scandinavian Studies, 1991–2002
Private antiquities broker, 2003–present
Last known place of residence: London, United Kingdom

"Academic," Yasha said. "A lot of good education in that head. Though that was before—" The Russian make a slashing motion across his throat.

Oh yeah, that settled my stomach. I set my coffee down, too.

"He hadn't been an academic for nearly ten years," Ian said. "He'd spent the time since then as a private broker. That could cover up a lot of shady dealings."

Kenji clicked more keys. "I'll send it up to Bob and Rob in Research; if there's dirt, they'll dig it up."

"Better copy the boss lady," Ian said.

"Already done. I'm too pretty to be the breakfast special."

"Whoever sent her the letter that went poof would be way ahead of you on the menu," I told him.

Kenji arched one dark eyebrow. "Poof?" Minus the funky haircut, he looked disturbingly like a young version of the Mr. Spock candy jar he kept filled with wasabi-covered peas.

"Incendiary," Ian clarified. "Delivered to her home."

Yasha muttered something under his breath in Russian. I didn't understand the words, but they sounded impressed.

"He must be a major talent with an equally major death wish," Kenji noted.

I just stood there being confused. Ian noticed, and surprisingly, explained it to me.

"Sending an incendiary note to Vivienne Sagadraco took balls and then some," he said. "Sending one that could elude her detection took scary skill. And sending it to her at home was just nuts."

"So . . . the guy with the scarab tattoo and without a head was working for a magically talented nutcase."

"Or he could have been freelancing on the side and his boss took offense," Ian said. He gave me a sidelong glance. "Like somebody else I know."

"Not gonna let me forget that, are you?"

He jerked his head toward the screen. "Considering what happened to that guy, should I?"

"No, I don't believe you should."

Kenji turned his chair so we'd all have a front row seat for what was about to happen, then he leaned back, removed the top of Spock's head, and started popping wasabi peas like he was eating popcorn at a movie.

"Regardless," he said, "Ollie had information on his computer that Dr. Falke—or whoever he was working for—wanted in a bad way."

"Can you hack into Ollie's computer?" I asked.

Kenji stopped popping and just looked at me.

"Sorry. Let me rephrase that. *Have* you hacked into Ollie's computer?"

"Yes. Nothing even remotely interesting. Whatever this guy was looking for, Ollie didn't keep it on a computer, or at least not that one."

Yet another reason to pull Ollie out from the rock he'd crawled under.

On the screen, Falke stopped clicking keys and started listening. On the opposite screen, the camera focused on the front door showed me and Ian coming into the shop. Falke had heard the bell ring above the door. The camera captured video only, so while we couldn't hear the word he spat, we saw it just fine. He listened for a moment longer, then having apparently determined that we weren't coming upstairs, he went back to what he'd been looking for, but did it a lot faster.

Seven and a half minutes had passed according to the clock in the corner of the screen when a huge shadow fell over the man.

The creature had been in the office the entire time.

I'd been in Ollie's office before tonight. It didn't even have a closet, so there'd been nowhere for the thing to hide. Dr. Falke had been nervous enough when he'd heard us, but apparently he hadn't heard a ten-foot-tall monster so much as breathe before it started killing him.

"I didn't know veils could hide sound," I said in a small voice.

A single muscle twitched along Ian's jaw. "Apparently this one can."

Yasha spat a single word in Russian. I didn't need a translation for that one.

Dr. Falke must have heard the floorboards creak when we did. The screams started right after that—when the poor man had seen what was about to kill him. The screams were silent in the video, but we'd gotten to hear it at full volume and in person.

Now I was grateful the camera didn't record sound. I'd heard it once, and it'd probably be the soundtrack for my nightmares until something even scarier came along. The camera's field of vision was only what was directly in front of the window. Ollie's office wasn't all that large, so even if Falke had had a chance to run, there'd been nowhere to go, and in a matter of seconds, blood spattered in a sheet across the window, and even Kenji stopped eating.

The monster was too fast—for Falke and the camera. It was almost like the thing knew it was being filmed and stayed just out of sight. When the slaughter stopped, the only movement visible through the bloody window was the overhead light swinging back and forth.

A massive shadow loomed over the office door. The monster was standing just out of our view. Waiting.

It had heard us running up the stairs.

I instinctively froze. I knew I was watching a recording, but that didn't stop my survival instinct from telling me not to move or even breathe. Knowing that thing had been on the other side of the door from us was entirely different from actually watching it. My knees felt a little weak and I found a chair and all but fell into it.

The monster made its escape out the window, easily leaping down into the alley two stories below, too quick for the camera to catch anything other than a blurry shadow. Suddenly something dark passed across the lens of the camera mounted on the roof of the building across the alley from Ollie's office.

"Now *this* is the scary part," Kenji said.

The camera automatically refocused. Filling the screen was an eye divided by a vertical slit pupil. The eye narrowed, and a blink of that monster eye later, the screen went blank.

I just stared. "The second monster."

"Safe bet," Kenji said. "I wouldn't want to run into either one in a dark alley."

"Kanil already did," Ian muttered.

"My guess is that whatever it was ripped the camera out," Kenji said. "We'll need to fix that." More clicking. "I'll get the job req started."

I blew out my breath. "Crap. Time to go find Ollie."

Ian nodded. "The sooner, the better."

"I am your driver," Yasha told Ian. "Dragon lady wants you to have both hands free."

"What for?" I asked.

"Keeping you alive," Ian said. "Whoever sent the boss that letter could have sent that thing to kill Adam Falke, or it could have been acting on its own. Either way, I think she's right—our mastermind can't risk those two things being found before New Year's Eve. Kanil Ghevari was sharp; I can't imagine anything that could've come up on him without him knowing. And you saw what it did just now. It's got veils stronger than anything I've ever heard of." Ian stood and instinctively checked to make sure his gun and knife were where they were supposed to be. I suspected he had more. My partner looked down at me, his dark green eyes unreadable. "Only one person here can see through those veils."

I knew what that meant. "That would be me."

"Unfortunately, yes. And the worst you've had to deal with so far has been a gang of horny leprechauns." He reached for his coat. "We need to go."

I stood. "I have some ideas about where Ollie might be."

"Good. But we're making a pit stop first."

"Where?"

His scowl told me he didn't like what he was about to say. "To see Sam and get you a real gun."

# 5

JUST for the record, a real gun loaded with silver bullets is a lot heavier than a plastic water pistol filled with tequila.

While we had no way of knowing if silver bullets could take out either monster, they would work on many of the supernaturals that the monsters' host could have at his disposal and possibly send after us.

It was eight o'clock in the morning, and Ian, Yasha, and I were staking out Li Fong's just off Mott Street in Chinatown. We'd been here an hour.

It hadn't taken me long to figure out where Ollie was likely to be. I used simple logic then simply followed the bouncing ball. Almost every time I'd come to see him, regardless of the hour, Ollie had take-out boxes from Li Fong's scattered around on the counter or his desk. For Ollie, Chinese food was comfort food. I was a hot and sour soup aficionado myself, and no one made it better than Li Fong, so I was a regular customer as well.

Ollie had to have heard what happened last night at his shop; and if so, he was in hiding. Or he'd come to open his shop this morning, seen the police crawling all over the place, ran away, dug a hole, and pulled the dirt in after him. Regardless of which scenario Ollie was operating under, he needed comfort and Ollie had two means of comfort: money and food. He got twitchy at the mere thought of having to go for long without either one. The police still had his shop closed and surrounded with crime scene tape. That meant no money today for Ollie—and probably not for the rest of the week. He was probably holed up somewhere agonizing over the thought of all the potential after-Christmas shoppers he was missing out on; though most stores ran specials on tacky Christmas sweaters, not shrunken heads and vampire stakes. If he couldn't be making money, food had just been bumped up the list to his number one comfort. And that meant Li Fong's.

Ollie had an apartment off Canal Street. Not surprisingly, he wasn't there this morning. Considering the type of people he did business with, it'd be in his best interests to have a hidey-hole on the side. For Ollie, there was comfort in proximity, so he'd want to be close to his food source. There were rooms for rent above some of the restaurants and shops close to Li Fong's, so I was betting that Ollie was hiding in one of them. And he had to be one of Mr. Fong's best customers, so if Ollie wanted takeout first thing in the morning, Li would accommodate him.

I was quite proud of myself for my train of thought. What made it even better was that Ian had agreed with me. Though after sitting for the past hour, the shine had started to fade from my choo choo and my butt was asleep.

"Who orders Chinese at eight in the morning?" Yasha asked.

Ian shifted uncomfortably in his seat. "A man who thinks it might be his last meal."

We sat some more, and watched and waited for almost another hour when there were signs of life just inside the front door of the still-closed restaurant. A tall and lanky teenager came out and shut the door securely behind him, insulated delivery carrier in his hand.

Finally.

"That's Scott, Mr. Fong's grandson and delivery boy," I said. "Looks like Ollie just ordered breakfast."

I reached for the door handle; Ian's hand over mine stopped me.

"But we'll lose him," I said.

"We won't lose him," Ian said. "And if we wait, he won't see us—which is the point of following someone."

Scott went less than a block, stopping in front of a narrow brick building with no windows and what looked like a steel door. Balancing the takeout in one hand, Scott punched numbers into a keypad.

I swore. "See? Now we can't get in. If we'd followed him when I—"

"Not a problem." Ian kept his eyes on Scott, and extended his hand back to Yasha, who flipped open a small case attached to the underside of the dash.

"One super-secret spy gadget coming up," the Russian said.

He passed something to Ian that was about half the size of a smartphone, and Ian wrapped his gloved fingers around it before I could get a good look.

Ian started to open the door. "Okay, Mac. We're going to get out, and once you have a clear view down the street in both directions, I want you to take a good look. I'll check out the humans; I need you to ID any supernaturals who don't look like they're minding their own business." He opened the door and got out. "Let's go."

"I will make sure no one follows you," Yasha said. "Let me know if this Ollie does not want to leave. I will help change mind."

Ian grinned. "I'll do that."

The market down the street had opened, and two clerks were setting up a fresh fruit and vegetable display just outside the door. Despite the freezing temperatures, folks were out and about, opening their businesses, shopping, or just getting outside. The sun was out for the first time in days, and people were taking advantage of it. Unfortunately, they were all bundled up like they were setting out on an Arctic expedition. I could see through veils, but I couldn't see through five layers of sweaters, coats, boots, hats, and scarves wound around faces so only their eyes were peeking out. And since most everyone I saw was wearing sunglasses against the snow glare, I couldn't even see eyes. It was funny; I could see the supernaturals' auras floating around them, so I knew what they looked like. But the humans all looked like loaded and walking coatracks. I didn't know what the heck the humans were up to; but the trio of gnomes, the two elves, and the one troll seemed intent on their own business.

"Clear?" Ian asked.

"As far as I can tell."

We crossed the street as quickly as the icy slush would allow. When we got to the door, Ian pushed a button on the device and held it up against the keypad. It beeped, and Ian turned it around to look. A tiny display showed the keys glowing in various degrees of brightness. Ian quickly pushed the keys beginning with the dimmest to the brightest.

"Heat detector," Ian explained. "The key showing the faintest glow was pressed first, the brightest, last."

"But it's freezing out here and Scott was wearing gloves."

"It's that sensitive. Though at this temp, it wouldn't get a reading after about two minutes."

The door clicked and we were in.

I glanced over at Ian. Black leather coat, black jeans, black boots, black watch cap, unshaven face set on scowl.

"Could you at least try to look harmless?" I whispered. "You'll scare Scott."

We were in a relatively short hallway with four doors, two on each side. Scott was standing in front of the farthest door, hand raised to knock. Good. Ollie hadn't answered the door yet. Scott saw us and recognized me. I gave him a big smile and a little finger wave. He'd seen me in Ollie's shop before in addition to delivering to my apartment. Which boded well for the success of what I was about to try.

The kid's mouth gaped open. "How did you—"

"It's okay, hon," I said as casually as I could. "Ollie told me the code. He's expecting us." That last part had to be true. Ollie wouldn't be hiding in what was essentially a vault if he wasn't expecting visitors.

Scott visibly relaxed—and I reminded myself to breathe.

"What's he owe you?" I asked.

"Twenty-five ninety-eight."

I whistled.

"He ordered the lobster Cantonese, six crab rangoon, four eggrolls, and a—"

I held up a hand. "That more than explains it." Ollie was going all out on his last meal.

I turned to Ian. "Pay the man."

"What?"

"And give him a big tip. Scott's putting himself through NYU."

Ian reached for his wallet, muttering under his breath. "Ollie'll pay me back if I have to turn him upside down and shake it out of him."

Scott pocketed the cash and emptied his delivery bag on a table in the hall then knocked on the door for me. "Li Fong's," he shouted. Then he grinned, winked at me, and left.

We heard at least three dead bolts slide back plus an iron bar.

Ian rolled his eyes.

Ollie cracked open the door to peek out, saw me, and his eyes widened. But Ollie's survival instinct was no match for Ian's determined steel-toed combat boot.

"Scott, you little—" Ollie shouted.

"Miss Mac tips better than you," Scott called back over his shoulder.

"I told you being cheap was going to get you in trouble," I told Ollie as Ian forced our way in. "This time it might save your life."

Oliver Barrington-Smythe was on his fourth egg roll and third crab rangoon. I was on my second wave of nausea. I made a mental note never to eat Chinese food for breakfast.

"You have to believe me," he said around a mouthful of

egg roll. "I didn't know Adam Falkenburg would break into my office, and I have absolutely no idea why he would have a photograph of you."

I didn't have to believe him, but I did. However, the late Dr. Falke's trust didn't go nearly that far. He'd added a couple of extra letters onto his last name just to keep Ollie from knowing who he really was.

What I couldn't believe was why Ollie would even consider having what Dr. Falke had been in the market to buy. My nausea might have been caused by something other than the smell of Chinese food in the morning. I thought monkey brains had to be the nastiest thing Ollie had for sale.

I was wrong.

Oliver Barrington-Smythe was in possession of a mummified and preserved monster arm.

Dr. Adam Falke had been looking to buy one, and Ollie had it to sell.

That didn't explain why the Danish historian and archaeologist had broken into Ollie's office to get at his computer, and it did nothing to clear up why Falke had a picture of me. But it did confirm that no object was too bizarre or disgusting for Ollie to try to make a buck on it.

My British friend and his aliases had a pricey lifestyle to support, and had no qualms about what he did or who he conned to keep himself in the style to which he was accustomed. However, pricey didn't necessarily mean tasteful, as was evidenced by a toupee that sat on his head like a squirrel with Taser-styled fur. I didn't think Ollie was particularly vain; he just knew he looked like Humpty Dumpty without his rug.

Ollie was digging into the lobster Cantonese with a spork. "Falkenburg told me he represented an interested party who wanted to buy the arm."

Ian and I exchanged glances. We both knew that Ollie's interested party had to be the same person who had sent Vivienne Sagadraco a present that went poof.

"There's a head that goes with it. He wanted that, too. It's a matched set."

I experienced wave of nausea number three. "Well, of course. You couldn't break up a set."

"Do you have the head?" Ian asked.

"Not yet," Ollie said. "Though I've got a meeting set up at noon with the man who does."

"How big is the arm?" I asked.

"As long as you are tall." He gave me a quick up and down, re-calculating. "Then again, probably longer."

"Does it have claws?" Ian asked.

Ollie nodded around a mouthful of lobster Cantonese and held up his spork. "About this long."

"Keep eating," Ian told him and motioned me over to the corner of the room. "Falke's employer sent him to get the arm and head from Ollie. For whatever reason, the monster killed Falke. He's dead, but his boss still wants those parts . . ."

"And the only person who knows their whereabouts is our egg roll connoisseur over there." I looked at Ollie and shook my head. "He might as well have painted a bull's-eye on his forehead."

There was a grim glitter in Ian's eyes. "Not if we get the arm and head first."

He walked back over to where Ollie had just popped the last crab rangoon into his mouth. I followed.

"Where's the arm?" Ian asked Ollie.

"Certainly not anywhere near me. I showed Falkenburg a photo of the arm which I let him take with him. He damned well wasn't getting the arm until I got my million pounds."

I raised an eyebrow. "Pounds?"

"Falkenburg was based out of London. If he had to be in the land of the barbarians—no offense Mr. Byrne—"

"None taken. Yet."

"It made him more comfortable to deal in real money. It helped to establish trust. I like my high-end clientele to feel comfortable doing business."

"Nice," Ian said. "For the second and last time, where's the arm?"

"Certainly not in my gallery. I don't keep any higher quality merchandise there."

That was the truth.

"I've had clients try to take items without payment." Ollie smiled up at Ian. "I'd be delighted to take you to the arm—as soon as you deposit a million pounds into my account . . ."

I wasn't surprised that Ollie tried to fleece us for the money, but I was shocked that Ian didn't clear Ollie's kitchen table of everything, including Ollie.

Ian smiled, though there was nothing friendly about it. "As long as you have that arm, you're a dead man walking. Tell me, Ollie, what is the price of *your* arm—*and* your head? Give the arm to us and we'll make sure the very well-connected person holding the leash of the thing that ripped your late client to shreds knows that you don't have it anymore. That should keep your head on your shoulders for a little longer."

Until he pissed off the next criminal mastermind who had their own personal hit-monsters.

"You must understand, Mr. Byrne, I'm a businessman. I can't make exceptions for—"

Ian took his phone from his pocket. "You heard what happened to Dr. Falkenburg, correct?"

Ollie nodded and swallowed the last mouthful of lobster Cantonese with an audible gulp.

"Words don't do it justice." Ian walked around the table, pulled up a chair, and sat right next to Ollie. A little physical intimidation went a long way—it went even longer with gruesome photos. "A friend helped us get these pictures from the NYPD crime scene investigators. They do good work."

Ian used his index finger to scroll through the photos, and Ollie got pastier with every flick of the finger.

"Most of these really need no explanation," Ian said. He paused and turned his phone vertical, and then with an exaggerated puzzled expression, turned it back again. "I'm not sure which way is up on this one." He took his fingers and expanded the photo. "Oh yeah, that's it. There's your overhead light fixture with a rather long piece of intestine hanging from it."

Ollie's now-empty take-out box dropped from his suddenly nerveless fingers as his other hand went to his mouth. He fled to the bathroom.

Ian pushed a button on his phone and held it up to his ear. "Yasha, we'll be right out." I detected the barest hint of a crooked grin. "Yes, there will be three of us."

# 6

WE were on our way to Brooklyn to pick up an arm and see a man about a head.

Ollie had a meeting at noon at Green-Wood Cemetery with the seller's agent to finalize the details about buying the head. Ian pressured Ollie for his contact's name and details. Ollie reluctantly replied. Now all we had to do was get Ollie to the cemetery on time.

Ian had called Kenji and told him that we'd not only found Ollie, but also the two things that Falke and his boss had been after. Kenji relayed the information to the boss lady, and needless to say, Vivienne Sagadraco was intensely interested. To ensure that we kept what we were about to acquire, she'd dispatched a security team to the storage unit in Brooklyn. They would be waiting when we arrived. Dragons didn't fool around when it came to protecting things that they acquired—be it gold, gems, or a monster's body parts.

Yasha exited off the Brooklyn-Queens Expressway, onto Atlantic Avenue, went about two miles, and turned left into a small industrial complex. The sign on the storage unit office read "Climate-controlled units available."

"I take it you sprung for climate controlled?" I asked.

"Naturally."

"Thank you."

Even in winter, I'd imagine a mummified anything had a scent you didn't want to experience.

Yasha pulled up to the keypad on a pole, just in front of the gates. He looked in the rearview mirror at Ollie.

"Code."

Ollie hesitated, then sighed. "Eight, two, five, seven, three."

Apparently giving away a mummified monster arm for free was tough for Ollie, even if it meant saving his own.

Yasha punched in the numbers, there was a loud click, and the gate started to slowly roll back. Meanwhile, Ian was trying to see everywhere at once, and doing a fine job. As far as I could tell, no one had followed us. Unfortunately, that included our security team protection.

"Shouldn't our guys be here?" I asked.

Ian's silence was answer enough.

"Any chance they did some kind of ninja commando thing and are waiting for us at the unit?"

Silence again, this time with crickets.

I didn't put my hand anywhere near my gun; Ian would probably confiscate it if I did, but a real gun was a comforting weight under my coat.

The gate rattled to a close behind us, and Yasha drove to unit number 313. While I wasn't fond of the number, 666 would have been worse. Ian kept his eyes on the gate until it closed, while it had occurred to me that those ninja commandos could just as easily be from the opposing team.

The road that went around and between the buildings hadn't been plowed, but Yasha didn't let that slow him down.

He grinned at me in the rearview mirror. "No problem. Is like Siberia."

"You've never been to Siberia," Ian said, his eyes still scanning for any movement other than our own.

"True. But does not mean is not like Siberia."

Until now, Yasha hadn't said a word since Ollie had joined us. He had limited any and all communication to glares and scowls. I would have said it was his and Ian's version of good cop/bad cop, except right now, Ian wore the same expression. On second thought, it was how Ian always looked when he had to deal with Ollie—or almost anyone else for that matter.

Ollie directed Yasha to the front of a two-story building with a pair of iron-bar-reinforced glass doors. Inside was what looked like a freight elevator and a steel door that probably led to stairs.

"Looks like the only way in," Ian said to Yasha. "Did you see any fire exits?"

"Nyet."

"Where's your storage unit?" Ian asked Ollie.

"Second floor, last one on the left."

Ian just looked at Ollie.

Ollie raised his hands defensively. "If someone came in to randomly rob units, mine would be the last one they'd get to."

Ian's expression didn't change, and I knew neither did his opinion of Ollie.

"It doesn't seem like such a good idea now," Ollie admitted.

"I've got news," Ian said. "It wasn't a good idea then."

"I stand guard," Yasha said. He got out of the SUV and pulled a sawed-off shotgun out from under his seat.

"And keep our exit open," Ian told him.

Yasha grinned crookedly. "Don't I always?" He looked at me and his grin broadened. "Scream if something jumps at you."

I tried for a grin; it felt more like a grimace. "Don't I always?"

There was another keypad mounted on the wall next to the doors.

"Same code?" Ian asked Ollie.

"Yes."

Ian keyed in the code, the lock clicked, and we were in.

Ian had insisted that we take the stairs.

Ollie had started to complain, took one look at Ian's face, and kept his mouth shut.

I took the stairs whenever I could. Not because it was good for me . . . well, actually that was the reason, but not why you'd think. Ever since Ian had told me about getting trapped in an elevator by three shapeshifters who'd chosen to be giant rats for the evening, I had a newfound appreciation for the StairMasters at the company gym.

The stairwell and elevator doors opened into a single, long hallway that ran the length of the building. Ollie's unit was at the far end, next to the lovely dead-end concrete wall.

"Same code?" Ian asked Ollie.

"Yes."

Ian sprinted to the end of the hall, leaving me and Ollie to keep up. He punched in the code on yet another keypad, reached down, and lifted the rolling steel door.

We were hit in the collective face by dust and that pungent, musty smell that always signaled "really old stuff" to my nose. I sneezed. I was allergic to dust and mold, which wasn't a potentially fatal condition—unless you found monsters for a living, creatures that generally didn't lair in hypoallergenic conditions. People who sneezed didn't sneak very well.

Ian looked around inside the unit; his expression a perfect mix of disgust and disbelief. "Ollie, we need to have a serious talk about your choice of inventory."

So this is where Ollie had stashed the Egyptian mummy that had been in his shop—and two more to keep it company. There was also a more modern coffin that was hopefully empty, though thankfully closed. There were also chests, unidentifiable things, and various-sized cardboard boxes.

The dearly departed residents of his storage unit didn't bother Ollie at all as he squirmed his way to the back. We didn't need to tell him to hurry. The inside of Ollie's storage room wasn't the only thing that resembled a tomb. It was entirely too quiet out here, too. A mausoleum kind of quiet. Just like Yasha had never been to Siberia, I'd never been in a mausoleum, but I instinctively knew what one felt like. The creeps were the least of what I felt.

The sound of intense rummaging came from behind Ollie's mummies.

"Got it," he announced.

Have you ever noticed that when one big thing went right, everything else went straight to hell in a take-out box?

There was a heavy thump on the roof directly above our heads, immediately followed by more thumps farther back toward the elevator. Someone was on the roof, several someones, actually.

I froze. "Our guys?"

Ian's gun in his hand told me otherwise. Shotgun blasts from the front of the building where Yasha was confirmed it. The big Russian was good, and a werewolf, but there was only one of him.

Ian ran down the hall to cover the stairs and elevator. "Move it!" he shouted back at us.

My survival instincts had kicked in, and they sure as hell weren't telling me to run *toward* gunfire, but the way we'd come in was the only way out.

Before Ian could reach the end of the hall, both the elevator and stairway doors opened and three white camo-clad and armed men stormed through.

Not men.

Ghouls.

They'd look like men to Ian and Ollie, but my seer vision screamed—

"Ghouls!"

My brain did a quick flashback to SPI orientation. Ghouls ate human flesh, preferably while it was still alive; but in a pinch, corpses would do.

But either the pictures in the company manual hadn't done these things justice, or proximity magnified fear. Ghouls looked more or less like humans, but the resemblance ended there. Their eyes were solid black, but would roll over white like a shark when they fed. Their jaws were longer and their mouths wider to make room for jagged teeth. Their skin was a pasty whitish gray. But a more applicable problem in our case, they were next to impossible to kill. We'd had a ghoul from time to time back home, but I'd never run into a whole passel of the things.

Ian opened fire. The pair that'd come up in the elevator were hit and went down, one of the bodies trapped between the closing elevator door. Half a second later, both ghouls were trying to get up. Ian put another bullet between the eyes of the third ghoul that'd come up the stairs. He went down twitching, but the twitching didn't stop. Still twitching equaled not dead, or in his case, not dead again. More ghouls were coming through the stairway door.

Ollie was pushing his way out of the occult junk pile between the two upright mummies and was clutching what looked like a big gym bag. I reached in to grab him and the bag and pull them both out when one of the mummies fell out of the unit—and on top of me, knocking me to the concrete floor.

That mummy saved my life.

The unit's steel door slammed down, missing me by inches, and severing the mummy's legs at the knees. Ollie screamed from inside. I jumped up and grabbed the door handle, desperately trying to pull it up. It didn't budge. I panicked. The door must have locked.

"What's the code?" I yelled over Ollie's screams.

I jerked on the door again. Though if the door had been locked, it still would have had some give. This thing was anchored to the floor. I wasn't a weakling; something was keeping that door down.

Drowning out Ollie was the scream of metal being torn back as dust fell from the ceiling.

The roof.

Above Ollie's storage unit.

I pulled on that door with every bit of strength I had. What seemed to be fused to the concrete floor a second before now flew open.

The metal roof had been peeled back like a sardine can, exposing bright blue sky—and Ollie being hauled through the opening by two white camo-clad ghouls. They were attached to a hovering helicopter by a pair of quickly retracting zip lines pulling them up into the big chopper's open door. One ghoul had Ollie, the other had the bag with the arm.

Ollie was screaming, but I couldn't hear him over the rotors.

I pulled my gun and aimed it at the ghouls, then the helicopter. My hands were shaking so badly I couldn't get a fix on either one. The ghoul was holding Ollie in front of him like a human shield. The ghoul with the arm was safely behind the ghoul with Ollie. He saw me and grinned, his jagged teeth yellow against the white of his camo. Silver bullets wouldn't kill these ghouls, but they'd definitely kill Ollie.

The helicopter flew up and away before Ollie and his captors were even inside.

And I hadn't even fired a shot.

# 7

NORMALLY it wouldn't be easy to kick yourself while sitting in the backseat of a vehicle—even an SUV. But I had an advantage.

The seat next to me was empty.

Ollie wasn't there.

Because I'd failed.

I'd failed as a SPI agent; but worse than that, I'd failed Ollie as a friend. I'd never come right out and said that we'd protect him, and Ollie hadn't asked for it, because it'd been implied. He'd been depending on us, and since I'd been standing five feet away when the ghouls had ripped the roof off of that storage unit, that meant I was supposed to protect him.

I'd screwed up.

The first time I'd ever had a real gun out in the field, and I'd blown it. I might as well have had a squirt gun full of tequila. As a result of my inaction, Ollie was dead, or—knowing that ghouls preferred their human prey alive and kicking when they started to eat—right now he wished he was.

". . . they were headed northeast toward Queens," Ian was telling whoever he'd called at headquarters. "Looked like a

Sikorsky Jayhawk. Check with our guy in the coast guard and see if one's been decommissioned and sold lately." His eyes flicked to the visor mirror, glancing back at me. "No. No injuries." He paused, listening. "Yes, we're proceeding to Green-Wood. ETA . . ."

"Ten," Yasha told him.

"Ten minutes," Ian said into his Bluetooth headset. "I'll be meeting James Tarbert. Yeah, a guy who sells mummified monster heads. Check him out and give me a heads-up if there's something I need to know."

Not "*we'll* be meeting" or "*we* need to know," but "I." Looked like I'd had a chance to be a real partner, and I'd flunked the test.

Ian gave Yasha directions and then retreated into a full-blown silent treatment. Now I knew why Ian Byrne didn't want to work with me. I slouched down in the seat. And right now I agreed with him; I didn't want to work with me, either.

After a few miles, Ian spoke without turning. "You didn't have a clear shot."

I was leaning the left side of my face against the cold window. "It doesn't make me feel better, but thanks anyway."

"Wind, target position, helicopter speed—it all factors in. Besides, if you'd shot the ghoul, he probably would've dropped Ollie, and that wouldn't have been a survivable fall."

I slowly sat up. That hadn't occurred to me. Way to go, Mac. You could've converted Ollie from ghoul captive to rooftop pancake. Fat lot of good my back home gun experience had done me. Being able to clear a line of beer cans from an old washer would never save anyone's life, and I'd never actually heard of a deer taking a hunter hostage and using him as a shield while being hoisted into a helicopter. So I could hit a target. Big deal. That didn't teach me when to shoot, when to hold my fire; or if I did shoot, the why and how of that decision, a split-second choice that could mean life or death for another SPI agent, me, or a friend who was in the right place but at the worst time. Shooting targets was one thing. It was another thing entirely to shoot something with two legs—even if it was a ghoul.

When I glanced back up, Ian was regarding me solemnly in the visor mirror. "Your gun is for self-defense. You're the agency seer. Saving Ollie or anyone else isn't your job."

"And it's not your job to spot ghoul commandos," I told him. "But if you could, you'd do it, or anything else you needed to do. So maybe saving people should be at least part of my job."

Ian started to speak, and I raised my hand. "*If* necessary," I stipulated. "Or if needed."

Ian's phone beeped with an incoming call. I couldn't hear the caller's voice, and Ian kept his responses short. "That was our wayward backup," he told me and Yasha. "They were delayed by a frozen fuel line. They've gone ahead to the cemetery, and are establishing a perimeter around our subject. He just arrived."

Finally, something was going right.

"Was he carrying anything?" I asked. "Like a monster head?"

"No head."

"That would have been kind of conspicuous. Hopefully he won't send us to another storage unit."

"Pull over here," Ian told Yasha. "Keep the engine running; I won't be long." He gave me a look in the visor mirror.

I raised both hands. "Staying put."

I tried to see where he was going, but I lost him behind a mini mountain of snow, courtesy of the New York department of sanitation, that was piled on the side of Brooklyn's McDonald Avenue and topped by un-picked-up bags of garbage courtesy of the same city, same department. Between the weather and the holidays, public service was running a little light on the service.

After about five minutes, Ian got back in the SUV and handed me a respectable-sized bouquet of dark pink roses. "Here, hold this."

I met his roses with open-mouthed befuddlement.

"We need a reason to be in a cemetery," he told me. "A reason that'll ensure no one will get too close or ask any questions." He pulled what looked like a tourist brochure out of the glove box and unfolded it.

I saw the words "Green-Wood Cemetery" on the cover. I blinked. "A map? Of a cemetery?"

Yasha pulled out into traffic, such that it was. Though first he had to yield to a woman on cross-country skis who was making better progress than the cars.

"Green-Wood's quite the tourist attraction," Ian said. "They even have concerts."

"You're kidding?"

He folded the map to show one section and passed it back to me. I laid the bouquet across my arm like a pageant winner so I could take the map.

"Tarbert is supposed to meet Ollie on the cemetery's Nut Path off Hemlock Avenue," Ian told me.

"So the owner of a monster head wants to meet on a path named Nut," I said. "That's appropriate." I studied the map. Most of the avenues and paths were named after trees, bushes, flowers, and their various pieces and parts. There was a lot of twisty pavement on that map, so the cemetery's founders had to get creative with the names.

Yasha drove slowly past a pair of cast-iron gates on Twentieth Street near Prospect Park. The gates were closed, but there was a sign. "Use main entrance," Yasha read.

I squinted at the sign. "You can *see* that?"

"My eyes, they are very good." Yasha looked in the rearview mirror and flashed me a tooth-filled grin. "The better to see you with, *moja dorogaja*."

Russian werewolf humor.

"Reinforcements dead ahead," Ian said.

Considering where we were going, I could have done without the "dead" reference, but I was glad to see a big white Suburban parked on the other side of the street, hopefully packed to the spare tire with SPI commando-ninja-badass monster fighters and all their implements of destruction.

One guy got out.

Okay, that was disappointing.

He crossed the street to where we'd pulled over. There wasn't much by way of traffic, which was good, because he didn't look. Not that he needed to. He was big enough that cars had more to fear from him, like a month's stay in the body shop.

"Able to crush small cars with a single stomp," I murmured.

Yasha coughed a single chuckle.

The guy didn't glance down to check for icy patches on the street. It looked like his combat-booted feet just crunched right through to the pavement. I recognized him. He'd been on a takedown team for a hydra in a Chelsea apartment building laundry room. Small space, big mess, most of it made by the man coming around to Ian's window. He was at least a foot taller than me. Biceps the size of my thighs in my fat jeans, bull neck, and bald head. Kind of like Mr. T without the bling.

I wasn't disappointed anymore.

Ian lowered his window. "Calvin."

The big guy nodded. Not easy to do without a neck. "Captain sent me to escort you in."

"Good. Hop in next to Mac."

He did, and me and my bouquet full of disguise ended up scrunched against the far door.

"Pounded any interesting critters lately?" I asked as Yasha pulled back out into traffic.

"A redcap tried to pass himself off as Santa Claus out in front of FAO Schwarz last week. Those little bastards can run." Calvin grinned. "This one ran right out in front of a city bus."

"Ouch."

"We don't mind getting help from the MTA."

I nodded in approval. "Citizens' tax dollars at work."

Calvin turned to Ian. "Captain Norwood wanted me to tell you we're on comms." He tapped his ear once, and I saw the earpiece communications unit. "Usual channel."

While Ian was getting his own earpiece in place and testing it with Calvin, Yasha turned left onto Fifth Avenue and another left soon after into Green-Wood Cemetery.

I stared in goggle-eyed wonder. "*This* is the entrance to a cemetery?"

It was a Gothic wonderland extravaganza with two massive arches for entry and exit topped by three towering spires.

I looked down at the brochure and did a quick scan. Five hundred acres, one of the largest outdoor collections of nineteenth-century statuary and mausoleums, National Historic Landmark, yadda, yadda. Impressive. I glanced up as we passed under the largest Gothic arch. I saw a small sign next to a door.

I blinked. "Gift shop?"

"Cool T-shirts," Calvin rumbled.

Note to self: come back here when the snow melts.

Yasha went left on a neatly plowed and salted Battle Avenue.

The cemetery maintenance workers had done a good job plowing Green-Wood's roads, though most of the paths to the graves remained untouched. The larger monuments and headstones were easy enough to see even while snow covered, but any ground markers were completely buried and were neck-breakers waiting to happen.

"Pull over when Battle Avenue intersects with Hemlock," Ian told Yasha.

I looked down at the map. "That's still quite a walk to the meeting place."

"It's as close as I want to get," Ian said. "Since Ollie's not with us, I don't want to spook this guy."

Yasha pulled over to the right side of the road and opened his window before turning off the engine.

He saw my quizzical look.

"You find trouble, you scream, I hear and obey."

We could all only hope that none of the above happened.

I didn't know how many maintenance workers Green-Wood had on any given weekday between Christmas and New Year's, but I suspected it wasn't many; so I was surprised to see at least six men wearing Green-Wood coveralls working to clear paths near our meeting place. Two were working specifically on the Nut Path. Considering that the path was on a hill, I was grateful for their attention to detail.

"Looks like a skeleton crew," Yasha quipped.

I rolled my eyes.

The big Russian shrugged. "Someone had to say it."

"No, someone didn't."

"They're our men," Calvin told us.

"Wearing Green-Wood uniforms?"

Ian replied. "For some reason, the people we deal with prefer meeting in places like cemeteries instead of the corner Starbucks."

I got out and did a quick look around. According to the map, the area was far enough from the main entrance and close enough to the middle of the cemetery for privacy—or to be cut off. With the weather, I didn't think there'd be any other visitors here today, but I was wrong.

An elderly man stood next to a headstone, while a younger man, possibly his son or grandson, knelt to clear the snow from the name and dates on the front. An older lady was walking up the side of the hill overlooking Nut Path toward a grouping of headstones, a bouquet of white lilies in one hand, the handle of a black purse in the crook of the opposite elbow. She had on sensible boots, a bright blue coat with matching hat. She kind of looked like the Queen of England. A young couple were walking slowly away from us, the man with his arm tight around the woman's shoulders, their heads together. There were a few others nearby, but I couldn't see them well enough to get any details.

To get to the path, Ian and I would have to cross a section of undisturbed snow with several ominous lumps beneath the surface—ground markers just waiting for me to trip over them.

Ian saw where I was looking. "Walk exactly where I walk."

"What if you fall over something?"

"Then don't walk where I walk." He paused. "Oh, and Mac?"

I stopped and looked up at him. "Yes?"

"We'll work on it."

"Work on wha—"

"The new part of your job."

I bit my bottom lip against an incoming smile.

Ian raised a finger. "The *possible* new part of your job, and only when you're ready—and only when necessary."

I tried not to look as excited as I felt. "Agreed. And thank you."

He held my gaze for a second longer, then turned and started trudging up the hill, shaking his head and muttering to himself.

After a few minutes walking uphill—and a few stumbles, mostly mine—we arrived at the small hillside mausoleum where Ollie's contact waited.

According to the brochure, Green-Wood had almost 600,000 permanent residents. Ollie's contact fit right in.

He was dead.

Instead of meeting with Ollie, the head salesman had met his maker. Though on the upside, at least he still had his head.

Ian swore, then started talking fast and pissed into his comms.

The dead man was on the ground, lying on his side with a single stab wound to the chest, and the snow under him bore a disturbing resemblance to a cherry Slurpee.

The small mausoleum was nearly surrounded by a waist-high hedge. Our guys would have seen anyone who had come in, unless they'd been less than three feet tall. I stepped around a marble bench to get a better look at the rest of the body, and saw something more disturbing than Slurpee snow.

Next to the man's body was a bouquet of white lilies.

Dammit.

I ran around behind the mausoleum, to the backside of

the hill. The Queen of England was halfway down the hill, and she wasn't carrying white lilies anymore—but I saw the handle of a knife vanishing into her purse.

The sweet, little old lady was a cold-blooded killer.

That was all the proof I needed. I threw down my pink bouquet and took off running down the hill, quickly discovering there was something I needed very badly, but didn't have.

Traction.

I fell, rolled, and came up sputtering. "Old lady . . . blue coat," I yelled back to Ian. I scrambled to my feet, slipping and sliding, but making progress. Gravity was both my friend and worst enemy right now.

The woman may have been little, she may have been old, but there was nothing wrong with her hearing. What had been a quick, but dignified walk, turned into a run, and unlike me, she didn't fall down. And if she had, with my luck she'd have titanium hips.

And her big Buick—seemingly the preferred transportation of old people everywhere—was waiting for her at the foot of the hill. All of my backup was also at the foot of the hill—on the other freaking side.

I couldn't let her get away.

Ian was coming down the hill behind me. "Subject is an elderly woman in a blue coat and hat," he said into his comms.

"She looks like the Queen of England," I screamed back at him.

Ian didn't add that to his description.

The Buick roared to life and the old lady floored the gas, sending up a spray of slush and road salt in its wake.

Then I saw my salvation. A tractor. A big one. With a raised snowplow attached. Also big.

But first I had to reach it.

I could wait for Ian and risk having the killer escape, or I could do something that I was qualified to do.

I could drive the hell out of a tractor.

There were entirely too many grave markers lurking just

below the snow's surface on that hillside, and my feet were doing a fine job of finding every last one of them. I'd made two face-down snow angels and one outright sprawl. It was nothing short of a miracle that I made it to the bottom of the hill without two broken legs.

I scrambled up onto the tractor's seat. Fortunately, the keys were in the ignition. I guess the maintenance worker who left it there figured that if you can't trust dead people, who can you trust?

I turned the key, and the engine choked and sputtered. "Come on, come on, come on, come on . . ."

The ignition caught and the engine turned over. I popped off the brake and slammed it in gear, the engine growling in response. I grinned and growled with it.

"Don't mess with country girls," I snarled at the fleeing Buick.

My screwup time was officially over.

The Buick had gotten a head start, but it couldn't go cross-country.

I could and I did.

In a little over twelve hours, I'd been assaulted, arrested, interrogated, nearly fired, and a friend had been kidnapped—all because of some moldy monster parts. And now a man I hadn't even met yet was sprawled on the ground with a hole in his chest, lilies in his arms, and this blue-haired bitch was responsible.

I jerked the wheel to the left, sending up a plume of snow as I sped across the cemetery on an intersection collision course with the Buick. I didn't think the residents of the graves I was driving over would mind. Heck, I kind of got the feeling they approved. I lowered the snowplow to Buick-ramming height.

I briefly considered that this was likely to hurt, but since I was still a SPI employee, I still had plenty of major medical to use, and the thought that I might need it in the next few seconds didn't bother me nearly as much as I would've thought. Besides, there were plenty of our people around to see to it that I got to a hospital.

For the record, I had no idea what happened after the initial tractor-met-Buick moment, but I apparently left the tractor seat at some point.

I landed a goodly distance away from the tangled pile of tractor/car, but fortunately my flight had been stopped by possibly the only snowdrift not to contain a headstone. The tractor's front half was on top of the Buick's back half, reminding me of the aftermath of a monster truck rally I'd once been to.

I could hear shouting as our agents closed in. The old lady climbed out of the car, dazed, and her hat askew, with that purse *still* crooked over her arm. She made a run for it.

Oh. Hell. No.

I got to my feet, found my good friend Traction, and together we tackled Ma Parker.

The black patent-leather purse went airborne, and with a word no blue-hair would ever utter, let alone shriek, she scuttled after it. I grabbed the back of her coat in both hands and jerked her back. Messy wrestling ensued. I ended up on top of the woman and raised my fist back to punch, and froze. What was I doing? I couldn't punch an old lady! I looked down at that sweet little face, and hesitated a split second too long. Sweet turned to savage, and just before her fist hit the side of my head, I saw a glint of metal on top of her dainty kid glove.

Brass knuckles.

She caught me with a right cross that made me see the royal jewels. When my brain stopped ricocheting against the insides of my skull, the woman was free and again clawing for her purse.

This time I got her in a choke hold, but not before she clamped her teeth down on the inside of my arm. My coat had come off at some point during the fight, so all that was between my skin and her teeth was a sweater. The sweater was thick, but damn if it still didn't hurt. I screamed and started hitting her with her own hat.

Ian smoothly scooped up the purse, completely ignoring us.

"Hey!" I yelled.

"You're doing great," he said. "Keep it up."

Ian opened her purse and looked inside. "What have we here?" He emptied it on a nearby marble bench. "I've always wondered what the queen carries in her purse. A knife complete with fresh blood, a pack of tissues, peppermints, and one lipstick." He picked up what looked like a large key, large and old. Two modern-looking keys shared the ring with it. "What have we here? A key to a Green-Wood mausoleum." He waved the key and smiled at the now growling old lady. "I think we're about to find what we came for." Ian rummaged around inside the purse, checking for anything else. When his hand came out, it wasn't empty.

A flash drive.

"And maybe more than we bargained for," he murmured.

# 8

FOR the first time this week I was grateful for the ice and snow—as a pack for the left side of my face.

I made yet another snowball and held it to my head. My hand was numb from holding snowballs, even through gloves that were supposed to be waterproof.

Yasha handed me the confiscated brass knuckles, saying "Hair of dog. Is that the phrase?"

"Close enough." I slipped them on the hand not holding the snowball. Nice fit. I put my glove back on over them. At least I had a trophy for my trouble.

Calvin, who—conveniently for me—had been an army field medic in Iraq, deemed my brain to be non-concussed.

"Though if she'd been fifty or sixty years younger, I would have advised a trip to the ER," he said with a completely straight face. "The guys were taking bets on the winner. Half were betting on the old woman."

Yasha nodded in agreement. "The babushka is a biter."

"Though nice style points there with the hat," Calvin added. "We've never considered using hats as weapons. Maybe we should add it to our training."

"I'd break every bone in my hand if I punched you," I said. "You realize that's the only thing saving you, right?"

The SPI commando with no neck gave me only one upward twitch of his lips. The man was a master of self-control.

I was in the SUV with Yasha and Calvin. Ian was outside on the phone. After relaying what had happened, he was doing very little talking and a whole lot of listening.

We had an awkward situation. If you could call having a dead body literally on ice and the knife-wielding granny who'd done the deed in nonpolice custody awkward. Which, legally speaking, was leaps and bounds beyond awkward. Right now we were probably breaking laws I'd never even heard of. Our guys had removed the tractor from the car. If you didn't get too close to either one (say within twenty yards or so) both looked perfectly fine, as far as average vehicle condition went in New York.

"This is the second murder scene I've walked in on in less than twenty-four hours," I said. "Is that a company record?"

"Is not even close," Yasha told me.

"Good."

"Though I think is record for newbie."

"Great. Glad to know I'm making a difference."

"And I know is first time SPI agent use tractor to catch killer."

Calvin coughed, though it sounded more like he choked on a laugh.

I ignored him with as much dignity as I could muster, considering I had the imprint of the Queen of England's brass knuckles on the side of my head. I looked out the window at my path of demolition and sighed.

While the destruction was still there, our team in their Green-Wood maintenance coveralls were not. Only two remained. They were flanking the assassin who was seated on the bench Ian had used to go through her purse. Her hat was back on her head, and while dented, was more or less in one piece. Her blue coat was draped around her shoulders and doing a nice job of hiding the handcuffs from any curious passersby. Fortunately for us, there weren't any.

Ian got off the phone and came over to my open window. While I had been icing my head, Ian had made a quick trip back up to the body.

"Was it him?" I asked.

"License and credit cards confirm that he's James Tarbert from Tribeca."

"I wonder how Ollie knew him?"

"Right now, we can't ask either one of them. The name matches the one on the key, so I'd say he was using the family mausoleum for more than dearly departed relatives."

"Once the police locate his next of kin, he'll be joining them."

Ian nodded. "As soon as we're out of here, the Seventy-second Precinct will get an anonymous call about a body in Green-Wood—one that's *not* in a coffin. Captain Norwood will get the flash drive back to headquarters. Kenji will let us know what's on it."

I inclined my head toward Tarbert's killer. "What about her?"

"The team will take our geriatric Golden Gloves winner in for questioning and find out who hired her. Hopefully she'll know. A lot of the time contract kills are arranged without a face-to-face meeting. Maybe we'll get lucky and she'll at least have a name."

I hesitated. "What if she's not in the mood for a chat?"

"She'll talk, and afterward she won't remember a thing."

"Uh . . . do I want to know how they're going to do that?"

"Probably not. But it sounds worse than it is. We have people who are very good at what they do—getting information with no pain or injury to the suspect."

"Kind of like a Vulcan mind meld?"

"Vaguely. She won't remember a thing after stabbing the guy and before turning up on the Seventy-second's doorstep, carrying her black purse full of evidence. As soon as she's dropped off, another anonymous tip will be called in."

"To tell the cops to go look out their front door?"

"Basically."

"You've done this before."

"Many times."

"And it always goes as planned."

"Without fail."

"I've never been involved before."

"I'm very much aware of that. I'm trying to think positive."

I looked out at the tractor and Buick. "What about the mess?"

"The boss is a patron of Green-Wood," Ian said. "She'll make a donation that will more than repair the damage caused by"—he leveled a stare at me—"an unknown teenager who took a joyride on a tractor. Or if you're feeling really guilty, I'm sure she'd be willing to take it out of your pay."

I winced. "I'd be as old as the queen over there by the time it's paid off."

"Which is why the boss will take care of it."

"Is she going to be mad?"

"Probably. But she's an ends-justifies-the-means kind of woman."

Yasha nodded knowingly. "Dragons, they are like that."

I took one last look at the squashed Buick. "Good to know. I think."

The white Suburban pulled up on the road closest to the bench, and the two agents escorted the little old lady to it. When the SUV pulled away, Ian opened my door and I scooted over so he could get in. Calvin was already in the passenger's seat.

"We gonna go get ourselves a monster head?" I asked Ian.

He shut the door and buckled in. "Affirmative. Grab it and get out. The tip about the body won't be called in until we're clear, but with all the noise you made—"

"Catching the killer," I reminded him.

"Yes, but the Seventy-second is only a few blocks from here, and it wouldn't take much—"

Calvin half turned, his index finger on the comms unit in his ear. "The captain says two Green-Wood security cars are heading this way."

"—to get the police involved," Ian finished with an I-told-you-so look. "Looks like they'll be getting that call sooner than we'd like."

Yasha needed no further encouragement and got us moving. He glanced in the rearview at Ian. "Would be helpful to know where we are going."

"Sorry, buddy. Keep going straight. Calvin, hand me that map in the door."

Calvin tossed it back, and Ian found where we were now, used his index finger to trace a path to where we were going, and directed Yasha to our destination. It was conveniently close to the maintenance entrance and exit from the cemetery, away from Green-Wood security, and far away from the newly dead Tarbert and the newly destroyed tractor and Buick.

"Can I see the key?" I asked Ian.

He handed it to me and I turned it over in my hand. It had been bronze before age had given it a verdigris patina. It had the name "Tarbert" in raised lettering on the rounded end. The other two keys were definitely modern, but they had also darkened with age.

"It's got a family name on it and looks old, but how did you know it was a key to a Green-Wood mausoleum?"

"Seen them before."

"Another knowledge perk of our chosen profession?"

"You got it."

"And where the mausoleum is?"

He held up his phone. "As close as a quick search on Green-Wood's website. There's only one listing for Tarbert, and it's a mausoleum. Section sixty-one, Hill Side Path, off Valley Avenue." He looked closely at the side of my head. "You all right?"

"Sure. I get chocked in the head with brass knuckles all the time." I was starting to lisp either from swollen or frozen lips; I must have gotten hit there, too.

"When we get there, I want you to—"

"Let me guess. Stay right where I am."

Ian almost smiled. Almost. "I was going to say that if you're up to it, you can come with me."

I almost dropped my snowball.

"You've earned it," he said.

A reward was usually a good thing. What kind of reward was going into a mausoleum to look for a mummified monster head?

Ian and I made our way through the snow to the Tarbert family mausoleum. As the path name indicated, it was set into the side of a hill. The branches of a massive evergreen sheltered most of the mausoleum, so the snow wasn't piled up against the door. Equally lucky for us, the area around Valley Avenue was deserted. No maintenance workers, no guests, no homicidal old ladies—but best of all, no security or police, at least not yet. Yasha and Calvin were keeping watch, and the only sound was the crunch of our boots in the snow.

I took a deep breath and blew it out in a blissful sigh. "Nothing but dead people."

"Excuse me?"

"I'm glad that there's nothing but dead people around. They're perfectly behaved."

"You sure about that?" Ian's eyes twinkled wickedly as he turned the key in the lock of the brownstone mausoleum. A lock that shared the door with a massive horned lion's head clenching a knocker in its fanged mouth. "Maybe we should knock first."

"So that's your idea of humor?"

Ian grinned and gave the bronze door a solid hit with his shoulder to get it open. "Just keeping it real for you, newbie."

We went inside.

There were five stained glass skylights in the shape of a pentangle that weren't visible from the outside. The evergreen's branches overhead had kept them relatively free of snow, giving us at least some light to see by. From what I could tell, the mausoleum looked a lot bigger on the inside than it appeared on the outside. It occurred to me that I didn't have a flashlight.

"Crap. Do you have a flashl—"

"Of course." Ian started pushing the door closed.

"Wait! Don't—"

He closed the door before I could stop him.

"We have the key," he assured me, "and it can't be locked from the outside without it. It's a *dead* bolt."

"And the laughs just keep coming."

Ian locked the door and shined his light around. "I think so." He kept his voice low. There was no one in here to hear us, but the location seemed to demand whispers. "And if security or the police start searching the entire cemetery—and eventually they will—Yasha and Calvin will leave until I call them back."

"Leave? As in leave us here? I didn't hear you tell them that."

"Didn't need to. It's standard operating procedure. With them gone and the door closed, unless anyone looks closely for footprints, no one will know we're here."

"Why doesn't that make me feel warm and fuzzy?"

"Because you have no sense of adventure."

"Do so."

"Where?"

"At the moment it's MIA, but I have one."

"Right."

I followed the track of Ian's flashlight. "I expected cobwebs."

"Ever been in a mausoleum before?"

"Nope. The past day has been full of firsts."

Ian's light revealed a pair of oil lamps set in niches on either side of the iron door.

"Got a lighter?" I asked.

He smiled and took one out of his pocket.

"You don't smoke," I said.

"I don't, but you never know when you'll need to set fire to something."

I ignored anything that might mean, and removed the

glass globe. Ian flicked his Bic, lighting one lamp, then the other. Both were only half full of oil, but hopefully we weren't going to be here that long.

Beside one of the lamps was a key identical to the one we'd used to get in. The name Tarbert was on this one, too.

"Why is there another key in here?"

"In case one of the Tarberts wasn't dead when they were put in here," Ian said. "Paranoia was popular with the Victorians. Doctors back then occasionally jumped the gun declaring someone dead."

I quickly put the key right back where I found it, and tried not to think that a Tarbert had actually needed to use it.

The lamps illuminated the front part of the mausoleum, but the back was still in shadow.

There were six urn niches on each side of the mausoleum door, stacked three high and two across, some with names and dates engraved in their stone fronts, others empty and waiting for another Tarbert to die and be reduced to ashes.

"An extra key wouldn't do *them* much good," I muttered.

The most recent internment was dated a month ago. Dr. Jonathan Tarbert. I looked at the birth date and did the math. He'd been only thirty-eight.

"Did you note James Tarbert's birthday on his license by any chance?" I asked Ian.

"I took a picture so I wouldn't have to." Seconds later, his face was illuminated by the glow of his phone. "Thirty-eight."

"And date of birth?"

"September seventh."

I indicated the urn niche. "The month, date, and year are exactly the same as the mausoleum's newest tenant. Whatcha wanna bet Dr. Jonathan here was his twin brother."

Ian shone the flashlight on the marble panel. "Damn. Died last month."

"Or was killed. It could be worth looking into."

"People generally don't drop dead in their thirties without help."

Ian resumed surveying the mausoleum. Farther back

from the urns were the coffin-sized niches. All had names with birth and death dates, the oldest dating back to 1851. I hoped James Tarbert had wanted to be cremated like his brother; the coffin section was strictly "no vacancy."

I swallowed. "Any of those look big enough for the head of a ten-foot-tall monster?"

"Not to me." Ian shone his light around. "In fact, nothing in here says 'monster head container' to me."

The interior of the mausoleum was symmetrical down to the decorative vases holding matching dead flowers.

The drawers—or whatever they were called—for the coffins were also stacked three high. Three on one wall, three on the other. The back wall had a total of six, stacked three high and two across, like the urn niches.

The only thing that didn't come in matched sets was the single square column in the exact center of the room. Each of the stone column's four panels had to be at least two foot across.

I slowly walked around it, scanning it from top to bottom. "Is it just me, or is this column needlessly big?"

Ian looked up at the ceiling. "And it doesn't appear to be structurally necessary."

On each panel, at points exactly between the floor and the ceiling, were stone replicas of the bronze horned lion's head that was on the door. Their mouths were open like they were roaring. The lions were more or less at eye level, on a person of normal height. Ian had to duck his head to see inside the mouths. He aimed the flashlight's beam inside.

"Nothing there," he said. He repeated the exam on the next two, leaning to look closer at the last lion. "You might be on to something," he murmured. "There's a place in here for a key." He took the mausoleum key out of his pocket and stuck it and half his hand into the lion's mouth. "I'm thinking that . . ."

There was a click and the entire panel opened on silent hinges.

Ian shone the light inside and then down. The column was hollow, with a hole in the floor just wide enough for one person, with what looked like a modern aluminum ladder descending into darkness.

"Being in a mausoleum's not bad enough," I said, "now we get to find out what's in a dark pit underneath one."

"A chamber under a mausoleum is called a crypt," Ian told me.

"Lovely."

"I'll go first."

"I'll let you."

Ian began his descent.

"Why would anyone have a second way out in a mausoleum?" I asked.

"Could be the same reason the Tarberts left oil lamps and an extra key."

He reached the bottom of the ladder, shining the flashlight around. There weren't any shouts or gunshots, so it must not have been too bad. My skin started prickling when I realized that my only source of light was two sputtering oil lamps, and my company was seventeen dead Tarberts.

Ian's voice echoed eerily from below. "I think we need a bigger truck."

I quickly knelt on the floor next to the hole. "What is it?"

"They say you can't take it with you, but one or more of the Tarberts sure tried."

Curiosity may or may not kill cats, but it motivated me. "I'm coming down."

"I thought you would. Put out those lamps before you do."

I did, and on my way down the ladder, I heard a click like a switch being flipped, and honest-to-God lights came on down below. Ian gave an impressed whistle.

I reached the bottom and looked around. I was impressed, too. Impressed and intrigued. The room was twice the size of the mausoleum above it, and the floor, walls, and ceiling were concrete, like a bomb shelter or a bunker. There were sturdy metal shelves containing wooden crates and locked metal cases. Some of the crates smelled like new wood. There was a door at one end. It was steel. Serious industrial steel.

Ian saw me looking. "Yeah, this is new. Probably within the last few years. From the looks of that door, they didn't want anyone getting in."

"Or anything getting out."

"I'm betting one of the other keys on the ring unlocks that door."

I looked up at the way we'd come down. "It must. All this couldn't have been brought here through that hole."

Ian continued his examination. "There's no dust. This place almost qualifies as sterile."

Every crate had what looked like brown duct tape over words that had been paint stenciled onto the wood. The same tape was on the same place on every crate—possibly covering the same words. Ian peeled back the tape on one of the crates.

"Property of U.S. Government."

A second and third crate said the same thing.

"At least none of these crates are big enough to hold the Ark of the Covenant," I said.

"Good, because I didn't bring my fedora and bullwhip," Ian said, smoothing the tape back into place.

I spotted a crate that wasn't big enough to hold the Ark, but it was plenty large enough for a monster head. "How about this one?"

"Looks like the most likely candidate." He pulled out what looked like a Swiss Army knife on steroids. One of the blades wasn't a blade at all, but a thick, flat piece of steel. He stuck it under the corner of the crate.

I gave it a dubious look. "You're sure that thing can—"

Ian responded by popping the wooden corner straight up. "Easy as a bottle cap."

Under the obligatory packing peanuts was a wooden box, more like a chest, actually. Really old and really fancy.

There was a word carved into the lid. At least I assumed it was one word; all of the letters were together.

"You wouldn't happen to read ancient whatever, would you?" I asked.

Ian took out his phone and snapped a quick picture.

"Nope. But I know a guy at headquarters who does. Two guys, actually."

"Bob and Rob?"

"That's them." He scrolled down a list of numbers and tapped the screen once. "And . . . no signal." He quickly climbed the ladder and stuck his hand with the phone through the hole and up into the mausoleum. From up there, it probably looked like Thing from *The Addams Family* was trying to make a crypt-to-headquarters call.

Ian ended up climbing all the way up into the mausoleum. "There we go. Sending now." Then he called Yasha and gave him a quick rundown of our situation. About a minute later, he came back down.

"Going to wait for Bob or open it now?" I asked.

"Now."

There weren't any locks on the wooden chest, just an iron latch. I wasn't the only one who stood as far back as I could, while still being able to get a good look at what was inside. I didn't think standing on tiptoe and raising my eyebrows would help me stand back farther and see higher, but I did it anyway. I couldn't imagine anything hidden in a crypt with "Property of U.S. Government" stamped on its crate being anything good.

Ian opened the box.

We looked inside.

Holy Mother of God.

The monster's head was lying faceup, surrounded by a nest of the same matted and coiled hair that I'd found clutched in Adam Falke's dead fist. The head was gigantic, the face easily the size of the top of a fifty-five-gallon drum. Its features were vaguely human, partially reptilian, but it was the teeth that I couldn't look away from. The closest I'd ever seen was while watching Shark Week on the Discovery Channel. The lips had dried and pulled back from a mouthful of teeth that were triangular like a shark's, but that went to a sharper point. Behind the first row of teeth was an equally large second row, followed by an only slightly smaller but even sharper third row. Supporting the demonic dental work were massive jaws that looked like they could easily bite a man in half. The scent coming off of it was musty like Ollie's mummies, but there was also a hint of fishiness.

"It's the same smell that was in Ollie's office."

Ian nodded. "And the same hair."

"Ollie said the arm he had came from this thing," I said. "If the hair matches what I found with Falke, the claw found in Kanil Ghevari's body probably does, too."

My left brain was working out the logical part of what that meant. My right brain had already figured it out and had started whimpering. This thing's descendants had gutted and ripped apart Adam Falke and Kanil Ghevari.

This thing's descendant had been on the other side of the door from us in Ollie's office.

Ian's jaw tightened. "Let's see if the boys have anything for us. One word couldn't take long to look up." He climbed the ladder and his hand repeated its Thing impersonation. Almost immediately, his phone buzzed with an incoming text.

"Shit," Ian swore softly.

"I take it they knew what the word was, and it wasn't a very nice one."

Ian came down the ladder and showed me the screen. "Said it was Old Danish."

I stared in disbelief at the name glowing on the screen.

Grendel.

# 9

"WHERE'S Beowulf when you need him?" I managed.

"A name on a box doesn't mean that this is the actual Grendel," Ian said. "Or even if there *was* a real Grendel."

"It doesn't mean it's not—and that there wasn't. And whoever sent the boss lady that letter mentioned monsters from literature. According to my high school English teacher, *Beowulf* is literature, and Grendel most definitely was—or is—a monster."

Ian gave me a flat look. "I'm trying to be optimistic here."

"My optimism went bye-bye when you opened that lid."

I suspected Ian's had at least taken a brief sabbatical, but since he didn't say anything else, neither did I.

"How we going to get it out of here?" I asked.

"Certainly not the way we came in. Which leaves whatever's behind Door Number Two back there. It's wide enough for every crate in here."

I threw a wary glance in the door's direction. "Whoever made this room didn't want what was behind that door getting in here. And considering what's in here, that doesn't say good things about what's out there."

Ian crossed the room and lifted the bar. "Only one way to find out."

I had the urge to have my gun out and leveled at that door when it opened, but since Ian didn't seem to feel the need, I squelched mine. I didn't want another gun-related screwup today.

It was a narrow room. Ian's flashlight showed it to be arched, bricked, and old. Cobwebby old.

"There's your cobwebs," he said. "Happy?"

"Thrilled."

There was a switch on the wall inside the vault next to the door. Ian flipped it. A long line of bare lightbulbs hanging from a single cable stretched as far as I could see.

It wasn't a room. It was a tunnel.

"Interesting," was all Ian had to say.

"At least there's cobwebs," I said. "It means nothing's been down here in a long time."

"We *are* under a cemetery," he replied. "Not everything moves cobwebs."

"Funny."

"Not funny. Accurate. Not everything we hunt moves cobwebs."

I stood absolutely still. "That wasn't in the company manual."

"Not everything is." He pocketed his flashlight. "Let's see where this goes, then I'll get Yasha and Calvin to help move the head."

We left the door open behind us and I counted the paces as we went. It gave me some idea of how long the tunnel was, but it did an even better job of helping me focus on something besides being in a narrow, decrepit tunnel that ran under a nearly two-hundred-year-old cemetery. I walked in the exact center of the tunnel, and if I could have pulled in my shoulders, I would have. The hair on my arms knew without a doubt that there were bodies buried on both sides of us.

"Are we going away from the cemetery or deeper into it?" I asked.

"Actually we should be almost out by now."

Another fifty-seven steps put us at the end of the tunnel—and in front of another door, if you could call it that. It looked more like a hatch on an old battleship. It was metal, the rust blending in with the surrounding brick wall. Instead of a knob, there was a latch that looked like it'd snap in half if you tried to use it.

A low rumble shook the walls around us, followed by dust falling from the brick above our heads.

"Subway," Ian said. He carefully gripped the latch and turned it. The door opened with a pop and a hiss of air—air that in comparison made the monster head smell like the roses I'd carried around Green-Wood.

"Dang." I wrinkled up my nose and tried to breathe through my mouth.

Ian stopped. Being directly behind him, I had no choice. Then he stepped aside, giving me a view that I could have done without.

"Looks as bad as it smells," he said.

A men's room.

At least it used to be. The urinals were still on the walls, but the rest of the space appeared to have been converted to a storage room. It didn't look like it'd been used for its original purpose for years, but apparently some smells never completely go away.

Ian noted my confusion. "Not many public restrooms in subway stations anymore."

"Too gross?"

"That and too little funding and too much crime."

The other side of the hatchway we'd come through was basically a door-sized section of tiled wall, the grout perfectly aligned with the edges, so that when it was closed, no one would ever know that there even was an opening there.

Ian was doing an up close and personal examination of the door, lightly rapping on the tiles with his knuckles.

"What are you doing?"

"There's got to be a lock or latch on this side," Ian said. "I can't see someone going to all the trouble to put an exit here that they couldn't get in through as well."

A couple more knocks revealed what sounded like a hollow tile. Ian used his fingertips to press around the tile's outer edge. He found the magic spot, and the tile popped open on silent hinges revealing a keyhole and a small door handle.

"Clever," I said. "Think the key that opened the door on the other end will fit?"

"Don't see why not." Ian gave it a try. It was a perfect fit.

He closed the door in the wall, locked it, and clicked the tile back into place. "That'll do until we can get back here with Yasha and Calvin to do a pickup."

I made my way across the former restroom/present storage room, and pulled on the exit door handle.

Locked.

That wasn't good.

Then I saw the dead bolt. Ian came up behind me, key ring dangling from his fingers. "We've got one more key that has yet to have a lock."

I stepped aside to let him try. "Here's hoping . . ."

It took a little key wiggling and maneuvering, but the dead bolt reluctantly slid aside. Ian opened the door just enough to see out, and apparently didn't object to what he saw and pulled it the rest of the way open.

The subway station was full of people bundled up against the weather topside. Across the platform was an orange-tiled section of wall that said "25th Street."

"I'll be damned," Ian said. "We're a block from Green-Wood's main entrance." He inclined his head in greeting to a woman with an appalled expression who'd just seen the two of us come out of what had once been a subway men's room. The station was busy, but no one else even batted an eye—at least the other women didn't.

"How convenient," I said, catching the knowing smirks of several men, whom I proceeded to stare down. "Yet, creepy and disgusting."

"There has to be another exit from that tunnel," Ian said. "There's no way those crates and cases were hauled through one of Brooklyn's busiest subway stations and into a locked storage room."

Even the most jaded New Yorkers would notice that.

Ian took out his phone, looked down at it, and blew out his breath in annoyance. "When are they gonna make a phone that can get a signal in a subway?" He crossed the platform to a pay phone, and I stuck close. Ian quickly made the call, and I recognized Yasha's mobile number. I was standing right next to him and I still could make out only a word or two over all the noise around us.

"Was he surprised when you told him where we were?" I asked Ian when he'd hung up.

"Yasha's not the surprised type."

We waited, and it said a lot about Yasha's creative parking skills that we didn't have to wait long. He and Calvin came down the stairs into the station carrying tool boxes and wearing a pair of navy coveralls like our agents at Green-Wood had worn, but instead of the cemetery's logo, the patch on the left side of his chest said "Sarkowski Plumbing."

Matching outfits. Cute.

"Aren't those the same coveralls our guys were wearing in Green-Wood?" I asked.

Ian nodded. "We keep coveralls and a selection of company patches in all of our vehicles," he said. "Velcro. Tear one off, slap another one on. Quick and virtually unquestioned access."

"Uh, but the restroom is closed," I said. "Storage rooms don't need plumbers."

Ian indicated the men's room door. The sign over the door said Men; there was nothing to indicate it was anything else. "Some are still open; most aren't, and a lot of the time, they don't have signs saying otherwise."

"Mean trick to play on someone who has to go."

"Other than the one we just came out of, have you ever been in a subway bathroom?"

"No."

"Trust me; the mean part would be having to use them."

Yasha and Calvin ignored us completely, but as they passed us, Yasha said, "Half block west," and headed straight for the men's room. Calvin hung a Closed for Maintenance sign on the door, and both men disappeared inside.

"What the hell was that?" I asked.

Ian pressed something into my hand. "Here's a key to the SUV. Yasha parked half a block west. I want you to get in and lock the doors. We'll be there within twenty minutes."

"You don't have a uniform."

"I will when we come out. Right now, I'm just a guy who needs to take a leak and thinks signs don't apply to him."

"How are you going to haul a monster head in a crate out of there?"

"Tell anyone who gets in our way that it's a busted toilet."

"That'd stop my questions."

"And anyone else's. Always does." His expression turned doubly serious. "Go directly to the SUV and don't stop for anyone."

Ian turned on his heel and headed purposefully toward the men's room, a man on a mission.

This was one time when I was perfectly fine waiting in the car. I had no desire to go back through a claustrophobic tunnel that went under a cemetery. Also I'd be sharing the backseat with a monster head in a box soon enough; I didn't feel the need to rush it.

While sitting would be more than welcome, I'd really rather do it someplace other than an SUV parked in sub-freezing temperatures. I hadn't eaten since the pre-dawn stale doughnuts at headquarters, so just the thought of food set my mouth to watering. Even Kenji's wasabi peas would be manna from heaven right now. Note to self: fighting ghouls and running down a little old lady killer with a tractor really takes it out of a girl.

I went through the turnstile and up the stairs to the street in search of hot food and even hotter coffee. I knew I wouldn't have to go far to find either one. New Yorkers liked their coffee, and they liked having places to get it close by, regardless of where they happened to be at any given moment in their day or night. Before I even got to the top of the stairs, my nose told me that coffee was close; and where there was coffee, there were baked goods. Since this was Brooklyn, those baked goods were sure to include bagels. Though at this point, I wasn't going to be picky. I'd eat cardboard if someone smeared cream cheese on it.

It wasn't hard to spot the behemoth black SUV. Yasha had parked it almost on top of a pile of snow left at the curb from the latest plowing, and it had one of those magnetic signs on the driver's side door that said "Sarkowski Plumbing." Unfortunately it was in the opposite direction from where my nose insisted that there was coffee. The SUV wasn't going anywhere, but I was making a detour.

The line at the coffee shop wasn't long, and soon I was headed back to the pile of snow with the giant SUV perched on top with a mega grande mocha latte in one hand and a hot, whole grain bagel packed with honey walnut cream cheese eagerly clutched in the other.

I climbed the mini mountain, got into the SUV, locked the doors, and happily hunkered down to do some serious eating, but not before burning my tongue on the nuclear-hot coffee.

I glanced over at a newsstand and saw it.

Oh no.

Today's issue of the *Informer.*

The headline screamed at me and anyone else with working eyeballs and a taste for the bizarre.

*SoHo Sasquatch!*

To make it even worse—if that was remotely possible—there was a photo of the monster in all its grainy glory. Apparently SPI wasn't the only one with cameras around Ollie's shop. The resolution wasn't the best, but it was good enough for a front page, smack-you-in-the-face headline. And if the *Informer* had it on their front page, it'd be only a matter of time until someone got themselves slaughtered in front of witnesses, any or all of whom could be taking pictures or video and instantly uploading them to Twitter or YouTube. If they hadn't already . . .

Crap.

I took out my phone and searched Twitter and YouTube, then Googled "SoHo Sasquatch."

Nothing.

For now.

The stack of the *Informer* was twice the height of what it usually was. It looked like they'd printed plenty of extras. My old editor would want to entice as much money as possible from the sensation-loving public. It was half past two in the afternoon; that stack must have been huge when it'd been delivered this morning.

I put down my bagel, took my coffee with me to cool it down, and climbed out of the SUV to get a copy.

It read like a fluffed-up police report, and seeing the name on the byline, I knew it'd been fluffed up with silicone.

I'd been my editor's favorite reporter because I was a good reporter who got the story. Scuttlebutt had it that Trixie Shaftner was now his favorite, but for completely different reasons. Trixie was good at getting people to talk to her—especially men. Her sources were bigger and higher up than mine, but then so were her boobs. All she had to do was aim her girls at them, and the poor, besotted bastards were one question away from becoming her next "source close to the investigation."

I gave the article a quick scan to see if Trixie had managed to get anywhere close to the truth.

The article was sensational, panic inducing, and full of gruesome details—vintage *Informer.* Sounded like Trixie had gotten her hands on the coroner's report or had rubbed her bounty up against one of the first responders, or both. Falke's method of demise was described with near ghoulish glee. The coroner believed the weapon to be a curved knife, like a sickle. Trixie said that Falke's slash wounds were caused by claws, and that his arm had been torn, not cut, from his shoulder.

One point for Trixie.

She had the same information that we did on Falke's background, but there was nothing on why he had been in New York. She also didn't know what Falke had been doing in the proprietor's office at Barrington Galleries when he was murdered; and of course, all efforts to locate Oliver Barrington-Smythe led to a dead end. In an unexpected and imaginative twist, Trixie all but accused Ollie of being the Dr. Frankenstein/

mastermind behind the monster, and inferred that his gallery was a front for occult criminal activity.

Ollie? A criminal mastermind?

Snort.

Nice try, Trix, but no cigar.

Conveniently, Ollie wasn't around to refute her story or sue the pants off of her and the *Informer.* Though if he were here, he'd just stay open extended hours to take financial advantage of his notoriety, and offer tours of his office at twenty bucks a pop.

The official police statement was that a body was found and that they were currently investigating.

I had coffee in one hand, the tabloid in the other, and was drinking the former and reading the latter while walking across an icy sidewalk back to the SUV. It was multitasking at its finest. It was also what kept me from seeing the yuppie vampire stroll right up next to me and put a vice-clamp grip on my upper arm.

"Fools and their money are easily parted," he murmured in my ear.

He was wearing sunglasses. Oakleys. That kept his eyes from doing a repeat of trying to hypnotize like he'd nearly done last night.

I did some panicked fumbling through my brain's filing cabinet for what I knew about vampires and daylight. Younger vamps couldn't take the light at all. Middle-aged ones could be out in the light, but "time to turn so you don't burn" was literal with them. Vamps older than five hundred years had no problem being out and about during the day, but shades were advisable.

In addition to sunglasses, the yuppie vamp had every square inch of skin covered—suit, tie, wool coat, gloves, and scarf. Only his face was exposed, but it was shaded under the brim of a stylish fedora. Middle-aged variety. Check.

I'd like to say that I didn't do a repeat of my stand, stare, and stammer bit from last night. I'd like to say it, but I couldn't.

"The sun doesn't agree with me, either," I eventually heard myself say.

The vampire took the *Informer* from me then firmly linked my arm through his. "I thought as much with your kind." He said the last two words as if they left a bad taste in his mouth. "Then you will be agreeable to finding a more private place to continue our conversation." He tossed the tabloid in the nearest trash, which was really where it belonged.

I wasn't running this time; and with my arm locked down, I couldn't. Besides, vampire or not, I'd seen him rip the ass out of his pants. That and knowing what color underwear he wore took a little of the edge off my fear. It was also broad daylight and we were in the middle of a relatively crowded street. If I had to, I had a scream that'd put a banshee to shame.

The vampire jerked me in closer, facing him. "Is the package in place?"

"What?"

"My package. Is it in place?"

I resisted the urge to look down at the front of the vampire's pants. "Uh . . . yes?"

"Good." His fingers curled in a crushing grip around my hand. "Now explain to me why you apprehended the assassin and delivered the keys and flash drive into SPI's hands?"

I didn't know him, but he obviously thought he knew me. Plus, the homeless guy knew Ian. This was officially beyond confusing.

When in doubt, go with the truth. "She killed our source." I remembered Ian dumping out the contents of the purse. "The SPI agent took the keys, and I didn't know about the flash drive."

"Tarbert had far outlived his usefulness, and paid the price for his greed." He lowered his face to mine, and I could smell whoever he had for breakfast. "The head of the beast does not matter to me, but if you do not wish to share Tarbert's fate, you *will* retrieve that flash drive."

"I . . . I don't think I can do that."

"You derive great enjoyment from toying with me, demon. Perhaps our employer is correct and you have outlived your usefulness as well." He adjusted his grip on my arm to get a better hold. "Your behavior has become increasingly erratic, and the risk of exposure is too great."

A black van with blacked-out windows pulled up to the curb. The door slid open. I caught a glimpse of two men in black suits, white shirts, black ties, and sunglasses, putting off a serious *Men in Black* vibe.

"Get in," the vampire ordered.

It didn't matter where you were from—backwoods or big city—you didn't get into a van full of strange men, and they didn't come any stranger than this.

I didn't act. I reacted.

With a scream that could be heard for blocks—probably above and below ground—I punched the vamp in the face with the hand holding the scalding coffee. I'd forgotten until that moment that I was still wearing the brass knuckles under my glove. I felt teeth break. The vamp's hold on me loosened, and I yanked my arm free, inadvertently knocking off his hat and sunglasses in the process.

Now the vamp was screaming, too—burning from coffee and the sun, and bleeding from broken teeth, including one fang.

I ran and kept running, down the stairs into the subway station, slowing only enough to swipe my MetroCard at the turnstile. I rounded the corner and was going full speed when I hit the men's room door with my open hand and plowed into Ian, knocking him to the floor and landing on top of him. Yasha and Calvin were carrying a crate now marked "Defective Toilet." They looked just as stunned as Ian, minus the pain.

I panted to catch my breath. "Need any help?"

# 10

WE were in the SUV headed back to Manhattan. Yasha was driving and Calvin was literally riding shotgun. Ian was in the backseat with me, and Grendel's head was in the cargo area right behind us. When we'd gotten topside, there had been no sign of the vamp, van, or MiBs. Heck, even the vamp's blood was gone. And the people on the street were acting like nothing had happened. I had to hand it to them; it took a lot to ruffle New Yorkers.

"When he asked if his package was in place, I told him yes."

Calvin shot me a bemused look.

"Yeah," I said. "That was my first thought, too. And 'yes' seemed to be the answer he wanted. When I'm dealing with crazy people who can rip my throat out with their teeth—or who want to take me to a mystery employer who thinks I've outlived my usefulness—I tell them what they want to hear."

In addition to freaking out over nearly being kidnapped, my skin was trying to crawl off and hide from a mummified monster head sitting mere inches away. I turned in the seat to put my back to the door. I didn't care if the thing didn't have a body; I wasn't taking my eyes off of it, but it didn't stop me from finishing my bagel. I had my priorities. What I didn't have was any coffee to wash it down with, but who needed caffeine when you had adrenaline.

I'd given them the *Reader's Digest* condensed version of the *Informer* getting wind of our monster problem, but a word-for-word report of my encounter with the vampire. As a former reporter, I was good at remembering exactly what someone told me, especially when it involved personal threats of the fatal kind.

Ian's response when I finished was to run his hand over his face. "Let me get this straight. The dead guy from Ollie's had your picture in his pocket, and now this vampire—also from last night—thinks that you and he work for the same person."

"That person couldn't possibly be Vivienne Sagadraco, could it?"

Ian didn't even dignify that with an answer.

"Hey, I'm still new here. Just checking."

"Did he give any indication of what was in the package and where it is?" Ian asked.

"None." And I could've smacked myself for not asking. "I wanted to ask, but if I had, he'd have known I wasn't the person he thought I was—whoever that is. And he acted like I should know what he was talking about, like I'm in cahoots with these people—whoever they are."

"How could vampire mistake you for demon?" Yasha asked.

I threw up my hands in an I've-got-nothing gesture.

"I'm more concerned about how he knew exactly where you'd be last night and today," Ian said. "Maybe once Kenji gets a look at what's on that flash drive, we'll have a big piece of the puzzle and some of this will start to make sense."

"Nothing that's happened since this whole thing started has made sense," I told him.

"Is true," Yasha agreed.

Ian shot the Russian a look. Yasha ignored him.

"We have Tarbert's killer in custody," Ian reminded me. "Our people are the best. If she knows who hired her, the name of her contact, and where the drop point was for the flash drive and those keys—they'll get it out of her."

I leaned back and ate the last bite of bagel. "I'd forgotten about the mausoleum and crypt keys. And the vampire said that the head of the beast didn't matter to him." I tried to put the pieces together in my head. "Adam Falke wanted to buy the arm and head; now Falke's dead, probably killed by the beast the vampire was talking about. Ollie was going to get the arm and buy the head to sell to Falke. And now Ollie's kidnapped and the guy selling the head is dead."

"We have the head," Ian said. "And the flash drive."

"And ghouls took Ollie and the arm."

"In a decommissioned military helicopter."

We all thought about that.

As I swallowed the last bite of my bagel, my fear gave way to anger. "And just what the hell did he mean by 'my erratic behavior'?"

Ian just looked at me. Yasha and Calvin stared straight ahead and didn't say a word.

I glared at all of them.

"We'll check in with Moreau when we get back to headquarters," Ian said. "See if he has any leads on who the vampire is."

A vampire that thinks that I'm working with him, the same vampire who orchestrated at least one murder—and possibly two. I could hardly forget the pieces of Adam Falke scattered around Ollie's office—a victim who was carrying a blood-spattered photo of me.

I thunked my head against the window. This couldn't be good for my next performance review.

The monster head was a big hit at SPI headquarters. People in white lab coats immediately surrounded the box labeled "Defective Toilet" and whisked it away.

Ian went in search of Alain Moreau. I went in search of answers. Alone. By myself. Without having to account to Moreau for dealings with shady vampires, men in black in black vans, and erratic behavior. I'd have to talk to him eventually, but it wasn't going to be now.

There was something I could do to help that I was actually good at.

Get to the bottom of a story.

There'd been three murders in two days, and two of those killings had been committed by a ten-foot-tall monster with five-inch claws who'd come to town not as a tourist, but to eat the tourists, and anyone else who looked tasty. Connected to all that in some way was a team of ghoul commandos who'd taken Oliver Barrington-Smythe. Ollie wasn't just a source; he was a friend. Occasionally obnoxious, but always a friend. It may not have been my job to save him from those ghouls; but dammit, it was my job to do everything I could to help get him back. And the thing I did best of all was to stick my nose where it didn't belong. One of my dad's best hunting dogs had gotten a piece bitten out of her nose by a raccoon that way, but it hadn't stopped her from doing what she'd been born to do.

I was a hunter, too, only I tracked down information, waded through facts and rumors, picking through the truth and lies—until I'd found all the pieces of a puzzle and could put together a picture of what had really happened. Like one of Dad's hounds on a scent, I wasn't going to let anything throw me off the trail. Yes, a scarab-tattooed guy who'd been carrying a picture of me had gotten himself gutted, but if we didn't get to the bottom of this by New Year's Eve, more people would die; a lot more.

And it was growing increasingly likely that I could be one of them.

I went to my desk in the far corner of the bull pen.

There'd been a decorative addition since this morning.

A toy model of a tractor sitting on top of a crushed model car.

Embarrassing news traveled fast.

I looked around for the culprit. As I did, clapping, whistles, and cheering came from every agent in the bull pen. I even got some standing ovations. So I did the only thing I could do. Smiled, waved like a gymnast after a successful dismount, and sat down.

I slunk down behind my computer monitor, but the smile stayed.

It was my second piece of coworker-supplied desk flair.

When an agent did something particularly memorable in the field—intentionally good or unintentionally mortifying—their fellow agents made sure their actions didn't go unrewarded.

You weren't truly a member of the team until you'd been gifted with desk flair.

My smile turned into a goofy grin. To paraphrase the immortal words of Sally Field: they liked me. They really liked me.

My first piece of desk flair had been a leprechaun figurine wearing a gold crown. He looked like the cute, little guy on the Lucky Charms cereal box—that is if you ignored the tiny pair of pants that someone had sewed that were down around his ankles—and the itty-bitty dangly bits someone had made out of Play-Doh. Multiply that leprechaun times five, and that was the event that marked my first time out in the field as a SPI agent.

SPI wasn't normally in the bodyguard business, but as a favor to the local Seelie Court, a team of SPI agents had been assigned to escort a soon-to-be-married leprechaun prince and his bachelor-party buddies for a night on the town. Those three wishes the leprechauns would've been forced to grant if they'd been captured? They held unlimited power if they came from a member of the royal family. Wishes certain creatures of the Unseelie Court would've stopped at nothing to get. Hence the SPI bodyguard detail.

Well, the prince didn't want bodyguards.

A fun fact to know about leprechauns: a human's gaze can hold them prisoner. However, the instant the human looks away, the leprechaun can vanish. So where was the first place the prince and his roving bachelor party wanted to go? A strip club. SPI's agents are highly trained and disciplined; but take five male agents into a strip club and tell them they can't look?

The prince and his boys had flown the coop before the first G-string dropped.

Leprechauns are masters of disguise and can make themselves look like anyone. So we had five magically disguised leprechauns running amok and unguarded through New York's adult entertainment establishments, and yours truly was the only SPI agent who'd been able to see through their glamours.

That night turned into a race against agents of the Unseelie Court as we hit New York's strip joints, searching for a pack of horny leprechauns looking to get lucky.

We eventually found them in the Bronx. They'd gotten the munchies and staggered into a thankfully empty McDonalds.

The hobgoblin owner had met us in the parking lot, and while Ian got him calmed down, I went inside.

Bad call.

The leprechauns weren't wearing glamours; and by this point, they weren't even wearing clothes. Every last one of them thought that, like the Lucky Charms guy, they were "magically delicious." His Highness even asked if I wanted to rub his charms for good luck.

After I'd Tasered him smack-dab in the Happy Meal, the others saw the wisdom in putting their pants back on.

For Tasering the happy parts of a Seelie royal, guess whose Taser-carrying privileges were revoked in the political poop storm that followed?

I eventually replaced my Taser with the tequila squirt gun when I learned that for ninety-nine percent of supernaturals (leprechauns being the exception), Tasers just tickled.

It was a hell of a night for my first day on the job.

I typed in my computer password and got to work. I opted to start with a Google search rather than going directly to the *New York Times* and the *New York Post*. The *Times* gave you the facts; the *Post* dished the dirt. I wanted both, but since I didn't know whether Tarbert was a New Yorker like his brother, I opted to cast a wide net first.

I was pretty sure the rest of his family lived in New York—or had. I'd imagine that a Green-Wood family mausoleum with occupants dating back to 1851 was about as local as you could get. Nowadays, it didn't matter where you had lived and died, your family could have your remains put on the next available flight back to the family plot. Or in the Tarberts' case, the family mausoleum. I hadn't seen one up close before, but I knew expensive when I saw it.

I kept seeing James Tarbert lying dead in a cherry Slurpee. Why would someone take out a hit on him? And why and how had his brother died only a month before? I glanced around the bull pen and up at the catwalks. I didn't know where our Vulcan mind meld people had their cube farm, but I suspected they wouldn't bring suspects here for questioning—unless they didn't plan on letting them go. And Ian had said they'd be dropping Tarbert's killer off at the Seventy-second after they were finished. Ian wasn't one for volunteering information, but he'd never lied to me, either.

I Googled Jonathan Tarbert and got more than I'd expected—or ever dreamed.

For starters, Dr. Jonathan Tarbert wasn't a medical doctor; he was the research and development/inventor kind. He graduated at the top of his class from MIT, then promptly vanished into the subterranean corridors of the government sector.

And he was a native New Yorker, all right. The Tarberts had provided their city with five generations of seamy, steamy, back-stabbing entertainment that read like a soap opera. As I sat back and scrolled through the more promising stories, I wished I had some of Kenji's wasabi peas to pop while I perused all that juicy copy. Rich, beautiful heiress marries ambitious financier, and they have twin sons. The first is a brilliant scientist and gets snatched up by the government, but the only thing the second-born twin was brilliant at was getting his hands on other people's money. Now both sons were dead, James murdered, and Jonathan was . . . I clicked on his obit in the *Times* . . . killed in a fire in his lab at GES, Inc. That didn't sound like a government lab.

"Must be good stuff," said Ian from directly behind me.

I squeaked, jumped, and knocked the tiny tractor off the little car, which bumped the danglies off my leprechaun.

Ian noted the tractor/car addition to my desktop diorama with approval. "That was fast."

My two pieces of flair were cute. Ian's vast collection looked like they'd come from horror movies and slasher films.

"Looks like you've got a decent start," he said, indicating the info on my screen. "What'd you find so far?"

"The Tarberts are local, rich, and could've given the Borgias a run for their money—or their lives. And Dr. Tarbert was a government researcher, who doesn't appear to have died in a government lab, who coincidentally had 'Property of U.S. Government' crates hidden in a secret room under his mausoleum."

Ian pulled his chair over next to mine. "What department was he with?"

"Unknown. His last place of employment was GES, Inc."

"Which stands for . . ."

"GES, Inc."

"Generic enough."

"Yep."

"Know what they do there?"

I shook my head. "I haven't gotten that far. I'm still on the 'who did what to whom and for how much.' The Tarberts knew how to make money—or at least how to get their hands on it. They were perfectly fine taking it from others, but apparently what they really liked was snatching it from each other."

"Any fatalities from all that snatching?"

"At least once a generation one of them would off the other, sometimes twice if they were feeling ambitious." I turned from my screen and looked up at him. "You thinking that James might have killed Jonathan?"

Ian booted up his computer. "I've called an old buddy of

mine at the NYPD. He's going to check if there were any suspicious circumstances surrounding Dr. Tarbert's death. He'll e-mail when he has something. While we wait, did you find anything on the newly late James Tarbert?"

"He was the second born, so Jonathan had the silver spoon, and it seems he also inherited the brains—and the family fortune. James barely graduated from Harvard with a degree in finance. That their dad was an alumnus and major donor might have helped. James worked at Enron, and then was let go from Enron. The last few years he's been making the rounds of small investment firms as a consultant."

"No trust fund?"

I shook my head. "The Tribeca address on his license is for a one-bedroom apartment. The senior Tarbert died five years ago. Jonathan got the money, and James got an allowance that'd be enough to keep a tasteful roof over his head, and if he wanted more, he'd have to work for it. The society pages were all over that."

"I get the feeling James's career goal was to work as little as possible."

"And let everyone else do the work. None of his consulting gigs lasted longer than six months."

"Married?"

"James, no. Jonathan, yes. Tia Sebastian. Divorced last year. That event also got a nice amount of coverage." I clicked a few keys and brought up a photo from their wedding. "This is from when they could still be called 'the happy couple.' "

"How much did she get after the divorce?"

"Nothing, courtesy of a pre-nup."

"Ouch."

"And seven months later, Jonathan's dead."

Ian's computer dinged with an incoming e-mail. He rolled his chair over and opened it. "Looks like I owe Jerry a beer."

"Jerry?"

"Precinct buddy." Ian scanned the e-mail. "Hell, I owe

him a beer *and* lunch. He came through in spades. Sent the full investigator's report."

I scooted over to have a look.

Dr. Tarbert looked just like his brother James: brown hair, kind of pale, average-looking features. I couldn't tell what color his eyes were from the police report photo, but I got the feeling he had a lot going on in his gray matter. He kind of reminded me of a professor I'd had in college—intensely focused on his subject, and the rest of the world might as well not have existed. Intense. Yeah, that was it. Intense and intelligent.

There was a lot of police-speak in the report, and I didn't know what half of it meant. "Care to translate?"

"They didn't have to cremate Dr. Tarbert any more than he already was," Ian told me. "He died in a fire, a hot one, completely destroyed his lab. The CSI team found traces of a body at the scene; barely enough to fill an evidence bag, let alone an urn." He scrolled down some more. "They found the slag of the good doctor's Rolex among the bits and pieces and the burnt-out shell of his Mercedes in the parking lot. The detectives had two witnesses who saw Dr. Tarbert enter his lab about twenty minutes before the fire started. One of them called nine-one-one."

"Jeez, what kind of lab did he have?"

"Whatever it was, I doubt if it was supposed to have military-grade accelerants in it."

"They're thinking arson?"

Ian nodded. "With Tarbert inside. Whoever doused that lab didn't want anything left."

"You thinking little brother James?"

"That's exactly what I would be thinking except that he alibied out, which is why he was dead in Green-Wood rather than alive in prison. He was in White Plains the night of the fire, and the witnesses at the scene didn't see anyone other than Dr. Tarbert in the area."

"What about the ex-wife?"

"In Europe when the lab burned."

"Does she have enough of her own money to pay for a little murder and arson?"

"Unknown, but we can find out."

Yasha came out of the break room carrying a massive mug of coffee and heard Ian's last comment. "I take it death not accident?"

"Not unless Tarbert accidentally sprayed down his lab like a charcoal grill then started tossing around lit matches," Ian said. "The case is listed as an unsolved homicide." He paused. "Of course, there's another possibility."

"What's that?" I asked.

"That wasn't Jonathan Tarbert in that lab. No body to speak of, and not enough DNA on what was there for testing."

"Faked his own death?"

Ian shrugged. "I've heard of stranger things."

I thought for a few moments. "Today, his twin brother gets himself killed while waiting to sell a monster head to Ollie, and while carrying a flash drive that a vampire and his men in black were willing to kill me to get. Is there anything in that police report about the kind of research Tarbert was doing?"

Ian clicked quickly through the pages. "No info on the research, but a couple of guys in suits were the ones answering the detectives' questions—or more like deflecting their questions." He smiled. "But they couldn't avoid identifying themselves. Department of Defense."

We both looked over at Kenji's still empty computer command center.

"We need to know what's on that flash drive," I said.

"Kenji has it," Ian said. "I passed him in the hall. He was just coming out of a meeting."

"Meeting about the flash drive?"

"Possible. Though Kenji prefers to work at his own station."

"Maybe someone does not care what Kenji prefers," Yasha said.

I did some math. "Okay, we've got a *possibly* dead researcher, probably Department of Defense, and his lab was definitely destroyed. Underneath his family's mausoleum are crates with 'Property of the U.S. Government' on them." I stopped, baffled. "Who in the government would want a monster head? And why hide a bunch of government crates? Dr. Tarbert's dead. Well, maybe. Little brother starts selling off the inventory—and the mysterious contents of the flash drive—and gets himself killed for his efforts." I sat back. "We need to know what else's in those crates. The Tarbert brothers were the last of the family, so those boxes don't belong to anyone now—unless Dr. Jonathan puts in an appearance from beyond the grave."

"I would imagine they still belong to the government," Ian said.

"It's a big government." I grinned slowly. "Until we know what's inside, we won't know who to return them to."

Ian actually gave me a wink. "Which is why a SPI team is emptying the crypt as we speak."

Alain Moreau appeared silently on the other side of my desk. I squeaked and jumped again, but didn't have anything left to turn over on my desk.

"Madame Sagadraco and the rest of the team are waiting for you in the main conference room," the vampire lawyer said without expression. "Follow me."

"Team?" I whispered to Ian. "That doesn't sound good."

"Because it never is."

# 11

THE main conference room at SPI headquarters resembled a scaled-down version of the Security Council Room at the UN. I'd been in here only once before. Meetings in this room were super secret, hush-hush, and meant that the supernatural crap had hit the fan big-time. Needless to say, not many people wanted to be called into a meeting in here. It looked like telling the boss about my adventure in Brooklyn would have to wait.

A massive U-shaped table dominated the room, with the light from a pair of projectors—one mounted in the ceiling, the other in the floor—coming together to form a hologram of SPI's company logo, a stylized monster eye with a slit pupil. The eye slowly spun, a placeholder for whatever visuals the boss was going to use in the meeting. Plush and pricey executive office chairs were spaced every few feet around the table, a closed folder at each place. There were only two vacant chairs. Vivienne Sagadraco stood at the open end of the table, arms crossed, remote in hand, perfectly still, waiting. I hoped we hadn't kept her waiting for long.

"Be seated," she said without moving, or looking at us.

With a dragon's sense of smell, she wouldn't need to look to know who we were.

We did as told, and Alain Moreau took his usual place in the shadows behind Vivienne Sagadraco.

The others seated around the table had given us a quick glance when we'd come in, then put their collective noses back into the contents of the folders in front of them.

I recognized everyone. Some I knew; others I'd only seen but had been told their names and what they did.

Kenji Hayashi was sitting directly across from us. Ian caught his attention and gave him a questioning look. Kenji nodded once and held up two fingers with the flash drive between them, before tucking it safely back in his shirt pocket.

That was a relief. It'd be even more of a relief if he'd already looked at it, but when Vivienne Sagadraco asked you to a meeting, you came.

In addition to Kenji, both of SPI's monster hunter/commando commanders were there, meaning that the combat boots were about to hit the pavement. One of those commanders was a woman, as were many team members on both squads. SPI was an equal opportunity employer of combat badassness regardless of sex, species, or dimensional origin.

Ian and I had a copy of the folder and the contents that had everyone else in the room grimly enthralled.

I opened it. Reports and crime scene photos—both ours and the NYPD's. SPI had people in the police department who kept us in the loop on cases that involved monster perps. Our people had taken the photos of Kanil Ghevari. The cops had done the honors on what had been left of Dr. Adam Falke. I hadn't seen the aftermath of the first murder, but I'd seen more than enough of the second so that I didn't feel the need to linger over the visual records of either one. There was also a copy of the text of the letter that the adversary had sent to the boss.

"Ladies and gentlemen, thank you for coming on such short notice," Vivienne Sagadraco said. "You've all been briefed on recent events. I've called you here because I have just acquired new information that escalates these events to a critical level. As you know, the killers left behind physical evidence at both crime scenes: a claw at the first murder and a lock of hair at the second. These, combined with an artifact recovered today by Agents Byrne and Fraser, led me to contact my counterpart at SPI Scandinavia, Lars Anderssen. He was able to provide a wealth of information." She paused. "Most notably, confirmation of what we are dealing with."

Everyone looked up from their gory photos at that.

"Director Anderssen sent us this." She pointed the remote at the empty area in the center of the table. The SPI eye logo vanished, and in its place a nightmare formed from its clawed feet to the top of its leathery head. The boss clicked once more, and the hologram began to rotate slowly so everyone could get the full effect.

A full effect I could have gone the rest of my life without.

The monster was gigantic, corded with muscle, and with what looked like veins protruding just under the surface of its skin. I couldn't tell if the skin was mottled or extensively tattooed. The only difference between the face presented on the hologram and the head we'd found in the box was that it wasn't desiccated and mummified. It had the same hair, facial features, and mouthful of razored teeth. The monster's legs were powerful and its knees slightly bent, but it was the arms and hands that really got my attention. Long and thick with muscle, they extended almost to the creature's knees, each ending in a hand that could easily encircle my entire waist, and tipped with claws that could have shredded Ollie's office door like toilet paper and gutted the two of us with one swat.

All the little hairs on my arms stood straight up, and my bagel threatened to come back up the way it'd gone down. I suddenly felt light-headed and realized that I'd forgotten to breathe. I glanced around the room and saw I wasn't wearing the only stunned expression at the table.

"This creature is called a grendel," Vivienne Sagadraco said. "It was named after two of its ancestors featured in the epic poem, *Beowulf.* Their present-day habitat is the mountains and caves of Norway and Sweden near the Arctic

Circle. As with many supernatural hunters, the encroachment of modern man has forced many away from their preferred habitats. When *Beowulf* was written approximately twelve hundred years ago, grendels lived as far south as the marshlands of Denmark. As the human population spread, they moved northward and adapted to colder climates. From what details I could give him, Director Anderssen believes that we have a male and female."

"Shit," drawled one of the commanders, a Louisianan named Roy Benoit. "Grendel *and* his momma."

A couple of chuckles made their way around the table.

Roy had grown up in the swamps of southern Louisiana in a long and proud line of gator hunters. He'd done a stint in the army, become a ranger, then done a longer stint in Iraq. He saw things over there that convinced him that humans weren't the only alpha predators walking on two legs on this green earth. He'd come straight from Iraq to SPI NY, and was a natural as a unit commander.

"If I recall correctly," Benoit continued, "the monster in *Beowulf* liked it quiet. Loud, drunken partiers—whether Vikings or Times Square tourists—really piss it off."

"I believe they were selected for precisely that reason," Sagadraco said. "According to Director Anderssen, while they can and do hunt alone, grendels prefer to hunt in pairs or small groups. They display a keen intelligence and tactical precision in pursuit of their prey. Our adversary—at least for now—is somehow able to influence the grendels' aggression, or at least direct it. For those of you unfamiliar with the poem, after Beowulf killed Grendel by tearing off his arm, Grendel's mother attacked Heorot Hall to retrieve her dead son's arm and exact vengeance. Beowulf tracked Grendel's mother to her lair, killed her, retrieved the arm, and decapitated the dead Grendel."

She aimed the remote at the grendel hologram, clicked a button, and it vanished. If only the real thing could be dispatched as easily.

"The events of the past forty-eight hours," Sagadraco said, "imply that their descendants have a desire for vengeance of the eye-for-an-eye variety. They are now in our city committing murder, and taking heads and arms as trophies. We can theorize that the mummified body parts were intended as payment or a reward of some sort for the grendels that were brought here. However, we lack proof for that hypothesis; so for now, it remains a theory." She paused meaningfully. "Director Anderssen insists that these are primitive creatures that would not have the ability to veil themselves from sight and sound. This means that our adversary must somehow be providing them with the means to do so."

"The last thing we need is a pair of independent, strategic-thinking monsters prowling the city hunting for their ancestor's missing body parts." The speaker was Sandra Niles, another team commander, who'd come to New York by way of Jamaica.

"Do we have any leads as to who's behind this?" Ian asked.

"Unfortunately, no," Sagadraco said. "The team of ghouls who took the arm and Mr. Barrington-Smythe could be working either for our adversary or for an as of yet unknown party."

Sagadraco aimed and clicked the remote again. Where the grendel had stood was now a holographic map of the lower half of Manhattan.

"The first murder—that we can directly attribute to our subjects—was in Chinatown," she continued. "The second was in SoHo. That doesn't mean that the monsters and their controller are in Lower Manhattan, but Times Square is close enough that we can safely narrow our search parameters."

Red dots appeared at each of the three locations then a glowing blue line linked the dots to form a triangle.

"If the grendels choose to hunt on the surface tonight, there will be more killings, and more risk of additional exposure," she added. "Unfortunately these creatures are not sluggish during the day." Sagadraco turned to SPI's resident cryptozoologist. "Dr. Milner."

Dr. Henry Milner took the boss lady's place at the front of the room, as well as control of the remote. Control of the room was another matter entirely. I'd met him during my first week at SPI, and knew him to be more comfortable studying creatures of the night than interacting with people during the day. He cleared his throat nervously, clicked the remote, and the map of Lower Manhattan came back, only this time it was flat like a tabletop with red, green, and blue glowing lines descending in a seemingly endless tangle below the surface.

I knew what they were. Tunnels and pipes. I felt a pair of eyes on me. Vivienne Sagadraco was regarding me with an assessing gaze.

"The red represents subway tunnels, the green are the city sewers, and the blue are the major waterlines and storm overflow drains," Dr. Milner was saying. "There are more than eight hundred miles of subway tracks and thousands of miles of sewer tunnels running under the city. While grendels historically preferred warm temperatures, they have adapted to colder climates, meaning they could be anywhere down there."

Ian's expression was grim. "As are many of the city's homeless."

"Unfortunately, yes." Milner pressed a button on the remote and the bottom two-thirds of the hologram's tunnels vanished, still leaving an impossible amount of real estate for our people to cover. "Based on surveys done by ourselves, the police, and the city's social services department, many of the city's tunnel-dwelling homeless can be found in the levels that are far enough down for concealment, yet close enough to the surface for access." He paused uneasily. "Director Anderssen said that while grendels are carnivores and will eat any warm-blooded animal, their prey of preference is humans. Their physiology is such that they thrive in an environment where they have ready access to humans. As a result, grendels have been hunted down and rendered virtually extinct in the Scandinavian countries. Our present situation proves that there are a few remaining."

"So how do we kill 'em?" Benoit asked.

"Due to their size and speed, not easily," Milner replied.

"The information Director Anderssen sent says that their skin is essentially armored scales," Sagadraco said. "Impervious to most weapons, unless the entry point is beneath one of the plates. One would have to be preternaturally skilled with a bladed weapon or lucky beyond belief with a firearm. Even if the skin is penetrated, the musculature beneath is capable of healing all but the most grievous of injuries. The only sure way of dispatching the creature is by decapitation. The grendels' speed and strength make getting close enough to do any of the above all but impossible." She smiled. "However, we deal with the impossible every day, and I have every confidence in your abilities."

Benoit gave the boss a crooked grin. "Why, thank you, ma'am. We aim to kill."

"Lars and a team of specialists are on their way now and will arrive by eleven o'clock this evening. They have had experience with grendels, and have agreed to serve as consultants on this mission." She leveled a glance around the table. "We will give them our full cooperation."

There were nods of agreement, some more reluctant than others. Each of our people had the highest qualifications for the job they did—and the lowest tolerance for outsiders coming in to potentially tell them how to do it. The boss knew that, hence the proactive admonition.

"However, we have two other problems that cannot be solved by accurately placed silver or steel." She held out her hand and Moreau gave her a copy of today's *Informer.* I didn't blame her; I wouldn't want to hold the thing any longer than I had to, either. "One of our city's tabloids has captured a photo of one of the grendels."

I felt an overwhelming urge to slink down in my chair. Just because I didn't work for the *Informer* any longer, didn't mean that I wasn't still embarrassed by having once been employed by them.

"Fortunately for us," Sagadraco added, "this tabloid does not enjoy a reputation for sterling journalism."

"Amen," I said.

There was light laughter around the table.

"Though, in our favor," Sagadraco added, "the photograph is grainy, and the *Informer* is known to have faked or embellished photos in the past. Also to our benefit, the police believe Dr. Falke's murder to be the work of a sickle-wielding serial killer who plagued this city several years ago."

That was new. I glanced at Ian. He nodded once in confirmation.

"Rumors benefit us now," the boss continued, "but in a city of this size where nearly everyone carries the means to photograph or videotape anything they see, it is only a matter of time before the grendels are a secret no longer. If this happens, supernatural beings will soon be exposed by legitimate sources that people trust and believe." She frowned. "A copy of the letter I received is in your folders. It all but directly states that our adversary's intent with these creatures is to release them into Times Square on New Year's Eve. Our challenge is great. We have a little more than twenty-four hours to locate two grendels in hundreds of miles of tunnels before midnight on New Year's Eve. If we fail, it will literally be there for the world to see. If we fail—real monsters will become known to mankind, undisputed proof that supernatural creatures exist will be provided to millions at once, inciting a worldwide panic." Vivienne Sagadraco took a deep breath and looked in the eyes of each man and woman seated at the table. "Ladies and gentlemen, what would follow would be open season on *all* supernatural creatures."

The dragon lady's mood was grim enough after the meeting without me adding to it, but just like the vamp's offer, ignoring this wasn't going to make it go away.

Immediately after the meeting adjourned, Roy Benoit approached the boss, and they were now deep in discussion. Ian caught Alain Moreau's attention. The lawyer crossed the room to us.

"We need to speak with the boss after she and Roy are finished," Ian told him.

Moreau's pale blue eyes regarded me with absolutely zero

expression. "I was about to request the same of you and Agent Fraser on behalf of Madame Sagadraco." He opened a door behind us that appeared to have been part of the wood-paneled wall. Inside was a small conference room with a table and six chairs. With a pale, elegant hand, he indicated that we precede him.

Once we were inside, he closed the door. "Please be seated."

We did. Ian and I sat on one side of the table, with Moreau and his iPad on the other. Except for the fact that the iPad wasn't a file folder, the setup felt uncomfortably like the precinct interrogation room from last night.

Ian started to speak, and Moreau held up a hand. "Madame has requested that we wait for her."

Ian sat back, with him and Moreau wearing identical poker faces.

Oh boy.

With the faintest of clicks, the door opened and Vivienne Sagadraco came in the room. The three of us automatically stood.

"Please be seated," she said. Moreau held a chair out for her.

Ian spoke before Moreau could. "Ma'am, after we left Green-Wood this afternoon, the vampire Mac encountered last night tried to kidnap her near the Twenty-fifth Street subway station—an abduction with the intent of killing her. He acted as if he knew her, but Mac had never seen him before last night."

Moreau didn't blink an eye. The only reaction from Vivienne Sagadraco was to lean forward and steeple her long fingers in front of her face.

"You don't seem surprised," I ventured carefully.

"I assure you, Agent Fraser," the boss said, "today has been abundantly full of surprises—every one of them unpleasant."

I smiled weakly. "Sounds like my day, ma'am."

Vivienne Sagadraco settled back in her chair. "Why don't you tell me about your day, Agent Fraser?"

After I found enough spit to swallow, I did. I left nothing out, and relayed the conversation with the vamp word for word. Then Ian and I told them what we'd discovered about the Tarbert family.

"Where is this flash drive now?" Sagadraco asked me.

"Kenji Hayashi has it. I don't believe he had time to look at it before the meeting, so he's probably doing it now."

"The assassin from Green-Wood was unable to shed any light on the identity of her employer," Sagadraco said. "The transaction was completed by leaving instructions in an obscure volume in the main branch of the New York Public Library. The payment was deposited in a library coat locker. Our examination uncovered that the assassin works there part-time."

"A librarian?" I blurted.

Vivienne Sagadraco's eyes went cold and hard. "I would think you of all people, Agent Fraser, would not be fooled by outward appearances."

I felt the blood rush to my face, and I had to clutch my hands under the table to stop them from shaking. The boss was pissed—at me—and while I had no idea why, I think I was about to find out.

"Unless we discover otherwise, we will assume that the assassin's services were secured by the vampire you encountered." Sagadraco paused. "I have learned a great deal today, and not all of the unpleasant revelations came from Director Anderssen." She cast the barest glance at Moreau. "Alain?"

"I have discovered the identity of our traitor," Moreau said. He touched the iPad's screen and turned it so we could see the photo. It was the vampire from last night and today, bundled up like he had been today, smiling and shaking hands with an equally happy-looking woman with a blond ponytail and wearing an all-too-familiar green sweater.

It was me.

# 12

IT took me a good five seconds to find words, another five to get them out. "Ma'am, that ain't me."

I cringed to myself. Way to sound like a hick to the boss, Mac. You can take the girl out of the mountains, but fear of being eaten by your dragon boss brings out the mountain in the girl.

"This photo is from a surveillance camera mounted outside of Saga Partners Investments," Moreau said. "This particular scene was recorded at eleven thirty-five yesterday morning at the café across the street."

"That's him, but it's not me."

"Who is he, Agent Fraser?"

"That's the vampire from SoHo last night and Brooklyn today. Those were the only times I've ever set eyes on him in my life."

You have to believe me, I wanted to shout. But they didn't have to believe me; they had photographic evidence smack-dab in front of them, complete with a date and time stamp, and I couldn't prove otherwise. The homeless man was the only witness last night, and today the vampire was gone by the time we came up from the subway station. Hell, either him or one of his MiB buddies had even cleaned up his blood first.

I'd been set up.

This was officially a nightmare.

I locked eyes with Moreau. "You know who he is, don't you?"

Without taking his eyes from mine, he touched the bottom of the screen again, and the photo changed to a scene I didn't recognize, but it was the same vampire. "Charles Warrenton Fitzpatrick the Third. He previously worked for the CIA as a handler."

I froze. "Handler?"

"A point of contact for their undercover agents."

Just when I thought it couldn't get any worse.

Someone was setting me up to not only be fired, but probably killed, if not by the vampire CIA agent, then by my own employers. I was shaking in my snow boots, but I was also mad as hell. Whoever had painted a bull's eye on me wasn't here, so I turned my anger on the vampire in the room with me. "So what is it that I'm supposed to be all happy about with this Charlie Fitzpatrick?"

"Unknown," Moreau said.

"You mean unknown until you get it out of me."

Silence.

"We're merely seeking an explanation, Agent Fraser," Vivienne Sagadraco said.

Then they'd turn me over to the Vulcan mind meld people.

"You said *previously* a CIA handler," Ian said to Moreau.

"That is correct."

"Who's he working for now?"

"Unknown. But it appears he is working in a similar capacity."

"You said this was taken at eleven thirty-five yesterday?" Ian asked.

"Correct."

"The photo of Mac in Adam Falke's pocket, did you

discover when that was taken while reviewing the break room tape?"

"I did." Moreau brought up the security camera's version of that photo on his screen, the one where I had a cookie in each hand. The date was yesterday. The time was 11:00 a.m., which gave me plenty of time to get across the street for some vamp schmoozing. Great. Just great. I resisted the urge to kick something.

Ian indicated the tablet. "May I?"

Moreau slid it over to him.

"Is this icon for the break room video?" Ian asked.

Moreau nodded. "For a twelve-hour period beginning at six yesterday morning through six last night."

Ian glanced at me, then his attention was back on the tablet. "Mac, you said you ate cookies several times yesterday."

"Yes." I failed to see how bringing up my cookie addiction could do anything but get me fired and/or killed quicker.

Ian fast-forwarded the video until I appeared again. The time indicator read 12:15. Again it left plenty of time to get back from the café across the street.

A small smile creased Ian's lips. "Makenna Fraser is no traitor. But then I already knew that."

He isolated the three photos and dragged them so that they were side by side.

"What do you see, Mac?" he asked me.

I leaned in for a closer look. There I stood in the first photo eating a cookie, with another in my hand lined up to be devoured next. Powdered sugar was sprinkled down one side of my sweater. At least in the third photo I was only eating one cookie. Aw jeez, I hadn't even wiped off the powdered sugar from the previous cookie raid.

Wait a minute.

My eyes went to the middle photo of me and the yuppie vampire. The vampire was in profile, but my twin was almost facing the camera straight on. I could clearly see the front of the sweater.

"No powdered sugar," I said, almost to myself.

Ian sat back and crossed his arms over his chest. "Not one speck." He showed Moreau and the boss. "It's on her sweater in the exact same place at ten and twelve fifteen in the break room, but not at eleven thirty-five across the street."

"I didn't have time to go to lunch," I remembered, "so I had another cookie."

"Security has your hand scan indicating that you left at eleven thirty-one and returned at eleven fifty-five," Moreau said.

"I was at my desk during that time," I said. "Check the bull pen video. I may have cookie issues, but I'm no traitor."

Alain Moreau and Vivienne Sagadraco exchanged a concerned glance.

Moreau lowered the tablet. "I no longer need to check. It was not you."

"You have our apologies, Agent Fraser," Vivienne Sagadraco told me. "I had hoped there was a logical explanation. Now we have one."

I was even more confused, if that was possible. "Apology accepted, ma'am. But there's not a damned thing logical about that second photo. It's not me, but she could be my twin. She's even wearing the same clothes."

"Not your twin, Agent Fraser. Your doppelganger."

"My what?"

"A doppelganger is the paranormal double of a living person," Sagadraco said.

"I've been xeroxed?" I heard myself ask.

"Historically to see one's doppelganger was a harbinger of death. In modern times, they are often used to take the place of a person for nefarious purposes."

"Framing me for corporate treason is plenty nefarious."

"Yes, it is."

"And this thing is so perfectly me that it replicated my handprint well enough to get in and out of headquarters?"

"A doppelganger assumes not only the appearance of its victim, but all of its mannerisms and thought processes as well," Moreau added. "A perfect copy."

"Thankfully for me, minus the powdered sugar."

"An experienced doppelganger can easily convince even a victim's closest associates," Sagadraco said. "We've been infiltrated more cleverly than I ever suspected."

"If the traitor is a shapeshifter who looks like me, then who took that picture in the break room of me eating cookies?" I asked. "I think I would have noticed if my twin was standing ten feet in front of me clicking away with her phone. Someone else would have noticed, too."

"The angle at which it was taken suggests that the photographer was standing outside the door," Moreau said, "just to the left—an area that is not covered by the security camera. It is doubtful that is a coincidence. This thing knows our security system."

"So, my doppelganger has an accomplice?" I asked. "Or another stolen identity. Could someone here have gotten themselves a new body for Christmas, and decided that yesterday they needed to be me?"

"Fortunately, that's not possible," Ian said. "Doppelgangers are at the top of the shapeshifter food chain, but they can still change into only one person at a time."

"What do doppelgangers look like normally?"

"Amorphous blob pretty much covers it."

Ick.

Ian's expression darkened. "Doppelgangers usually kill the person whose appearance they replicate to avoid discovery. If you're going to make a copy, it's risky to leave the original behind."

"Apparently my being alive to take the blame was worth more to the thing than the risk of it being caught."

Ian brushed his finger across the tip of his nose.

"Doppelgangers are perfect for spy and infiltration work," Moreau said. "I had heard rumors that the CIA had recently begun using them. Simply replace the person and act in their stead. Spies, CEOs, political and world leaders—the perfect infiltrator with endless possibilities."

I blinked. "The CIA is using supernaturals?"

"Another rumor." Moreau glanced down at the photo of

me and the vampire ex-CIA handler. "One that seems to have just been verified. Another benefit to using doppelgangers is that doppelgangers are exceptionally strong, supernaturally so. That strength is not diminished regardless of the form they take."

"Why have a doppelganger impersonate me? I don't know or have access to anything that would be useful to the CIA or anyone else."

"Perhaps it is not what you know," Vivienne Sagadraco said quietly, "but what you are."

"A seer."

"The *only* seer in our New York office, and one of only five in the entire company. Aside from yourself, we have one seer in our Canadian, Scandinavian, British, and South American offices. The Scandinavian seer will be accompanying Director Anderssen. The Canadian, British, and South American seers are unavailable. The Canadian is still recuperating from a Sasquatch encounter gone extremely wrong. The British seer is assisting in a rabid gryphon outbreak in Wales, and the South American is somewhere in the jungles of the Amazon on vacation and out of contact."

"So aside from the Scandinavian, I'm all we have. And if you thought I was a traitor . . ."

"There would be no seer available in all of the Americas on the eve of what could be a world-altering, catastrophic event. Monsters are real, and billions of people will witness it as it happens live on television or the Internet on New Year's Eve."

Ian leaned back and his chair creaked. It was the only sound in the room. "That's not a coincidence, either."

"No, I don't believe it is, Agent Byrne," Sagadraco said. "These two grendels are somehow veiled against sight and sound. Our teams would never know what hit them. But at midnight on New Year's Eve the world could witness it all. Alain, we must determine what damage the doppelganger has done to our security while masquerading as Agent Fraser—and any other form it may have been using. Determine if it brought any kind of package into this building. Review the hand scan records for agents arriving or departing early or late for anything that stands out from their normal routine. Any sickness or offsite appointments that were requested at the last minute or that ran longer than requested. Start with the senior security and science staff and work your way down until you find any anomalies. Personally select a few nonhuman agents to assist you."

"What good would—" I began.

"Doppelgangers can only duplicate humans," she told me. "For some reason, supernatural physiology impairs accurate duplication. Unfortunately, our uninvited guest has probably already eliminated the person they originally used to gain entrance. I imagine they've been with us for some time. Alain, have all of the security tapes been reviewed?"

"No, madame. Just the break room and the Saga Partners Investments cameras. I stopped once I found what I was looking for."

Me making nice with my presumed handler.

"Have security review the tapes for the past forty-eight hours, looking for Agent Fraser," the boss instructed. "Note the time and location of each instance. Agent Fraser, please provide Alain with your whereabouts for the same time period, both here and outside of headquarters. We will go back further if necessary. I want to know where that doppelganger has been and what it has done."

"I'll have a report for you within the hour," Moreau said.

"I'd also suggest checking the Saga video further than Fitzpatrick's meeting with Mac's doppelganger across the street," Ian said. "He could've left soon after—or he could've had a meeting with his handler or his employer."

Sagadraco nodded in approval. "Excellent idea, Agent Byrne. Alain?"

"Added to the list, ma'am."

"We need it done quickly, and we also should monitor the Saga camera overlooking the street in case Mr. Fitzgerald pays our doppelganger another visit." She paused thoughtfully. "Get that new employee in Research to assist you, the one with four pair of eyes. Bob has reported that he's very adept with them and is an excellent multitasker."

"Yes, ma'am."

Sagadraco turned to me. "For your safety, Agent Fraser, I want you to stay here until these issues are resolved."

"With my doppelganger running loose?"

She raised an elegant brow. "And Mr. Fitzpatrick and an unknown phantom organization on the prowl out there? One creature inside SPI as opposed to an unknown number outside."

"Good point, ma'am."

"We can protect you more efficiently here. Agent Byrne will remain with you at all times. By the time Lars and his team arrive we will have the most probable locations for the grendels and begin our search. I need you to be with them. They are bringing their seer. You'll deploy with the teams. I can't risk having you abducted or murdered before then."

"I wouldn't like that either, ma'am." I had a disturbing thought, even more disturbing than possibly running into my evil twin in the ladies' room. "It's dark outside. There's been two killings in two nights. These things hunt when it's dark, and our Scandinavian grendel experts are somewhere over the North Atlantic right now."

Sagadraco glanced at her slender, diamond watch, as did her dragon aura. Dragons liked their sparklies. "On the contrary, they should be landing by nine o'clock tonight."

"But in the meeting just now, you said—"

Her eyes glittered with a hint of humor. "I say many things, Agent Fraser—some of which are intentionally inaccurate."

"I wondered why you invited me to a meeting if you thought I was a traitor."

"I sincerely hope it is not the case, but the doppelganger could very well have been one of the other people in that room. They represent my best and most valued people. Everyone who was in that room is now privy to the fake time and place of Director Anderssen's arrival."

"The fake time five hours from now."

"I am having all of them watched," Moreau said. "If one of those in that meeting attempts to contact anyone outside of SPI within the next few hours, that communication will be monitored, intercepted, and if it is suspect, swiftly acted upon."

Vivienne Sagadraco smiled, predatory and eager. "Meanwhile, I will investigate the CIA angle. I have a few contacts who should be able to provide the information we require on former-Agent Fitzgerald."

She stood, as did Ian and Moreau. I kept my seat. After nearly being fired, killed, and knowing I had a doppelganger who'd damned near made both happen, my legs were a wee bit on the wobbly side.

Sagadraco nodded curtly and left the room.

Grendels without. Doppelgangers within. And my dragon boss chomping at the bit to sink her teeth into a vampire ex-CIA agent. This was shaping up to be one hell of a holiday weekend.

Ian stopped Alain Moreau outside the conference room.

"Mac and I are going over to the Full Moon for a quick bite to eat."

"Madame Sagadraco requested—"

"I know what she wants, but my partner and I haven't slept and have barely eaten in twenty-four hours. The Scandinavian team will be here soon. Between now and then, our seer needs food and rest. Any objections?"

"None, Agent Byrne. However, I must insist that you take at least one guard with you; preferably two."

"I won't need the help, but Yasha and Calvin are welcome for the company. Are they acceptable?"

"They will be adequate."

The two men held eye contact for a couple of seconds, and then Moreau nodded curtly, turned, and went about his business. I guess in alpha male speak that meant Ian had won this round.

Ian saw me trying not to smile.

"What?"

I raised my hands. "Nothing, nothing at all. By the way," I added quietly. "Thank you."

"Dragons and older vamps forget that we mere humans have to eat and sleep. You're not going to be any good to anyone if you're too tired to see straight. Hunger and fatigue will get you killed."

"That's not what I was thanking you for; though I haven't eaten in so long I think my stomach's forgotten what food is. Thank you for saying that you knew I wasn't a traitor—even without the powdered sugar."

There was an awkward silence.

"I call it like I see it," Ian said.

"Well, thank you for seeing me that way. I appreciate it." Then I remembered that the boss wanted me to give Moreau a rundown of where I'd been and when I'd been there for the past forty-eight hours. "Dang it, I promised Moreau that list of my whereabouts."

Ian put a hand on my shoulder and firmly turned me in the opposite direction. "And he can wait another hour to get it. Let's grab our coats and get out of here."

# 13

AT the end of the block, two buildings down from the café, which I swore I was never setting foot in again, was the Full Moon.

If I had to pick a place to eat a last meal, the Full Moon would be it. The barbeque was slow cooked, the burgers were rare, the steaks tartar, and the regulars were furry. The Full Moon also had the distinction of having one of the best collections of single malt scotches in the city, scotches that'd put even more hair on a werewolf's chest.

Bill and Nancy Garrison were a nice werewolf couple who'd come from North Carolina to spread the gospel of barbeque to the heathen Yankees—and to give homesick Southern werewolves a taste of home. I came for the pulled pork platter, banana puddin', and sweet tea.

The Full Moon billed itself as New York's Official Werewolf Bar. They even had a gift shop up front. The place was dark wood, dim lights, and decorated with every werewolf cliché the Garrisons could come up with. Werewolf movie posters hung on the walls, werewolf movies ran on the big screen TVs, and on Friday and Saturday nights when the mundane came in, Warren Zevon's "Werewolves of London" was in heavy rotation on the state-of-the-art sound system. In my opinion, Bill and Nancy's booming business had been a flash of brilliance. Hide in plain sight.

They still had their Christmas decorations up. My favorite was the life-sized fake werewolf looming in one corner. In honor of the holidays, he was wearing a festive scarf that Nancy had knitted and a red Rudolph nose. The bloodred light from the nose shone up into its glittering eyes. Christmasy, yet with creepy bonus points.

It was a little after six o'clock on the night before New Year's Eve, and the place was already packed. Werewolves made up a big part of the dinner crowd, but with three days until the full moon, the younger werewolves would be sticking close to home—something to do with lack of control. I could see where being in a packed restaurant would cause control issues in the younger werewolf set—especially with all those two-legged, warm-blooded potential meals crowding the bar area.

Yasha and Calvin cleared a path through the bar like the bow of a destroyer through a sea of rubber duckies. I could see Yasha's nostrils flaring at all the meaty goodness; you couldn't blame the man for sniffing.

We didn't have to wait for a table. The Full Moon was a favorite place for SPI offsite meetings, so the Garrisons kept a reserved sign on a quiet booth near the back—or as quiet as the place ever got.

Ian pulled Yasha and Calvin aside. He spoke briefly, the two other men nodded, and then took a seat at a nearby section of bar. Ian slid into the booth next to me.

"What's all that about?" I asked.

"I want to talk to you without anyone overhearing."

"That doesn't sound good."

He answered me with silence.

"You're supposed to tell me I'm wrong."

"Can't do that." He looked up and sat back. The waiter took our drink order, and since we knew what we wanted, he took our food order as well. Unlike other couples seated together, Ian and I weren't on a date, and we most definitely didn't have time to relax and have a leisurely dinner. But I wasn't about to let a pair of rampaging monsters cheat me out of dessert. I'd get that banana puddin' to go if I had to.

As soon as the waiter left, Ian's attention was on me.

"Do you know how I started working at SPI?" he asked.

"Not one for small talk, are you?"

"Not normally; and certainly not now."

I sat back in the booth. "I haven't heard."

The edge of a smile appeared. "You mean you couldn't get Yasha to tell you."

Busted. "Or Calvin or Kenji or anyone else." I shrugged. "Digging up info no one wants out there is what I do."

"Well, you can stop snooping. I need your cooperation, so you need to know."

"Cooperation?"

"I thought it might work better with you than 'obey.' "

"You thought right. Let me guess, this cooperation would be with you."

"Correct. Though how I came here isn't good dinner conversation, but we're out of time."

"Not much about SPI is fit for the supper table. I can take it." Maybe. Probably not. But I wasn't about to tell Ian that. I'd made enough mistakes to make myself look incompetent in the past day and I wasn't about to add anything else to it.

"Almost four years ago, my partner and I responded to a call of a robbery in progress at a high-end jewelry store."

"NYPD?" I asked.

"Yeah, I was still on the force then. It was a silent alarm, so we knew there was a possibility that we'd show up while the perps were still there. They were there, all right."

"Let me guess, not human."

"Ghouls." Ian paused. "Had you dealt with ghouls before you came here?"

"We'd have one pop up occasionally back home."

"No swarms?"

"Swarms?"

"That's what a group of ghouls is called."

"That's a new one on me," I said. "I thought it kinda odd that they'd work together like they did at the storage place, but I was too busy at the time to ponder it much."

"There's about as many ghouls in the world as vampires and werewolves," Ian told me. "And they're just as organized. That night in the jewelry store there were five of them. Though when me and Pete got there, we only saw three; and they were wearing masks, so we didn't know what they really were. I called for backup. Pete didn't want to wait. He'd looked around back. There was a white van with a dint in the driver's side door. It fit the description of a getaway vehicle used in a robbery the month before, this time at a pawnshop known to carry high-end jewelry. The pawnshop owner and his wife were there when the robbers hit." Ian paused, a muscle clenching in his jaw. "They'd been tied up and taken into the back . . ."

With a sickening dread, I knew what was coming next.

"They cut pieces off of them. The medical examiner said it had been done slowly, one then the other, and then back again until they both bled out. They never found the pieces."

Ian didn't need to say it. We both knew what had happened to those missing parts, and those parts had probably been eaten while their victims had been forced to watch.

"So we knew we were dealing with the same crew. Pete had known the husband and wife from the pawnshop. It had been on his old beat. He wouldn't wait; he said he couldn't live with himself if they got away, not after what they'd done, what they'd keep doing unless someone stopped them."

Ian paused and sat back when our drinks arrived. With barely a flick of his thumb, he popped the cap off of his longneck; and with suddenly shaky hands, I peeled the paper off my straw and put it in my sweet tea.

Ian took a long pull from his beer, set his bottle down, and raised his eyes to mine. "Pete went in."

"What did you do?"

"I did what a partner does; I backed him up. The ghouls were waiting. They must have been disappointed at first when they saw there was no one to slice up this time, so they waited for us. We'd seen three in the shop, but there were five of them and two of us. Pete thought he'd gotten the drop on them. Ordered them to take off their masks. The leader did, and he laughed while he did it. Then we saw what they were. Pete froze."

"No." Like me saying that could make it go back and not happen.

"The leader was on him before I could even react, fangs tearing at his face and throat. I shot the thing, and kept shooting. He raised his face from Pete's throat, covered in my partner's blood, smiled, and told me to be patient, I was next. I emptied two mags into those things and they didn't even flinch. Then three of them came after me. I hadn't seen their fingernails until then. I fought . . . and they cut me up. When I was in the hospital, the investigators assigned to the case tried to tell me that they'd used switchblades. I knew the truth. I knew what I'd seen, but I also knew enough to keep my mouth shut to avoid getting transferred upstairs to the psych ward. One night I got a visit from Vivienne Sagadraco."

"Who made you an offer you couldn't refuse."

"An offer I jumped at. Lying in that hospital bed, I'd sworn to myself that I'd get the things that had butchered my partner, and I couldn't do it working for the NYPD. The lady offered me a job, and after I got out of the hospital a month later, I took it."

"Did you get those ghouls?"

"Oh yeah. Paid back with interest."

"Ian, I'm not going to freeze at the sight of ghouls. Just because I didn't take that shot—"

"This has nothing to do with this morning. This is about being smart and staying alive."

"I chase little old ladies. I don't chase ghouls, and I sure as hell won't chase a grendel."

"Which is precisely what the boss is telling you to do."

"It's seeing through that veil—or whatever those things are using—and telling the team where they are."

"It's putting yourself within killing distance."

"It's my job." Here it comes, what Ian really thought of

me. I was going to beat him to it. "And you don't think I can do it."

"You're plenty qualified—as a seer." He leaned forward. "Mac, this situation is a first. I don't know how monsters supposedly that primitive are making themselves invisible, but they shouldn't be able to. Whether you're responding to what sounds like a routine call—or a hunt in dark tunnels for two grendels—a situation can go to shit in the blink of an eye. It takes less time than that to get killed. If you put someone who's not trained on the front line, bad things will happen. Maybe not the first time, but eventually, they will happen."

My mouth suddenly went bone dry. "And I'm not trained."

"Not for this. Not even a little. SPI's never given their seers combat training. They don't think it's necessary." He paused and took another swig of beer. "Combat training's a hell of a lot more than necessary when you're hunting monsters that rip off heads and arms, and gut you with one swipe."

I sucked down half a glass of sweet tea through my straw.

"You'll be with me," I said.

"I was there with Pete, too."

"And you're saying Pete would still be alive if he'd listened to you and waited for backup."

"I don't know that for sure."

"But you think it."

"Yeah, I think it. I think it all the damned time."

"My grandma thinks that good comes out of bad. If you and Pete hadn't walked in on those ghouls, Pete might be alive now—and you might still be with the NYPD."

"Your point?"

"I've seen the stuff on your desk. Your desk flair would give me nightmares; I can't even imagine what you had to do to earn all of it." I was silent for a moment. "You've done a lot of good here, and a lot of people are probably alive because of it. You would've never had a chance to do those things if you'd still been a cop. There's plenty of men who can be good cops, but it takes a man who's a lot more to storm the gates of Hell before lunch."

Ian's teeth flashed in a brief grin. "So Yasha *has* been talking."

"Who knew the gates of Hell were in Hoboken?" I looked down at my tea, suddenly uneasy. "And if you hadn't been here, the boss might already be looking for my replacement."

Ian put his big hand over mine. "The boss made you my responsibility; it's my job to keep you alive. Pete was my partner; he was my responsibility."

"You can't blame yourself for that."

"What happened that night was something I could've never predicted. Neither one of us was ready for five ghouls. But I know what's out there now. You're my partner, so I'm going to make damned sure you're ready."

"Uh . . . it's a little late for this time."

Ian sat back, pulling his hand back with him, leaving mine bare and cold. "Yeah, it is. After this—and there *will* be an after this—we start work." His lips twitched at the corners. "I can guarantee you're not going to enjoy it; but when I'm finished with you neither will any monster that crosses your path. Or at the very least, they'll get one hell of a shock."

I felt a grin coming on. "So you think you're that good of a teacher?"

"I know I am." He paused. "And I think you'll be that determined of a student."

I smiled. I couldn't help it. "So you're going to teach me to be a badass?"

"I'm a teacher, not a miracle worker. Let's start by teaching you how to stay alive. In the meantime, until this is over, it's about survival. I'll never be farther from you than I am right now."

Our food arrived and we ate. And in my relief at knowing Ian would be sticking with me, I found I actually had an appetite.

We'd finished eating, and Ian had paid the humongous bill—Yasha and Calvin had eaten like it was their last meal, too—when Nancy Garrison dropped by our booth.

Make no mistake about it, Nancy was a ferocious werewolf, but as a human, she was perky personified. Heels, stylish pantsuit, and her ever-present pearls—she was a Southern steel magnolia who just happened to go furry and fanged once a month.

"How was everything?" she asked.

"Fabulous as always," I said. "And today, it was much needed."

Nancy's perky faded a little. "I'm hearing that something's about to hit the fan."

"We're going to do everything we can to keep that from happening," Ian told her without elaborating further.

Nancy and Bill were clued in, and they knew about SPI, but unless events directly affected specific supernaturals, company policy was to keep the details under wraps. Nancy knew that, too. I'd always thought it was that whole don't-incite-a-public-panic thing. The Full Moon always threw their own New Year's Eve party, so Ian knew that the Garrisons wouldn't be going anywhere near Times Square tomorrow night.

"You should come bowl with us sometime," Nancy was saying.

I looked from Nancy to Ian and back again. "Me?"

"Yes, dear," Nancy said. "You."

"Bowl?"

"Since you've got your own ball and everything. Or are you already in a league?"

"I don't bowl. I mean I have, but I suck at it, and I sure don't have my own ball."

"I could've sworn I saw you carrying a bowling bag into work the other day."

Ian and I traded a glance.

"Which other day?" I asked.

Nancy thought for a moment. "Day before yesterday."

"You're sure?" Ian asked.

"As sure as I am that I saw a bowling bag."

"What color?" he asked.

"Red and white. Vintage looking. Like something from

the fifties. Nice bag." She looked at me. "Are you saying that wasn't you carrying that bag?"

"I'm saying some*thing* was carrying that bag that wasn't me."

Nancy's big brown eyes suddenly flashed gold. "You've got a doppelganger making trouble for you?" Those gold eyes said loud and clear that my doppelganger had better pray it never crossed Nancy Garrison's path again—on a full moon or any other time.

Jeez, did everyone know about doppelgangers except me?

I nodded. "In spades."

"Honey, those things are nothing to mess with." Then Ian was the target of those gold eyes. "You sticking close to this girl?"

"Don't worry," he assured her. "When I guard a woman, she stays guarded."

Nancy barely nodded, signaling that she acknowledged his ability to do that. Barely.

"I'll be fine," I assured her.

"You be careful."

"As much as I can."

I waited until Nancy had moved on to the next table. "You thinking what I'm thinking?"

"Since SPI doesn't have a bowling alley, I probably am."

"It's the package that CIA vampire was talking about."

We didn't have to say anything else; we were both thinking the same thing.

A bomb.

Or since we were dealing with supernaturals—something even worse.

# 14

THE four of us ran down the block, across the street, and back into Saga Investments. Ian had tried getting Moreau on his phone, and when he didn't answer, he tried Vivienne Sagadraco. No answer. No voicemail.

Meanwhile my mind was racing. What if being seen as me wasn't my doppelganger's main reason for being sent to SPI? I didn't know anything about bombs, but I was pretty sure you could get a whole lot of boom into a bowling bag. If the vampire ex-CIA agent worked for the adversary and hired the doppelganger to infiltrate SPI, delivering a bag full of boom was a distinct possibility. They'd turned a pair of grendels loose on New York. We wanted to stop the grendels. So following the bouncing logic ball, one could assume that they'd want to stop us.

Hence a big boom.

In the bull pen, things were still business as usual. Nothing ticking, no smoke, no fizzing fuses or however it was that bombs did their thing.

But something was going on, something big.

Kenji Hayashi's work area had become a hive of activity

for those of the brainy persuasion, the folks at SPI who rarely came out of their labs.

"Looks like we've got an answer on that flash drive," Ian said. "Mac, find out what the deal is. Yasha and Calvin, stay with her. Don't let her out of your sight. I'm going to find the boss and Moreau." And he was gone, running for the stairs.

The lab folks around Kenji's computer were equal parts excited and . . . okay, they were just excited. I stood back a little, waiting for the brainiac brouhaha to die down enough to ask Kenji what he'd found on that flash drive.

"Don't think I've ever seen the lab rats this excited," Calvin noted.

Those that weren't gathered around Kenji's screen, talking, debating, and arguing nonstop, had broken off into white-coated clumps, scribbling on tablets—both the paper and electronic kind. One enterprising group had commandeered a whiteboard, filling it with numbers, symbols, and diagrams that made absolutely no sense to me, nor I suspect to anyone with less than three math or engineering degrees.

"Whatever it is, they do seem to be enjoying themselves," I said.

I caught Kenji's attention, and the tech elf stood and pushed his way out of the human and nonhuman crush of his fellow science nerds, and made his way over to us.

"So what's got the smart kids in a tizzy?" I asked.

Kenji was grinning like it was Christmas morning. "Just the coolest thing ever. The actual *working* schematics for a device that renders its wearer visually and audibly undetectable."

"Uh . . . you mean unseen and unheard?"

"That's what I just said."

"Not unless you're in Mensa."

Kenji's dark eyes sparkled with geeky joy. "It's a cloaking device. The thing's small enough to fit in the palm of your hand, and will conceal anyone wearing it—from sight *and sound*. Eat your heart out, Romulans."

"It works like a veil?"

"It takes a veil about fifty giant leaps forward. Veils just project an altered appearance; this thing can conceal you completely."

"So how does it work?" Calvin asked.

"We understand about eighty percent of the science involved, but it's got some woo-woo crap going on that we haven't figured out yet."

I just looked at him. "Woo-woo crap?"

"Magic." Kenji scowled. "It's looking like we're going to have to call in the Merlin types up on the fourth floor."

"That's a problem?"

"It is when the head of the sorcery department's a pompous asshole. Tries to take over every project he's called in on. Thinks just because he's a couple hundred years older than the rest of us that makes him smarter. All it means is he's had more time to piss off more people."

I thought back to the grendel we'd seen on the surveillance video. Adam Falke hadn't seen or heard the monster looming in the corner. Then when Falke started screaming, it was obvious that he had.

"Does the device have a switch of some kind?" I asked.

Kenji nodded. "A button. A simple on and off."

"Then if the grendel picks up a weapon while he's invisible, would the weapon be invisible, too? Or would the cloaking device only cover the grendel itself?"

"Like I said, this thing's made of twenty percent Grade-A woo-woo crap. We have no idea what it can or can't cover. Yet."

"Sounds like we will find out hard way," Yasha muttered.

"Some of the best scientific discoveries happen in the field."

Calvin snorted. "Unless something in the field eats them first."

Kenji shrugged and grinned. "Maybe if we can get the grendel to wear a natty dressing gown and sunglasses we'd be able to see him."

"You lost me," I said.

Yasha smiled and nodded. "Claude Rains. *The Invisible Man.*"

"A werewolf that likes classic monster movies," Kenji noted with approval. "Borderline ironic, yet cool."

I grimaced. "So . . . you have to be *naked* for the device to work?"

Kenji gave me a flat look. "I don't know. I was trying to make a funny, lighten a tense workplace situation. See prior statement regarding mysterious woo-woo crap."

"Well, do you know if it's buildable?"

"Buildable, and probably built," Kenji said. "The files for these plans were dated from four to six months ago, covering conception through revisions, testing, and final product."

"By chance did the plans have the inventor's name on them?"

"They sure did. Dr. Jonathan Tarbert."

"Who was killed three months ago," I mused. "Maybe. Late brother of the definitely dearly departed James Tarbert. My vampire buddy said Tarbert's brother got himself killed because of greed. I wonder if he was peddling his late brother's invention for fun and profit?"

Kenji whistled. "That wouldn't have made Dr. Tarbert's employer happy at all."

I went still. "That wouldn't be the Department of Defense by any chance?"

He nodded. "Affirmative. Said so right on the plans. And the DOD is *so* not known for their sense of humor."

An outraged squeal came from Kenji's computer. One of the white coats had made himself at home in the elf tech's chair. "Dude!" Kenji shouted. "Don't touch her there." He gave a long-suffering sigh. "Engineers. Gotta go."

"The MiBs in the back of that van didn't look like they appreciated a good joke, either," I told Yasha and Calvin.

"Sounds like that ex-CIA vampire has been dipping into the DOD toy box," Calvin noted.

Yasha frowned. "Sounds like crazy person who made grendels not seen or heard already did."

My phone rang. It was Ian. He'd found the boss and Moreau in the main lab.

The crates had arrived from the Tarbert mausoleum.

SPI's lab was normally a busy place. Tonight only two of the senior research staff were there with the boss and Moreau. Every available tabletop was covered with open crates, and the air was thick with smells that didn't agree with what I'd just eaten—or with the rest of me that didn't like being around dead things.

That's what was in every crate I could see from where I was standing.

Dead things. Dead supernaturals to be exact, displayed like hunting trophies.

Human skulls with fangs. Some were just the jaws—lowers and fanged uppers. Vampires.

Massive wolflike skulls and pelts. A few skulls had been taxidermied. Werewolves.

Baby dragons preserved in jars or in cross-sectioned eggs. Skulls of adults, and stuffed younger and smaller specimens.

Plus a whole bunch of other deadly looking creatures that I couldn't identify.

And grendels. More grendels. One of the long crates contained yet another grendel arm.

With each crate was documentation saying where they'd been killed or collected, and if photography had been available at that time, there was photographic proof of the successful hunt. They ranged from high-resolution, full-color digital prints, all the way back to grainy, turn-of-the-last-century sepia tones.

Photographic and scientific proof of the existence of supernaturals. Predatory and dangerous supernaturals.

All packed in crates stamped "Property of the U.S. Government."

It was a tabloid editor's wet dream.

It was SPI's worst nightmare.

I tried to put it all together in my head. The CIA was knowingly using vampires and possibly doppelgangers. A dead research scientist for the Department of Defense had a collection of supernatural predator hunting trophies hidden under his family mausoleum, and, at the time of his murder, had developed and perfected a device to render anyone—or anything—that wore it invisible and inaudible.

Right now, a pair of grendels were murdering their way through New York, unseen and unheard by their victims. Tomorrow night, the same individual who had sent Vivienne Sagadraco a taunting letter was going to aim them at Times Square and a crowd of nearly one million people.

Oh holy hell.

Ian came up beside me.

"This is about much more than a pair of grendels," I murmured. I had to force my eyes away from the crates and their gruesome contents. "Kenji told the boss what he found on that flash drive?"

Ian nodded, his mouth tightened in a grim line. "As soon as he had confirmation."

"You tell Moreau that my evil twin is a bowler?"

"I did."

"And?"

"He's about to tear this place apart until he finds that bag or what was in it. The new guy in Research found that you arrived twice at work yesterday—once with the bowling bag, and once without."

"I was without."

"That's what I told him. When you and your doppelganger left yesterday afternoon, neither one of you had a bag."

"Oh shit."

"Yeah."

"We've got CIA, DOD . . . so who the hell is doing this?"

Vivienne Sagadraco's cool voice came from behind me. "At this point, neither, Agent Fraser." Her gaze swept the tables and their contents, her steely eyes lingering and narrowing in barely contained anger at the sight of the baby dragons. "My source inside the intelligence community was able to tell me that the seed of this evil germinated in the minds of former employees of both organizations—but it was a CIA task force that was formed to investigate the feasibility of using, shall we say, unconventional weapons."

"Supernaturals?"

"Yes. This task force proposed to exploit the talents of certain qualified creatures—whether voluntarily or through coercion—against the enemies of this nation."

"That's crazy."

"So were many government projects. The Philadelphia Experiment is merely one that comes to mind. But your opinion is similar to that of senior CIA officials charged with finding projects to eliminate due to budget cuts. This particular project was deemed to be highly dangerous with little chance of success, so the project and its funding were discontinued, the task force disbanded, and its members either resigned or were reassigned. As far as the CIA is concerned, that was the end of it."

"Looks like some of those people ignored the memo," Ian said.

"I can say with virtual certainty that all of the task force 'ignored the memo.' We have closely examined the backgrounds of each of the seventeen individuals involved. All are either supernatural creatures or humans extraordinarily gifted in the dark magical arts. I believe they were assembled with a purpose, and used their positions within these agencies to act openly."

Ian shook his head in amazement. "All the resources they needed were there for the asking. They operated with the full funding and cooperation of the U.S. government."

"Was the vampire that's been following me on this task force?" I asked.

"He was one of those who resigned." Vivienne Sagadraco pulled a photo from a folder and held it out for me and Ian to see. "This woman was the head of the task force."

I instantly recognized her. I'd seen her in another photo less than an hour ago; only in this picture she was wearing a cocktail dress instead of a wedding gown.

"Jonathan Tarbert's wife was the head of the task force?" I shook my head. "Well, that certainly explains a lot."

Vivienne Sagadraco raised a silvery eyebrow. "Tarbert's *wife*?"

"I found their wedding photo earlier."

When the boss spoke, it was almost to herself. "My, she did go to extraordinary lengths, didn't she?"

I looked closer at the ex-wife and ex-CIA agent and my mouth fell open. "Is that what I think it is?"

The woman wore a multi-strand pearl choker with a carved, pale blue oval stone in the center, carved in an all-too-familiar shape.

"It is," the boss said, "if you think it's a scarab identical to the one used to seal the letter to me, and the tattoo on the palm of Adam Falke."

I slowly sat back. "She's the adversary."

"Correction, Agent Fraser," Vivienne Sagadraco said, her eyes hard and locked on the woman's face. "This woman is *my* adversary, and the adversary of every principle I founded SPI upon."

"You know her." I didn't ask it as a question.

"Only too well. It was my misfortune to share a nest with this creature, and not very amiably."

I was stunned. "Your sister?"

Sagadraco nodded once. "I have not seen her since 1914. We had . . . a disagreement; it was but the latest of the many we have had. The scarab adaptation is new. However, she always did have a fondness for ancient cultures similar to our own—and for her given name. Tia is a shortened form of Tiamat."

I went very still. "As in the dragon goddess Tiamat?" I saw Ian's surprised expression. "I've flipped through Kenji's D&D books."

"Though in Babylonian mythology and in actuality, Tiamat does not have five heads," Vivienne Sagadraco told us. "Which is fortunate, because it has always been sufficiently challenging for me to deal with the single head that Tia does have."

My mind boggled at how old that made my boss. "That makes you . . ."

Vivienne Sagadraco smiled, though it was tinged with sadness. "A woman who is well aware of her age."

"Excuse me, ma'am. I didn't mean to—"

The boss—the dragon lady—waved a dismissive hand. "I take no offense, Agent Fraser."

"Do you believe that Jonathan Tarbert was involved?" Ian asked.

"Unknown. The task force was strictly CIA. Dr. Tarbert's research was for military applications—*human* military. And I cannot see Tia taking a human into her confidence. Her arrogance would prevent such a partnership. However, I can easily see Tia obtaining and exploiting the results of his research."

I started running over the facts; trying to put the whole picture together in my head. "Tarbert's lab burns down with him in it, and the flash drive with the plans turns up in the hands of his dead brother. Kenji said that the plans were four to six months old, and that from the notes, the device had been built, tested, and perfected."

"Given that we have ample evidence of invisible and inaudible grendels, that conclusion is correct."

"Your sister has the device," Ian said. "We have the plans. Plans that ex-CIA agent Fitzpatrick was willing to kill Mac to get for his boss/your sister. At least she can't make more devices."

Vivienne Sagadraco nodded once. "At least not easily. Though given time, she could reproduce them by disassembling the one that is in her possession. However, we would be foolhardy not to proceed under the assumption that Tia has more than one device at her disposal."

"What does she want to get out of this?" I asked.

"Tia has always resented having to hide her nature from the world. The hazard with having a civilization worship you as a goddess is that you begin to believe as they do. The Babylonians were correct in naming her the goddess of chaos. Chaos and power are all that my sister is capable of loving. She employs manipulation as a means to an end, and does absolutely nothing without a reason. I believe she has found a new game that not only offers her entertainment and power; it will also enable her to destroy what I have done here at SPI. While far from her main goal, it no doubt would bring her great satisfaction. We protect humans and supernaturals alike. Tia would tear away the illusions, exposing humans to the reality of the supernatural world. In order to be out in the world in this present age, she has been forced to exist in a human body, and to live within its limitations. I am quite content; but make no mistake, my sister is not. She has told me that for a dragon to endure life as a human was the same as a human forced to suffer as the lowest worm."

I let out a low whistle. "Your sister doesn't have much use for us, does she?"

"Actually she has expressed two uses for humans: as slaves and as food." Vivienne Sagadraco's expression darkened. "In this century and the last, humans have developed technology that surpasses what was previously considered to be magic. They can defend themselves, even from a creature as formidable as my sister in her dragon form and at her full power. Her most earnest desire is to change this. Her letter to me said that humans weren't at the top of the food chain and would soon know it. She also said that New Year's Eve would mark the beginning of an enlightened new age."

"That's one thing I don't get," I said. "Okay, there's a lot that I don't get, but why would your sister send you a letter essentially telling you what she's going to do?"

"Pride and arrogance. She will use the devices and the grendels in the most public way possible. Tia knows that I won't sit by while monsters savage untold numbers of people. Knowing my sister as I do, I can surmise that she acted within the limitations of her human form, gained employment at the human agency that would give her the best access to what she needed to accomplish her ultimate goal—to put into motion events that would reduce the human race to what they once were, and what Tia believes they should be again—slaves and food."

"Why not do it herself?" Ian asked. "Turning dragon and dive-bombing Times Square on New Year's Eve would certainly make a statement, cause chaos, and it'd be a hell of a lot easier than wrangling grendels."

"My sister would only appear and risk herself in such a way under the direst of circumstances. Simply put, grendels are vicious killers of humans, are visually terrifying and virtually indestructible. Times Square on New Year's Eve is one of the most heavily policed events in the world. Thousands of what are essentially soldiers, heavily armed and well trained to react instantly to any type of attack scenario that they can imagine."

"I bet they haven't trained for grendels," I said.

"Precisely. Which would cause a level of panic that has never been seen by so many at the same time. It would be broadcast live around the world."

"Spooking the entire human herd," I murmured.

"An apt analogy, Agent Fraser," Sagadraco said. "No one would feel safe. Armed with the devices, Tia and her allies could launch attacks from anywhere at any time. Fear would turn to paranoia. People's confidence in their law enforcement, military, and governments to protect them would falter and quickly fail. Those with her on that CIA task force represent my sister's longtime allies. Creatures who resent hiding themselves from humans; who want to hunt and feed openly and as often as they wish. Humans with extraordinary magical gifts twisted by greed and evil, who resent hiding their dark powers."

"There are certain vampire covens around the world that would gladly ally themselves with Tiamat," Moreau said. "As would virtually all of the ghoul swarms and demon hordes. If Tiamat is successful tomorrow night, they would acknowledge her leadership and pledge their allegiance to her and her cause. Armed with the devices, they would be capable of appearing and vanishing at will. Humans would live in constant fear, banding together, never sure when or where the next attack would come from. Life on Earth would become a living nightmare."

"My sister would consider it heaven on Earth," Vivienne Sagadraco told us. "Tiamat fights to win. It is a fight that humans and supernaturals alike cannot afford to lose. I have failed to stop her before. We cannot fail to stop her now."

# 15

POLITICIANS are right about one thing: budget cuts can be dangerous. Slash the funding to the wrong people, and you get a bunch of disgruntled, supernatural ex-CIA spooks going into business for themselves.

Combine that with my doppelganger having hidden a bowling bag full of unknown and potentially deadly contents somewhere in headquarters, and I had enough nerves to qualify for a nervous breakdown.

Vivienne Sagadraco had ordered headquarters emptied of all nonessential personnel. Which in SPI parlance meant the only agents who stayed were either experts in all forms of combat should the doppelganger still be here, those with the nasal talent needed to sniff out potential bombs, or the lab people and engineers still unraveling the workings of Dr. Tarbert's "cloaking device" as they'd taken to calling it.

And then there was me.

One, the boss deemed it too risky—even with a bomb possibly in the house—to send me home. Two, if my doppelganger was still here and using one of Tarbert's devices, I'd be the only one able to see her—if I could see her at all.

My seer ability enabled me to detect veils, wards, etc., produced either by natural or magical means. I had absolutely zero experience with anything mechanical. Everyone still in headquarters—including me—hoped that I could. One way or another, we'd be finding out the answer soon enough.

I briefly squeezed my eyes shut against an incoming headache. There were just too many unanswered questions. And the longer they stayed unanswered, the longer we stayed screwed.

Vivienne Sagadraco very much wanted to have a chat with my doppelganger. So much so that when she ordered the nonessential folks out, everyone had to scan their palms before any exit would open for them and them only. The boss wasn't taking any chances that my doppelganger would activate her cloaking device and try to sneak out on somebody's coattails.

As to finding the explosives, who needed bomb-sniffing dogs when we had werewolves on staff?

Yasha and the five other werewolf agents who were working tonight had undergone extensive training to identify and locate the various pieces, parts, and ingredients that could go into making a bomb.

I tried to sit and relax, but the latter wasn't happening, so the former was impossible. This much stress called for a sugar hit. I looked down at the carry-out container of banana puddin' from the Full Moon sitting on my desk. I needed that puddin'. But first I needed a spoon. And milk. I had to have milk. I pushed back my chair and stood. "I'm fixin' to go for milk," I announced. "Anyone else want something?"

I went into the break room, got a spoon out of the drawer, a glass out of the cabinet, opened the fridge door . . .

. . . and stared.

My doppelganger hadn't brought a bomb in that bowling bag—or even a bowling ball.

Ollie Barrington-Smythe's blood-spattered toupee was perched on top of a honeydew melon.

And to make it extra festive, a fruit knife had been plunged through the top like a Lizzie Borden hatpin, and a face had been drawn on in black Sharpie that actually looked like Ollie.

As my vision went sparkly and my knees weak, my only thought was that my doppelganger was an artist. Who knew?

The combination of that and everything else left me with an overwhelming need to find a chair, sit down, and put my head between my knees.

"Ian." I said it as loudly as I could while folded double in a chair.

Nothing.

"Ian," I called again, going for more volume this time. "I found what was in the bowling bag."

I heard more than one pair of booted feet running in my direction, and since I knew they were friendlies, I left my head right where it was and watched the light show behind my eyelids.

There were two obscenities, one guffaw, and an eww.

Ian's hand was on my back. "Breathe."

After about a minute, the sparklies started to go away. Breathing wasn't particularly easy, but then I was wadded up in a chair. Air was way overrated anyway, especially when it smelled like overripe melon and something that must have been toupee glue.

"Is it Ollie's?" Ian asked.

My voice was muffled between my knees. "Oh yeah."

"The blood appears to be fresh; as to the claw marks, ghouls would be a safe bet."

"Oh goody."

"Though generally if kidnappers send a part or piece, it means the victim is still alive."

"Generally?" I asked.

"Mostly."

I slowly sat up. Minor sparklies, but no whirlies or woozies. "Aw jeez, my milk is in there."

"It's on the other side of the shelf."

"From a bloody toupee."

"Look on the bright side," Ian said. "At least she didn't leave you a body part."

I stared sadly at the hairy melon that was even shaped like Ollie's head. I felt my eyes start to tear up. "The toupee might be the only thing they didn't eat."

"There's not enough blood for it to have been fatal," Ian hurried to assure me. "But the melon and toupee couldn't have been what was in the bowling bag."

I sniffed. "Why not?"

"Your doppelganger brought the bag in early yesterday morning."

"And Ollie wasn't kidnapped until around eleven," I realized. Duh.

"Right. However, the blood on the toupee is relatively fresh, and people have been in and out of this fridge all day."

I slowly stood up. "Meaning if I just now found it . . ."

There was a gleam in Ian's green eyes. "She's still here."

Vivienne Sagadraco's voice came from the doorway. "I understand our intruder left a calling card."

The boss was probably accustomed to receiving actual calling cards from her butler on a tiny silver tray. I got a melon wearing Ollie's rug on a chipped plate.

"You could say that, ma'am."

"I believe I just did."

"Yes, ma'am."

Ian told the boss his theory about the doppelganger's present whereabouts.

"Alain?"

"Yes, madam?"

I jumped. Moreau was standing right behind me.

"Lock down the complex. No one else leaves or enters."

"Consider it done." The vampire left to carry out her orders, as silently as he'd come in. Creepy.

I started to slip past her and out the break room door.

"And where are you going, Agent Fraser?" she asked.

"I'm going to find me and kick my ass."

"You will stay here."

"But ma'am, I wanna help find—"

Vivienne Sagadraco held up a hand. "You can best do that by remaining here. That way there will be no confusion as to the doppelganger's true identity if you are not dashing about the complex complicating matters."

"Meaning no one will accidentally kill you while looking for her," Ian said.

"But if I stay with you, you'll know I'm me," I insisted. "If she's wearing that cloaking device, you won't see her. I'm the only one who might be able to. Moreau said doppelgangers have supernatural strength, so wouldn't it be good to see something like that before it finds you?"

Ian and the boss both regarded me with narrowed eyes, meaning that they didn't like it, but they knew I was right, at least a little bit; though I wasn't stupid enough to say so out loud.

"Your argument has merit," the boss admitted. "I will consider your request." She turned on her fashionably high heels and left the break room. "Commander Benoit," she called out into the bull pen, "I want the doppelganger taken alive. I have questions and that creature has answers. I want those answers."

"Understood, ma'am. One doppelganger conscious enough for questioning coming up."

I started to leave, but was stopped by Ian's hand on my arm.

"Wipe that smirk off your face," he said.

"I'm not smirking." Then again, maybe I was.

"If she says yes—and if she does, she's wrong and I don't agree with her—you will do *exactly* as I say."

Normally, I would've argued with him, but with what he'd told me during dinner, I knew he was afraid. For me. For fear of another partner disregarding caution and getting themselves in a situation that was way over their head. It had taken a lot for him to tell me what had happened. I also remembered his promise to teach me how to survive those situations. He didn't have to make that offer or tell me what had happened to him and his last partner; but he had, and both meant a lot to me.

So the least I could do—at least for now—was to toe the line.

"Understood," I said.

Ian's eyes widened in surprise then narrowed in suspicion. "You can understand something but still not do it."

"Okay, then let me rephrase that. I will be a good and cautious partner and follow the directions of a senior—and more experienced—agent."

Ian's expression was dubious to say the least.

"Really," I said.

Ian raised an eyebrow.

"And truly." I raised a hand. "Scout's honor . . . um, even though I was never a Girl Scout."

"Let me guess, too many rules?"

"I never made it past Brownies. On our first campout, there was a fire drill, and I fell, rolled down a hill, and into the lake. There were scrapes, cuts, possibly a concussion—"

*"I found bowling bag in trash next to incinerator,"* said Yasha's voice over Kenji's speakers. *"Is empty. Does not smell like bomb."*

Ian and I ran out into the bull pen.

Vivienne Sagadraco reached over Kenji and keyed the mike. "Can you identify it?"

A pause from Yasha. Then a long sniff. Then another pause. *"There is smell, but I do not know it."*

"Take it up to the lab," the boss told him. "They'll tell us what it is. Mr. Hayashi, do you have those sightings compiled yet?"

"Aye, aye," Kenji told her then looked over at me. "I need to know which of these are you, and which ones are not. Looks like you were all over the place yesterday."

I pulled up a chair beside him and looked at the big, segmented screen.

"Once inside, I spent most of my day either at my desk, but I was in the break room, uh . . . several times getting cookies." I lowered my voice. "Or in the ladies' room . . . because of all the coffee and milk I had with those cookies."

"It looks like your doppelganger went damned near everywhere else. She's been in nearly every part of the complex, a few times going just out of the security cameras' range."

"Identify the places where she was out of range," Sagadraco said. "All of them."

"The hall behind the armory, locker rooms, labs, and of course, the incinerator."

Ian maneuvered around behind Kenji's chair. "Got a floor plan handy?"

"Coming right up."

Lines and boxes crisscrossed on the screen. Kenji touched the screen in the five places, each area highlighting as he did.

"For one, they're spread out," Ian muttered. "Good blast radius."

Kenji shot him a look.

"*If* you're a bomber."

I noticed small squares in each area. "What are those?"

"Air vents."

"Bombs in air vents?"

"Could be gas." Roy Benoit had paused on his way out of the bull pen.

"Commander," the boss said, "take your people and coordinate with Commander Niles and her team. I want each of those areas thoroughly searched."

Roy and his heavily armed monster-hunting commandos moved out to split up the search duties with Sandra and her folks, leaving me and Ian high and dry. Ian showed no reaction one way or another. I was more than a little disappointed.

Kenji spent the next few minutes scanning through the still photos from the security cameras, images rolling past too fast for me to see. The elf tech didn't seem to share my problem. The scrolling screen was making me dizzy, so I looked away. As soon as I did, Kenji stopped scrolling.

"Wait," he said to himself. "What's this?"

I leaned over. "What's what?"

"Another photo. Is that you?"

I looked closely. "Looks like me; but since I don't recognize where it was taken, I probably wasn't there."

The lights flickered. In the bull pen and on the five floors above it.

I froze. I wasn't the only one.

"Is that . . . normal, but just really bad timing?" I asked quietly.

We all watched as the lights on each level and catwalk above and surrounding the bull pen, flickered again then came back on, but at less than full power.

"Mr. Hayashi, identify the source of that power fluctuation," the boss said. She touched what I'd always thought was an oversized pearl earring, and spoke. "Commanders Benoit and Niles, report."

I looked closer. The "pearl" was held in place by a gold mount, the end of which curled around her earlobe and into her ear. Nice. That had to be the world's most expensive headset.

While she listened, Kenji's fingers flew over the keys. "It's the south tunnel generators, ma'am. But all the readings from the control panels are normal, no fluctuation."

The boss exhaled on a growl. "Naturally, I just evacuated the maintenance staff," she muttered.

"I can run diagnostics from here, ma'am," Kenji offered.

"Do it."

"By the way, those generators are next to the HVAC control room," the elf tech told her. "The same place the doppelganger was at approximately nine this morning in the photo I just found."

Sagadraco nodded as she listened to either Roy or Sandra on the other end.

Kenji leaned toward me. "HVAC is heating, ventilation, and air conditioning," he whispered to me.

"I know what that is," I whispered back.

"Just making sure. We're ten stories underground. Our air comes from the surface and is circulated out through those big-ass exhaust fans outside the north tunnel entrance."

Ian was intent on the schematics of the south tunnel area that Kenji's search had called up. "All of which lead to air ducts," he murmured.

Kenji nodded. "In every room of the complex."

Vivienne Sagadraco finished speaking into her headset, and turned to me and Ian. "Agent Fraser, you're about to get your wish, though I think you should be more careful what you wish for. One of Commander Niles's teams is closest to that location and will be backing you up. However it will be another ten minutes before they can get there. Agent Byrne, arm yourself and your partner and investigate that power fluctuation—and find out why that doppelganger would have been down there."

# 16

THE HVAC control room didn't look anywhere near as important as it sounded. Yes, there were some impressive-looking switches and panels with lots of blinking lights, but all that was behind some seriously thick glass in its own little room. The only things out here with us were pipes, covered cables, metal cabinets, and a whole mess of concrete and steel.

There was no sign that my doppelganger was here or had ever been here.

The toe of my boot kicked something small, sending it bouncing with metallic plinks across the concrete floor, until it hit the far wall.

It was plenty light enough to see, but we'd brought flashlights that felt more like steel clubs and had beams that would probably strike you blind. The flashlight was a heavy and reassuring weight in my hand.

I walked over and shone the beam of my flashlight down on the tiny piece of metal.

Ian glanced up from his inspection of the closest control panel. "What was it?"

It was just a screw.

I aimed my light up and around, searching for what it'd come off of. "Something down here's lost a screw."

Ian refrained from commenting.

I located a square of dark in the shadows close to the ceiling. An open air vent. A metal grate hung from the one remaining screw. It looked like there'd been three others that'd fallen out—or had been removed.

I stepped back. Way back.

I spoke without turning. "Houston, we have—"

"I see it," Ian said quietly, coming up behind me.

"Okay," I said. "I'm only like five six, so that's all my doppelganger has to work with heightwise. Kenji didn't have a picture of her haulin' a ladder in here, so how would she have—"

"True." Ian had gone down on one knee to search the floor. He came up with two more screws in the palm of his hand. "But these haven't been on the floor for long. See how the screws' heads are dull, but the threads aren't? These were taken out recently." He went over to stand in front of the wall just to the right of the open vent. "Put down your flashlight and come here."

I did.

He squatted down. "Get on my shoulders."

"What?"

"Put your legs over here"—he tapped each side of his chest—"and sit on my shoulders. I'll stand up and you shine your light in there."

"And a bomb blows up in my face."

"There's not a bomb in there."

"But up in the bull pen, you said—"

"*This* vent would be a bad place for a bomb. If your doppelganger was carrying around explosives or gas, she wouldn't waste them in there. So far, she hasn't been stupid. Come on. We're wasting time. Lean forward, brace your hands against the wall, and climb on."

I got behind him, put one leg over his shoulder and hesitated.

"What's wrong?"

"Um . . . if I put my other leg over, what's going to keep me from falling over backward?"

"Me." He clamped his big hand over my shin, essentially anchoring my leg from the knee down against his chest. He was right; my leg wasn't going anywhere. "Now put your other leg over and sit up straight—and stay still. I'll do the rest."

"Uh . . . I don't think the wall's gonna work for my hands, could we—"

Ian's sharp exhale told me he'd lost his patience when I'd lost my coordination.

"It's not my fault I've never done this before."

"Just grab my head."

"Your what?"

"My head. Wrap your hands around the top of my head."

I did as instructed.

"Not my eyes, my head!"

I moved my hands up and put my other leg over his shoulder. Ian grabbed my leg and started to stand.

I squeaked as I felt myself start to topple over. Ian's grip tightened on my legs, and I clutched a double handful of his hair. I steadied myself, my hands not doing a very good job of holding on to the top of Ian's head.

I didn't dare to breathe, let alone move. "You need longer hair."

He ignored me. "Ready?"

"As I'll ever be."

Ian stood. I stayed on. It was nothing short of a miracle.

To my relief, he stopped about three feet away from the wall, and my head was perfectly aligned with the opening.

"Here." Ian handed me his flashlight.

I took it and aimed the beam straight ahead, illuminating the shaft.

There was definitely something in there, in some kind of pile. I couldn't quite make out what they were, but since the pile wasn't moving . . .

"Move a little closer."

Ian did.

I couldn't tell how many there were, but they were brown, each about the size and shape of a baked potato. I looked closer.

They weren't bombs or nerve gas canisters.

They were eggs.

And they had hatched.

"Bad news," I said. "You were right. It's not a bomb."

"Well, what is it?"

"They. It's a 'they.' About ten, I don't know, maybe twelve . . . eggs."

"Eggs?"

"Eggs. Hatched eggs."

"What kind?"

"Nothing I've ever seen before." I had a sudden urge to run and keep running. "Let me down. Let me down now."

Quicker than I could react, Ian released my legs, reached behind his head, grabbed me around the waist, swung me down, and had me tucked tightly under his arm. His other hand held his gun.

I scanned the floor directly below me and didn't dare move. "Where is it?" I hissed in a whisper. "Do you see anything?"

"Not yet."

I had no idea why we were whispering. If there was something down here with us, they knew we were here. As long as I was tucked up under Ian's arm like a sack of chicken feed, I wouldn't be able to do a thing about it. Though I was grateful to have my feet off the floor. I had to stifle the urge to twist around and climb Ian like a tree.

"Put me down."

He did.

I'd dropped my flashlight and it'd rolled into the corner, stopping at the base of some kind of metal cabinet. I ran after it, and reached down to snatch it off the concrete floor. If there was ever a time I wanted a steel club, it was right—

I yelped and yanked my hand back, scrambling backward, tripping over my own legs in the process.

The back of my hand was bleeding from a two-inch gash. Must have raked my hand on the base of the cabinet yanking it . . .

A raspy hiss came from the shadowy corner . . .

. . . and from the air vent opening.

Ian put himself between me and whatever they were. "Get to the door. Get out."

I hesitated.

"Move!"

The things came at us, and Ian opened fire.

A creature launched itself out of the open air vent and into the tangle of pipes that ran above our heads. I only got a glimpse. It was about a foot tall, with pale mottled skin slick and glistening, with spindly and impossibly long arms and legs. Another one leapt effortlessly to the top of the cabinet. It perched there, its yellow eyes glittering in the shadows. The thing rolled its bald head on ropy shoulders as if stretching, its mouth yawning open to reveal multiple rows of needle teeth, flexing its thin, spidery fingers, claws curved to razor points. Claws that were red with my blood.

It looked like . . .

It couldn't be.

A baby grendel.

I opened my mouth, to shout, to scream, but nothing came out, not even a whimper.

The grendel's eyes focused on us and it hissed, a hood of folded skin flaring around its neck.

Ian shot at the slick face. The grendel was gone before the bullet got there. Simultaneous attacks came from the open air vent and the sound of claws on metal scrambled by inside the ductwork directly overhead. I was sure that every last one of them would star in my next nightmare, if I lived long enough to have another one.

Ian reached out, prepared to throw me toward the door, but I was already running.

We escaped into the hall, and Ian slammed the reinforced steel door.

I was all but jumping in place. "Lock it! Lock it!"

Ian spat a curse. "The dead bolt's been broken off."

I desperately looked around for something to block the door with. There was nothing, absolutely nothing in that hall that would do us any good.

The door handle began to rotate downward.

On the other side of the door came the scrabbling of claws on concrete—a *lot* of claws.

Ian and I stared.

Then we ran like hell.

The male and female grendels had been busy since they'd arrived in town, and they hadn't been seeing the sights. My doppelganger had brought grendel eggs in that bowling bag.

"Kenji, we've got grendels," Ian was shouting into his headset. "Repeat, grendels. Little ones, spawn. Unknown number. Eggs were in the HVAC vents, and the sons of bitches are fast. We're in the hall coming away from—"

Ian skidded to a halt and I plowed into him from behind. Then I saw why he'd stopped.

Countless glowing yellow eyes, and the baby monsters they belonged to, were completely blocking our only way out.

Ian raised his gun, his voice low and steady. "Mac, get your gun, pick your targets, and go for head shots."

I swallowed, and drew my gun. My hand was shaking so badly I almost dropped it. I gripped it tighter. Ian saw.

"Relax your grip and your shoulders. Pull the trigger on the exhale. You can do this."

Agent Ian Byrne. Poster child for calm.

Me. Poster child for panic.

I heard clicking behind us. I spun, going back-to-back with Ian, gun leveled.

Four grendels had stopped about twenty feet away, watching us, chittering amongst themselves.

"Four behind us," I managed.

"Okay. I'll take these. Those are yours."

As if by unspoken signal, the grendels rushed us.

I only got off one shot before the first grendel reached me.

A clawed hand clutched my ankle, latching onto my boot, trying to pull itself up. I stomped on the hand, and fired at another grendel skittering across the floor at me. It squealed as a spray of pink erupted from its side, but kept coming, its eyes brightly glowing like sunstruck flame, eyes shining with a single-minded hunger.

Squealing, hissing, eyes gleaming with a yellow light. I fired at every last one of them. I could've sworn my shots were on target, but the spawn were fast. Too fast.

A grendel latched onto my leg, above my boot, its claws raking their way up my leg through my jeans, hooking into my skin. I wanted to scream, but the only sounds I could make were choked gasps, as if the thing was clutching my throat, not my thigh. It was that high now, and coming faster toward my face. It got a grip on my belt and launched itself onto my shoulder, the throbbing pulse in my neck within reach of its jagged, razor-sharp teeth, teeth that were clicking together in eager anticipation.

My right hand was slick with blood and my gun slipped out of my grip and landed on the floor. I grabbed the grendel with both hands, trying to keep it away from my face, its squirming body cold and slick in my hands. I held it out away from me as it twisted and wriggled to get at me. I gripped it tighter. It squealed. So did I.

It took both of my hands and all of my strength just to hold on to the thing. I wanted to kill it. I needed to kill it, but if I let go, just with one hand, even for an instant, the grendel would be at my throat, claws and the barbed spurs that curved from its bony heels slicing me to ribbons.

If I was lucky, I'd bleed to death before the whole pack started to eat me.

I didn't dare turn to check on Ian, but gunfire and squealing grendels told me he was at least holding his own.

Which was better than I was doing.

I threw the grendel, slamming it into the wall. Not even dazed, it clung there, defying gravity and then physics as it scampered up the wall and across the ceiling like a freaking gecko, launching itself again at my face with chittering glee.

It exploded in a single bullet-induced spray of pink mere inches from my face.

Ian.

Ian had looked away from the grendels attacking him to help me. It was the opening the things had been waiting for.

They swarmed him.

Then I saw it. Recessed in the wall was one of those fire hose boxes—with an ax.

I scrabbled and stumbled toward it, clawing desperately to get the glass door open, my hands fumbling at the handle. I got it open and pulled at the ax.

It was latched to the back wall of the case.

I screamed in terror and frustration.

A grendel dropped from the ceiling onto my shoulders, and I fell forward into the coiled fire hose. The whole thing came loose, wrapping me in hose. The nozzle came free last, hitting me in the head. I grabbed at the nozzle and the grendel that was holding on to both it and me.

And somehow I turned on the water.

Instantly a blast as big as my arm shot from the end of that nozzle, the water pressure slamming the grendel that'd been holding on to it into the far wall. The hose whipped around me like I was wrestling the world's biggest snake, knocking me to the floor, sending the spray to the ceiling, walls, and floor. I held on to the nozzle for dear life, and aimed it directly at the grendels swarming Ian.

The water blasted the grendels and sent them rolling down the hall, end over end. Then as quick as they'd come, they vanished.

I loosened my grip on the nozzle, releasing the lever that I'd been holding down, and the hose slowly deflated. I was sprawled in the middle of the hall, soaked to the skin, teeth chattering, and gasping for what air I could find. I still clutched the nozzle in a double-fisted, white-knuckled grip. Ian climbed to his feet and staggered over to me, dripping blood from multiple wounds, and dropped into the puddle by my side.

"Nice shootin', Annie Oakley."

I tried to suck in enough air to make words. I finally just gave up and nodded.

Sandra Niles and her team came charging down the hall, guns held at the ready.

Ian stood. I staggered to my feet.

Sandra's sharp, dark eyes were taking in everything at once. "Where are they?"

For all that, there were only two dead grendels on the wet floor. That meant there were at least nine others in the complex. Though if my doppelganger had Tarbert's device, there was no telling how many eggs she'd brought in.

SPI headquarters had been turned into a monster nursery.

# 17

"HOW many?" Sandra asked.

"A dozen," Ian said, wincing as her team medic cleaned yet another slash on his back. "Probably more."

We'd moved to a more easily defendable—and drier—part of the bottom level of the complex. It'd been only minutes since the grendel hatchlings had vanished, though I knew they couldn't be gone. Since we knew nothing about what grendel bites and scratches did to humans, Sandra had ordered her people to stand guard while the team medic quickly saw to the worst of our injuries and at least cleaned the others.

Ian had stripped off his soaked shirt and sat on the floor next to me in his jeans and boots. Dry clothes would have to wait. Most of Ian's injuries had been from the waist up. Mine had been pretty much everywhere, though the worst was a gash on my right thigh. The medic had cut off the right leg of my jeans near my upper thigh so he could stop the bleeding. I felt like a lopsided Daisy Duke.

"This needs stitches," he told me, "but butterfly bandages

will hold it for now." He was putting a bandage over the butterflies. "Try not to tear them loose in the meantime."

"I don't plan to; but I'm pretty sure the hatchlings have other ideas."

"I can't believe those things had just hatched," Sandra said.

"Considering when the doppelganger brought them in," Ian said, "they probably hatched in the last twelve to twenty-four hours. Their armor's still soft, which is the only reason bullets can still hurt them. I don't know how long it takes for it to harden."

I couldn't get the image of the dead grendel out of my head. Its mouth gaped open in death, revealing not three, but four rows of triangular, sharklike teeth. The arms and legs were spindly and hadn't developed the heavy musculature of an adult, but that didn't mean they were weak. Far from it. I hurt all over from numerous bites and scratches, a hurt that had escalated to a three-alarm blaze after the medic had swabbed what felt like alcohol on all of them.

Sandra Niles was listening intently on her headset. She scowled. "Let me put you on speaker."

Kenji's voice came over a tiny speaker set somewhere near the shoulder of Sandra's body armor. *"Mac, you there?"*

"Yes."

*"According to the security scanner, you just came in through the north tunnel entrance."* He paused. *"Holy shit. You brought a friend."*

Suddenly sirens went off and red flashing lights strobed all around us. An automated voice came over the wall speakers. *"Intruder alert at the north tunnel access. All security personnel immediately report to the north tunnel access."*

Ian got to his feet and had to help me to mine. It isn't easy to stand when you're trying not to move one of your legs.

We were at the south tunnel entrance. Going north would take us away from the baby monsters and toward another, larger one. Though right now, I'd take one monster on the other side of the complex over an unknown number of smaller ones that were right here with us. We passed several wall-mounted air vents. They all still had their screws, but if those things started unscrewing and dropping to the floor, I was running, butterfly bandages be damned.

Sandra had sprinted to the nearest corridor intersection—and its wall monitor. They were placed throughout the complex for things like announcements and briefings. At the moment, it showed a rotating 3D SPI logo.

"Kenji, I'm at monitor A-5," Sandra told him. "Give me a visual on the north tunnel."

The live video feed came on almost immediately. Static cut in and out for a few seconds, then cleared to give us a good view.

The camera looked down on my doppelganger. She was wearing a sweater identical to mine. Again. A massive shadow moved directly in front of the camera, blocking the lens.

"How high up is that camera?" I whispered to Ian.

"It's in the corner, back section of the loading dock, it's ten feet."

And the thing my doppelganger had let in blocked the camera completely. As it moved away, the camera pivoted to follow, and refocused.

Those of us who'd been in the conference room briefing knew what it had to be, but when it moved into view, we all watched in stunned silence.

It was a grendel. An adult. The conference room hologram brought to terrifying life. And everyone could see it.

It was gigantic, with small armored plates completely covering its body. They were steel gray edged in black, which was what had given it a tattooed appearance. The grendel was corded with muscle, but wasn't bulky with it. This was lean and powerful muscle, the kind made for speed and strength. It was a predator, a skilled and lethal hunter of its preferred prey—humans. The grendel's arms were as big around as my waist, maybe more. One hand could easily engulf my entire head and flip it off my shoulders with its thumb like popping the top off a bottle of beer.

The video feed flickered and then came back.

I gasped and froze.

Sandra bit off a curse. "They're gone. Both of them. Where the hell did they go?"

I looked at her in disbelief. "They're right there."

"What?"

"Right there." I spread my hands wide in front of my face. "The thing's head fills up the entire screen." That wasn't all it was doing. The grendel's glowing eyes felt like they were staring straight at me, then its lips pulled back, exposing teeth like triangular razors. A knot formed and twisted in my stomach. It wasn't just showing me its teeth.

My eyes locked on the scene before me. "It's smiling at us."

"Kenji, pull up the loading dock camera," Sandra ordered. "Aim it on that hallway."

*"It's empty,"* Kenji reported. *"Nothing there."*

"We can't see them," Ian said quietly. "But Mac can."

He believed me. I was beyond grateful. "It's wearing a collar or necklace with a round, thick disk. Here." I reached up and touched the hollow of my throat. "And it knows we're watching. I got a glimpse of the doppelganger, but now the grendel is blocking the entire lens."

As if the thing could hear me, the grendel put its hand in front of the camera lens, flexing its hooked claws into a fist and then extending them, like a boxer before a fight, giving me a good up-close look at what it would be using as it slaughtered its way through the complex. A wet coughing sound came from deep beyond the rows of teeth, then another, and another. I recognized his voice. I'd heard it before, in Ollie's office after it had gutted Adam Falke.

The grendel was laughing.

"Can you hear it?"

Ian shook his head.

Damn. So much for whether my seer abilities extended to mechanical/woo-woo devices. I knew I should be grateful they did, but watching a monster invade SPI headquarters was the last thing I wanted to see.

The grendel reached out, wrapped its massive hand around the camera, and plucked it right off the wall.

*"Great,"* Kenji spat over the speaker. *"The camera picks now to futz out on me."*

I found my voice. "The camera didn't go out, Kenji. The grendel ripped it off the wall."

*"Excuse me?"*

"The grendel ripped the camera off the wall. I can see it. I wish it wasn't there, but it is. Kenji, is Tarbert's device about the size of a hockey puck?"

*"Yeah."*

"The grendel's wearing it on some kind of collar. Metal. My doppelganger is probably wearing one, too."

As far as I could tell, the grendel was naked, but my doppelganger had been wearing clothes. My clothes. So that shot down the possibility that you had to be naked for the cloaking device to work. What a relief. If my doppelganger had to be naked to be invisible, and turned off her device in front of anyone at SPI, since she was an exact copy of me, my coworkers would know what I looked like starkers. If that happened, I'd have to resign out of sheer mortification.

"Kenji, for God's sake, shut down those sirens," Sandra said. "We know we have a shit storm on our hands; we don't need sirens telling us. And get rid of those flashing red lights. The damned things are going to give somebody a seizure."

That was when the lights went out.

All of them.

A few seconds later, the battery-powered emergency lights came on. They were spaced down the hall, leaving some awfully big patches of dark.

Sandra keyed her mike. "Dammit, Kenji, not all the lights. Just the red ones."

Silence.

Silence so complete that I could hear the buzzing in my ears. I remembered Kenji saying that we were ten stories underground. We were now three stories below that.

Thirteen stories below Lower Manhattan.

In the dark.

With monster toddlers who wanted to eat us. And one massive monster who'd probably eat any and every SPI agent it came across.

"My comms are out, too," Ian said. "And the air system just went."

My mind raced for answers. One grendel. One doppelganger that looked like me. Why had they been sent here? Inflicting violence and gruesome death was a given, but against who? The doppelganger now knew SPI like the back of its shapeshifting hand. Was it a guide for the grendel? If so, where was it taking it? The instant that question popped into my head, I knew, or at the very least I had a damned likely theory.

"Tia sent her sister a present," Ian murmured next to my ear, nearly reading my mind.

"And the spawn are just a distraction," I said.

"Sandra, we have to get up to the bull pen," Ian told her. "The grendel's going after the boss."

"How do you—"

"I can't explain. Just trust me. The eggs and spawn are a diversion to get your people and Roy's away from Vivienne Sagadraco. It's no coincidence we're on the far end of the complex from where that grendel came in. It was sent after her. She can fight it as a dragon, but not if she can't see it. That grendel will tear her to shreds. We've got to get Mac up there; she can see it."

My throat caught in midswallow, so I just nodded.

Everyone at SPI knew that the boss was a dragon, but she probably didn't want it known that her sister was trying to kill thousands of New Yorkers and tourists, and light a fuse that could start the next world war, this time between humans and supernaturals.

I finished my swallow with an audible gulp.

"Not much we can do to help her with what we have," Sandra said. "Let's get up to the armory. I don't know if grendels can see in the dark, but we'll assume they can—at least better than us—until they prove otherwise. Since we're some of the only people left in this place, those spawn'll follow us. To them, we're food." She smiled in a flash of white teeth. "So as of right now, we're fast food. Move out."

We entered the black hole that was the stairwell.

With the power out, the only way up was the stairs, and what passed for emergency lights were entirely too dim. Ian had brought extra ammo, but I only had what my gun had, which thanks to the spawn was now empty.

That and our injuries had relegated us to the center of Sandra's team. Though I knew the real reason. I was the only one who could see the cloaked adult grendel. All the extra ammo in the armory wouldn't do much good without me to tell them where to shoot. I'd never had to do that before, and I had absolutely no clue how to direct the fire of a commando team to hit something they couldn't see and that would possibly be attacking a dragon they couldn't risk hitting.

We'd paused while two of Sandra's team quickly scouted the next level.

I got as close to Ian as I could without getting in the way of his gun arm. He, like everyone else—except for me—carried their weapons lowered but ready. Since mine was empty, I'd holstered it. And if I'd had any bullets left and needed to shoot anything, I would've handed it to someone who could reliably hit a moving target.

"Ian," I said in the barest whisper. I wasn't afraid of the grendel spawn hearing us. I didn't want the team to know what I was about to ask.

"How do I tell them where the grendel and doppelganger are? Nine o'clock, three o'clock, left, right?"

"Whatever's logical. Short is best."

Logical? We were running toward a ten-foot monster and my evil twin who knew I could see them—or if they didn't, they'd be clued in real quick once I started telling people with guns exactly where they were standing. They weren't going to be happy about that.

I think I conveyed all of the above perfectly with one expression, even in the almost complete dark.

Ian's silence told me that I'd raised a valid concern. "Stay calm, stay focused, do the best you can," he eventually said. Then he gave me what he no doubt meant to be an encouraging smile. It wasn't. "I'll be there with you to watch your back while you protect the boss's front."

Not long ago, I'd been chomping at the bit to find me and kick my ass. Now I wasn't so eager. My doppelganger could do more than kick my ass, and she'd brought the grendel that'd gutted Adam Falke to help her do it. I had no doubt whose name came after the boss's on today's to-gut list.

I gave Ian a terse nod that conveyed a lot more confidence than I felt.

Ian smiled grimly and held his fist out.

I sighed, made a fist of my own, and bumped it with as much bravado as I could muster, which wasn't nearly enough to do what I had to do.

The scouts reported the all clear, and we continued our climb.

We got to the armory on the main level without being attacked by the grendel spawn. Not a one of us trusted it. If we didn't get ambushed now, it probably just meant the little critters had something more fun in mind.

Sandra had half of her team stand guard while the others geared up. Ian ran to a big metal locker and started ransacking it for whatever he was looking for. When he found it, he threw it at me, and I caught it with my face.

Pants. Better than that, dry pants. With both legs intact.

Ian followed it with a thick pullover shirt that I managed to catch with my hands.

They were both black, the pants had lots of pockets, and the shirt was padded.

"You're not accessorizing them," Ian said. "Just put them on. Quick."

I glanced around. We were in one, big room.

"There's no dressing rooms," he said, "and no time for modesty. Just strip and change."

Ian pulled out identical clothing and shimmied out of his wet jeans and skivvies, right there in front of God and the world.

And me.

"Sandy," Ian called, standing there showing what had to be the best set of buns in the tristate area. Damn, you could bounce a quarter off those things. "Mac needs a vest."

"On it."

Seconds later, Sandra was pushing something into my hands. A bulletproof vest. She flashed me a quick smile. "Concentrate, Mac."

I was concentrating. On my partner who was flashing more than a smile.

Sandra's team had grabbed body armor, bigger guns, and more ammo. The second half of the team came in while the newly armed and armored folks took their place standing guard, and I hadn't even taken off my boots.

Body-hugging jeans were nice, but not when they'd soaked up three times their weight in water. I'd gotten them unzipped, but they weren't going any farther. Then there was my bandaged thigh to contend with.

As I struggled, Ian appeared next to me, dressed and armored.

I gaped at him. "How'd you do that so fast?"

"Repetition. And motivation not to have those toothy bastards catch me with my pants down. We're out of time." Ian grabbed the waist of my jeans on the side of my bandaged leg in one hand, pulled them as far from my hip as he could, whipped out a knife, and sliced the Daisy Duke side of my jeans clean off—including panties.

"You need help with the other side?" The words were all business, but his eyes had darkened.

I quickly held up my hands. "No, no. I got it."

One tug from me sent the rest of my jeans—with undies—to the floor in a wet plop.

Meanwhile, Ian had grabbed the fatigues and unzipped the legs from the ankles to midcalf, then went down on one knee in front of me, eyes steadfastly on my feet.

"Don't need to take off your boots," he said, "just stick your feet in."

I did before he decided to cut anything else off of me.

"Does going commando make me one?" I asked hopefully.

Ian let out a low laugh. "I wish it was that easy."

While Ian took care of the zippers and ties on the bottom of my pants, I got my wet sweater over my head and wiggled into the dry one so fast that if anyone saw anything, they didn't see it for long.

In the minute it took Sandra's folks to grab their gear, Ian had changed his clothes and mine. He held up the vest for me and I stuck my arms in and fastened the front.

"No time to find armor for you," he said. "But that'll at least protect your vitals. Let's go."

# 18

THE grendel might have been a present for the boss from her sister, but it had left presents for us.

There were five deep gouges down the length of the walls of the corridor leading to the bull pen. It was obvious what it had done. The grendel had reached its arms out and scored the walls at least an inch deep as it had stalked toward the bull pen doors and its destination. The corridor was easily ten feet across.

The grendel's claws had raked through that wall like it'd been a piñata.

"It's marking its new territory," Ian growled.

That wasn't all it had done.

There were two bodies in front of the bull pen doors. They'd been torn open, gutted, and dismembered. The arms and legs had been carefully placed next to the trunk of the body they'd been torn from—but facing the wrong way. The heads—a man and a woman—had been cleanly severed and set on their own chests, the dead eyes facing us. The bodies had an uncountable number of small bites taken out of the flesh.

The spawn had been here. They'd gotten ahead of us.

Sandra spat a curse. "They were Roy's people."

It was a warning.

But most of all, it was meant to terrify, to paralyze.

It sure as hell worked for me.

It also really pissed me off.

I hadn't known their names. Like me, they'd been relatively new. They had been standing guard at those doors to prevent what was now beyond those doors from getting in. From the bullet holes pocking the walls, the amount of blood saturating the carpet under the bodies from one side of the wall to the other—and up the walls and onto the ceiling—they had stood their ground, determined to do their jobs.

They had been butchered for doing them.

They were heroes.

I didn't want to die.

I didn't care about being a hero.

But, like those two fallen security agents who'd been slaughtered and staged in front of those doors, I was going to do my job.

With Sandra's team leading the way, we went in.

Vivienne Sagadraco was a dragon.

I'd known it, I'd seen the aura of her true form, and I'd known it was big.

But damn.

The SPI bull pen extended five stories above the main floor.

Vivienne Sagadraco's head came to the third story, and the width from one side of the atrium to the other was enough to accommodate her wingspan. By having the complex built with five stories, she'd allowed herself enough room to take off and hover.

She was doing that now.

It still didn't put her out of the grendel's reach. Propelled by its powerful legs, the grendel leapt and sank its claws into Vivienne Sagadraco's hip, the force of impact and the grendel's weight pulling her down almost to the floor, where not one piece of office furniture or equipment remained intact.

It'd all been stomped to bits.

The spawn waited below, leaping impatiently for dad to bring down dinner. And yep, it was definitely male. When your skin doubled as armor, clothes were kinda redundant.

And I was the only one who could see him.

Ian swore a blue streak.

I snarled in frustration. "When this is over, you're gonna train me with a gun 'til I can shoot the ticks off a bear."

"Count on it."

The boss had to know what was attacking her, but she couldn't see it, and barring a lucky slash or bite, there was only so much she could do against a monster assassin she couldn't see or hear. She could only fight back when it latched onto her, and the grendel was too smart to stay in one place for any longer than it took him to add another wound.

The spawn surrounded its parent, putting a ring of baby monster death between Vivienne Sagadraco and any possible help.

Roy and the rest of his team were killing the only things they could see to aim at—grendel spawn—or at least they were trying. They were highly trained and their bullets hit what they were shooting at, but there were no explosions of pink this time. The spawn's armor was hardening. Our folks had to be using everything in their arsenal. Silver, lead, brass—the metal didn't seem to matter. The spawn were either too fast to hit or too armored to penetrate.

"How the hell did they get ahead of us?" Sandra shouldered her weapon and took aim at where she thought the adult grendel was. "Just what we need, the little bastards are problem solvers fresh out of the egg." Her dark, sharp eyes were trying to pinpoint the adult grendel's location based on Vivienne Sagadraco's reactions and counterattacks. She held her weapon ready, but didn't dare fire for fear of hitting the boss. "Talk to me, Mac. Help me out here."

I didn't know what to do, or what was even possible. The

grendel wasn't mindlessly attacking. Any shot taken would risk going through the grendel and into the boss. He never presented himself as a clear target. The boss's body was always behind him, so there wasn't a good or even a decent shot to be had. How was I supposed to direct fire at that?

It wasn't like I could point and scream "Shoot!" Quick as our people's reflexes were, by the time they fired, the grendel would be gone and their bullets would tear into the boss. We couldn't take even the slightest risk of hitting Vivienne Sagadraco with bullets.

I stopped.

Bullets.

Perhaps I didn't need to use bullets to help the boss.

The grendel was both invisible and buck naked. My budding theory—and hopeful plan—didn't involve putting a natty dressing gown on the monster, but it might work just as well to help our shooters see their target. I didn't know if it was possible—based either on the laws of science or woo-woo crap—but there was only one way to find out.

I sprinted to my desk, which by being in a corner had escaped being squashed. What I was looking for was right where I'd left it, leaning against the wall beside my desk.

And it was loaded.

Grandma Fraser always said a gun ain't gonna do you a lick of good if it ain't loaded for what's most likely to come lookin' for you.

My semiautomatic paintball rifle had a hopper full of neon yellow paintballs, ready to take down the Research Department—or hopefully tag the grendel that was trying to eat the boss one bite at a time.

If it worked, then the experts at putting real bullets where they needed to go would be able to see him.

The worst the boss could get from me was wet. Normally it'd be a bad career move to shoot your boss with a paintball gun, but I figured that if it got her out of her present predicament, Vivienne Sagadraco wouldn't mind an accidental splatter or two—or six.

I slung the rifle's carrying strap over my shoulder and grabbed an extra bag of balls. Apparently my plan was obvious to Ian. My partner hadn't asked any questions, and was at his desk stuffing things in his pockets too fast for me to ID them.

"Second floor catwalk?" he asked me.

I shot a glance at the combatants. "I was thinking third. Let's go see if we can't paint ourselves a grendel."

Ian charged up the stairs four at a time. With my shorter legs, it was all I could do to take two. He paused at the door to the third floor, waiting for me, his back to the wall beside the closed door.

"Ready?" he asked.

I nodded.

Ian quickly opened the door, paused a fraction of a second to make sure nothing was waiting to take his face off, then darted around the corner, gun held low and ready.

Getting closer to the fight—and the grendel—only made it even more obvious that a twelve-gauge shotgun might get this thing's attention, but it wasn't gonna do much else. The grendel was only about twenty feet away, and Vivienne Sagadraco's eyes were level with the catwalk's railing. When the grendel's hands opened to slash, I saw nails the size of steak knives. And judging from the boss's injuries, the thickest dragon hide was obviously no match for razor-sharp grendel claws.

A powerful downdraft from Vivienne Sagadraco's wings nearly knocked me over the railing. I swore. I hadn't considered wind strong enough to send my itty-bitty paintballs all over creation, but it wasn't going to keep me from firing every last one I had.

While I wasn't all that picky about where I landed my paint, ideally I wanted them where a direct hit by real ammo would do the most damage.

Head, face, and throat.

The cloaking device was at the base of the grendel's neck. Number one target. If our shooters could destroy the device, the boss could destroy the grendel. And for a backup target, splattering paint in the thing's eyes would have the double benefit of marking two of the only visible places that weren't armored, as well as temporarily blinding the thing.

I aimed, fired, the combatants shifted the battle a foot to the left, and my first volley of paintballs hit the boss in the back, smack-dab between her wings.

I winced and aimed again. "Sorry, ma'am."

The grendel looked at me, and made a sound I instantly recognized. The same wet, coughing laugh we'd heard in Ollie's office.

It was unnerving as hell, though him looking at me gave me the best chance I was likely to get to paint his face. I snapped my rifle up to my shoulder.

Primitive or not, the grendel realized on some level what I was doing. Giggles turned to growls, and *I* became *his* number one target. His powerful legs pushed off from the floor, propelling him straight at me.

I instinctively squealed and jumped back, my hands gripping the rifle. That gripping included my trigger finger, and paintballs popped from the muzzle in a rapid-fire stream, busting open on contact with the grendel's face, head, and chest, and forming a fine-looking bull's-eye splatter pattern if I did say so myself.

"See that?" I shouted to Ian. In response, my partner grinned, raised his gun, and opened fire.

My handiwork made the boss right happy, too. A triumphant roar split the air enough to shake the catwalk as Vivienne Sagadraco tore into her attacker, and from below, SPI's commandos opened fire.

I was so intent on the goings-on below that I didn't see the arm come around from behind me until it pulled tight in a choke hold around my neck.

My doppelganger.

In all the commotion over the grendels, I'd forgotten about her.

With a snap of her other hand, she easily knocked the paintball rifle out of my hands and over the railing, leaving them numb and even more useless than they already would have been against her. Moreau had been right about a doppelganger's strength. With one arm around my throat and the other gripping my upper arm, she started dragging me backward, using me as a human shield, to where the grendel and Vivienne Sagadraco still battled.

After a moment of confusion followed by realization, Ian raised his gun, panning the area behind me, desperate for something to shoot at.

The doppelganger jerked me back against her. I couldn't breathe, let alone fight back. Something the size of a hockey puck pressed between my shoulders, almost against my neck, and I knew the grendel wasn't the only monster wearing a cloaking device. As she pulled me along with her, I caught sight of a holster strapped to her thigh.

In an instant, I knew what she was going to do. I was the only one who could see her. She could put a bullet into one of Vivienne Sagadraco's eyes at point-blank range. If that didn't kill the boss instantly, she'd fall to the floor where the still-in-the-fight grendel and what was left of his brood would finish her off.

I got my hands up to the doppelganger's arm circling my throat, trying to get my fingers around her forearm and pry it off my windpipe. I twisted and struggled and rammed the heels of my combat boots down on her insteps. You name it, I tried it; nothing worked.

My doppelganger merely tightened her arm around my throat. "I wanted to kill you from the first, but she wouldn't let me. Stupid human cattle," she spat. "Only good for feeding the beasts."

"Shoot her!" I croaked to Ian.

"Yes, clumsy human, shoot me," she called mockingly to Ian. "He can't hear or see me." The doppelganger jerked me back against her. "Shoot me and blow your partner's brains out, or what little there are."

She dropped one hand down to her holster and I let go of the arm about to crush my windpipe. I had one chance before I passed out or she snapped my neck like a Sunday dinner chicken. I reached behind my neck and grabbed the collar that held the cloaking device and pulled with every bit of strength I had left. I had to get it off of her.

At that instant, Ian's hand came around from behind his back, and a round and dark object came flying directly at my face. What the hell?! Instinctively I winced and closed my eyes. A second later, I heard and felt a wet splat followed by an enraged scream from my doppelganger.

Black spots bloomed on the edge of my vision, and I suddenly pitched forward as the collar snapped off and into my hands. I felt myself falling, the thought only half registering through my air-starved brain; so fortunately I was only half-conscious when my face hit the floor and broke my fall.

I groaned and rolled to see the doppelganger's face and head splattered with what I could only call chicken-shit green. I knew then what Ian had gotten out of his desk drawer.

Paint grenades.

As Ian opened fire on the doppelganger with bullets instead of paint, something slammed into the catwalk, and suddenly I was rolling and sliding. I didn't know which way was up, down, or sideways. But when I no longer felt the cold metal of the catwalk, I knew I was going down. Way down. Falling through three stories of empty space toward a pack of hungry baby grendels. By the time my survival instinct kicked in, I was screaming and it was two inches too late to grab the edge of the pitching catwalk.

My scream was cut short when a massive clawed hand snatched me out of the air.

Vivienne Sagadraco.

I instinctively grabbed one of the boss's scaled fingers that was the size of my arm, and held on, prayed, screamed, and fought the urge to be sick, all at the same time. The boss spun to intercept a grendel attack from behind, swinging me around to give me a quick and blurry tour of the entire bull pen like I was on the Scrambler from Hell.

I was beyond nauseous with all the dropping, swooping, and flying; but I'd rather be sick than eaten by the grendel spawn that were leaping up to grab my legs whenever I came within reach. All the monster scenery flew back and forth before my eyes as nauseating streams of color.

Ian was shouting at me from somewhere above, but I couldn't hear a word he was yelling while being whipped around. I groaned, dropped my head to the boss's scaled finger, and tried to hold on to her finger and my barbeque dinner as tightly as I could.

The sudden stench like rotten fish made me look up to see where I was.

The male grendel's bloody face was inches from mine.

I drew breath to scream and the boss yanked me away just as the grendel's steak knives raked through the air where I'd just been.

Vivienne Sagadraco flung her right arm out full length and dropped me on another section of catwalk. This one wasn't moving or even tilting.

Oh God, I loved this catwalk. Rather than kiss it, I just tried real hard not to throw up on it.

The weight of someone running toward me pounded and vibrated the catwalk against my aching head. The pounding stopped and strong hands pulled me up.

I forced my eyes open. Ian's face came into focus, then out again.

"Stop moving," I said blearily.

"I'm not moving."

I clutched at his arms. "Then stop me from moving."

"I've got you; you're not going anywhere."

Too bad nobody told the catwalk.

The only warning we got was groaning metal and the popping of support cables as the rest of the catwalk went down, and us with it.

Something hard and cold whapped me in the head and everything went mercifully black.

# 19

I think it was the quiet that woke me up—and the dark that freaked me out.

Dark could mean any number of things, and in my mind right now, all of them were bad. That is, until I felt the pillows under my head and a blanket snuggled around me. I couldn't imagine Papa Grendel tucking me in, unless it was to roll me up in the world's biggest piece of bacon.

There was a click and a small light came on. A bedside lamp. I blinked my eyes into focus and saw Ian sitting on a cot next to the narrow bed I was on. He appeared to be in one piece. Tired, scruffy, with a mild case of bed head, but in one piece.

I lifted my blanket and looked down at the rest of me. I was wearing what looked like scrubs. "My third outfit today. Do I have you to thank for another wardrobe change?"

One side of his mouth curved up. "The company doc and her medic took care of it this time. She stitched up your leg and the cut on your head while you were out."

I touched the fresh bandage on my head and winced. I felt like death warmed over and served up. "I can tell."

"The painkillers must be wearing off. Do you need more?"

I held up a hand. "I'm good. I think I'd better go with lucid over loopy." I pulled myself up against the pillows. "We fell off the third floor. How are we even—"

"Alive?" Ian gave me a little crooked grin. "The boss managed to catch you *and* me. Said she wished her employees would stop falling off of things at inconvenient times." The grin vanished. "Unfortunately she couldn't catch you before you grazed your head on a steel cable."

I got out one chuckle before I had to grab at my head to make the pounding stop. "How is she?" I whispered against the throbbing.

"Dragons heal quickly. And after you marked the grendel for everyone, the boss could see him just fine."

"I do seem to recall a triumphant-sounding roar."

"You made the boss very happy."

"She got him?"

Ian shook his head. "Got away. Moved so fast no one could get enough bullets in him to bring him down."

"Damn."

"Yeah, but we're tracking him."

"The spawn?"

Ian hesitated a beat. "Disposed of."

"By Roy and Sandra?"

"The boss took care of it."

My brow creased as I tried to figure out what he meant.

"Turning dragon and exerting herself as she did, she needed to . . . replenish her strength."

My lip curled. "Replenish as in she *ate* them?"

"She did leave the two from the HVAC room intact for Lars Anderssen to see. Right now, she's . . ."

"Digesting?"

"And sleeping it off."

"What about my doppelganger?"

"No longer a problem for anyone," Ian assured me.

"Nice move with the paint grenade." I paused. I wasn't sure how I felt about my partner being able to open fire on something that looked exactly like me. "Uh . . . after I pulled the device off, you could see her—looking just like me—and you didn't hesitate to fill her full of lead."

"Silver," he corrected me.

"Whatever. You didn't feel . . . odd . . . about doing that?"

"Mac, I knew she wasn't you. I know what a doppelganger looks like—"

"An amorphous blob."

"An amorphous blob that brought that monster into our house, was going to put a bullet through the boss's head, and snap my partner's neck." His voice was tight with unused rage. "I could've put every round I had into that thing and still slept like a baby afterward."

"Um . . . thank you?"

A little of the tension went out of his shoulders. "Sorry."

"No, no. It's okay. I mean, who wouldn't want their partner to kill their murderous amorphous blob twin for them?" There was a second or two of awkward silence. "Where's the cloaking device I tore off the doppelganger?"

"Kenji found it. The fall broke it, but he thinks they can repair it. He and a team of engineers are working on it now."

There was a little digital clock on the bedside table. It was 3:54. In the ever-lovin' morning.

New Year's Eve morning. Holy crap.

"How long was I out?" I asked.

"Out for only thirty minutes. Asleep for the next four hours."

"Why didn't you—"

"You needed the sleep." He patted the cot he was sitting on. "I caught a few winks myself once Calvin came in to relieve me."

"Relieve?"

"From watching over you."

"You watched me sleep?" Usually I'd think a man watching me sleep was creepy. With my normally stoic partner doing the watching, it was kinda sweet. "Isn't watching me sleep on the excitement meter somewhere above watching paint dry and below golf?"

"I'm learning that when I take my eyes off you, all hell's liable to break loose, so watching you is safer for everyone."

I had no idea how to respond to that, so I simply changed the subject. I glanced around. The room we were in looked like a college dorm. "Where is this?"

"Sandra's quarters. She and Roy each keep a room here for multiple shifts or emergencies."

I didn't have to ask which one this was. "She doesn't need it?"

"Sandy's a busy lady right now; she's overseeing the cleanup."

"The bull pen looked like a war zone."

Ian shook his head. "Cleanup as in making sure there aren't any more eggs. She hasn't found any. Two of our werewolves got the scent from one of the dead spawn and have searched every place an egg could be hidden."

"Where's Yasha? Is he—"

"Out with the rest of our werewolves tracking that grendel. Yasha was at the north tunnel entrance when the big male tore through there. He tried to stop him, but all he ended up with was a mouthful of grendel scales."

I made a face.

"Which gave him the grendel's taste *and* scent. The wounds the thing got in the bull pen sent him running back to wherever home is."

"The nest."

"That's what we're hoping. Find out where they are, gear up, and go end this. The boss has notified Lars Anderssen about the eggs and spawn. He'll tell us all we never wanted to know about grendel spawn." Ian stood. "In the meantime, if you're up to it, Sandra found you a fourth outfit for today." He smiled. "With accessories—body armor."

# 20

EARLIER it'd been a swarm of spawn. Now, we'd been invaded by a horde of Vikings. This horde had arrived in a big private jet from Oslo; but other than that, they sure looked like Vikings to me, at least via my experience watching the History Channel.

Judging from the equipment and gear they had with them, I could see why the team from SPI Scandinavia hadn't wanted to get into the country via JFK or LaGuardia—or go anywhere near an airport security, customs, or TSA checkpoint. Their jet had landed at a private airstrip in Westchester County. Considering their cargo, they'd had to.

Every last one of them was tall, blond, and buff. Way buff. But instead of leather and chain mail, they wore black fatigues and had unloaded cases of matte black body armor. Instead of swords and axes, they had . . . well, swords and axes. Add to that a war's worth of automatic weapons, flamethrowers, and what looked like Godzilla-sized barbed spears, and Director Lars Anderssen and his team looked ready enough to take on the newest residents of New York's sewers.

I was in the subterranean parking area just outside the SPI complex, along with my official bodyguard, Ian, and Yasha, my unofficial guard werewolf. Yasha and the other two werewolf agents had gotten back from their tracking mission only about half an hour ago. After getting a taste of a grendel, and the primal excitement of trying to track it to its lair, the big Russian's eyes had gone gold and stayed that way. He also looked a little hairier, though maybe that was due to a lack of shaving rather than an abundance of wolf.

The Vikings weren't the only ones decked out like cover models from *Soldier of Fortune*.

My eyes involuntarily flicked to the midsection of Ian's black Under Armour T-shirt that was tight enough to outline every can in his six-pack.

"Why bring so much?" Yasha asked. "We have guns."

"A man likes to have his own," Ian replied.

"It would've been nice if they could've been here earlier," I muttered. The Scandinavians had landed a little after nine o'clock as scheduled, but icy road conditions had made getting into Manhattan from Westchester County a challenge, even with the snow chain–equipped SUVs the boss had sent to pick them up.

"For this kind of party," Ian said, "better late than never. The real fun hasn't even started yet."

Vivienne Sagadraco's petite human form suddenly appeared behind Ian, regarding me with expressionless eyes. The only sign that the last few hours had been anything except business as usual was the boss leaning on an elegant cane, its grip a silver dragon's head.

"Exemplary work, Agent Fraser."

"Thank you, ma'am," I managed to say. I gestured vaguely in the direction of wherever she'd been injured. "How are you?"

"Passably well. Well enough to do whatever is needed. And yourself?"

"Uh, good. I'm good."

She seemed to expect more.

"And I'm ready to get this done," I added with enthusiasm. Jeez, I sounded like such a dork.

She gave me a sharp nod. "Commendable. Agents Byrne and Kazakov, you also have my thanks. The actions of the three of you this evening exemplify the sterling qualities that all our agents should aspire to."

Both men gave a bow of their heads. "Thank you, ma'am." I quickly followed suit.

Vivienne Sagadraco crossed the parking area to speak with the SPI Scandinavia director.

Ian lowered his voice. "I'm ready to get this done?"

I cringed. "I know. You've got one more job as my partner."

"What's that?"

"Save me from myself."

"Spawn and doppelgangers I can do, but saving you from yourself is too tall an order for any man."

There were nine Scandinavians—and half of the men looked like they'd walked out of a Viking romance novel cover shoot. The team included two women—one with a long braid and the other who actually made a military cut look good. Both of them had that whole Valkyrie/Norse goddess thing going. And the one with the short hair had an aura showing me that the Norwegians also had a werewolf on their team.

A garage-door-sized section of the wall rolled up. Beyond was the combat teams' briefing and staging area. SPI commanders Roy Benoit and Sandra Niles came out into the parking area along with their teams. They'd already fought round one of the battle. Two hadn't survived, and others had been injured, but they were all here. The New Yorkers and Vikings stepped up to greet each other—but mainly to size up the competition.

"I love the smell of animosity in the morning," Ian murmured.

One of the Scandinavians, who was slightly older than the others, crossed the parking area floor to meet Vivienne Sagadraco. They exchanged handshakes and did that double-cheek-kissing thing then spoke in low tones. Judging from the Scandinavian director's serious scowling, he was getting the expanded version of our rapidly growing problem. At one point, the man turned his head and looked directly at me, and his eyes narrowed appraisingly. Seems I'd just been introduced as the agency seer and self-appointed painter of monsters. Without further expression, his attention went back to the boss, leaving me with no idea if he approved of what he'd seen, though I suspect he was less than impressed. I had that effect on people. His blond hair wasn't long, but it wasn't buzz-cut short, either. His beard was neatly trimmed. He looked fit, but not in a brawny way. He was the shortest among the Scandinavians, but he towered over Vivienne Sagadraco. Though mere hours ago, she would've towered over every last one of them combined.

"Director Lars Anderssen, I presume?"

"In the flesh," Ian confirmed. "Good man. Knows his business. I'm going to assume that he wouldn't have brought those men and women with him unless they knew the same. Considering our situation, I'm going to be very disappointed if any of them prove me wrong."

The boss lady and Anderssen handled the team leader introductions, and our people helped the visiting team get their gear inside. The briefing room had chairs lined up in rows with a table, screen, and whiteboard at the front of the room. Everyone quickly found a seat.

"Based on the data from the DNA samples we were able to provide from the claw and lock of hair," Vivienne Sagadraco told us, "Director Anderssen's science team in Oslo has narrowed the age of our two grendels to less than a hundred years old, which confirms that they are of prime mating age, and were probably selected by our adversary because they are a breeding pair."

I wondered if she had told Lars Anderssen who the adversary was. Regardless, she still wasn't sharing that information with anyone else.

Anderssen stepped forward. "The way in which the first victim, the goblin Kanil Ghevari, was killed and the relative absence of blood found at the scene, suggests that the attack was by the female. Female grendels must consume blood for weeks after spawning to replenish their strength; and as they are large creatures—larger than the males—they require an equally great quantity."

Holy crap. I turned to Ian. "Larger?" I mouthed.

Then with dawning horror, I recalled the photos in the folder from Kanil Ghevari's autopsy. There'd been teeth marks around the stub of the goblin's remaining arm. The female grendel must have used it like a straw and drained him like a freaking juice box.

Sandra half raised her hand. "Director Anderssen, how many eggs are we talking about?"

"Anywhere from twenty to thirty eggs—in *each* clutch."

Silence.

Roy Benoit swore. "There's more than one clutch?"

"Grendels lay three clutches of eggs over the course of three days, with one clutch expelled every twenty-four hours. The incubation period is approximately forty days."

Several of our experienced people began to mutter. Roy softly swore again. I completely agreed with his word choice. The doppelganger had put the grendel eggs in the air duct a day before they'd hatched into armored killing machines. Nothing had any right to grow that fast and be that deadly mere hours out of the egg.

"Twenty plus thirty equals bloodbath in Times Square," Ian murmured.

"As each clutch hatches, the parents move the spawn to a section of the nest cave where they've been stockpiling food," Anderssen continued. "The food usually keeps the hatchlings from eating their brothers and sisters that are still in their eggs. If there's enough food, everyone lives. If there's not enough, that'd be good news for us and we could be looking at a much smaller problem—quite literally, as grendel growth rates are dependent on their food intake. More food available equals maximum growth potential. However, I can't see anyone going to all the trouble to import a pregnant grendel, and not ensure there'd be plenty of food for everyone."

"Preferred food?" one of our people asked.

"Humans," Anderssen said. "With our female being less than a hundred years old, this could very well be her first nesting. If so, the first clutch will be smaller in quantity, with more eggs being laid in the second clutch, and the greatest number coming in the third." The Norwegian inclined his head in the boss's direction. "I understand from Director Sagadraco that part of a clutch had been planted here and hatched, but has been eradicated. Also, the male gained access to the complex, but was injured and escaped. Unfortunately for us, these creatures' rate of healing is as prodigious as their strength. The male should be fully regenerated by the next time we encounter him."

"And really pissed," Yasha muttered.

That earned some chuckles.

"Can you tell which clutch we're dealing with by examining the eggshells and remains?" Sagadraco asked.

"My science officer can," Anderssen replied with a nod to the long-braided Valkyrie type. "You kept both?" he asked the boss.

"Naturally."

"Not refrigerated?"

Sagadraco shook her head once. "Contained in a triple-thick kill bag to contain the blood and scent." She reached down to the floor behind the table, and using only one hand, lifted and plopped an honest-to-God body bag on the table. Apparently grendels weren't the only supernaturals who healed quickly.

The Scandinavian science officer extracted some latex gloves from her pack, and snapped them on before unzipping the body bag. She studied the contents, and then carefully shifted through the bits and pieces.

The bag had done a fine job of stifling the stink—until it was opened. I was glad we'd chosen to sit toward the back of the room.

"These spawn were approximately twelve hours old when they were killed," the science officer said. "Apparently these specimens lacked sufficient food; they should be larger than this."

Ian and I exchanged glances. We were the "sufficient food" the grendel toddlers had lacked.

"They appear to have been dead a little less than eight hours." The blonde lifted one of the eggs out of the bag. It was brown and leathery looking, and the shell, if you could even call it that, appeared to have been torn from the inside rather than cracked and broken.

"These are definitely from the first clutch," she said. "The shells from subsequent batches will be softer, and quicker to lay." She held one of the more or less intact bodies in her hands. I tensed. The thing's yellow eyes were open and it didn't look dead to me. "Had this one survived, it would have been three-quarters the size of its parents by this time tomorrow."

The Scandinavians didn't react. We Americans sat in stunned silence.

"Which means we have bad news and not-so-bad news," Anderssen said. "The second clutch has likely already hatched, and is feeding and growing, but the third clutch is still in their eggs."

"After hatching," the science officer continued, "the young must feed at least every two hours. Should their food source be plentiful, the young ones can easily grow to adult size within forty-eight hours, but with five times their appetite during that time. As to possible locations of the nests, the parents would want their young to have quick and easy access to a food source. However, they would also want their nests to be in a perpetually dark and warm place. They also cover their nests in whatever organic matter is available."

Roy snorted. "There's plenty of *organic matter* where we're headed. It's like a swamp down there."

Anderssen nodded. "The spawn will feed on what they can find in the sewers then quickly be drawn by the scent and noise of prey to the surface. The eggs themselves aren't easy to destroy. A flamethrower can do the job. Or exposure to concentrated acid."

"Since our adversary is so confident of her success," Vivienne Sagadraco said, "we can assume that the nest has been well hidden or veiled from sight—and that they are being heavily guarded."

"She?" Roy asked.

"We have recently discovered that our adversary is a woman."

"Pack it up, boys and girls," Roy drawled. "We're screwed."

That earned a couple of snorts.

"Our adversary has much at stake," the boss continued. "For her, the show starts at midnight on New Year's Eve." She paused. "That's tonight. If there are additional killings today, the city still has time to cancel the celebrations. She cannot afford that. She has gone to too much trouble to let the grendels disrupt her timetable. Regardless of the actual scenario we are faced with, we will accomplish nothing and fail the citizens of this city—human and supernatural—if we do not find the grendels and their spawn and eliminate them before they make their presence even more known to the public."

I wondered if Vivienne Sagadraco would be sharing the whole story with Lars Anderssen. Though as Ian would no doubt say, it didn't change the mission: go, find, kill.

The boss nodded and an agent who I could have sworn hadn't been there moments before opened a door on the other side of the room, and a familiar aroma wafted through. In anticipation of what was to come, my mouth curled upward in a smile of pure bliss. Our two monster hunter teams wore the same expressions. The Scandinavians sniffed the air and nodded approvingly.

"We have a long day and night ahead of us, so I have ordered food brought in," Vivienne Sagadraco said. "We will continue our briefing while we eat."

# 21

SPI was putting in a small onsite cafeteria complete with kitchen. While it was a few weeks away from completion, it was finished enough for Bill and Nancy from the Full Moon to put out one heck of a spread. Bill and Nancy were werewolves, and most of their staff were nocturnals, so fueling SPI commandos with a pre-hunt meal wasn't anything out of the ordinary. They'd done it before. The Full Moon staff had pulled a couple of tables together against one wall for the buffet line, and at the front of the room was a laptop on a table next to a wall-mounted, wide-screen TV, making our pre-mission briefing look more like an off-site corporate meeting complete with the requisite mind-numbing PowerPoint presentation.

Yasha had already cozied up at the far end of one table with the blonde Scandinavian werewolf. Nowadays, single werewolves had all of the social benefits of humans, including online dating sites. But in Yasha's line of work, he had to be even more circumspect than a run-of-the-mill banker who went furry once a month. I didn't blame him a bit for grabbing a little one-on-one time to socialize and talk shop with a like-minded and identically employed lady.

Ian and I were seated near the head of one of the tables near the boss, Roy, Sandra, and Lars Anderssen. Bill had served up plates of his famous jalapeño alligator bites down the length of both tables, and Roy was digging in with gusto. He'd told me once that he liked eating critters that could eat him—and said they tasted even better when he got to kill them himself.

Sandra stood and went to the laptop, clicked a couple of keys and a map of the lower half of Manhattan appeared on the screen. She gave a short whistle and the chatter died down.

"With intelligence gained from three of our agents who attempted to track the male grendel back to his lair, we've narrowed our search perimeter to a twenty-block section of Midtown that includes Times Square. Considering that we know the adversary's plan is to release the grendels into the crowds at midnight tonight, we've now excluded the locations of the two known attacks in SoHo and Chinatown as the possible nest site." Sandra moused over the map, connecting the dots in a glowing red triangle. "Based on intel provided by Director Anderssen, this area is the most likely nesting place for our grendels. It gets warm down there; and with all that water, it's warm *and* humid. If our out-of-towners are looking for a dark and cozy place for their nest, one of nine locations within this area could be our winner. We've got watchers among the local paranormal community. They've reported signs of ghoul activity on the surface that correlates to our nine potential sites. So that's where we'll start. Good news for us is that these areas aren't highly trafficked, either by city maintenance workers or the homeless population. That also increases the likelihood that the grendels are nesting there. They wouldn't want their nest to be disturbed, even by potential food."

Sandra clicked a few more keys and a green rectangle appeared over Times Square, overlapping the red triangle in places.

"This is the seventeen-block security perimeter for New Year's Eve," she said. "Even before nine eleven, security has always been tight. Now the NYPD and the feds prepare as if Times Square is one, big terrorist bull's-eye. There are thousands of police on foot patrol, admittance checkpoints, mounted police, bomb-sniffing dogs, helicopters with infrared, and counter-snipers on strategic rooftops. All manhole covers in the protected zone are sealed. Underground security includes the addition of five hundred security cameras to the subway stops at Times Square, Grand Central Station, and Penn Station. Plus there's a new network of about three thousand closed-circuit security cameras in Lower and Midtown Manhattan. For crowd control, there are sixty-five metal pens to limit where the people stand, letting the NYPD keep a path clear for emergency vehicles. Add to that plainclothes police officers in the pens blending in with the crowd. The federal, state, and local boys and girls have the place covered tight. We have agents in with the local law enforcement. They know what to look for and will report if they find anything suspicious."

The boss lady stood. "We must assume that since the adversary and many in her organization are ex-CIA that she could have people in place among the federal authorities, which makes it even more imperative that our presence not be detected by *any* outside law enforcement and security personnel. She knows that we will be coming after the grendels, and she *will* be ready for us. Our adversary needs only one grendel to surface tonight in front of one television camera. The damage will be done. If over fifty succeed . . . people will die and what we have dreaded for so long will begin." Vivienne Sagadraco was silent for a moment. "Tonight there will be the noise of a million of those people, the scent of a million bodies. It will be torment for the creatures. Their reaction to disagreeable auditory stimuli is extremely aggressive. There will be no controlling them regardless of what means is now being used. The grendels will strike out at the source of that torment. And once blood is flowing . . . though at that point, I expect our adversary won't be interested in controlling them anymore. They will have served their purpose and would be expendable. Our goal tonight is for us to eliminate them first."

Director Anderssen nodded. "Anyone who went to all the trouble to import a pregnant grendel has arranged protection for those eggs. Count on having more to contend with than just grendels."

Ian raised his hand.

"Agent Byrne?"

"She's got at least one team of ghouls working for her. Professionals."

"And they're veiled," I added. "At least veiled enough to pass for human."

Silence.

With a human you just had to worry about being shot or stabbed. A ghoul was fast and strong enough to just yank you into a dark corner and start eating you, and probably no one in this room knew that better than Ian.

"If we don't find them, when the time comes to move, these grendels don't need a connecting tunnel to where they want to go," Anderssen said. "They're perfectly capable of making their own. I've seen a grendel claw through steel plate. So regardless of what is blocked off or sealed, these things can get into your Times Square any damned way they want to."

"We will deploy in three teams," Sandra said, "each taking a slice of the search area and three of the potential nest sites. We'll be concentrating our search in the deepest parts of the tunnels. If you encounter a grendel of any age, kill it. If you find the nest, call for backup before beginning extermination." She stepped back, yielding the floor to the Scandinavian director.

"There will be three of my people with each team. We know what grendels leave behind and can show you what to look for: territorial clawing on walls, footprints, scent, droppings, urine, saliva. Grendels are droolers, especially when they're eating. Our ideal killing zone will minimize the space the grendels have to maneuver. Preferably a dead end—a solid one. Hit them with high-intensity light, immediately followed by spears. Our spears are specially equipped with a firing mechanism for twelve-gauge shells peppered with silver. They've proven effective at penetrating a grendel's armored torso and blowing them up from the inside." Anderssen paused. "However, the point of penetration must be beneath one of the armored scales. They are overlapped and tightly spaced. Speed and accuracy are critical to success—and survival. It's imperative that we find them first. Grendels can move in almost complete silence when they're hunting. You don't know it's there until it hits you, and you'll probably bleed out before your brain knows you've even been hit. Grendels are killing machines, with the intelligence of a human being." He paused with a small smile and sidelong glance at the boss lady. "At least on our better days. And the strength of . . . well, you've seen what it can do. As to their speed, a grendel can do sixty-five kilometers an hour out in the open. That would be forty miles per hour for you Americans. They're sprinters rather than long-distance runners, but when they can move that fast, a sprint is all they need to do. They have much the same olfactory senses as a shark, and a similar dental structure with three to five rows of teeth. Their hearing is acutely sensitive. We have reason to believe they can hear a human heart beating."

"No wonder loud noises piss them off," someone muttered.

"And NVGs will be useful for getting around down there, but thermal imaging won't do us a damned bit of good," Anderssen continued. "Grendels are whatever temperature their surroundings are, as are ghouls. So other than the rats, chances are we'll be the only warm-blooded things down there. As to their reproductive habits, grendels lay eggs only once every fifty years. SPI Scandinavia has a policy of destroying any nests we find, but it only takes one successful hatching to keep them going. Since their reproduction cycle occurs so seldom, grendels are extremely protective of their young. And we know for a fact that mated pairs can communicate telepathically; this ability is especially strong while hunting or protecting their young."

"We know three things for sure, ladies and gentlemen," Anderssen concluded. "We will encounter armed and trained opposition. The adult grendels know we will be coming." He paused. "And unless we find that lair and nest before the last clutch hatches, *we* will be the closest food source."

Someone's stomach growled.

There were chuckles and sputters of laughter all around, at least from those who had enough experience to routinely go looking in the dark for hungry monsters.

"What's the significance of the mummified head and arm?" Ian asked.

"Fortunately, even at the height of their population, grendels have never been plentiful," Anderssen replied. "Their life expectancies are in the five- to seven-hundred-year range. The grendel of the Beowulf legend could very well have been the grandfather of one or even both of those here."

"Brother and sister?" Roy asked.

"Grendels do not share taboos that are common to humans."

"Apparently."

"Grendels keep the corpses of their dead," Anderssen said. "This head and arm—if they are from their father—would be of great value to them as a tribal relic."

"Could those have been used to lure them here?" Sandra asked.

"A lure would not have been necessary," Anderssen replied. "Grendels have been hunted for as long as humans have known of their existence—and grendels have fed almost exclusively on humans for at least that long. They now live in the most inhospitable parts of Norway and Sweden. There are not sufficient humans in those areas to sustain them."

"And New York City has over eight million humans," Sandra said.

Anderssen nodded. "And countless places in the tunnel and sewer system in which to hide and thrive. Warmth, shelter, and a nearly unlimited food supply. If grendels had a heaven, this city would be it."

# 22

IT was three months until Easter, but I was going on an egg hunt. And instead of baskets, the SPI NY and Scandinavia commandos were carrying guns, knives, flamethrowers, and spears with tips that went boom. The men looked like they'd been chiseled from solid rock; and the women could've been stunt doubles for Sigourney Weaver in *Alien*. Every last one of them was badass to the bone.

Me? Well, I was a Sigourney wannabe.

We were divided into three teams, each assigned to a slice of the pie that was the likely nesting zone. Two of the three teams had a seer and a werewolf tracker. All three teams had one flamethrower, one subway tunnel expert, and two Viking types packing the grendel-gutting spears.

My first mission underground was going to be searching for a creature that was as smart as a human—and that had little ones to feed. Little ones that could eat enough human flesh to be adult-sized monsters within two days.

We were in the team locker room gearing up. Earlier I'd worn a bulletproof vest, but this was my first time in full body armor. It was hot and heavy, and not in a good way.

The thought of going into the claustrophobic sewers wearing claustrophobic armor made me want to hyperventilate, and I wasn't even wearing the helmet yet.

"This doesn't bode well," I told Ian who was helping me get strapped and buckled in. I gave him the condensed version of my phobic triggers.

"Just think of it as a claw-resistant shell against grendels," he said.

"Yeah? Well, then I know how a lobster feels." I poked myself in the chest. It did seem sturdy enough. "Not claw *proof*, huh?"

"It's not in the plan for you to be finding out."

"But what if the plan—"

"Then you run." Ian indicated a switch on the suit's belt. "There's an oxygen tank built into the back. Press this button here if you need a hit."

"Need?"

"Air can get nasty down there with fumes that aren't lung friendly. If your brain's not getting enough oxygen, you can start seeing things that aren't there."

"Just as long as I can still see things that *are* there."

"If you start seeing little flickering lights, flip the switch."

"And the tanks are safely under the bulletproof armor, right?"

"Right."

"'Cause it'd really suck for a stray bullet to hit that tank and blow me up."

"I got news; it'd suck for the rest of us around you, too."

I was armed with one gun and one knife, both in shoulder holsters: the gun was loaded with silver-peppered bullets, the knife with silver-infused steel. And I'd been forbidden to use either one unless I found myself separated from the rest of the team with a grendel about to bite my head off.

However, I had full permission to use my other weapon.

My paintball rifle was slung over my back.

Before she returned to the bull pen that would be the communications center for our mission, Vivienne Sagadraco had told the assembled teams what we could be up against in regards to the cloaking devices. Since we had no idea how many were in the adversary's possession, we would not be taking any chances. I could see any grendel or ghoul that might be making use of the newfangled technology. The look she'd given the assembled commandos dared any of them to make a joke about my armaments. However, that didn't stop the Scandinavians from ribbing their seer who was sporting a paintball rifle of his own. Poor guy. Ian had offered me paint grenades, but I turned him down. To say that I throw like a girl was an insult to girls everywhere.

Ian noticed my wistful glances at everyone else's Rambo-ready real weapons. "You're not trained yet."

"And if I get gutted down there, I never will be."

"Your job is to see the monster, and mark it if we can't see it. Our job is to kill it. You're qualified to do your job; we're not. We're qualified to do our job—"

"I get it. It doesn't make me feel any less naked, but I get it."

He finished fastening my armor, his hands lingering on my shoulders. "We're not going to let our seer get killed—and I'm not about to lose my partner. Speaking of which, you have a tracking chip in your armor."

I tried to smile. "Y'all are just afraid I'll pull a Barney Fife and shoot somebody's foot off."

"That, too." He took my gloved hand and moved it to another switch on my utility belt. "And this is for your headlamp."

"I've got a light? Excellent."

Ian patted the top of my head. "It'll be right up here, built in to your helmet. Low, medium intensity, and retina frying. The switch is there."

"Let me guess, when you have to wear something like that, it's a given that your hands will have better things to do than hold a flashlight. Like hold a gun."

He gave me a flat look. "Right—for the rest of us. Nice try, though."

I shrugged. "I may not be trained, but I am persistent."

"That you are." He continued with my equipment inventory. "You have an emergency light here, mounted to the forearm of your gun hand, which you will—"

"Not be using for anything other than a paintball gun," I said for him.

"Right again. But as a point of instruction for the future, the more distance you can keep between you and your target and still take it out, the better."

"That's why our spears are so damned long," said one of the Scandinavians. He stuck out his gloved hand that wasn't holding a spear. "Rolf Haagen. I'll be with your team."

Ian shook it, then I did. It felt like shaking hands with a steel mannequin.

"It's not mine," he said. "Neither is most of the arm up to my elbow. Finnish ice dragon took a taste of me a couple of years back. I took his hide for this," he said cheerfully and kicked his gear bag. "Payback pays, or at least it makes a great set of luggage." He held up his arm. "If I lose my hardware, I'll just get a new one. I'm due for an upgrade. Maybe I can make a grendel choke on it."

An up-close look at the spear showed four thick hooks spaced around the shaft about ten inches below the point.

"Keeps what you've got on the business end from pulling its way down to eat your face," Rolf said with pride.

"Helpful feature," I said.

"More than once." He grinned and clicked the two sections of the spear's shaft together. It was solid sounding.

"That'd definitely hurt sliding through someone's guts," I noted.

"We didn't come here to tickle them. A lot of Old World monsters needed old kill methods. Tonight we make SPI history." The Viking commando looked entirely too eager. "No one has ever killed a grendel in the dark—except for some Danish guy named Beowulf, and he just tore off the beastie's arm and it bled to death at its mother's house." He snorted with derision. "That's not a kill. So that 'First Dark Kill' position is open. I think my name would look good on that plaque in Oslo." He gave us a maniacal grin and clapped

Ian on the shoulder, hard enough to rattle *my* teeth. "Let's go, kill, and return to drink to our victory."

Sounded simple enough, and the last part sounded fun, at least the returning part.

My job was even simpler.

If the grendels were wearing Tarbert's cloaking devices, my job was to find them before they found us, point them out or paint them up, get the hell out of the way, and let the shooters and stabbers do their thing. If the grendels weren't cloaked, just get and stay the hell out of the way.

Yasha came over to us wearing a T-shirt, shorts, and flip-flops. I knew what that meant. The Russian would be going werewolf for our expedition.

"Listen up," Anderssen boomed and I jumped. "My people line up over here to get fitted with your comms. Our New York hosts have gear designed to work in the tunnels. We'll all be on the same secure channel. Once we're inside, no unnecessary chatter. Team leaders will check in with me every ten minutes. Report any sightings as they happen."

"Will a girly scream work?" Rolf asked.

"It's always worked for you in the past," a huge, blond-bearded commando shouted good-naturedly. "Why change now?"

Chatter was good. Chatter kept me from thinking about going down into unknown miles of tunnels to hunt down monsters that only I'd be able to see—armed with a paintball gun.

"By the way, people," Roy said, "try to avoid shooting anything vital that will cause maintenance people to come down to fix. That includes anything that looks like an electrical switching box or anything with a pipe. We don't need civilian company."

The Scandinavian woman leapt down from the back of the truck that'd brought their equipment from the airport. She'd turned wolf in the privacy of the back. Her fur went from dark blond to silvery highlights. Yasha smiled slowly, liking what he saw. The female wolf stood preternaturally still, regarding the Russian, her amber eyes glittering in what I swear looked like playful challenge. By now, everyone was watching. Yasha smiled, kicked off his flip-flops, and smoothly stripped out of his T-shirt, earning catcalls, wolf whistles, and applause.

Then he dropped his shorts, and buck naked, turned right there in front of everyone. Muscles stretching, bones popping, claws extending, hair growing. When he'd finished, he threw back his head and neck—that had enough dark, rich red fur to qualify as a mane—and cut loose with a bone-chilling, triumphant howl.

The Scandinavian woman had sat back on her haunches with a panting, wolfy grin to enjoy the show.

Yasha the werewolf shook himself vigorously, settling his reddish brown fur around him, and grinned back.

"We're ready, sir," called out a voice from just inside the tunnel access doors. Two of our people each held a spray nozzle connected to a tank.

I looked over and groaned. Others groaned and swore. The Scandinavians just looked confused.

Roy grinned. "Time to get spritzed with some of that fancy New York City toilet water."

Back home, toilet water could mean perfume. Roy meant toilet water. Literally. Though with my luck, the grendels would think it was seasoning.

Our people reluctantly lined up to get sprayed down front and back.

Rolf caught a whiff of what was in those tanks. "What is—"

"Eau de Sewage," Roy told our guests. "Not the real stuff; it just smells like it. Can't have the beasties picking us out from anything else down there. Least not until we're close enough to give 'em a proper welcome to town."

"Okay, teams," Anderssen said. "Let's form up, get coated, and move out. The clock's ticking."

You could get anywhere in the city via the subway. Using the tunnels, so could monsters—and so could we.

We boarded the two troop transport trucks SPI kept in

its fleet for getting commando teams closer to where they needed to be without being seen by the public.

The abandoned subway tunnel SPI had paved and adapted for its use led to the Hudson River in one direction, up toward Midtown in the other. The Midtown section ended just before West Twenty-third Street. From there, the tunnel narrowed, and we were on foot. Grendels were nocturnal, but in the New York underground, it was always night. Man-made electricity was all that held primeval darkness at bay. Topside it was just after eight o'clock on what'd been forecasted to be a bitterly cold morning. New Year's Eve morning. Under Manhattan, it was always dark and warm, at least warmer than it was out on the streets.

Ideally, we'd find the nest with the adult grendels in one of the nine target sites, catch them both by surprise, and the bionic Viking and his spear would do their thing and he'd get his name on a plaque back in Oslo.

Roy Benoit led our team; Sandra Niles headed the second, and Lars Anderssen the third. Roy was a lead-from-the-front kind of guy—or as was the case now, a lead-from-beside-the-werewolf kind of guy. Yasha had tracked the male grendel earlier, so he and his nose had the point. I was behind Yasha and Roy with Ian at my left shoulder, Calvin at my right. Rolf and the second Scandinavian spearman, a third Scandinavian, and one of our commandos, a former Marine named Liz brought up the rear with the flamethrower. If anything tried to sneak up on us, Liz would turn it into something resembling the gooey center of a s'more.

I'd been in subway tunnels before, but not in what was below. Yasha led us through the levels with the garbage, bizarre and otherwise, and into passages that looked like no one had been there since they'd been scooped out of whatever the underbelly of Manhattan was made of. The tracks in the subway tunnel we were in had been abandoned, but only by trains. Trash was expected. An office chair on casters sitting perfectly level in the middle of the tracks? Not so much.

Over the next who knew how many hours, we paused for

quick MREs and brief breaks for the trackers to scout ahead. We found one of the likely nest sites. Empty. Sandra's team located two more. Likewise empty. At this rate, by the time we found the actual nest, we'd be too exhausted to do anything about it. As we continued the search, Yasha and Roy took us past tunnels that branched off into what could have been uncharted darkness, and around shafts in the floor that could have fallen all the way to Hell's waiting room for all I knew. Left to my own devices, I would have been lost after the first two levels. Who was I kidding? I'd have been hopelessly turned around as soon as I got out of the truck.

I didn't know how far we'd gone or how much time had passed when Roy called a halt and keyed his mike that was linked to the comms we all wore in our ears. "We've got a junction here. Both eventually get us to one of the possible nest sites. Mac, I need your eyes and Yasha's nose. Tell me if our visitors have recently used either one. Let's go to low lights, people."

Yasha and I moved forward, Yasha slightly in front, but still giving me a clear view. The Russian werewolf padded several paces into the tunnel—far enough to register scents that weren't us—and stopped. His deep breaths frosted the air. I stood back far enough to give him room to work and took a good look around. The tunnel descended like a boarding ramp for an airplane and then curved slightly at about the same distance. If Yasha couldn't smell it and I couldn't see it, there was nothing there.

I keyed my mike. "Nothing, sir."

Yasha growled low in his throat, which I took to be a frustrated no.

We proceeded to the second tunnel. After about fifty feet, there was a concrete landing with metal stairs descending into darkness, stairs only wide enough for one person at a time. If we went this way, we'd have to go single file. Yasha stepped out onto the concrete landing and went perfectly still. I could just make out the fur bristling along the ridge of his spine.

I stood off to the side. I didn't need—or want—to go any

farther. I couldn't see anything, but I could feel it. Something was below. Waiting. That feeling had nothing to do with my seer ability; it was the primitive instincts of a human in the presence of a predator. I trusted those instincts. I turned my head toward Roy and nodded.

Roy stepped between me and Yasha and onto the first stair. It creaked. It wasn't loud, but for what we were hunting, it was loud enough.

"Looks like the surprise party's over, folks," Roy said. "Yasha and I will take point. Calvin and Rolf, you and your pig sticker cover our six. Mac, wait until we're at the bottom before you follow; these stairs don't sound stable. Keep your senses wide open and sweep that floor for anything that even thinks about moving. The rest follow after you. When we reach the bottom, we'll go bright. I want to see every rat turd down there."

They quickly made their way down the staircase. Roy and Yasha in the lead, Calvin at his back, followed by Rolf. I scanned below and beyond for any sign of ambush, but saw nothing. I started down, Ian protectively behind me, and the other three kept watch on the tunnel behind us.

Our helmet lights pierced the darkness. The stairs went down at least two stories; the floor at the bottom mostly hidden in shadow. To our immediate right was a concrete wall; to our left a vast open space, interrupted midway by a catwalk roughly even with the halfway point of the stair. I couldn't see where it came from or where it went. I aimed my light down and could just make out the shape of torn-up subway tracks. Still no visual confirmation, but I was still getting that primeval warning system thing that scrawny dinosaurs must have gotten right before a T-Rex came charging out of the trees.

Or in our case, a whole forest worth of concrete and steel supports.

We all made it to the bottom without the stairs collapsing or walking into an ambush.

Roy's sharp eyes were determined to see where his high beams couldn't. "Talk to me, Mac."

"Still no visible targets. Sorry."

"Don't be. I'm sure that'll change any second now. Yasha?"

The Russian indicated the junction of the tracks with his nose.

Roy gave a curt nod. "We'll cover you."

Yasha moved silently to the center of the vast space, stopping where the tracks merged—and where he was in full view of the four tunnel openings. He faced each of the four in turn, letting the air, and the scents they carried, wash over him. Then without any indication of what he'd sensed, he quickly trotted back to where we waited.

As Yasha approached us, his eyes glittered amber and gold. It was no trick of the light.

A werewolf's nose knew blood when it whiffed it.

When he reached us, he turned in the direction of the tunnel opening in the left corner.

The pitch-dark left corner.

"Estimate of our location?" Roy asked Calvin.

The big commando studied a device attached to his forearm armor. "Less than three hundred yards to the next possible nest site." He nodded in the direction of the left corner. "That way."

# 23

AFTER no more than fifty feet into the tunnel, the heat and humidity felt to me like they were climbing to sauna levels. Grendels might have liked it here, but I sure didn't. I would've loved nothing more than to strip down to my tank top, but only Sigourney could survive a monster attack wearing nothing but her skivvies.

We could all smell it now. A sharp odor, a combination of ammonia and copper. My nose instantly told my brain what those two smells were—and more importantly, what they meant, but to avoid scaring myself any more than I already was, I pushed the babbling realization into a closet in my head and slammed the door. Similar realizations were happening to the rest of the team—minus the babbling.

It was urine at a level that couldn't possibly be human, and blood that probably was.

As we followed the tunnel downward, the air grew hotter. And stinkier.

Rotten meat.

"There's a scent difference between things that wander

down holes and die," Rolf said quietly, "and things that are dragged down holes and slaughtered."

As food for grendel spawn.

He shined his light on an object lying on the tracks.

A running shoe. It wasn't as bizarre as the office chair, but it made me wonder why only one?

I wondered until I saw the bloody sock lying flat on the left rail, still in the shoe—and a snapped-off leg bone still in the sock.

I flipped my oxygen switch and took a couple of deep breaths. I was having sparklies that didn't have a thing to do with bad air.

Roy keyed his mike. "Benoit to teams. We have likely grendel activity." He looked down at his GPS. The other two team commanders had the same device. It showed the positions of all three team leaders with pulsing red dots. "We're approximately one block from the center of Times Square."

*"This is Anderssen,"* came the Scandinavian commander's voice through our comms. *"I am being told that we can be at your location in twenty minutes."*

"Roger that, Lars," Roy said. "We'll proceed, but we'd appreciate the company when you get here."

*"Niles checking in,"* Sandra said. She didn't sound happy. *"I'm thirty—repeat three zero—minutes from your location."*

"Sandy, darlin', looks like you're gonna miss the shindig." Roy's expression didn't match his tone. He wasn't happy, either. "I'll try to bring you a souvenir." He took his finger off the mike switch. "Circle the wagons, folks. I want eyes on every patch of dark down here. If that mama monster laid her eggs down that tunnel, there's a heap of meanness waiting for us. We're taking this nice and easy." He caught Rolf Haagen's impatient scowl. "You'll get your chance to play with 'em, son. Don't jump the gun and you'll get the fun of surviving, too."

"Unless you're in a hurry to get to Valhalla," Ian said.

Rolf shrugged. "My ancestors can wait another day to meet me."

I was willing to wait until the other team got here *and* the cows came home, but the monsters weren't so patient.

Yasha raised his head and sniffed the air. He growled.

A few seconds later, the rest of us smelled it, too. It was the dead-fish-at-low-tide stench from Ollie's office. It wasn't quite as overpowering, but it was definitely the same overripe odor.

Rolf's nostrils flared as he breathed in the scent, and a slow smile spread across his face. "Definitely grendels."

"Yasha, can you follow that stink?" Roy asked.

The Russian werewolf didn't dignify that with a response. He sniffed in a semicircle then started down a side tunnel.

There were no steel and concrete columns where Yasha and his nose led us, just plenty of pipes and claustrophobia.

"It looks like Hell's jungle gym down here," Ian whispered.

The larger pipes, the circumference of fifty-five-gallon drums, were stacked two and three high, mounted on metal frames that kept them off the floor and separated from each other, creating what was essentially a wall of pipes. The aisle between them gave us enough room for three of us to walk side by side, but left us next to no room to maneuver. And I wanted room to maneuver worse than I think I've ever wanted anything.

"Do grendels climb?" Roy asked Rolf.

"And jump," he replied, his sharp blue eyes sweeping the rafters of smaller pipes above our heads. He silently extended the spear to its full length, locking it in place with the barest of clicks; the other Scandinavian spearman followed suit.

The tunnel broadened into an open area, if you could call something the size of two subway cars sitting side by side open. The pipes curved at various points, in seemingly all directions, basically turning the place into a maze. Beyond where we were standing, all I could see was a lot of dark.

The tiny hairs on the back of my neck quivered, sending a shudder down the length of my body. I breathed through my nose, trying to stay calm.

Roy's attention never wavered from the shadows in front of us. Some of our people found that patch of dark mighty interesting, too. Experience must breed a sixth sense when it came to things that went bump in dark places.

I couldn't pick anything out from the shadows yet, but they were close enough that I could smell the leftovers of what they'd been eating—a sharp, coppery tang. Blood. Then I detected a shimmer in the dark, like a heat mirage on a road. It was too dark to see the actual grendel, but my seer vision was picking up the effects of the cloaking device.

Oh hell. Here we go.

"Cloaking device in use," I said. "From ten o'clock to two." The shimmer darted through the dark into the forest of pipes, so fast that my mind couldn't confirm what or how many my eyes had just seen.

Grendels are sprinters, Anderssen had said.

I swallowed hard. "It's moving."

Calvin and Rolf took up position with Roy on the front line. Yasha dropped back to stand with me and Ian.

Ian had his gun up, tracking the shadows to our rear. "I've got a couple of ghouls playing hide-'n'-seek back here. I can see them. No cloaks or veils, so they're not being too shy."

Liz immediately staked out that patch of concrete as her own, the nozzle of her flamethrower glowing with an eager blue flame. The second Scandinavian spearman joined her.

Roy was perfectly still. "How many grendels?"

"Just one that I could see," I said. "Could be more."

"Adult?"

I had no clue. I shook my head. "Moving too fast."

The Cajun actually shrugged under his armor. "We knew it wasn't gonna be easy." He already had a huge handgun in one hand; and with his other, pulled out the biggest Bowie knife I'd ever seen. He saw my eyes widen and grinned. "Gator gutter. In case one of 'em wants to slow dance. Calvin, lay down some light, both directions."

Calvin lit two flares, and with a major-league effort, threw one ahead and one behind, far enough to show us anything that'd be coming at us.

With Ian and Yasha flanking me, I froze as an adult grendel—shimmering with the effects of Tarbert's cloaking device—stepped out of the shadows and into the flares' light. No one else could see it.

Oh shit.

It was the one from headquarters. The male. With no wounds, scars, or indication that he'd ever been in a dragon fight. His scales glowed like blood-dipped armor in the flares' light. His gleaming yellow eyes were locked on me. I was the one that got away.

My paintball rifle was pointing down, my index finger against the trigger guard. The grendel knew I could see it. I knew that if I so much as twitched, he'd be gone back into the shadows—or on top of me. I stayed absolutely still, kept my eyes locked on the grendel, and tried to speak without moving my lips. "Roy, male, dead ahead, twenty yards."

In one smooth and deadly move, Roy brought his pistol up and fired three shots precisely where the thing's head was . . . had been.

The Cajun snarled. He knew he hadn't hit it, and that it'd been gone before his bullets even got there. "Faster than a speeding bullet," he said between clenched teeth. "Bunch up, people. I want coverage in every direction. You're now weapons free."

I'd learned that was military-speak for "If you see it, kill it." Problem was, I was the only one who could see it.

I held my breath and waited for the grendel to put in another appearance.

I didn't have to wait long.

Four of them, six, nine, then a dozen and more. From every direction.

Ghouls, not grendels. Nest guardians.

They weren't veiled, so everyone could see them.

They were also smart, swift, and sadistic. Though with something that liked eating its dinner while it was still alive, that last one was a given. In my opinion, it also said a lot about an adversary who hired them as her thugs-on-call—and as nannies for newborn monsters. They'd ditched the white camo for black, and had likewise ditched any effort to disguise themselves as human.

The team opened fire with enough silver to bring down double their number.

Naturally, the ghouls fired back.

Whether I heard, saw, or just felt the air get heavy over my head, my lizard brain told me to look up. Now.

I did.

A ghoul leapt.

I didn't think. There was no time. Suddenly everything went into that slow-motion thing that was your brain's way of giving you one chance to figure out how not to die horribly. With roars and unearthly shrieks, the ghouls on the ground rushed us. I dimly heard the team opening fire all around me. My hand moved with agonizing slowness, going for my real gun, but hitting something else on the way there.

My headlamp switch. Scalding bright light flash-fried the ghoul's vision as I jumped aside, so instead of landing on me, the ghoul pancaked on the concrete floor. Ian double-tapped the ghoul in the back of the head.

I barely heard the gunshots with all the adrenaline pounding through me. I tried to look everywhere at once, desperate to find the grendel, and my headlamp spotlighted another ghoul about to jump. Ian fired exactly where my beam pointed. I might not be a sharpshooter yet with a gun, but I could aim the hell out of a flashlight.

"Stay together!" Roy shouted.

Like I was gonna cut myself from the herd. I scanned the tangle of pipes for more targets. They were everywhere, but they were too fast. I panicked. Where the hell was the male?

"Lars, we are under attack," Roy said through his comms. "Ghouls and grendels."

There was a hiss then a roar as an arc of fire erupted from Liz's flamethrower, sweeping flaming death across three of the ghouls. The things ran and leapt out of range, with no damage whatsoever. A pair of ghoul arms reached through the pipes, grabbed the second spearman by an armor strap, and jerked him repeatedly against the wall of metal. The man was flush against the pipes, too close to use his spear. He dropped it and drew his pistol, firing through the spaces at what had him pinned. Calvin snatched up the spear and drove it between the pipes. The spear jerked in his big hands, the point caught in something on the other side. Calvin pulled the spear's trigger, immediately followed by a muffled thump and a high-pitched scream.

One less ghoul.

The floor shook beneath our feet. The still-cloaked male grendel landed squarely in the middle of the aisle.

Behind us.

I fired my rifle in a steady stream of neon yellow directly at the thing's head.

Just like with Roy's real bullets, the grendel was gone before the paintballs arrived.

Ian and Roy both followed the paintballs' path like tracers. Before Ian's first bullet reached him, the grendel's armored scales flattened against his body and the silver bullets seemed to just bounce off. He roared in rage, not pain, and leapt into the rafters.

Deep, raspy laughter drifted down to me.

Ian had hit him, and it hadn't done a damned thing but laugh.

A black-gloved hand with razored nails protruding from the fingertips reached down and snatched Rolf Haagen into the air and into the dark nest of pipes over our heads. Several seconds of furious snarling, pounding, and clanging ended in a scream that rose into a gurgling shriek. Then there was a thud as Rolf landed in a crouch a few feet away, covered in ghoul goo, clutching a bloody spear, and grinning like the happy berserker he was.

Another ghoul appeared, silhouetted in the dying flares' light. It didn't even crouch; it just sprung, covering the distance between it and Roy in one leap. Its feet hadn't even touched the ground as the Cajun's blade flashed in a blur of motion as it sliced cleanly through the ghoul's wrist, missing its throat by less than an inch.

We were moving toward the nest, but not nearly fast

enough. I had no idea how long we had been fighting, probably less than two minutes. The twenty minutes it would take Anderssen's team to get here might as well have been an eternity. We didn't have twenty minutes. We might not even have ten the way things were going. Calvin had lit another flare and hurled it down the aisle toward where we thought the nest was. There was an opening in the fighting, and Liz took it, Calvin at her back with me right behind him.

The flare's red glow cast flickering shadows into the room. Liz swept the room with the flamethrower, hopefully making anything inside less likely to kill us for a few seconds. Our headlamps lit the space bright as day. It took my brain an extra few seconds to process what I was seeing.

A mound of mud and trash with about two dozen indentations dug into it, like an egg crate made of garbage.

They were all empty. No hatched eggs, no shell fragments. Nothing.

The eggs had been moved.

They'd known we were coming.

It had been a nest.

Now it was a trap.

# 24

THIS was bad.

The eggs had been here and now they were gone.

Liz's swearing was doing her Marine training proud; it was almost poetic. I wanted to scream a few choice words myself, but it'd be like throwing out a dirty limerick after a Shakespearean sonnet. I'd just embarrass myself.

Not only was the room empty, it was also worthless to us. It would have been a good place to barricade ourselves in until reinforcements arrived. However, the room didn't have a door—at least not anymore. It was metal, thick, and should have been standing until the second coming. It wasn't standing now. It'd been ripped off its hinges by something that had sunk its claws into the steel, gotten a good hold, and let 'er rip.

Like a certain female grendel desperate to get her eggs out before we got in. I looked around. This didn't strike me as a particularly good nesting spot. I shrugged inwardly. What did I know about monster maternal urges? Compared to a Norwegian ice cave, this place might have looked like a five-star resort. Odd behavior aside, the bottom line was that she'd known we were coming. Though she could've easily heard or smelled us. After a certain point in the tunnels, stealth was no longer at the top of our list of concerns.

"Sir!" Calvin shouted to be heard over the fighting.

Roy finished hacking the head off the ghoul closest to him before sparing a quick glance back at us.

We'd thought that the ghouls had been protecting the nest, but judging from the lack of eggs and the number of ghouls, it appeared they'd been funneling us down to this room. My helmet light showed me that going past where we were would only get us so far. Beyond the dark was a dead end.

It was an ambush.

The fighting was entirely too close to the empty nest room. Ian and the others were being pushed back with the intent of forcing them into this room and then turning where we stood into a death chamber.

I looked down. Other than our boot prints, there were no tracks leading in or out.

"Anything?" Liz called back. After her initial crème brûlée treatment of the room's interior, Liz had stationed herself at the door, lighting up any ghoul her flames could reach.

I scanned the room with my light, making sure nothing waiting to eat me was lurking in a dark corner. Dark, dank, and mildewed. I sneezed. Great. I had everything I needed to survive a monster attack, but I didn't have a Kleenex to my name. And encased in body armor the way I was, I didn't even have the option of using my sleeve, disgusting as that would have been. I just sniffed and carried on. I moved around the room, searching for some sign or smudge of slime to tell me the way those eggs had been taken out. Even though they weren't here anymore, I didn't want to turn my back on that nest, even if it was empty.

Then I saw it. A seam in the concrete wall that didn't line up, and dirt that had been scraped away when this section of wall had been opened. Not that long before, it seemed, due to lack of new dust. Hopefully it was a way out.

"Bingo," I whispered.

Calvin quickly joined me. "Find something?"

"Possibly." I crouched down to get a closer look. A tiny piece of broken pipe had gotten stuck down near the floor, keeping it from closing completely. I wedged my fingers in between the slabs of concrete and pulled.

It didn't budge.

One of Calvin's big hands reached around me and took a try. Even he had a hard time getting that loose section to move. It ended up taking both of Calvin's hands and all of his effort to open it, confirming that whatever had carried those eggs out—or played doorman for whatever did—was probably stronger than Calvin. I shoved that thought aside, and pressed my back against the wall next to the opening. Calvin stood opposite me, using the door as a shield, and when nothing jumped out, he stepped quickly into the opening, shining both helmet- and gun-mounted lights inside, showing an area even smaller than the room we were in, almost like a bomb shelter. With Calvin covering me, we went inside. There weren't any cracks or seams in the wall indicating anything remotely resembling another way in or out. Just crumbling and flaking concrete.

I took a step back from the wall, snagged my heel on a chunk of concrete, and not used to the extra weight of body armor, fell flat on my ass. The floor cracked and broke beneath me. I yelped and kept falling—at least part of me did. Next thing I knew, I'd plugged a hole in the floor with my butt, floundering like I was stuck in an inner tube float—from my chest up and my knees down were the only parts of me sticking out.

I looked up at a surprised Calvin. "Found something."

The ghoul attack ended as fast as it'd begun. The male grendel had vanished before that.

No one on the team liked or trusted what either of those things implied.

Most of the team stood guard against a probable and

reinforced second-wave attack, while waiting for our own reinforcements. Ian, Calvin, and a momentarily back-in-human-form Yasha worked quickly to literally pry my armored butt out of that hole. It would have been beyond embarrassing if it hadn't been for the terror. In an inner tube floating down a river, usually the worst that could bite you would be a fish. I was presently having a flashback to the grendel spawn in the HVAC room, and my vivid imagination had them scurrying up from below right this very moment to attack my posterior parts.

Once the guys had popped me out, we saw that the hole was a shaft—or a chute that, for all we knew, went straight down to Satan's sitting room.

It was also where those eggs had gone.

Before we'd left headquarters, Yasha had taken big sniffs of the grendel spawn and their eggs. That's what he smelled now.

"So something just threw them down there?" I asked.

Yasha sniffed again. "Nose says yes."

"Anderssen said grendel eggs are tough," Ian said. "So I imagine a trip down a hole in the ground wouldn't be a problem. Heck, the kiddies might even enjoy it."

I barely heard him. My eyes were locked on that opening in the floor. The hole was small. Everyone on the team was big, at least bigger than the hole was wide.

Except for me.

Everyone looked at me.

I looked back.

"Nobody's going down there yet," Roy said to everyone's unspoken conclusion. "Calvin, you got any information on where that goes?"

The big commando shook his head. "According to the maps we have, there's not anything down there. However, the old Forty-second Street subway station is on the level above us."

That got everyone's attention.

"Old?" Roy asked.

"Built in 1932, but only used from 1959 to 1981 for rush hour trains. Abandoned now." He paused meaningfully.

"The present-day Forty-second Street/Times Square station is almost right on top of it."

"It'd be packed at midnight," Ian countered. "Our grendels need direct access to the street—without thousands of witnesses until they get there."

"I said *almost* right above it. There's a pedestrian tunnel and station entrance a quarter mile to the south. Back before Times Square got Disneyfied, it was a favorite hangout for junkies, pushers, and the homeless. After a crime spree down there back in 1991, they closed the tunnel and sealed it off. The homeless still find their way in."

"Providing an out-of-the-way, steady food source," Roy noted.

Calvin nodded. "Especially in the winter. And there's a stairway that goes straight down from that tunnel to the abandoned Forty-second Street station. Also 'sealed.' Once the grendels get to that closed station entrance on the street level, if that handiwork's any indication"—Calvin jerked his head back at the steel door that'd been torn from its hinges—"they'd have no problem accessing Times Square."

Roy indicated the shaft at our feet. "If those eggs are down there, we've got our likely access point. But we're running a camera down first." Roy popped open a pouch on his utility belt, taking out what looked like a drain snake with a knob on the end.

I shot a quick glance at the door. "Do we have time to—"

"We sure as hell don't have time to lose our seer down a hole in the ground," Roy said. "I ain't going back to the dragon lady with that story."

He unwound and lowered the camera into the hole, using the same viewer he had for the GPS. I looked around his arm. The sides of the hole were rough as if they'd been scooped out by a hand, a big hand, one that had even larger claws. It reminded me of a burrow.

Rolf stuck his head through the doorway. "Still no ghouls, no grendel, and no Lars."

Roy nodded absently, eyes intent on the camera screen.

"The shaft's clear down to fifty feet. It goes farther, but our cable doesn't."

Everyone looked at me again.

"Can't we just toss down a pair of grenades?" Rolf asked.

Roy shook his head. "Not until we know for sure the eggs are down there. No disrespect to Yasha's sniffer, but we need a confirmed kill."

Meaning I was going down. Hopefully just in the spelunking sense rather than that of impending doom.

"No grendel could've dug that," Rolf said. "It's too small."

"I've seen this before," Roy said. "It's ghoul work. They're like rats; there's nothing they can't fit through. Damned things just flatten out and squirm their way in."

"Ghoul nannies protecting the babies," I muttered. I leaned over and peered into the hole. "From the looks of things, I'll fit, but my armor won't." I took a deep breath. Down a pitch-black hole in the depths of subterranean Manhattan was the last place I wanted to go, but there was no other option. "Ian, get me out of this; we're wasting time."

My partner's hand gripped my arm. "Roy, I need a minute."

"Make it a fast one."

Ian's hand slid down from my upper arm and took my hand in his and pulled me away from the others and went to the corner of the bunker.

I beat him to whatever he was going to say. "No."

"No, what?"

"Whatever you're going to say. Save it. I have to go. You heard Roy; he needs a confirmed kill. So I go, confirm they're down there, you guys pull me back up, Rolf chucks in a couple grenades. Boom. Besides, there could be a veil over those eggs. No one else would be able to see them. I'm just taking a peek and getting the hell out."

His hand squeezed mine through my glove. "If you hear, see, or smell anything alive down there, you say the word and we'll have you out of there so fast you'll—"

"To quote Rolf: 'Would a girly scream work?' "

He smiled. "I'll take anything."

He and Yasha helped me out of my armor, and into a rappelling harness. I got to keep my helmet with the light.

"Uh, I've never rappelled."

Roy grinned. "You ain't rappelling. We're dropping; you're hanging on."

"I can do that."

Ian picked up my shoulder harness with my real gun and knife, and held it up for me to slip on. I did and he adjusted the harness so that it'd fit just me rather than over me plus my armor.

I met his eyes. His were grimly resigned, mine were questioning.

"If you need them, use them," he told me.

"They'd work even better than a girly scream."

"Damn straight." Ian tapped the top of my helmet. "Use your night vision until you get a look at what's down there. Don't let anything know you're there unless you have to."

Roy chipped at the wall nearest the pit with a gloved finger; bits of concrete flaked off. "Wall's not strong enough to hold even your little bit of weight."

"I'll anchor," Ian told him.

Roy nodded. "I'll pitch in. Calvin, you, too. No insult, son," he told Ian.

"None taken."

I was in black fatigues, combat boots, and Under Armour tank top. At least I got to keep my helmet with its ghoul-retina–frying light.

I tried a grin; it probably looked like a grimace. "Sigourney, eat your heart out," I muttered to myself.

"When you tell us to pull you up, tuck your upper arms to your sides and cross your forearms and hands tight against your chest, like this." Ian demonstrated, and I mirrored his action. He nodded. "Good. We'll be pulling you out of there fast, and I don't want to leave your skin on the walls on the way up."

I sat down on the rim of the hole with my lower legs dangling over the edge. I looked up. "You guys got me?"

"We're not letting go," Ian assured me.

They lowered me over the side, my weight entirely supported by three of the men I trusted most. That was the only thing I felt confident about.

As soon as my head dropped below the surface, I pressed my lips together against the whimpers that desperately wanted to get out—almost as desperately as I wanted to get out of this hole. I was determined not to lose it. If I did, the entire team would be listening while I did. I jumped over terror straight into petrified. I tried to tell myself it was like one of those water park slides, but I'd never liked the thought of going down one of those, either.

I had a comm link in my ear and a helmet and high-beam flashlight on my head, so I wasn't alone and I had light if I needed it. Scrapes were unavoidable, and twice I almost got stuck. I felt blood on my shoulders and upper arms. Blood that anything below me could smell like circling sharks.

I was chum on a rope.

What was probably minutes seemed like an eternity. I felt like I was being lowered down a monster's throat, a monster that was going to swallow and gulp me down at any moment. I watched my descent by tucking my chin down to my chest and looking under my arm, while clutching the rope with both hands. At first I didn't see anything but a whole heap of dark, then it started to lighten ever so slightly. I turned off my night vision, and let my eyes adjust. It was definitely lighter. Dim, but getting brighter as I descended. A light in a hole in the ground? I wasn't opposed to light, just suspicious until I knew what was making it and why. Being lowered down what was basically a packed dirt shaft was disorienting, so I couldn't begin to guess how far down the light was. Suddenly I stopped moving.

End of the line. Literally.

The rope couldn't go any farther, but I had to.

"Guys," I whispered into my comms. "I need another . . ." I looked down again and made my best guess. "Twenty feet of rope."

Silence.

I started to panic. "Hello?"

*"Sit tight,"* Ian said. *"We're rigging it up."*

Soon I started moving again. About a minute after that, my feet touched the bottom of the shaft, and a small tunnel branched off to the right. As best I could figure, the shaft had gone straight down, with the tunnel branching off the bottom of it like the letter L.

I squatted, and ducked my head down as far as I could, trying to peek out. It looked like some kind of room, size unknown. Contents even more unknown. The glow was coming from there, but it wasn't bright enough for me to see eggs, ghouls, or anything else that might be waiting for me—or waiting for anything warm-blooded and presumed tasty.

After much squirming and wiggling, I got myself turned around, head facing toward the light. Lying flat on my stomach, and using my hands and forearms, I pulled myself forward. I reached the end of the short tunnel, and was getting ready to take a look at what was beyond, when the dirt directly under my front half gave way, dumping me out face-first on a hard floor; fortunately it was only a few feet down, but it was far enough to knock the air out of me.

I must have made an "oof" sound, because the next thing I heard was Ian's concerned voice as if from far away. *"Mac! Mac, can you hear—"*

I pulled in some air and grunted as I rolled over on my side. "Yeah." I winced at the pain in my side. "I hear you. That last step was a dooz—"

I froze.

I was face-to-face with a pile of about-to-hatch grendel eggs. The light in the room came from a pair of Coleman camp lanterns, which shone right through the thin egg casings, showing me what was inside each and every one.

Squirming grendel spawn.

They must have sensed me. Their tiny scythe-tipped fingers clawed at the interior of their eggs. Holy crap, I could hear the things chittering from inside. The grendels in nearby eggs took up the cry, tiny razors clawing at the shells of their eggs.

Muffled sounds of an entirely different kind came from

directly overhead. I bit my bottom lip against a scream, and crab-crawled backward until I smacked up against the dirt wall.

Those two lanterns lit up the last thing I expected to see.

Ollie Barrington-Smythe gagged, hog-tied, and hanging suspended over the eggs like an edible crib mobile.

# 25

ALL I could do was stare in dumbfounded amazement.

When you're faced with more than your brain can process, you freeze up, probably to keep your body from doing something monumentally stupid while your brain's otherwise occupied. That was my theory. My fervent hope was that when my brain got past its deer-in-headlights moment, it'd send my body the signal to move.

I really wanted to move. I was nose to eggs with a mound of grendels; all of our mouths were open—mine in shock, the monsters' in hungry and hissing anticipation. I was probably only frozen there for a few seconds, but that would have been plenty enough time for anything that might've been in that room with us to kill and eat me if it was so inclined. Fortunately, the only things inclined were still trapped inside their eggs. Unfortunately, I had no clue how long they'd stay that way.

Remember that scene in *Jurassic Park* in the dinosaur nursery with the hatching velociraptor eggs? Such cute little sounds had come out of their tiny toothless mouths. Believe me, there was nothing cute or toothless about a nearly hatched grendel.

I didn't think the pair of camping lanterns in the room were there as nursery night-lights. Whoever was responsible for having Ollie strung up like a side of baby food beef had wanted him able to see what was going to eat him.

That was enough to send me scrambling to my feet.

Ollie was still wearing the absurdly expensive suit he'd had on the last time I'd seen him. My little British friend didn't look too much the worse for wear. He was bald as a cue ball due to his toupee presently sitting in SPI's break room. He had some cuts and bruises, and his suit was beyond all dry cleaning help, but other than that, not bad. However, the noises coming from behind Ollie's gag were simultaneously enraged and impatient. My movement and Ollie's squealing caused a chorus of ravenous chittering as every last grendel spawn started clawing and biting at the insides of their eggs, desperate to get to us. To add to my terror and sensory overload, Roy was yelling at me from inside my own head.

*"Mac, do you read? Dammit, girl, talk to me!"*

"I'm here." Now how to describe where here was, but more to the point, who I was here with?

As far as I could tell, the narrow room I'd landed in was cement—walls, floor, ceiling—with the exception of the way I'd come in. It looked like someone had taken a sledgehammer to the bottom third of a wall of six-inch-thick concrete. Other than Ollie and the eggs, the narrow room was empty, but it was obvious that it hadn't always been. There were metal brackets that looked to have once held cables against the wall, and what appeared to be big fuse boxes, rusted and empty now. I flipped on my helmet's high beams. The ceiling was high, about twenty foot worth of high. I had no idea what the room had been, but now it was a grendel nursery.

The way I'd come in seemed to be the only way out. There had to be another one. I'd had to shuck my armor to fit down that shaft. There was no way Ollie had come down the same way I had, and there was no chance he'd go up the way I'd come down.

I had a problem; though actually, the problem was worse for Ollie. The ropes that held him suspended above the nest had been rigged up with a pulley system anchored in the ceiling. The only way to get him down would be to cut him down. I didn't know how much pressure it'd take to pop one of those eggs, but I suspected Ollie's weight would more than do the trick. Unfortunately, it probably wouldn't be enough to squash the grendels inside.

*"Are the eggs there?"* Roy was asking.

"Oh yeah, but tell Rolf we can't use grenades."

At the word "grenades," Ollie's muffled scream rose into a not-so-muffled shriek.

Silence from Roy. Then, *"Why the hell not?"*

"The eggs have company." I paused and tried to do a quick count. I gave up at thirty. "More than thirty eggs about to hatch, and Ollie's hog-tied overhead as baby food."

*"Shit."*

"My thought exactly, sir."

I gave Roy and the others the basics of my dilemma. Though what to do wasn't the dilemma. Chucking a grenade down that shaft wasn't the only thing that was officially off the table; so was leaving Ollie behind to be eaten.

Ian's voice came over the comms. *"Mac, where's the door?"*

"Don't see one. No vents, ducts, or anything." That couldn't be right. There was air in here, and it was moving. What was coming off that pile of eggs smelled like the backwash off a hog farm, but there was something else in the air. It didn't smell that great, either; but it was familiar.

Damp and garbage. Problem was, that particular combination of aromas could have applied to anywhere in the city.

I shone my headlamp at the corner of the ceiling where the pulley holding Ollie off the nest was mounted. The air seemed to be coming from there. Then I saw it. A metal grate about three foot square with water dripping from it.

There was a metal ladder bolted to the wall, but it started at the grate and only extended halfway down. Far too high for me to reach. I'd seen nearly identical grates on the sidewalks near subway stations. Trains passing on the tracks below would send up blasts of air and noise. I wasn't standing above a subway station, but Calvin did mention something about . . .

"Ian, tell Calvin I think I might've found that abandoned subway station."

Ian's voice cut in and out then dissolved into static. I couldn't make out a word he said, and Roy sounded like he was talking to me from the bottom of a well. ". . . *are . . . way . . . do not go . . . wait . . .*"

Then silence.

Oh hell.

I scrambled into the hole in the wall and stuck my head up the shaft to get the signal back.

Nothing but a lot of dark and silence.

"Hello?" I called up the shaft.

No answer.

The shiver started at the base of my neck and ran clear down to my toes.

If they'd been attacked, I would have heard something, wouldn't I? Unless they'd been overwhelmed by grendels, ghouls, and spawn, and torn limb from—

Stop it. They're fine. You're going to be fine. If everything up there got carried off to hell in a handbasket, you're not gonna do yourself or Ollie any good by hitching a ride along with them. I took a deep breath. It's not a problem, Mac. They'll find you. You've got a tracking chip in your . . .

Armor that you're no longer wearing.

Dammit.

Either something in this room simply affected my reception, or the signal was being deliberately jammed. It didn't matter which it was, both meant I was on my own until reinforcements arrived. And they would arrive.

Unless they didn't.

My eyes went to the eggs which were starting to look

more like a pile of giant Mexican jumping beans. The egg closest to me had two slits that hadn't been there half a minute ago. A pair of claws appeared through the slits, and the baby monster slashed its way through the membrane that was keeping it from being first in the chow line.

Ollie was having himself a panic attack, and I was about to join him.

As far as I could tell, whoever had strung Ollie up had opened the grate, run the rope through the pulley, then lowered him until he was right above the nest. I couldn't reach the ladder on the wall, unless . . . I did some quick thinking. I had an idea. It might work, it might not, but it was the only idea my brain was giving me right now.

If I could cut Ollie down, I could pull down the rest of the rope that he'd been hanging from, Ollie could boost me up enough to reach the base of the metal ladder. I'd pull myself up, tie the rope to the ladder for Ollie to climb . . .

I stopped and snorted. Ollie shimmying up a rope? Might as well ask him to sprout wings while I'm at it. But the rest of my plan was entirely doable—unless I got to the top of the ladder and the grate was locked, welded in place, or it was too heavy to push up. It was pitch-dark up there, so I didn't know what I'd be climbing into . . .

"But if you don't *do* something and stop flapping your jaws," I snapped at myself, "you're gonna get eaten."

Motivation found.

No, Ollie wasn't the athletic type, but I think he'd find his inner mountain climber real quick if not climbing that rope meant being eaten alive. If a mom could lift a couple tons of car off her child, Ollie could haul his ass out of a concrete bunker.

Though none of that was gonna happen until I cut Ollie down.

I didn't know how much Ollie weighed, but I knew once I cut that rope, he'd come down. Fast. Smack-dab in the middle of that nest.

Not if the nest wasn't there, said the little voice in my head. You know the one. The voice responsible for telling your buddies, "Hey, y'all, watch this!" after drinking vast quantities of alcohol, and before doing something guaranteed to land your ass in the hospital. But just because I didn't want to move the eggs didn't mean that it was a bad idea. Actually, it was a very good idea. There were about thirty of them. Two dozen, plus a few extra. If they were chickens, it'd be less than three cartons.

Screw it. Just pick up the damned eggs, Mac.

Yeah, I was wearing gloves, but if one of those grendels picked the next two minutes to hatch, they'd bite through them like casings wrapped around sausages. I grabbed the egg closest to me, the one with the two claw slashes. If I put it on the bottom of the pile, I could bury it under its siblings. The grendel inside squirmed frantically to get out. I squeaked and ran and put the egg on what looked like a trash heap in the corner. It took every bit of control I had not to raise that squeak to a scream. On the next trip, I grabbed one egg in each hand. It doubled my urge to scream, but it'd get the job finished faster. After the fourth trip, the grendel squeals got louder, and my carrying turned into tossing and kicking.

After the last eggs left my hand and boot, and I had a landing pad for Ollie.

I took one look at Ollie's panic-stricken face and decided to leave his gag in for the trip down. The last thing either one of us needed was for the little British guy to go into loud and vocal hysterics the moment his mouth was unstoppered. Just because anyone hadn't popped in to introduce themselves as our captors didn't mean they weren't close by.

In response, Ollie went red in the face and squealed in indignation.

*"Shut up!"* I whispered emphatically.

I'd definitely made the right choice by leaving that gag in.

Suddenly the grate over our heads was lifted off. I doused my light and flattened myself against the wall—for all the good it'd do me.

Someone or something in black rappelled down into the room from the now-open ceiling grate.

I got my gun in my hand—the real one.

"Mac!" came an urgent whisper. Ian's whisper.

With shaking hands, I holstered my gun and started breathing again. I'd damned near shot my partner.

A couple of seconds later, Calvin followed Ian down.

I stepped away from the wall. "How did you find—"

"Not now." Ian unhooked himself from the rope, and quickly attached my harness to it. He looked up and gave a quick nod to Yasha and Rolf leaning over the edge of the grate opening.

"We'll get Ollie," Ian told me. "You leave. Now."

I pointed at the pile I'd made. "Hatching eggs!"

Ian nodded, and put both of my hands on the rope then squeezed them hard to tell me to hold on.

I'd barely gotten a good grip when Yasha and Rolf hauled me up and through the hole in the ceiling. Sometimes, it's good to be small.

Once topside, it was graffiti and garbage as far as the eye could see. Though the only light was Yasha's and Rolf's headlamps, and the occasional lightbulb down what looked to be a train tunnel. I was about to ask if this was the old Forty-second Street station when I saw a dingy, black-and-white-tiled "42nd ST." barely visible on the far wall.

Rolf was alert to any movement from the surrounding dark, and I knelt next to the open grate, willing Ian and Calvin to hurry. Yasha reached in to the pulley, unwound the rope holding Ollie, and he and Rolf quickly lowered him to the ground. Ollie started to flail around which only excited the spawn even more. Ian got in Ollie's face and whatever he said, made the little guy go pale; I could see it from here. The chittering from the spawn rose in pitch and intensity.

Ian cut the ropes on Ollie's hands and arms, leaving Calvin to take care of the ones on his legs and ankles. Ollie pulled his gag out and didn't make a sound. Thank God for small miracles. He must have known that what the ghouls had done to him would pale in comparison to what Ian would do if he even thought about opening his mouth.

Ian and Calvin hauled him over to the ropes and got him hooked up.

Yasha and Rolf hauled the much-heavier-than-me Ollie out of the hole with only minimal swearing. At least I assumed Rolf's angry hisses were Norwegian curses.

Once he was out, Ollie sucked in air to say or scream who knew what.

I clapped my hand across his mouth. Ollie complied. Miracle number two.

I glanced back at the now seething pile of eggs. The spawn were hatching and frantically clawing their way free of their eggs.

Ian and Calvin quickly pulled themselves hand over hand out of the concrete bunker/monster nursery. A group of newly hatched spawn scuttled on all fours to reach the ropes. It wouldn't do any good, but it was still all I could do not to reach down and start hauling on those ropes myself. When Ian and Calvin got within reach, Yasha and Rolf reached down, grabbed the drag handles on the back of their armor, and hauled them the rest of the way out. Half a dozen spawn were halfway up the ropes when Ian and Calvin detached the ropes from their harnesses, sending rope and grendels falling to the bunker floor. More spawn started jumping for the ladder, though "launched" would have been a better description, coming mere inches from reaching the bottom rung.

Rolf had a grenade in his hand, his blue eyes gleaming. He pulled the pin and tossed the grenade in the exact middle of the egg pile. I expected a boom. Instead there was a hiss and a loud pop as flames raced over the eggs that had just hatched, and those struggling to free themselves from their eggs. The insides of the eggs must have contained a fatty substance. It popped and crackled like bacon on a too-hot griddle.

I watched in disgusted wonder until the stench wafted up through the grate opening.

Rolf pulled another grenade from a pouch on his armor and dropped it straight down. He winked. "Incendiary grenades. That'll discourage the jumpers. Not to worry, I have the other kind, too."

Ian and Yasha quickly lifted and replaced the grate back over the opening and Calvin rolled what looked like a railroad pushcart on top of it. Calvin talked fast into his comms as Ian and Yasha got on either side of Ollie and hauled him to his feet.

Suddenly, my comms came back to life. All hell had broken loose somewhere.

*"This is Lars. I've got movement ahead."* Shouts and gunfire erupted in the background. *"Spawn. We've got spawn."*

*"Sandra here. Watch your six, Lars. They're behind you, too. Hang on, we're coming in."*

*"Tunnel's packed with ghouls."* It was Roy. *"Clearing a path to y'all now."*

Explosions filled my ears and shook the ground, knocking me on my butt and pieces of concrete from the walls.

Calvin gave me a hand up. "Lars's team found the main lair in a series of old maintenance rooms down there." He flashed a grin full of white teeth. "Sounds like we're missing quite a party."

I stared back at him, dumbfounded. None of the guys appeared to be in any hurry to get down there to help. "Aren't we going to help them?"

"They've got their job," Ian said. "We've got ours. The two adult grendels weren't in the lair."

Oh crap.

"What time is it?"

"Thirty minutes 'til midnight. We think they're already making their way to the surface. After we get Ollie close to the surface and cut him loose, we're going big-game hunting."

# 26

THE platform of the abandoned subway station was dark, dirty, and—aside from the occasional explosion in the chambers and tunnels beneath us—it was entirely too quiet. Broken wine and beer bottles littered the ground along with food wrappers, cigarette butts, aerosol paint cans, and discarded syringes.

To better listen for the adult grendels, we'd switched our comms to another channel. Calvin kept his on SPI's main channel to keep tabs on the faint booms still coming from below, and to know when—or if—we could be expecting company up here that we actually wanted to have. Since we'd been tasked with stopping two adult grendels, it would be nice to have more than five of us to do it.

Ollie had his back against the wall, knees clutched to his chest. At least he wasn't in a fetal position. However, he was babbling.

"What the hell's he saying?" Calvin asked.

Ollie's eyes were focused, but not on us. He had that thousand-yard stare that I'd heard sometimes happened after serious trauma. Being kidnapped by ghouls, hog-tied, and damn near fed to baby monsters certainly qualified.

Fortunately, I was fluent in panic attack.

"Ollie? It's Mac. You're safe." Though safe for any of us was relative right now. "You need to hush until we can get you out of here." I glanced at Ian in unspoken question. He nodded once. "We *are* getting you out of here, but you need to calm down. You understand?"

Ollie swallowed hard.

I figured that was about as much of a yes as I was likely to get.

"Calvin, what's the fastest way to the surface?" Ian asked.

"The stairs to that pedestrian passageway I told you about. The one that—"

Ian's warning glance cut him off.

I knew what he'd been about to say. The one the grendels would probably be using to get to the surface. A full-grown grendel was the last thing Ollie needed to see or hear about.

At the mention of a way out of his nightmare, any way at all, Ollie latched onto it like a life preserver. "I'll take it."

"You don't want to go there," I told him.

"If it's away from this bloody—"

Ian jerked his chin upward. "What about the main Times Square station?"

"There's a maintenance stairway," Calvin told him. "Down that hall and around the corner. Secured with a chain and padlock down here, and a dead bolt topside."

"Can you get through?"

Calvin spread his hands. "Please. You insult me."

"Do it. Let's get him out of here." The "and out of our hair" was strongly implied.

At this point, Ollie'd probably gnaw through those chains with his teeth.

We got Ollie up and moving. Knowing that he was on his way out brought back the ornery little Englishman that most of us knew, but only one of us liked.

Ian gave Ollie a pair of twenties. "When you're in the

station, get on a train and go. Direction doesn't matter. Just get as far away from Times Square as you can."

"The Full Moon," I told him. "On Thompson Street one block off West Third. Tell Nancy and Bill we sent you. They're good people. They'll take care of you."

Ollie's eyes went almost as wide as they'd been when we'd hauled him up. Terror mixed with distaste. "They're werewolves."

This from a man who sold shrunken heads and monkey brains for a living.

Yasha had just turned wolf again a few minutes ago and was standing guard down on the tracks, and while I hoped he hadn't heard Ollie, I knew he had. Fortunately, Yasha was of a mind that people with distasteful personalities didn't taste good. It was probably the only thing saving Ollie's nasty bacon right about now.

"They're. Good. Folks," I told him. I didn't care if he was traumatized. Rude was rude. "We've had this talk before."

Calvin took Ollie's arm and hustled him down the platform and out of sight.

I felt Ian watching me.

"And we've had *this* talk before," I told him. "Partners, remember? I'm here. I'm staying."

In response, Ian took a couple of steps into the shadows, and came back with a double armful of my armor, with my paintball rifle slung over one shoulder. "I know you're staying; that's why I brought all this up here with me."

He started helping me get geared up, and I grabbed a couple of pieces and started hurriedly putting them on myself. Standing there on those subway tracks, I knew just how a naked turtle would feel out in the middle of a highway. I tried not to think that shell or not, that turtle was roadkill as soon as the first truck came along—or, in my case, grendel. I'd rather see the headlights of an oncoming train on those abandoned tracks. It'd be less terrifying.

Yasha smiled a wolfy smile at us, then it turned into a predatory grin as he loped down the tunnel and into the darkness. A few minutes later, he appeared in the dim light, having doubled back to patrol in the opposite direction. He'd pause occasionally and raise his muzzle, letting the air currents flow over his nose that was the size of my closed fist. As far as fists went, it wasn't that big. As far as wolf noses went, it was enormous. He padded back to where we were, and with one smooth leap, landed lightly on the platform. He gave us a grumbling growl which I'd learned meant that he didn't find anything and he didn't like or trust it.

Ian jerked his head toward the platform. "Let's get you up there with Yasha." He kept his voice low as we climbed the short ladder. "The teams know where we are. As soon as they clean up, we'll be getting plenty of backup."

That'd be a lot of firepower to unleash directly below an in-use subway station. Not that I was against it. I was all for any and every kind of firepower we needed. "Won't they hear us up there?"

"No chance. Even if it wasn't New Year's Eve, that's one of the busiest stations in town, and tonight it'll be packed with thousands of rowdy people. We could be firing cannons down here and no one would know."

From what we'd experienced back at headquarters, a cannon might be the only thing that could put a dint in a grendel, and I wished we had one.

Calvin came running back to where we were.

"Ollie?" Ian asked without looking away from where he worked on my last few armor buckles.

"Gone."

I started. "What kind of gone?"

"Gone as in on a train." Calvin's face was set on scowl. "With his bitching about having to take 'uncivilized transportation,' he's lucky to have made it to a train."

Best I could tell it'd been at least five minutes since the last explosion. That could be good or really bad. One meant we'd have backup soon. The other meant we'd never see our coworkers again. I was gonna go with the first one.

Ian finished with my armor. His eyes searched my face. "You okay, Mac?"

There were all kinds of okay; and right now, I wasn't

any of them. Our backup needed backup, my main weapon was a paintball gun, and my real gun might as well have been loaded with BBs for all the good it was going to do me or anyone else.

"Just peachy."

"I need you to be on this platform."

"So I can be out of everyone's way?"

"So you can see down the tunnel in both directions, and blast their heads with paint. Eye shots if you can get it. Blind them long enough for us to kill them. And if you can't mark them, just fire on their position; we'll follow with live ammo. Calvin, you and Rolf take the northbound tracks. Me and Yasha will watch the south. Let's go to bright light."

I was stunned. We might as well stand in a spotlight. "Like the heat lamp over a buffet roast beef?"

Ian stopped and turned. "If those grendels are within a mile of this place, they know we're here. We're all that's standing between them and the ultimate buffet. Light's the only advantage we have and we're going to take it."

I couldn't argue with that.

The waiting began.

I didn't hear a peep from anyone. They were silent and focused, each getting ready in their own way for what would be coming for us from out of the dark. The guys had their game faces on, giving me no clue as to what was going through their minds. Well, except for Rolf. From the crazy-ass grin he was wearing, you'd think all of his birthdays—past, present, and future—had been tied up with a bow in this one moment.

Me? I was one of the first things Papa Grendel was gonna see when he cleared that tunnel. We'd tangled twice and he hadn't killed me yet, though neither of those times had been directly my doing; I'd had plenty of help both times. I'd never particularly cared for baseball, but "three strikes you're out" was stuck in a loop in my head.

Yasha growled low and deep in his throat.

"They're coming," Ian said, settling his assault rifle against his shoulder.

A roar only marginally softer than the lawyer-eating T-Rex in *Jurassic Park* shook the ground beneath our feet. It was louder than what I'd heard in the bull pen, but it was still some distance away. That roar was the grendel's way of announcing that he was coming to kill us horribly, so that by the time he actually got here, we'd be appropriately terrified, thus prolonging his fun.

I had news. I was appropriately terrified right now.

"Please tell me you guys heard that."

"No," Ian said. "But I feel the vibration. They're closing fast."

"He." I corrected him.

Rolf Haagen's face fell in disappointment. "Just one?"

"He's the only one roaring. It's the one from the bull pen and tunnel. Do all grendels sound alike?"

"No."

"Then it's a 'he' and he's coming right at you."

My little announcement of impending doom cheered Rolf right up.

Ian adjusted his shooting stance so he could fire in either direction. "Yasha, keep your eyes, ears, and nose on those southbound tracks. Grendels are silent hunters. One roaring in our direction probably means the female's sneaking up on us."

The crazy Norwegian was grinning from ear to ear. "This trip might be worth it after all." He reached over his shoulder and an instant later was hefting an honest-to-God broadsword. I hadn't noticed it before, which considering its size was saying a lot. The sword was matte black and had blended right in with his armor.

To supplement his gun, Calvin pulled a massive knife from a sheath that ran nearly the length of the big man's thigh. Rolf saw.

"That isn't big enough." The Norwegian gave his sword a fancy swing and tossed it to Calvin, who caught it cleanly. Rolf still had his spear, and an evil-looking rifle that he left slung over his back. "If he gets past me, don't let him get away. And take care of that blade; it's a family heirloom."

Yasha stood in the exact center of the tracks, his hackles rising along with his growls.

Deep, unnatural laughter came from the tunnel, closer now. I'd know that gravelly chuckle anywhere.

"It's definitely the male," I said.

"Shit," Calvin spat. He briefly tucked the sword under his arm, popped out what must have been a less than fully loaded magazine, and slammed home a new one. "This is getting old."

I moved up to the edge of the platform so I could have a clear view in both directions. Yeah, all the noise was coming from one end of the tunnel, but a whole world of hurt could be coming at us from the other.

Ian's eyes intently scanned the darkness. "Mac, let us know at thirty feet. Gentlemen, when she gives us a target, hit it with everything you have."

Yasha moved to stand with Ian in the grendel's path, positioning himself so he could cover the southbound tracks at the same time. He couldn't see the monster, but he had to be able to smell it. Though it didn't matter how sensitive your nose was, you couldn't fight by smell alone, at least not for long. Rolf and Calvin remained on the lookout facing the northbound tracks, and I was on what I deemed the grendel hunter equivalent of a deer stand, though this wasn't Bambi's dad coming at us. I gripped the paintball rifle, and dimly realized that Ian was treating me as a full member of our little team. To me, that said everything about the depth of the shit we were now standing in.

Shit that got a lot deeper when the grendel suddenly stood framed in the arched tunnel opening—and I hadn't heard a thing.

I swore and snapped my rifle to my shoulder, firing a steady stream of glow-in-the-dark paintballs. Some hit, most didn't, but what did hit was enough.

Almost immediately, an eruption of gunfire hit the grendel at nearly point-blank range.

There were plenty of hits, but little damage, even around the head. The grendel had darted out of range, with the last volley of bullets pockmarking the tunnel's concrete and steel arch.

The Norwegian was using quick and random attacks with the long spear, with Calvin doing the same with Rolf's sword. I had to hand it to Rolf; his poking had drawn blood and was starting to really piss off the grendel. Part of me admired that; but considering how close he had to get to inflict any damage, it just confirmed that he was nuttier than a passel of squirrels.

The guys were doing a good job at keeping the grendel boxed in, but only because the monster seemed to want it that way. He was either playing with us or buying time for his mate to join the fun. Or both.

Room to maneuver wasn't a problem; it was the obstacle course they were fighting on—uneven tracks, broken cross-ties, puddles, mud, trash. With the exception of the steel rails, the grendel's weight simply crushed everything it stepped on.

Yasha had joined them. If the momma grendel came at us from the southbound tunnel, he could break off and deal with it then. Now he was darting and retreating in coordination with his human teammates' attacks, working on the back of the grendel's legs below the knee. Hamstrings. Even with fangs the length of my longest finger, he couldn't get through, but he kept at it. Darting and lunging, same leg, same place, every time, trying to weaken the scales like a fanged battering ram to bite through to the muscle, hobbling it enough that Ian's bullets, Rolf's spear, or Calvin's sword could hit a sweet spot.

I yanked my gun out of its holster. Screw this. The grendel was tagged. My job was done, but it wasn't finished, not by a long shot. The grendel was a ten footer, my team was not.

I aimed. The monster's head was massive. How could I miss?

Easily.

Damnation, that thing was fast.

It didn't move far, arrogant bastard. It just kept shifting

and pivoting, staying in the meager light of the abandoned station, taking every bit of steel and silver we threw at it. I'd emptied my gun, managing to land two shots, one to the head, one to the shoulder; both had about as much effect as a mosquito bite. But rather than run, the thing stayed and kept playing with us.

Oh no.

I froze in realization, then ran to the edge of the platform to the mouth of the southbound tunnel. Even with my bright helmet light, there wasn't nothing coming at us from down there.

And there wouldn't be.

I remembered Lars Anderssen's words—a pair of mated grendels can communicate telepathically. The male was keeping us busy so the female could get to Times Square. Tia only needed one grendel to appear in front of those cameras at midnight.

With shaking hands, I fumbled for my mike. "The female isn't coming. He's holding us here 'til she can get to the surface."

Calvin spat a curse. Ian and Rolf didn't say a word, but they'd all heard me.

It didn't make any difference. None of it would. I'd emptied my gun to no effect. The guys were doing everything they could. None of it was working, but if they lessened by one iota the intensity of their attack, the male would slice them to shreds. Meanwhile the female was making her way to the street with its million people. When she got there, she'd probably send the "supper's ready" message to her mate, and it'd be all over.

We were trapped here. The amount of time we had to live would be determined by how quickly the female got to the surface. I knew it wouldn't be long.

As if the grendel could read *my* thoughts, a low, eager growl rumbled from the depths of his chest.

"Unfortunately, my aromatic friend," Rolf called out to the grendel, "we don't have all night. Playtime's over."

I stared in dumbstruck horror as Rolf Haagen released

the catch on his spear, telescoping it to half its length, and spread his arms to the monster.

"Come and get me."

"No!" Ian roared.

The grendel grabbed Rolf by the front of his body armor, and held him up so that they were face-to-face. Then the grendel slowly licked the Norwegian from chest to face with a black serpentine tongue. He probably didn't care what the Norwegian tasted like; he was just enjoying licking him like a Kevlar-coated lollipop while bullets ricocheted off his armored scales. The grendel smiled and opened his mouth, a gust of rotten air from his exhale blowing the Norwegian's blond hair back.

Neither Ian nor Calvin could get a clear head shot without risking Rolf, so they took anything and everything else they could get.

"That's it," Rolf was coaxing the monster. "Open wide. Show me where your gullet is." He shoved his right hand and forearm into the grendel's mouth. The grendel bit down and coughed, causing his mouth to open enough for Rolf to pull his now mangled mechanical hand and arm free.

The grendel's next cough was more like a hairball heave.

Rolf covered his head and twisted away . . .

. . . as the grendel's head and upper torso exploded.

Bits and pieces rained down including all that was left of the cloaking device and collar.

The headless corpse toppled forward, smacking with a ground-shaking thud onto the tracks, pinning Rolf under it.

I jumped down onto the tracks, grabbing a section of grendel, doing what I could to help Ian and Calvin move the remains. The thing shifted enough for Yasha to get his front fangs into the pull straps on Rolf's armor and drag him free.

Calvin was laughing; Ian was swearing—both at Rolf Haagen.

Not only was the Norwegian alive, he was beaming. He staggered to his feet, surveyed the destruction, and let out a loud whoop. "My last grenade. Never go into a grendel's maw empty-handed." He looked up. "Beowulf, my brother," he called, apparently toward Valhalla. "Now *that's* a kill."

Flashlights and the sound of running booted feet were coming toward us down the tracks. Fast.

More booted feet from the opposite direction.

Backup. I exhaled in relief.

Calvin was more vocal. "It took you long enou—"

"FBI! We have you surrounded."

The men appeared out of the tunnels and passed the dead grendel with barely a second glance.

I had a horrible, sinking feeling in the pit of my stomach. The leader stopped and I could just make out his profile in the light.

The vampire ex-CIA agent.

# 27

THE feds weren't feds, either—unless the FBI had started recruiting ghouls.

I didn't dare make a sound. I touched Ian on the shoulder. When his eyes met mine, I tapped one of my incisors with my index finger, hoping that was the universal symbol for vampire. Now, how to pantomime "ghoul"? They were veiled, and to the guys, they'd look human. They needed to know they weren't. Screw it. I stood on tiptoe and put my lips to Ian's ear. "And ghouls."

Ian leaned in even closer, then went absolutely still.

I did the same for exactly the same reason.

We both had guns pointed against our heads.

"The young lady said 'ghouls,' Detective Byrne," came an urbane voice from behind me. "Or I believe it is now Agent Byrne, isn't it?"

I couldn't see the speaker, and with a gun to my head, fear trumped curiosity. Ian looked as if he'd seen a ghost, the kind that haunted, day and night, and never left.

"Those sibilant consonants will betray you every time, Agent Fraser," the vampire, Charles Warrenton Fitzpatrick

III called to me across the tracks as we were all disarmed. "Even without preternatural hearing, they're nearly impossible to miss. But don't blame yourself for your capture; like our grendels, we've long known you were here." With exaggerated distaste, he stepped around the remains of the male grendel. "Even without the barbaric fireworks display." He looked to where Rolf Haagen was slowly getting to his feet, blood that hadn't been there thirty seconds before running down his temple. I'm certain our female guest will want to meet and eat the one who killed her mate."

Rolf spit out a mouthful of blood, and made sure every ghoul within reach shared the bounty before being knocked back to the tracks and his hands secured behind his back.

"We received word that a team of 'Scandinavian terrorists' had entered the country," the vampire continued. "I would think that to be an oxymoron. It was most accommodating of your comrades in arms to pay a visit to our nursery. It made collecting you all so much easier."

Calvin had been subdued, but a ghoul had paid for the privilege with its life, or whatever it was that ghouls had.

There was no sign of Yasha. That fact, and that fact alone, kept hope alive and kicking.

A pair of ghouls wrenched Ian's hands behind his back—or they tried to. One earned a head butt for his efforts. The ghoul guarding Ian pressed the muzzle harder into Ian's temple, and I heard the double click of handcuffs.

"Please don't make him shoot you, especially not in the head," the man behind me said. "It would be a needless waste of such a delicacy."

A shiver ran through me. Humans—at least normal ones—didn't consider people brains to be food, much less a delicacy. Zombies did; but zombies weren't much for conversation. Damn the gun. I turned my head and looked.

The urbane speaker was also a ghoul.

At least that was what it wanted to look like. The face was a blur of images, layered one over the other, constantly shifting. Only the dark eyes remained constant.

Eyes I recognized—as well as the seemingly endless

layering of faces. The last time I'd seen them was from beneath a tattered hat in front of a liquor store in SoHo.

The homeless man. The man who'd told me to give my regards to my partner. He knew Ian, and Ian knew him, and not in a good way.

I should have shot him in those eyes with tequila when I'd had the chance.

Either the creature could read minds or my recognition was obvious. His dark eyes sparkled in pleasure and he gave me a broad smile.

"You do remember me, Miss Fraser." To my seer vision, his dental work was an ever-changing array of teeth and fangs—from two incisors to four, from a mouthful of seemingly curved needles to human teeth. They had all been real enough at one point in time or another. The images were layered one upon another, stretching back into infinity, like looking into a wall of fun-house mirrors.

"You're not a ghoul," I said.

"Oh, but I am. At least to Agent Byrne. Please tell me you remember our encounter," he said to Ian. "I look back upon it with great fondness. Is she aware that your partners have shortened life expectancies?" Then those now black eyes were on me. "Agent Byrne believes that he has unfinished business with me. I perceive it as an interrupted meal."

"God damn you to hell," Ian snarled.

"You already tried to expedite my trip, remember? I certainly have not forgotten, as I am equally certain that you have not forgotten me. It was so very flattering to hear that I was instrumental in putting you on a new and exciting career path. Those of my kind are rather like cockroaches—a distasteful comparison, but an apt one. We can come back from virtually anything." The soul of murder was reflected in his flat black eyes. "What you did to me was extraordinarily difficult to recover from, but I found the thoughts of exacting prolonged vengeance from you to be the best curative of all."

Ian's hard face was carefully expressionless but I could feel the barely contained fury radiating off of him in waves.

In that moment, I knew who the creature had to be. "The leader of that gang of pawn and jewelry shop robbers."

"Agent Byrne, your newest partner is both delectable *and* perceptive. Gang is such a common term, Miss Fraser. I prefer to think of us as entrepreneurs with a common business goal. I am surprised that you told your new partner about me, Agent Byrne. I don't usually frequent base establishments such as pawnshops; however, this particular merchant had an item I had long searched for."

"What are you?" I asked. "You're not a doppelganger."

He laughed, a mixture of voices, none of them natural, all of them monstrous. "Not even on my worst days. Tonight, I'm a ghoul. Tomorrow?" He shrugged elaborately. "It depends on who or what the situation requires."

Charles Fitzpatrick gripped the back of my neck in a hand that felt more like a steel vise, and half carried, half dragged me away from Ian. With a gun muzzle in my back, he forced me up the ladder and onto the platform, then all but threw me against the bars of the old subway booth. I tripped over some discarded aerosol paint cans and went down hard.

"Get up and lace your fingers behind your neck," the vampire ordered. "Unfortunately, we are short of restraints, but I know I can count on your full cooperation."

When I made no move to comply, the ghoul that'd cuffed Ian embedded his fist hard in Ian's stomach, sending him to his knees.

I complied.

"Now couldn't that have been accomplished without discomfort to your partner?" The humor vanished from his eyes and Charles Fitzpatrick looked like the cold reanimated corpse that he was.

"I see your fang grew back," I noted. "Sorry I had to do that, but you didn't give me a choice."

"I do not believe that you are truly remorseful, Miss Fraser," Fitzpatrick said, his voice soft and low, his words for me only. "But I guarantee that you will be truly sorry before the sun rises tomorrow, and beyond—if you manage to last that long." He stepped up close to me and trapped my chin between two cruel fingers. "You're quite small and from the pallor of your skin, I imagine that you've never been a good blood donor. It's tradition to drink to the arrival of the New Year with a champagne toast." The vampire's eyes lingered on my throat. "I never liked champagne."

"That ghoul thing scared the hell out of you outside that liquor store, and now you're partners?"

"Mister Fitzpatrick was not supposed to be there that night, Agent Fraser," the creature called out, as he and his ghoul henchmen hauled Ian and the others onto the platform. "And yes, I can hear you. Nor was he given permission to feed from you. He was duly chastised for his disobedience and has worked most strenuously in an attempt to regain my favor."

The creature put just the slightest emphasis on "attempt," but I caught it, and so did the vampire, who'd gone a shade or two paler. Looked like somebody wasn't quite back in good graces yet.

We were waiting for Rolf and Calvin to be hauled up onto the platform. They were big guys, and even with ghoul strength, it wasn't a fast process.

I lowered my voice to the barest whisper. "Why?" I asked the vampire.

In response, Fitzpatrick raised a quizzical eyebrow.

"Why all this? The grendels? Slaughtering innocent people on international TV?"

The vampire glanced back at the creature, but apparently decided that he didn't care who overheard him. "Because, Miss Fraser, I am sick of hiding in the shadows, living among cattle such as yourself, pretending to be like them, meekly submitting to the wills of my 'superiors.' After tonight, I and those like me, will answer to no human, will no longer be dictated to by a species that is my food, not my master." He smiled. "And what I want, at least for tonight, is to play with my food—and soon to be paid handsomely and live like a prince while doing it. Times Square is merely the beginning."

"And with the world's eyes on Times Square, every last one of your potential allies will either see your demonstration tonight as it happens or hear about it within five minutes."

Charles Fitzpatrick smiled. "It will give a new meaning to the word 'viral.'"

"This is nothing but a live TV commercial for you."

"And we didn't have to spend millions on airtime."

I could see the crazy in his eyes. Bat-shit crazy. The evil kind. The kind with a business plan.

"Why kill Adam Falke?" I asked him.

"His loyalty was in doubt, so the male grendel was sent after him."

"And why did he have a picture of me?"

"Originally he was to be the contact for your doppelganger. He needed to know what you looked like." The vampire scowled. "After his fall from grace, the job fell to me."

"And Kanil Ghevari?"

"The device needed to be tested against a supernatural that was known for recognizing when a veil was in use. Goblins fit the bill."

Vivienne Sagadraco's friend had been gutted for a test.

Fitzpatrick checked his watch, slender, gold, and elegant. He raised his voice so the creature could hear. "Sir, it's fifteen minutes until midnight."

"Thank you, Charles." The creature crossed the platform to the stairs leading up to the closed pedestrian passageway—and the surface. "Guard our guests until midnight, then feel free to celebrate with them—in any manner you choose. All I require is that Agent Byrne remain unharmed until my return." He smiled at Ian, though it was more like a baring of fangs. "You will have to be patient only a few more minutes, Agent Byrne. But rest assured, *this* time, you will be next."

Essentially the same thing he'd told Ian in the pawnshop while he finished devouring Ian's partner.

The door to the stairwell opened and closed on rusty, unused hinges, and the creature was gone.

After he'd rung the dinner bell for the ghouls and Charles Fitzpatrick.

"Better bring him over here away from the others," the vampire ordered the pair of ghouls on either side of Ian. "You know he doesn't like someone else's blood splattered on his dinner." He turned to me. "Finicky eater," he explained. "Over there against the wall," he told them. "It'll be the best view in the house, Agent Byrne."

The ghouls brought Ian past where Fitzpatrick stood, and as he walked past me, he winked.

I tried to keep my face expressionless, but it wasn't easy when I wanted to drop my jaw.

What the hell was a wink supposed to mean? *He* had a plan? Was *I* supposed to have a plan? Was I supposed to be able to read his freakin' *mind*?

Then Ian made his move.

He crouched and pivoted, catching the ghoul at his right side with an uppercut to the midsection powerful enough to lift the ghoul's feet off the floor, and probably drive his stomach up into his chest.

It took me a stunned two seconds to realize that Ian had gotten out of his handcuffs. The "How the hell . . . ?" didn't matter now.

I made a move of my own.

I dove to the floor, grabbing what I'd had my eyes on since Fitzpatrick had dragged me over here—and since I'd tripped over them.

Cans of aerosol paint.

I came up with a can in each hand, and as Charles Fitzpatrick reached for me, I tagged the bastard smack-dab in the eyes with shamrock green and flamingo pink. He went to his knees, screaming, hands clutching his face. I kneed him in the nose and was rewarded with a sharp snap.

The ghoul writhing on the floor after Ian's fist had put him into a fetal position was my next arts and crafts project.

Ian was wrestling with his former captor for possession of his gun. Black blood oozing from the ghoul's left ear was testament to the effectiveness of my partner's left hook. Ian's lock on the ghoul's wrist changed from wrestling to aiming, shifting his weight to pivot the ghoul's body—and the gun—toward another ghoul running at Ian just as the gun went off, hitting it in the chest.

"Spin him," I shouted to Ian, aiming a paint can at it.

My partner obligingly spun the ghoul's face toward me and I gave him a bad case of pink eye.

I turned my attention where Calvin and Rolf were being held and stopped.

They most definitely did not need my help, or anyone else's.

Calvin had lowered his head, and like a linebacker, had hit a ghoul in the midsection with one massive shoulder, slamming it into a column. The big commando was still handcuffed, but he wasn't letting that slow him down one bit as he seemed intent on grinding the now unconscious ghoul into the concrete.

Yasha had rejoined us and had turned the three other ghouls into squeaky toys that weren't squeaking anymore.

Rolf Haagen was still handcuffed, but was sitting back against a wall bleeding, grinning, and just enjoying the show.

"How'd you get out of—"

"I always carry a pair of handcuff keys in my back pocket," Ian told me. "Never know when you'll need 'em."

I ignored everything that implied.

After all that scuffling, Ian was barely breathing heavy. I was gasping for air. Maybe it was the paint fumes.

Ian ran to Calvin, unlocked his handcuffs, and then handed him the keys.

"Yasha, you're with us." Ian grabbed my hand and all but yanked me off my feet toward the stairs.

There was only the three of us. Ian had a couple of guns and had snagged Rolf's sword; I grabbed my paintball gun; and well, Yasha *was* a werewolf, which was about the best thing we had going for us right now.

The stairs up to the closed and abandoned pedestrian walkway were only wide enough to allow two people to walk side by side or, in our case, run. Normally, when you had a sadistic mystery creature waiting for you at the top of the stairs, stealth would be the way to go. We had no time for stealth. Ian let Yasha take the lead since he was more qualified in werewolf form to take on anything of the paranormal persuasion. The stairwell ceiling was tall enough not to feel claustrophobic, but low and dark enough to be oppressive. The concrete had been bare and the only color came from steel pipe railings anchored to the walls along both sides of the stairs. That was then. Now, every square inch had been tagged by graffiti artists. The only light came from a pair of bulbs at the top stair of each landing. The walls were damp and glistening with water that had seeped through the concrete. Sections were splattered with rust-colored stains that I suspected were recent and had nothing to do with rust.

Yasha burst snarling through the double doors. What lay beyond smelled like a slaughterhouse, with the sickly sweet, coppery odor of blood. Nearly every surface of the passageway wore a coat of graffiti. In fact, some graffiti had been painted over to make room for later additions. Over the graffiti, blood was smeared and streaked on the walls of the abandoned passageway. It'd dried to a dull brown. Ahead was a pool of red, not fresh, but not old, either.

It had gone from a winter refuge for the homeless, to the grendels' and ghouls' own private meat market.

"You are resourceful, Agent Byrne, I will give you that."

The creature stood between us and a pair of open steel doors. Beyond, a short set of stairs led up to the street. The cold wind swept down the stairs, carrying the voices and shouts of hundreds of thousands of people.

"The female grendel is already out on the street," the creature said. "No one can see her, nor will they see her until midnight, when she's been instructed to disable the device that she wears. Once again, *Detective* Byrne, you're too late and too ineffective to save anyone. Such continued failure must be disheartening." He began leisurely walking toward us.

"Mac, go back downstairs," Ian said, never taking his eyes from the creature.

The creature extended one arm, fingers spread, and the doors behind us slammed, and the chains took on a life of their own quickly snaking between and around the door handles.

"Let her go," Ian said.

"I think not," the creature said. "What is it you humans say? The more the merrier?"

"Let her go, and the wolf—and I'll stay."

My heart kicked me in the chest. "No. You can't."

Ian never took his eyes from the creature that'd slaughtered and eaten his partner. "The offer stands. You said you wanted vengeance." His eyes glittered in challenge. "How bad do you want it?"

"You do drive a tempting bargain, Detective Byrne." His thin lips creased in a vulpine smile. "Agreed."

"Ian, no!"

The creature stepped aside with a flourish, clearing the way to the street. "But they will only have one choice of exit." His smile broadened. "And *she* will be waiting for them."

Ian hefted Rolf's broadsword. "Mac, go. Yasha, stay with her. When you get to the street, get the hell out of Times Square."

Yasha took my hand in his huge mouth. His fangs went beyond massive, but he never broke my skin. I also couldn't pull away.

The moment we were on the stairs, the steel doors slammed at our backs, the chains rattling on the other side as they wrapped the handles.

Leaving Ian alone with his worst nightmare.

# 28

ME and Yasha were alone on Forty-second Street with a million people.

The noise levels were deafening. My stomach lurched, and my breath came in gasping puffs in the freezing air. The shouts and cheering of a million people forced their way inside my head, the happy and blissfully ignorant cheering of people who had no idea what was stalking among them.

My partner was sacrificing himself to give us a chance to escape. I saw it as a chance to stop an invisible and virtually indestructible monster from wading into that crowd and turning those cheers to screams. I wasn't going anywhere. The cops might have the firepower to bring it down, but they couldn't see it. And once the blood started flowing and bodies flying, panic would spread from the epicenter that was the grendel. People would die who weren't anywhere near her as a panic-spawned stampede started in the desperation to escape Times Square.

And all that could keep those people from becoming corpses was a seer and a werewolf. I didn't have a plan, but

I wasn't going to stand by and let innocent people be slaughtered and trampled.

The stairs up to the surface from the pedestrian passageway had led to a now-mangled grate that the grendel had torn off and tossed aside. Yasha and I were in a fenced and boarded-up construction site where there didn't look to be any constructing going on. I wondered if Tia had arranged with any city businessmen she might have had in her pocket to have it cordoned off as a staging area for her special guests. The crushed padlock on the *inside* of the boarded-up chain-link gate, and the steel chains that had been pulled apart like so much taffy turned my theory into a safe bet.

There was a narrow crack between two of the boards. Yasha stuck his snout to the opening and started sniffing. I looked through.

Scaffolding flanked both sides of the building site. TV camera towers. The crowds had been blocked off from the area underneath, giving me and Yasha the cover we needed. The space between the two towers led right into the section of street kept cordoned off and open for emergency vehicle use. If something went wrong in a crowd of a million people, the good folks of the NYPD wanted a way in and out.

We started scanning the pens the NYPD always put in place on New Year's Eve to keep the crowds contained in manageable clumps. It looked like herds of cattle in a stockyard to me, and I imagine the grendel saw it much the same way.

If we couldn't stop that grendel from appearing at midnight and wading into the nearest crowd pen, adding a werewolf to the mix wasn't gonna make a hill of beans worth of difference. I was wearing my armor, which was good for personal protection, but bad for blending in with a crowd. Then I saw two of the law enforcement folks patrolling Forty-second Street. Their gear was similar enough to mine that I could look like I belonged. However their armor had NYPD on the back.

Something akin to an electric shock ran up my arm that had been touching Yasha's fur, and in place of Yasha the werewolf was Yasha the kinda/sorta German shepherd. I could still see Yasha's werewolf aura, but it was like a nimbus around his dog disguise. Good call. The only way Yasha could conceivably fight the grendel was as a werewolf, but to get out into Times Square called for every SPI werewolf's less threatening disguise—K-9 cop.

Yasha looked up at me with golden eyes, eyes that told me that whatever I was going to do to try to stop this, he'd be right there with me, and he'd go werewolf in the most public place imaginable if necessary to kill that grendel and save lives. I prayed it wouldn't come to that, but I had no idea how it could possibly go any other way. Then with one emphatic downward nod of his muzzle, a dog told a human to stay. Yasha pushed the gate open with his muzzle, squeezed through, and was gone.

Apparently, he had a plan or at least an idea. The clock was ticking, and it wasn't in our favor, but I stayed put.

Only a minute or so later, Yasha padded back to me; in his mouth was a dark blue ball cap with FBI in bright white on the front. I was already dressed more or less like a commando in solid black, with body armor that was similar enough to what I'd glimpsed through the fence to blend in. I took off my helmet and put on the hat, running my ponytail out the hole in the back. Not as good a disguise as Yasha's, but I was as official looking as I was going to get.

We quickly went out onto Forty-second Street.

Yasha stood tall, his head held high and alert, like a K-9 officer on patrol who belonged there. Hopefully, I was the only one of the million people here and billions watching who could see that the upstanding K-9 trotting purposely in front of the cameras, God, and the world, not only wasn't on a leash, but in reality was a nearly seven-foot-tall werewolf.

Finding our target would be the easy part. Even among a sea of humanity, a towering monster would stand out to me, even if she was invisible to everyone else.

Then I saw her.

The mother grendel.

I was ashamed to admit it, but I stood there and gawked in open-mouthed horror.

The female was a head and a half taller than her mate, her shoulders broader, her arms and legs more heavily muscled, her fangs bigger, her claws longer.

Better, stronger, faster.

Rolf and his bionic stump would hate that he missed out on this one. I wished the crazy Viking was here; he'd have a plan. It'd be just as crazy as he was, but at least he'd have one.

The grendel was taking full advantage of her invisibility to do a little window-shopping before midnight, stalking down the emergency vehicle access path, perusing the people in the metal pens like they were cattle for the slaughter. I wondered if the NYPD knew how accurately those metal pens helped make the comparison.

A voice reached me. The voice of a small child; small, but loud. A little girl in red coat and hood was perched on top of her daddy's shoulders, hitting the top of his hatted head to get his attention where she wanted it. On us.

"Daddy, Mommy, look at the *big* puppy!" she shouted. "What big teeth he has!"

She wasn't fooled by Yasha's K-9 disguise. Just our luck. A little seer in the making.

I sensed the Russian werewolf's "oh shit" and his German shepherd legs moved faster, and I ran to catch up.

*"There you are. My sister's seer eyes."*

I lunged forward, grabbing a handful of Yasha's fur, pulling him to a stop, and went down on one knee beside him.

"There's a voice in my head," I quickly said in his ear. This was weird, even by SPI standards. Hopefully anyone watching would think that the FBI agent and her K-9 partner just had a really close working bond.

I didn't feel like I was being watched, that I was in the center of a cross-haired target. I knew it for a fact. Running wouldn't help, neither would hiding, but that didn't stop me from wanting to do both.

*"Most countries have a monster that they use to frighten*

*their children. Behave or it will get you while you sleep. Most myths are based in reality. And what are a country's citizens but grown-up children? Fortunately for me, some fears never die."*

Tiamat. Babylonian dragon goddess of chaos. Vivienne Sagadraco's sister.

Inside my head.

At least her voice was.

Reason, or what I had left of it, told me that she was here. Not among the crowds. She was a dragon; she'd want to be above it all, enjoying the game she'd started, watching the pieces move about on the colorful, life-sized game board that was Times Square.

The one-sided conversation continued.

*"Primitive man lived in fear of the horrors that preyed upon them in the night. Man fears nothing in this modern age. In their arrogance, they deceive themselves into believing that science has told them all they need to know. They have lights to keep the darkness at bay, but their primitive fears are still there. They have forgotten what it is like to wonder what waits, red in tooth and claw, just beyond the light of their fires—or the lights of their cities. Their imaginations have been dulled by science—that explainer of all things. They do not know what hunts them, they do not believe how quickly they will die . . . but they soon will."*

Silence. The silence of bad things about to happen.

I jumped as a crackling in my ear almost burst my eardrum.

*"Mac? Can you hear me? Mac, come in."*

It was the most beautiful sound I'd ever heard.

Kenji.

"I can hear you." It was like I could breathe again. "I'm on—"

*"I know exactly where you are."*

Oh crap. "I'm on TV?"

*"No, the boss is keeping me posted. She sees you. Look up at the top of One Times Square."*

"One Times Square? Where the—"

*"The building with the big-ass ball on it? The one they're about to drop?"*

I looked. I saw the ball.

And I saw the dragon that was Vivienne Sagadraco perched regally—there was no other way to describe her—shimmering majestic blue in the spotlights trained on the dazzlingly lit ball covered with Waterford crystal.

Magnificent came to mind.

And invisible.

A million people here and billions around the world were watching that ball, but it was obvious that no one could see Vivienne Sagadraco.

My shoulders sagged in relief. "You fixed the cloaking device."

I heard the pride in Kenji's voice. *"Affirmative. Me and the boys."*

*"And girls!"* I heard shouted in the background.

My words came in a gush. "It's just me and Yasha. The teams were captured by ghouls and spawn and . . ." I stumbled on, unable to say "possibly eaten." "Calvin and Rolf are in the old Forty-second Street subway station, and Ian is alone fighting a ghoul that's not a ghoul, and—"

*"The teams are fine."*

"What?"

*"Roy, Sandra, and Lars just reported in. They ran into a little trouble clearing out the nest. They're on their way up to the old station, as I—"*

That son of a bitch vampire lied.

"Go get Ian!" I screamed.

Heads turned. A woman wearing an FBI hat, screaming into a headset, tended to make post-nine-eleven New Yorkers antsy. I quickly turned my head away and lowered my voice a few octaves. "He's in the closed pedestrian passageway. Calvin knows . . ."

I was talking to dead air.

"Kenji?"

No response.

"Kenji? Shit!"

I had my paintball gun, and the boss would be able to see a marked grendel, but I couldn't use it. At this moment, I had no doubt about the reactions of real cops to fake guns that they didn't know were fake—especially in Times Square on New Year's Eve where alert didn't even begin to describe the readiness state of the thousands of cops and feds in, around, and above the crowds. The moment I drew my real-looking paintball gun, six or ten of the gazillion cops would be on me like white on rice. Ian had been right. A real-looking fake gun could get you killed quicker than the real thing—or get my face ground into the asphalt while a real monster materialized and started eating people.

Hope flickered to life, and even severed communications wasn't going to crush it. There were a mess of folks depending on me. Ian was one of them. Whatever had happened to him—or whatever was happening to him—his sacrifice sure as hell wasn't gonna be in vain. And if I failed, I'd fail knowing that I'd done everything I could possibly do. No regrets.

I knew what I had to do.

Vivienne Sagadraco could fight the grendel. I couldn't. The boss knew where I was, so my job was to show her where the grendel was by the only other way available to me—by getting as close to the thing as possible, and grabbing it if I had to.

I spotted the grendel. "Bring it, bitch," I spat.

I suddenly smelled sulfur and was nearly knocked off my feet by a blast of air.

My lizard brain knew sulfur was bad, so it didn't consult with the rest of my mind on how to react to a downdraft on a night with no wind.

I dove behind a police cruiser as massive claws ripped through the space where I'd just been, leaving three, long gashes across the cruiser's hood.

Startled shouts and curses spread as sections of the crowd were buffeted with the downdraft generated by the wings of a huge red dragon that had dove down, leveled off over

Broadway, and damned near plucked me off the street like an owl going for a field mouse.

I frantically scanned the sky, but I couldn't see her for the glare of the TV lights; however, I could hear and feel her powerful wing beats as she gained altitude and momentum for another run.

Tiamat didn't get the chance for a second pass.

Vivienne Sagadraco must have seen the blast of wind flow and ripple over the top of the crowd and been able to track her sister's path of attack. She simply dropped off of the edge of One Times Square, spreading her wings just short of full extension. The boss was diving to intercept, but she was so large that dropping from the roof of a twenty-five-story building was like a bird hopping out of a tree.

The boss had the advantage of surprise, and she would only have it once.

The two titans collided in midair, barely three stories above the packed crowd in front of the main stage. The collision produced a shock wave that shook the steel gantry holding the stage lights, and rocked the street itself like an earthquake. People directly beneath the two battling dragons were knocked to the ground from the force of the downdrafts from their wings.

Vivienne tried to maneuver Tiamat higher and farther away from the crowds. When her sister didn't comply, Vivienne redoubled her attack with a roar that overpowered a million voices and the stage's probably million-amp sound system, but that only I could hear.

I shot a glance at the countdown clock at the bottom of the pole the ball would descend.

One minute, thirty seconds.

Tia broke away, the boss in pursuit. The red dragon banked to the right, the row of spikes at the end of her tail grazing one of the digital billboards, sending a spray of sparks down onto the crowd. With two beats of her mighty wings, Vivienne Sagadraco swooped beneath her sister, jaws snapping at Tia's underside, forcing her upward to escape.

The two massive dragons battled, climbing higher into the night sky.

Forty-five seconds.

I ran toward the female grendel who had ignored the roars and shrieks overhead and was nearing the pens closest to the stage. She leapt over a parked ambulance that was in her path, and when she landed, her weight cracked the asphalt beneath her taloned feet, the shock wave knocking more people to the street. Seen or unseen, the grendel was going into the crowd. Her clawed hand went to the front of her collar.

To turn off the cloaking device.

Oh no. No!

I ran toward her with no idea what I was going to do when I got there. The boss was busy fighting her sister, so my original plan was scuttled. It was just me. The grendel spun, slashing at me with her claws, catching on my armor, hooking it and me.

Thirty seconds.

Yasha surged past me, biting, tearing into the hand and arm that the grendel had used to reach for the disk on her collar. The people around us saw a K-9 officer snapping and biting something that wasn't there. I saw a werewolf savaging a monster.

"Rabies!" a woman shrieked.

Twenty seconds.

The grendel broke free, long strides taking her directly to the foot of the stage, to the people packed together in the metal pens, sheep for the taking.

The grendel stopped, reached up with her undamaged hand . . .

"NYPD! Freeze!"

It was directed at me, not the grendel. Yasha and I had finally gotten the attention we didn't want but couldn't avoid.

I ignored them and kept running toward the grendel, prepared to throw myself against that hand or somehow knock her off balance, anything to stop her.

Almost there.

Seven seconds.

I lunged, my shoulder slamming into the back of the grendel's armor-scaled knee.

Almost instantly, a downdraft knocked me off my feet as a giant claw grazed my back, sending me into a roll and throwing me against the bars of a crowd pen. I screamed in pain and frustration.

Five seconds.

I scrambled to my feet and stopped in open-mouthed amazement as Vivienne Sagadraco locked the talons that had knocked me out of the way securely around the grendel and swept her off the street, powerful beats of her wings working like the afterburners of a fighter jet as she fought for altitude. High enough and it wouldn't matter if the grendel disabled the device. No one would see.

Tiamat was nowhere to be seen.

Four seconds.

Booted feet caught up with me, and a cop grabbed my arms and pulled me aside.

"I've got her," he called to the others behind him.

I barely heard him as I stood and watched Vivienne Sagadraco carry the grendel farther up into the sky until they were barely visible, even to me. My eyes blurred with tears.

"We did it, Ian," I whispered.

"You have the right to remain silent," the policeman said. "Even though I know you can't."

*What?*

Three . . . two . . .

It was Ian.

. . . one.

Wearing a NYPD jacket and hat.

The crowd erupted and confetti came down.

I stared in relief and wonder. "How did you—"

"Later."

Over the past two days, we'd come close to dying any number of times. Coming that close makes you think. It was making me think right now about what I suddenly wanted to do and damn the consequences. I was shaking with terror and relief . . . and well, all that feeling had to go somewhere. Besides, everyone else was doing it.

I put my hands on either side of Ian's face, stood on tiptoes, and kissed him.

His lips were soft, he was warm, and damn, it was nice.

When I broke away, I was short of breath.

Ian was looking down at me, a mischievous grin flitting across his mouth. "Happy New Year, partner."

Over the sounds of celebration all around us came the joyous howl of a wolf.

# TWO DAYS LATER

IT was nine o'clock on Monday morning, and it wasn't exactly business as usual at SPI headquarters—for a lot of reasons.

The bull pen smelled like new office furniture and electronics. It was amazing what cashing in a couple of trinkets from a dragon's hoard could buy. The boss had everything delivered yesterday. Pre-assembled. On a Sunday. On New Year's Day. Like I said, cash speaks. Loudly.

About half of the desks and chairs had been brought up from the loading dock area, but were presently on the side of the bull pen that was the farthest from where welders were repairing various levels of the catwalks and railings.

I'd never considered welding to be that loud of a construction-type activity, but then I didn't have the preternaturally sensitive hearing of a werewolf.

Nor had I made the mistake of trying to drink the entire SPI Scandinavia team under the bar at the Full Moon on New Year's Day.

When Rolf Haagen had said he wanted to go, kill, and return to drink to our victory, he wasn't kidding—and apparently the bionic Viking had the liver to back it up. Wouldn't have surprised me if his liver had been man-made, too. Nancy and Bill had opened the Full Moon just for us yesterday, and SPI's agents from both sides of the pond had put an impressive dint in their single-malt scotch inventory—again, courtesy of cashed-in dragon hoard trinkets. The Scandinavians had invited us to Oslo for a Nordic-style monster hunt, and to consume vast quantities of aquavit. Hopefully they intended to wait and consume the latter until after we'd done the former. Though with that group, there was no telling.

Yasha gingerly rested his elbows on his desk and carefully placed his head—still wearing sunglasses—in his upraised hands. The sound he made was a mix of soft mournful howl and puppy whimper.

"You did it to yourself," I reminded him.

I'd come into the office today because Ian had promised to start my training.

Kenji had CNN and the Weather Channel streaming live on two of his computer screens—his being one of the few undamaged areas in the bull pen. I would have asked him to turn it up, but decided to be sensitive to my coworker's self-induced suffering and walked over to Kenji's desk.

"Amazing how people can explain away anything," the elf tech said, when I'd gotten close enough for him not to yell. I guess he was being considerate of Yasha, too.

I watched and listened, and was just as amazed. Jim Cantore was busy explaining how a nearly tornado-force downdraft could form on a virtually cloudless night with no major weather system within a hundred miles. Over on CNN, the earthquake that thousands had felt in Times Square and Midtown Manhattan on Saturday night was being blamed on a buildup of steam that had inexplicably released. Workers had been dispatched below the streets to find the culprit. Good thing our folks had cleaned up after themselves in the grendel nursery and old Forty-second Street station. And last, but certainly not least to the people who had been standing underneath it, the exploding section of Times Square billboard had been a short in electronics caused by yet another downdraft—or a large bird. They didn't have that one nailed down yet.

Conspicuously absent was any mention of monsters or giant dragons.

I caught a movement out of the corner of my eye at my desk.

Ian. Putting something over the back of my chair.

He saw me see him and stepped back with a crooked grin.

As I got closer, I saw what it was and laughed out loud.

"For the fastest tagger in the West . . . Side," Ian said.

I groaned at the bad pun.

Yasha groaned, too, but not for the same reason.

I had a new piece of desk flair. Slung over the back of my office chair was a Wild West–style gun belt, with an oversized holster on each hip; but instead of a pair of six-shooters, the holsters each held a can of spray paint.

I grinned like an idiot. "I love it." I felt myself blush a little. "Thank you."

"There's also that." Ian indicated a pink box with a gorgeous silver bow. "That wasn't there a few minutes ago."

"Moreau," Yasha said. He was sitting upright now, but he didn't look inclined to take off his sunglasses anytime soon.

There was a smell coming from the box—a really nice one for a change. And familiar. I smiled and bit my bottom lip.

There wasn't a card or a note, but I knew who it was from.

I looked up at the newly repaired windows of the executive suite. Vivienne Sagadraco, the dragon lady, founder and director of SPI, and my boss, stood framed in the floor-to-ceiling glass, her cane now more of a fashionable accessory than an orthopedic necessity. She smiled and bestowed upon me a single nod of her regal head. Her dragon aura did likewise.

I returned the smile and opened the box.

Cookies.

Iced and not iced, nuts and no nuts, and all with some form of chocolate. Except in one corner, separated from the others were delicate cookie confections, completely coated in . . . you guessed it, powdered sugar.

Needless to say, I ate one of those first.

I held out the box to Ian. "Want one?"

"I believe I will."

"Yasha?" I asked.

He held up both hands.

"Understood. Why don't I go put these on the break room table to share?"

"Is good idea."

"Three whole words," Ian said, impressed. He clapped the Russian on the shoulder. "Looks like you'll make it, buddy." He walked with me to the break room. "Heard from Ollie?"

"Oh yeah. He made it to the Full Moon just fine, and got home yesterday morning to find Detective Burton from the First Precinct waiting for him."

"I supposed it'd be too much to ask that he arrested Ollie?"

"Yeah, it would. Burton just took him in for questioning. In the end, he couldn't charge Ollie with anything other than being inconveniently absent for forty-eight hours."

"How'd Ollie explain that one?"

"House-sitting for a friend who was out of the country. Ollie was extra helpful and gave him the name and number of said friend, Humphrey Collington, for verification."

"Let me guess, one of Ollie's aliases."

"His favorite. And since the police had completed their lab work in Ollie's office, he was free to open his shop." I put the cookies on the break room table, the official permission and invitation in office kitchens everywhere to "eat these."

I chuckled. "Remember when I said that if Ollie hadn't been kidnapped, he'd be giving tours of the monster murder scene at twenty bucks a pop?"

"He's not."

"He is. Assured me that while he agreed that it was disgusting, he was just trying to make up for lost revenue."

"Yeah, right."

"Apparently money—at least for Ollie—is the best therapy of all."

"Did you tell him we had his rug?"

"Yeah, he doesn't want it back."

"Good choice."

"Not really. He's having another one made just like it."

There was an awkward silence as I knew what I wanted to ask, but not how to bring it up.

"Vivienne doesn't know anything about the ghoul," Ian said simply. "Either what it is or where it went, other than it was probably Tia's second in command, her boots on the ground, so to speak. Our interrogators haven't managed to get any good leads from Charles Fitzpatrick. Either he's good at being questioned, or he simply doesn't know anything. The boss thinks, and I agree, that he was only told what he needed to know. The rest of the organization has gone to ground. No sign of them. Vivienne thinks that since she carried off and killed the grendel, and that she runs the group that destroyed all the others, Tiamat will be back. She'll want revenge and not just from her sister."

I'd learned that the boss had badly wounded Tia out over the Hudson River, and to make it back to Times Square in time, she'd been forced to let her escape. Glad didn't even begin to describe how I'd felt about that decision.

"The boss told me that if there's anything her sister has, it's time," Ian was saying. "So we shouldn't expect immediate retaliation."

After Ian had agreed to stay behind with the ghoul in exchange for my and Yasha's freedom, he'd tried shooting the creature, only to have his silver bullets bounce right off. He fell back on the only other weapon he had.

Rolf's sword. The family heirloom.

Ian had never used swords before coming to work at SPI. But he'd gotten plenty of training since then. Since we fought some old-fashioned monsters, like Rolf said, sometimes Old

World weapons worked best. The creature had closed distance, and Ian had waited until the last instant to strike.

Rolf's sword had cut into the thing like hot butter. If it'd been any other night than New Year's Eve, all of Midtown Manhattan would have heard its screams.

The creature vanished, disappeared, ran back to whatever dimension it'd come from with its either figurative or literal tail between its legs.

Turned out that Rolf Haagen's family heirloom was one of those swords that had a name.

Gram.

His ancestor had quite a name, too.

Sigurd.

Lars Anderssen confirmed the bloodline. Dang.

I didn't know whether to be really impressed that I knew the descendant of a legendary hero of Norse not-mythology, or to be really worried for the safety and continued well-being of the Norse gods.

"Gram can kill dragons, right?"

Ian nodded. "The boss said she knew the moment Rolf brought it into the complex. Apparently that was one of the things Lars Anderssen was talking to her about when they first arrived. Letting her know it was here, and that he wouldn't have allowed Rolf to bring it except that it'd proven to be effective against grendels."

"And mystery ghouls."

"Thankfully."

"That makes two times you've hurt him bad," I said quietly.

Ian shrugged. "I'll just look over my shoulder more often."

Ian's tone was casual, but I knew he had to be more worried than he let on. The creature had been hungry for revenge after the first time. Now, vengeance had probably become its new life goal, if the thing even qualified as living.

"You can look over your shoulder," I told him. "But I've got your back."

His smile was warm. "Thanks, partner."

Impulsively, I reached down and took his hand. He didn't say anything else and neither did I. We also hadn't said anything about the New Year's Eve kiss, and that was fine with me, at least for now. Yeah, after my heart rate had returned to normal, I'd been a little embarrassed; okay, a lot embarrassed. I was sure it'd come up when the time was right—or the most awkward. I told myself that what had happened had happened, and there was no taking it back, not that I wanted to. It'd also been extremely nice, and I wouldn't be opposed to it happening again—under circumstances that didn't involve multiple near-death experiences.

We both tensed at the sound of heavy boot steps running toward the break room.

Calvin stuck his head around the corner. "We got a call."

Ian stood. I didn't know what I was supposed to do. I wasn't a commando.

Calvin grinned and jerked his head at Ian, but spoke to me. "My man here says you're ready for some on-the-job training."

I froze. "On the job?"

Ian smiled. "Training."

"We got report of a problem up at the Cloisters. Think I heard Roy say something about gargoyles. Fortunately, the museum's closed today, so we don't have to worry too much about being quiet."

I smiled, slow and probably dangerous looking. Ian didn't look like he minded.

I grabbed a handful of cookies. "Let's go."

## ABOUT THE AUTHOR

Lisa Shearin is the national bestselling author of the Raine Benares novels, a series of six comedic fantasy adventures. Lisa is a voracious collector of fountain pens both vintage and modern. She lives in North Carolina—the land of barbeque and sweet tea—with her husband, two spoiled-rotten retired racing greyhounds, and a Jack Russell terrier who rules them all.

For more information about Lisa and her books, visit her at lisashearin.com.

*Keep your enemies close—*
*and your exes closer.*

FROM NATIONAL BESTSELLING AUTHOR

LISA SHEARIN

# Con & Conjure

## A Raine Benares Novel

Ever since the Saghred—a soul-stealing stone that's given her unlimited power—bonded to Raine Benares, the goblin king and the elves have wanted to possess its magic themselves. Now both a goblin thief and Raine's ex-fiancé—an elven assassin—may be after her. To survive, she'll need the help of her notorious criminal family.

**PRAISE FOR THE RAINE BENARES NOVELS**

**"A roller-coaster ride through demons, goblins, elves, and mages... Will leave readers chomping at the bit for more."**

—*Monsters and Critics*